# EMPIRE RESURGENT

Robert Bruton

# EMPIRE RESURGENT

HISTRIA
FICTION

# Histria Fiction

Las Vegas ◊ Chicago ◊ Palm Beach

Published in the United States of America by
Histria Books
7181 N. Hualapai Way, Ste. 130-86
Las Vegas, NV 89166 USA
HistriaBooks.com

Histria Fiction is an imprint of Histria Books. Titles published under the imprints of Histria Books are distributed worldwide.

Library of Congress Control Number: 2024931051

ISBN 978-1-59211-434-4 (softbound)
ISBN 978-1-59211-447-4 (eBook)

For Betsy

Memor saepe, numquam oblivione delebitur

# FOREWORD

This three-part series offers a fictionalized account of two couples who lived during the glorious resurgence of the Eastern Roman Empire: Emperor Justinian, his Empress Theodora, his greatest general, Belisarius, and the general's wife, Antonina. Justinian the Great, the last truly Roman Emperor, began his reign with victories against the Persians and the Vandals in North Africa. Belisarius, one of the greatest generals who ever lived, enabled this new Roman springtime. He defeated the barbarians whose invasions brought about the fall of the Western Empire. The Emperor's and the general's ambitious wives, both former courtesans, are two of the most intriguing women of the Roman Era. Both were indispensable in the success of their husbands' careers and the transition to a society where women could play critical roles.

I have relied extensively on historical documents (particularly Procopius of Caesarea) to create a canvas to paint this picture. Where history is silent or obscure, I have filled the gaps with a literary narrative that generally aims to conform to the consensus of historians. Drawing on all known historical and literary accounts, I have attempted to reconcile narratives that made the most sense amidst conflicting versions of events. I have eliminated some characters who were part of the historical narrative while merging others.

The physical and spiritual despair that followed the veil of ash and the pandemic resembles Europe after the First World War. For that reason, I have borrowed much of the outline and metaphors that T.S. Eliot used in his epic poem, *The Wasteland.* In addition, I have used references from the treasuries of Sacred Scripture, patristic writings, Roman philosophy, world literature, and even modern cinema and music to illuminate the course of events and characters.

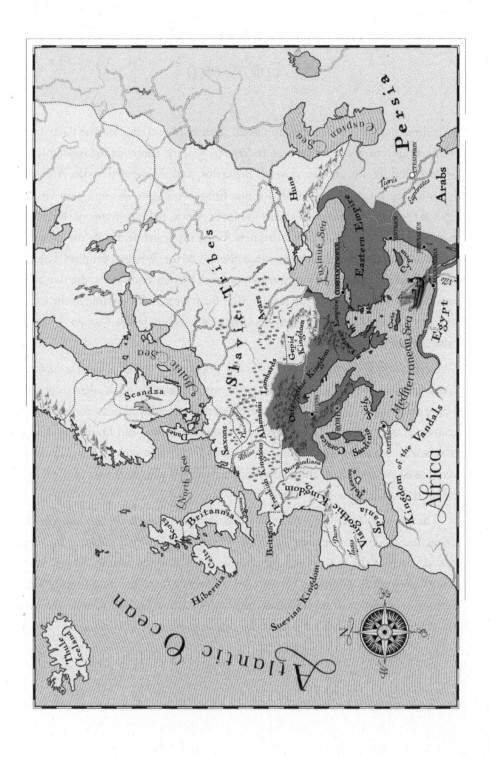

# CHAPTER ONE

# THE CHALLENGE

*People with good intentions make promises, but people with good character keep them.*

*Knowing what's right doesn't mean much unless you do what's right.*

— Theodore Roosevelt

*Roman Fortress at Dara near the Persian Border*
*26 June 530, A.D.*

They watched the ape-necked Persian giant emerge from the battle line riding a well-muscled chestnut horse. Impatiently, he moved back and forth along the Roman trench, just shy of the archers' range, taunting the Roman general and mocking his reluctance to accept the challenge of a duel.

"That Persian is at it again, General," Commander Pharas said to his old friend Flavius Belisarius. He gave Belisarius a grim but sympathetic look. Belisarius raised his eyebrows.

"What now?" He was no longer laughing at the daylong harangue.

"This time, he says he will cleave your skull and drink your wine from it."

Belisarius sighed and shook his head. "What kind of woman raises a child to talk like that?" He hunched over in his saddle as a feeling of nausea overcame him. A voice in his head suggested he would rather be in the Persian's saddle than his own. He knew that the leader of Persia's Ten-Thousand Immortals had every confidence his army would once again triumph over the Romans, as they had in every battle for the past century. He knew his chances of winning either in individual combat or battle were slim. He considered the short careers of the commanders before him who had either been killed on the battlefield or escaped, only to be disgraced or executed in Constantinople, a veritable graveyard for failed ambitions.

"When are the Persians going to attack, Pharas? What are they waiting for?"

"They're waiting for you to make the first move."

"We tried that at the battle of Thannuris and fell into pits. We're not doing that again."

"Agreed, but…"

"But what?" Belisarius interrupted before realizing that his impatience was worrying his staff around him. *Keep calm and keep your fears to yourself.* Three years on the Roman-Persian frontier had accomplished little more than a reduction of the size of his army. He looked around at his men. All eyes were on him, and they could not hide their apprehension as well as he could.

"The men and horses have been standing in the hot sun all day," Pharas said coolly. "They're in no condition to fight now." Belisarius nodded his agreement.

The two men looked over the hot and dusty border between the Roman and Persian empires. The formidable fortress of Dara stood behind them, a mile back, protecting their rear. Between the army and Dara, a thousand white tents littered the ground where the Roman army slept at night. A few fires around their camp prepared their evening meal, and the pleasant aroma left Belisarius feeling hungry. On their left and right were hills, too steep and covered with scrub for the cavalry to charge over them. Two miles off in front of them stood an army twice their size. Over them was a sun so hot that his men could not touch their armor without singeing their skin. Below them was the dry and dusty ground of Roman Mesopotamia, a productive land fed by mountains whose waters flowed slowly into the Euphrates River. *A green and pleasant land,* Belisarius thought; *they were safe — for now.* Pharas interrupted his thoughts.

"He is talking to you, Flavius." The two leaned forward in their saddles to hear the bombastic Persian.

"I have defeated every man I ever faced in single combat," he yelled in demotic Greek.

Belisarius turned to Pharas, "By his bulk, I'd say he is not boasting. What do you think he weighs? 250 pounds? He's as tall as his Nisean horse — maybe seven feet."

"Yes," Pharas said. "He's the vanguard of his cavalry unit, and if the boisterous encouragement of his fellows is an indication, he commands the respect of his army."

The comment made Belisarius shrink in his saddle. After the disaster at nearby Thannuris two years before, he wasn't sure what sort of respect he commanded. He had learned from that defeat but wondered if he had learned enough to change the outcome. The deliberation made Belisarius feel tired, and the conversation made him feel small.

Belisarius watched the Persian, in auriferous scaled armor and a golden helmet topped with a blue peacock panache on his head, taunt the Romans. "Send me your best warrior and let us fight to the death. The losing side quits Syria and returns home to the suckling breasts of their mothers." His guttural laughter bounced off the mountains and reverberated across the wasteland between the ridges and the fortified walls of Dara. The sounds of sycophantic foot soldiers joining in forced laughter only made his contempt for the Persians angrier. It seemed as though the valley itself echoed the taunts of the Persians.

"Don't disrespect our mothers," Belisarius murmured in a staccato fashion. His horse, Bucephalus, reared his head as though nodding in agreement. Belisarius pulled back the reins and spun his horse around in a circle, a habit of his whenever he grew irritated. He examined his rust-speckled armor and frowned. The white Ostridge plume in his helmet had broken in half that morning, making him feel ridiculous and angry.

He thought briefly of his counterpart, the Persian commander, Perozes, who would be watching this pretense in proud approval. He looked around nervously at the faces of Pharas and his men and saw that the unchallenged taunting was taking a toll on his army's confidence even as it seemed to raise the esprit de corps of the Persians. He knew the Persian was trying to goad him into making the first move. He watched the Persian giant remove his helmet and wipe the sweat from his brow and beard, waiting for the Roman response.

But no reply came from the disciplined Roman troops. Belisarius saw that his men grew weary of the charade even as he grew angry. They had been standing in the hot sun for twelve hours. He watched as a handful of troops passed out in the heat, and the water boys struggled to keep the army and the horses hydrated. The field around him reeked of sweat and horse piss. He wondered if his men thought him a coward for not meeting the Persian on the battlefield. As medics brought the passed-out men to the rear of the line, he looked at the low sun in the sky just dipping below the mountains in the west and turned to the handful of senior officers gathered around him.

"Tell me, Pharas, are the Persians going to attack this late in the day?"

"No, sir."

"Then tell the men they can return to their tents until the first light."

Hermogenes, the senior general on the staff, gave him a disapproving look that said his military training precluded dismissal of the army before sundown. Belisarius appreciated the old veteran's counsel. Belisarius knew that although he was commander of the army in the East, he needed Hermogenes's approval to hold the confidence of his fellow generals. He turned to Hermogenes.

"General, the Persians have watched us dig trenches for three days. They are not going to attack with less than an hour's light. They need to see the terrain in front of them."

Hermogenes seemed to accept this logic and nodded his cautious approval. Pharas delivered the message to the captains, who passed the word along. Starting with the rear-most ranks, the men returned to their tents. After an hour, only the front-most line and the generals remained. The entire valley was in the shade of the western mountain, which meant that there would undoubtedly be no attack. He had made the right call. A cool breeze cooled his head, and Belisarius wiped the sweat off his forehead and neck and made a sour face.

"I need a bath," he said.

"I'm glad you noticed," Pharas replied quickly with a grin.

"A cool bath will give me a chance to think," he said. "We cannot have our men just sitting in the sun for a third day while the Persian harasses them."

The weary cavalry officers dismounted their warhorses, walked a half-mile through the gates of the Roman fortress at Dara, and headed for the governor's palace. Belisarius stayed behind. The giant took notice and began again.

"Ahh, are you Roman boys going to take a little nap?"

"What's that peacock yelling about now?" Belisarius asked.

"I don't know, and I don't care," Pharas replied. "Aren't you coming? You need your rest."

"No, my duty is to these men. I'll come when every last one is off the field."

The mindless yammering of the giant faded until his voice was little more than a pulsating annoyance. Belisarius looked around at the long, grimy faces of the last line of men as they filed past him. These men needed much more than bread and water. They needed to be encouraged and know that their general appreciated them. Most of all, they needed their commander to be strong. As he watched the vanguard of the Roman line file past him under the weight of their bread-oven armor, he wondered if he could be enough for them.

Pharas whacked the butt of Belisarius's mount and pushed its rider forward to the fortress.

"Let's go! You smell like a barbarian," the barbarian said. A descendant of immigrants from Scandza[1] north of the Baltic Sea, Pharas was a tall man who wore his long, blond hair braided behind his ears. His fair skin, now freckled and bronzed by the hot Syrian sun, made his blue eyes glow like the port of an Ionian harbor. He and Belisarius had been playmates as children in the town of Germania[2] in Thrace, and he spoke acquired Latin with a Germanic Herulian accent that made everyone laugh.

From the Dara rampart, one of the Roman infantrymen called out to the taunting Persian, "The general is going to his bath! Leave him alone." Belisarius gave him a warm smile.

---

[1] Scandinavia.

[2] Thracian for hot springs. Modern "Sapareva Banya" in southwestern Bulgaria translates as steam bath.

The Persian beat his sword over his shield in furious protest, "When we conquer Dara, Belisarius will prepare a bath and breakfast for Perozes so that he can clean the filthy Roman blood from his body."

The infantryman put an arrow in his bow and pulled it back. "That arrogant bastard!"

"Hold your fire, soldier," Hermogenes commanded. "No one shoots until we give the order." The archers relaxed their bows. The fresh bread and hot stew aroma had taken the fight out of them. Three days of digging a quarter-mile trench needed rest.

"I hope you appreciate that we're getting this little demonstration instead of a battle," Belisarius said.

"Oh yes," Pharas said. "I look forward to showing the Persians that trenches can be used against them as easily as they were against us at Thannuris."

"How is morale among the men?"

Pharas hesitated.

"Be candid, Pharas."

"They all know our record against the Persians, and...." Pharas stopped again. "Their current commander, Flavius, remains yet... unproven."

"Indeed, I am," Belisarius said with resignation before walking past Pharas and into the governor's palace.

Belisarius considered ways to exploit the arrogance born of a century of uninterrupted Persian victories over the Romans. Twenty-five years earlier, in the last round of Roman-Persian wars, Rome had lost the frontier post at nearby Nisibis and had been in retreat ever since. The Romans had built the fort at Dara to protect the border and fled there after their defeat at the battle of Thannuris.

As Belisarius entered the bedchamber, he passed a mirror in the bath chamber and smiled ruefully at his reflection. His thick black eyebrows arched intelligently over his dark brown eyes. Women admired his curly chin-length black hair and his chiseled jaw, now partly hidden by ten days' growth. His muscular physique testified to a life of strenuous military training. He knew he looked impressive in his armor, but Pharas's words weighed heavily upon him. *Unproven.*

He looked fine but smelled like a pack animal and knew a good soak in the bath would do wonders for his mind. As he brushed his hair, he recalled how Spartans groomed themselves before battle since they might be preparing their bodies for the afterlife. He wondered if he was vainly doing the same. He smiled in the mirror as though smiling at death and liked the reflection staring back at him.

He looked forward to relaxing and washing the sweat off his back after the long, laborious march from Asia Minor[3]. Hot springs kept the Roman bath in use even in winter, but on a hot day such as this, he liked to take advantage of the *frigidarium*[4] and massage room.

Doric columns supported a windowed ceiling above the bath, and a mosaic depicting archers hunting wild rams graced the floor. The marble walls were adorned with statues, a rare touch of civilization in the dusty fortress town. The low sun poured through the arched window, forming light beams on the steam floating in the air. The sound of children laughing and playing in the nearby shallow pool reminded Belisarius of his childhood when he frolicked in the baths with Pharas. He wondered if these children would still be laughing the next day or sold into slavery by the victorious Persians.

As he walked into the dressing room, Pharas and John, both nude, raised their arms to welcome him. He laughed at the immodest way that the two strutted around the bath--almost as though they were unaware that they were unclothed. He remembered the first time he saw Pharas and John nude and how their hairy backs made them look like brown and black bears.

John was his best cavalry commander, a Christian refugee from Persian-controlled Armenia who joined the Roman army during the Iberian War to protect his people from Zoroastrian persecutions. He had a swarthy complexion and a thick beard that had once prevented a Persian sword from cutting off his chin. He knew that with John and Pharas, he could relax — and think.

---

[3] Modern Turkey.

[4] Latin for cold bath.

As Belisarius took off his sweaty tunic and stepped tentatively into the cool water, he said, "It's a shame we don't have a larger bath so the men...."

"Spare us your platitudes, Flavius, and get in the water," John said as he splashed the cool water upon him, "the men would want you to indulge in this. We need you at your best tomorrow. Besides, they are all bathing in the cisterns now."

Belisarius smiled gratefully. "Good. Still, I'm worried about the men, John."

John had a finger on the pulse of the men and could speak candidly to Belisarius. "The men always murmur about vast Persian numbers."

"Yes, but I don't like going into battle with the fear I see in their eyes," Belisarius said.

"That's not really what's bothering you, Flavius, is it?" John asked. "You're concerned the men have doubts about how young you are."

Belisarius's sad nod seemed to suggest he shared their concern. "Wouldn't you be concerned if you were in their shoes?"

Pharas laughed, "Don't think too hard about it, Flavius. You're the same age Alexander was when he conquered Persia."

"Yes," Flavius agreed, "but Alexander had proven himself by that point. John is right. I am the youngest general here, and many of these guys served with me at Thannuris, which didn't go too well."

"Things like that happen in war,' John said. "You know that. Yes, the cavalry deserted the infantry, and the Persians crushed us, but..."

Pharas interrupted, "That's because the cavalry fell into hidden pits the Persians left for them. General Cutzes's charge was reckless. We would never have escaped except for Flavius's quick thinking," Pharas said.

"Perhaps," Belisarius said, "but their fears of the Persians are well-founded. I cannot do anything about my age, but I need to do something to inspire the men."

"Like what?" Pharas asked with a look of concern on his face.

"Accept their challenge for a duel," John said as he checked the water temperature with his big toe.

Pharas gave him a stern look, "No! Absolutely not!"

As Belisarius, Pharas, and John relaxed in the water, Belisarius closed his eyes and drifted to a game he and his friends had played at the thermal baths in his native Germania. He remembered the natural geyser that erupted every few minutes to the cheers of delighted bathers. He recalled the stone slide his friends used as a watchtower in their child war games. He recalled how he would stand upon it looking out for "enemy Huns" at a time when the threat of a Hunnish invasion constantly hung over his quiet little town. He thought of the horrible afternoon twenty years earlier, when he had been playing with Pharas and his adopted brother, Sunicas. The chimes of church bells had interrupted their play and had rung violently, signaling another raid.

Young Belisarius had shouted out to his playmates, "Huns! Real Huns!"

As the teenage bathers fled through the streets toward their homes and mothers, they had passed screaming women, terrified children, and Huns on horseback, shooting arrows and stabbing the townsfolk with swords and pikes. The air had reeked of thatched roofs set ablaze and the iron stench of blood. The Huns rustled women into caged carts like cattle, and Hunnish archers had struck down men who attempted to resist. In horror, Belisarius had recognized his mother and Pharas's mother. Almost as soon as the Huns had arrived, they had disappeared into the woods.

Despite the fear in him that told him to run away, he told himself to be strong. His father had gone to the Persian front, leaving him to protect the family. He recalled the desperate looks on his playmates and knew this was not the time to lose his courage.

Belisarius snapped out of his trance-like state. "Pharas, do you remember that time when the Huns invaded our village?"

"Yes," Pharas replied. "You ordered Sunicas and me to follow the Huns and see where they took our mothers. I thought you were insane, and that the Huns would kill us!"

Belisarius smiled and closed his eyes again to relive the memory. He remembered Sunicas agreed with him and said, "If we don't follow the Huns, we will never see our mothers again."

"Let's go then," Belisarius had said, and the trio ran into the woods toward the threat.

The boys, who were expert trackers, discretely followed the Huns until well past sundown, tying pieces of their tunics to trees at eye level so they could find their way back in the dark. They stopped when they reached the forest overlooking the Huns' camp.

"What will they do with them?" Sunicas had asked. His quavering voice had betrayed his fear.

"They're Huns. So, they must be looking for ransom," Belisarius answered as if he were accustomed to such a situation.

"Ransom! We don't have a...."

"I know. So, the Huns will probably sell our mothers into slavery!" Belisarius had held a hand over his friend's mouth to keep his pain in check.

They stealthily cased the area and managed to steal a knife, a bow, and a quiver full of arrows from a drunken Hun who had gone into the woods to relieve himself. Two more drunken Huns guarded the cages. At the main campfire, their comrades were laughing, drinking the fermented mare's milk they called kumis, eating raw horsemeat, and brawling among themselves.

Belisarius remembered that he felt a knot, deep in his stomach, that made him want to throw up. He realized that his pursuit of his mother risked the lives of every woman in the cart and his two best friends. If things went wrong, he would soon be alone in the world.

"Damned Huns!" Belisarius remembered saying.

"Hey!" Sunicas protested, "I'm a Hun!" Belisarius's father had adopted Sunicas when Persian raids murdered his parents and left him homeless.

"Yes," Belisarius replied, "but you're a *Roman* Hun. These Bulgarian savages are not." Belisarius furrowed his brow and bit his lower lip — something he still did when deliberating a grave matter. Then, as now, he had assumed the role of leader — not because he wanted to, but because he had to. "We'll create a diversion, divide their forces, and take out the easy targets."

He remembered that they had practiced these maneuvers in mock operations many times, but at that moment, they would use the skills they had honed while playing and imitating their warrior fathers. He remembered that the price of failure would not be lost prestige, but lost lives. "We'll have to avoid a full confrontation since they outnumber us. If our plan succeeds, we'll free the hostages and run off with them!"

"Pharas," Belisarius had ordered, "quietly release all their horses from the pen. The noise should distract them. Sunicas, you are the marksman. Shoot the guards in the throats so they can't scream." He had pointed at two Huns.

Sunicas had given him a slightly irritated look. "What will *you* do, Flavius?"

Flavius had found himself bewildered by the question and realized that he hadn't worked this out yet. "I'm the strategic reserve," he had said with a laugh that put the trio more at ease. "I can't reveal my full plan because you might be captured and tortured for information." He had smiled nervously, and Sunicas rolled his eyes.

Belisarius then took a serious tone and asked sternly, "Can you do this?" The two had nodded. "When you've achieved your objectives, we'll meet at the cage, free the captives, and bring them home."

He remembered that while Pharas quietly released the horses, Belisarius had snuck up to the cage where the exhausted women had slept and whispered to the nearest woman who quietly woke his mother.

His mother's face betrayed pride and fear, "Flavius, how…."

"Shhh… I'll explain later." He had extended his hand through the cage and took hers. "Tell the other women to be quiet. I'm going to pass you a rope. You must all hold onto it, and we'll lead you out when the time is right."

He remembered looking up at the sky. A quarter moon shone just brightly enough that he could find the trail back through the woods without exposing them. He used the stolen knife to cut the ropes that secured the cage door.

Suddenly, the rumble of two dozen horses stampeding had awakened the sleeping Huns, who began to shout. Belisarius heard a "thwap!" followed by brief gurgling sounds, then silence. Another "thwap" told him Sunicas's arrows had found their targets. Both guards were dead.

"Now!" he whispered. "Go!"

The women stood up and grasped the rope.

Pharas led the women away from the camp, while Sunicas and Belisarius stayed behind to watch for followers. A quarter-hour later, they heard the thunder of hooves behind them. Belisarius ran back a hundred paces, and between two tall trees, he tied a rope at the height of a horse's shoulder.

He called out, "Hey! Are you looking for your daily wages?"

Three Huns had spotted him, pointed, and given chase. He had faked an escape and then ducked behind the trees. The rope unhorsed two of them as the Huns approached at full gallop. One had fallen dead with a broken neck, and Belisarius had quickly dispatched the other with a knife to his throat. He recalled that that had been his first kill, and while he expected to be conflicted about it, the moment's urgency allowed no time for introspection.

Seeing what had happened, the third Hun slowed his horse, drew back his bow, aimed at Belisarius, and loosed an arrow. It stuck in a tree just an arm's length from his head. The Hun drew another arrow and aimed. Frozen in fear, Belisarius had time enough to hope his mother would escape before he fell, but Sunicas put an arrow in the Hun's eye and ended the chase.

"You saved my life, Sunicas," Belisarius said as he snapped out of his stupor. "In gratitude, I offer you this fine horse."

"You love dividing the spoils, don't you?" Sunicas said with a grin. Belisarius grabbed the reins of the other two horses and scooped up the short lances the Huns had been carrying.

Riding two horses and leading the third, Sunicas and Belisarius had spotted a Hun aiming at the women, who screamed and ran faster. They had turned and charged the Hun with the short lances. Belisarius diverted him from Sunicas, who thrust his lance into the man's belly, then Belisarius lanced him in the neck, and he fell.

Belisarius looked for his mother but could not find her. He felt his heart racing and tried to control his breathing when he felt himself hyperventilating. Frantically, he asked Pharas where she was, but the boy shrugged his shoulders. Belisarius felt his heart rate increase and felt a shortness of breath. He felt his legs tremble underneath him.

Belisarius and Sunicas retraced the steps of the women across an open field. In a boggy area, he found a woman wearing his mother's red dress lying face down in the mud, circled in blood, an arrow in her spine. He remembered that day as the worst in his life.

An intense urge to run to her overcame him, and his stomach felt intolerably heavy. He dismounted and waded through the mud. "Mother! Mother!" When he had rolled her over, she slowly opened her eyes and struggled to catch her breath, gurgling. The arrow had penetrated a lung and filled it with blood. He had wiped the mud and blood from her face. "Flavius," she said, touching his cheek, "So proud of you. So brave… All safe?"

"Yes," he replied, his tears rinsing her bloodied face. "Don't leave me!"

"Promise me," she struggled to whisper, "never again!"

He nodded rapidly, too choked by grief to say that he understood what she wanted him to do. "I promise." He watched in sorrow as her soul's hold on this world slipped away, and she took one last dying breath. He was rocking her in his arms when Sunicas reached him.

"Flavius, we have to get out of here before the rest of the Huns find us," Sunicas urged.

Belisarius didn't move for a full minute. He wiped the blood around her mouth and kissed her tenderly on the lips. He gently closed her eyes, put his arms underneath her, gently removed the arrow from her back, picked her up, and stood up slowly and silently. Sunicas helped him lift his mother onto his horse, and he rode behind her. They headed back to the village to join Pharas and the freed women. From a distance, the freed women cheered the two young liberators until they realized their mother was dead in the saddle.

Broken, Belisarius dismounted with his mother and entered his smoldering, roofless home. He placed her on the charred remains of his dining room table, took off his cloak, and covered her, silently vowing to honor his mother's dying wish. This raid would never happen again, anywhere. He would dedicate his life to making the empire safe.

# CHAPTER TWO

# THE DUEL

*David said to the Philistine, "You come to me with sword and spear and javelin, but I come to you in the name of the Lord of hosts, the God of the armies of Israel, whom you have defied. This day, the Lord will deliver you into my hand, and I will strike you down and cut off your head.... The battle is the Lord's, and he will give you into our hand."*

— I Samuel 17:45-47

*Roman Fortress at Dara near the Persian Border*
*27 June 530, A.D.*

"Hey, Flavius! Have you fallen asleep in your bath?" Pharas asked, grinning.

"What was our commander muttering?" John asked. "Something about 'Never again. Never again?'" John asked Pharas.

"Yes," Pharas laughed. "He dreamed of his first kiss with that toothless Egyptian belly dancer at your wedding!"

The two generals laughed, startling Belisarius out of his reverie. He shook his head and rubbed his heavy eyelids. "Pharas? John? What's so funny?"

The two only laughed harder. Belisarius smiled embarrassingly. "When I heard the children laughing, I remembered why we're here. This town and these people are worth defending. The Persians have no right to this place, and they will destroy it."

Pharas and John stopped laughing and nodded, splashing cool water on their faces as if to sober up. "Indeed, the Roman retreat must stop here — today!" Pharas said sternly.

"No easy task," John added slowly.

"The question is *how?*" Pharas said.

"I know," Belisarius sighed. "We're responsible for the fate of Dara, but why should we think we'll fare any better than we did at Thannuris?"

"We have to," Pharas replied. "After the Persians sacrificed four hundred Roman nuns to the goddess Al-Uzza, I expect that those savages will either kill or enslave anyone captured at Dara." Belisarius nodded in agreement.

In the steam room, Belisarius inhaled the sweet incense burned to mask the body odors that drifted from the exercise and sweat rooms. A servant placed red-hot volcanic rocks on the center of the floor, then gently poured rosemary-scented water over them, filling the space with steam. Belisarius closed his eyes, inhaled, and smiled. It reminded him of a perfume his mother wore and somehow strengthened his resolve.

Half an hour later, they were in the rinsing room where a servant poured cold water over them. Belisarius avoided the temptation to shriek, and chuckled when he saw how much the servant enjoyed this part of the job. It reminded him of the days when his mother would bathe him and gently mock him for "being afraid of a little cold water."

Belisarius watched a swallow building a nest in an overhang as he shivered and dried himself. The bird studied the generals, seemed to dismiss them, and swooped to fill his beak with the cool water. The generals looked at each other and nodded their approval.

"It's a good omen, Flavius," John said. "Even the swallow shall find a home for its nest where she may lay her young."

Sunicas rushed into the room, disturbing the swallow, which flew away and interrupted the officers' serenity.

"Like a fluttering sparrow or a darting swallow, an undeserved curse will not land on its intended victim," John said to more laughs and a clueless Sunicas.

Sunicas was thirty, the same age as his childhood friends, but he looked much older. A long mustache shadowed his lips, and he had shaved the front of his head, giving him the appearance of a receding hairline while a black ponytail snaked down his back. He wore animal skins over most of his body, scaled armor protected his chest and back, and his fur cap resembled the traditional yurts in which his people had lived until the Persians destroyed them.

"Who is that prancing peacock to defy the armies of Rome?" Sunicas demanded. "Flavius, how long will you allow the Persian fool to insult us?"

"Until dawn, Sunicas," Belisarius replied, "The men need to regain their strength. We will be fighting soon enough. We should be grateful that our Persian guests haven't rushed into battle."

"If you have no more need of me," he said, "I should like to pick up the gauntlet on your behalf. I have earned a chance to distinguish myself."

"That you have, Sunicas," Belisarius replied, "but this Persian has challenged *me*."

"True enough, but we cannot send our top commander into a duel," Sunicas replied.

Belisarius smiled, raised an eyebrow, and looked at John. "I am thinking about accepting the challenge." John nodded his approval.

"Ha! You cannot beat him!" The cynical voice from the other side of the bathhouse belonged to Constantinus, lying on his belly while a domestic used a strigil to scrape dirt off his back.

Belisarius let out a long sigh. "We can always count on you for a word of encouragement."

"That's why they call him the 'black centurion,'" Pharas said as he looked in the corner of the bath where he saw Constantinus's black leather cuirass with purple trimming and a black plumed helmet carefully stacked on a rack.

Constantinus sat up, joined the generals in the bath, and began shaving his head. Pharas studied him with disbelief and said, "I suppose that when you are done making yourself look like Julius Caesar, you'll rinse your head in our bath water?"

Constantinus nodded, indifferent to the idea that Pharas did not want his colleague's head shavings stuck to his body when he emerged from the bath. Pharas rolled his eyes.

"That Persian is huge and fierce," Constantinus continued, "and I doubt his commander, Perozes, would have allowed him to taunt us if he doubts his chance of victory."

"Well, General, let's just say that I am intrigued about a David versus Goliath contest," Belisarius said.

John turned to Constantinus and the other bathers and said, "Flavius, if you unhorse this fire-worshipper, the Persians will see it as a bad omen. The sooner we finish this bloody war, the sooner our men can return to their families."

Belisarius rubbed his chin, "Agreed, John. I'll accept this challenge tomorrow. We could all use a good dose of martial spirit right now. The Persians outnumber us and have won every battle anyone alive can remember."

"God be with you, Flavius," Pharas said, striking his commander's shoulder.

Constantinus submerged his head in the bath water and vigorously rubbed his head. Pharas watched the event in disgust, jumped out of the water like a frog, and yelled, "By God's bones!"

The other generals gradually emerged from the bath less dramatically, but as Pharas departed, he kicked Constantinus's armor rack into the water.

"Damn you, barbarian!" Constantinus yelled as Belisarius, Sunicas, and John laughed at the display of intemperance and quickly left the scene before it further escalated.

Belisarius returned to his private quarters, laid his weary head on the bed and hoped to fall asleep, but he could not. That night, Belisarius's sweat-drenched body tossed and turned in his sinfully luxurious feather bed. His mind fixated on a terrible dream of a colossal Persian looking down upon him from a towering height. He heard the giant's voice inciting his comrade to show no mercy to the Romans. No matter how hard he tried, he could not arise from his vulnerable position on the ground. To his utter horror, he realized that his belly had been cut wide open, and rivers of blood poured out. The brute waved his sword above his head as blood ran down the hilt and his arm.

"And now I will destroy your entire army!"

Belisarius awoke to a transitioning sky. He wasn't sure if he had slept at all. John recognized this at once.

"Nightmares again, Flavius?" he asked with concern in his voice. Belisarius nodded. John helped his friend put on his scale armor, strapped his greaves to his shins, and placed his visored helmet on his head. "Nightmares can be terrifying, Flavius, but the real terror happens when you're awake." He slapped Belisarius on the chest, "We're taking down these Persians today, Flavius."

At that moment, Sunicas came through the door. "Flavius, send that creature back to his Creator!"

"God willing, Sunicas."

"And don't forget to take his Nisean steed. We're short of good horses."

"Yes, every infantryman wants to be a cavalryman, doesn't he?"

Belisarius left the governor's palace and passed through the city gate. All eyes were upon him, and he felt the weight of command like he never had. As he mounted Bucephalus and rode across the Roman line, his troops put down their morning meal, stood at attention for their commander, and erupted into cheers. Belisarius acknowledged their acclaim but found himself wishing he shared their good spirits. He felt tired from poor sleep and a weak breakfast that had refused to stay down.

As Belisarius rode past Constantinus, the general shook his head in disapproval. "I've had men flogged for this sort of charade."

He saw John standing beside the army chaplain, who beckoned Belisarius to dismount. The monk approached him with a jar of chrism and a hand raised. He put his thumb in the chrismaria and then pressed it hard into Belisarius's forehead, making a sign of the cross. "May you do what the Lord of Hosts requires of you, Flavius Belisarius. May He diminish your fears, fill you with courage, and keep you safe from all harm."

Belisarius thanked him, and the priest stepped aside. He inhaled the scent of the balsam and felt his spirit start to awaken. As John stepped in front of him, Belisarius smiled. "What do you have that can top that?"

John handed him a small sack. "I spent the morning collecting them from the riverbed."

Belisarius untied the string and opened the sack.

"Five smooth stones," Belisarius said as he recalled the story of David and Goliath. "Very fitting." He felt two tears of gratitude escape from his eyes as John warmly embraced him.

"Come back to us, Flavius, or Constantinus will be spitting on your grave."

"Thank you, John," Belisarius laughed, escaped the embrace, and remounted his horse.

The brazen Persian knight was already on the field, and as Belisarius appeared to face him, he lowered his lance, let out a battle cry, and charged at full gallop. Belisarius prayed, "Lord, give me strength." He leaned forward in the saddle and stirrups, kicked his horse in the ribs, and aimed his lance, unflinching as the Persian galloped toward him, then plunged it into the chest of the giant, who rolled onto the ground. The horse, now riderless, ran Belisarius down, propelling him ten paces back as his helmet somersaulted another twenty.

He struggled to get up, fearing the Persian would cut him down, but the giant lay on his back, weighed down by his heavy armor, as helpless as a tortoise turned shell-side down. Belisarius tossed his lance aside, pulled his sword from its sheath, and charged before the Persian could stand up. He recalled for a moment that this was the opposite of what had happed in his dream. He pressed his left hand into the man's fractured sternum while slashing his throat with his right so that he bled out in seconds like a sacrificial animal. Belisarius's exhilaration over his triumph was short-lived and soon replaced by grief.

Belisarius stood up and surveyed the lifeless body under him. "This day did not have to end like this for you," he said as sadness overcame him.

The Roman troops watching from their lines erupted in cheers and banged their shields, chanting, "Belsar! Belsar!" Few of his infantrymen spoke Latin well enough to pronounce his name correctly. He looked toward the Persian battlefront, hoping they would quit the field as promised, but he was not surprised to see them standing their ground. He retrieved his helmet and turned back to the

Roman line. When he was within a stone's throw, Pharas yelled, "Flavius, behind you!"

A second Persian knight cantered toward him. Fear gripped Belisarius as he realized the folly of turning his back to the enemy line. He mentally chastised himself for forgetting one of the critical rules of warfare: "Be ever on the watch for the opportunity to strike the enemy before he is ready." He turned around and saw a Persian bent over the giant's body.

"My son!" the Persian cried and stopped to mourn the corpse. In an instant, his sorrow turned to rage. He kicked his horse's ribs hard, lowered his lance, and charged at Belisarius, shaking the ground beneath him.

Belisarius cursed and wondered whether the Persians had planned an immediate follow-on attack if the giant had failed. He remounted his stallion and countercharged at full gallop, the white plume of his helmet streaming behind him. He leaned forward in his stirrups and blinked quickly as his eyes, dried by the sand and wind, blurred his vision. The two knights collided, deflecting blows with their lances so that neither could score a direct hit, crashing so violently that both horses and knights fell to the ground, their lances shattered.

Belisarius rose and frantically reached for his sword but found it was no longer in his belt. "*Deodamnautus!*" he murmured.

The Persian managed to get up on one knee and snapped his horsewhip. Belisarius charged him at a run, checking his belt for anything he might use to kill the Persian. As he felt nothing but John's little sack of stones, he laughed, wrapped his hand around it, and determined to transform it into a mace. He pulled his arm back and then quickly swung it forward, striking the Persian in the forehead. The Persian fell back and tackled Belisarius as he did so. Belisarius wrestled the old knight, got behind him, and held him by the throat as he kicked and thrashed. The weight of the Persian's armor prevented him from breaking free, and as Belisarius squeezed the life from him, his movements slowed.

Belisarius stood and raised the bag of stones above his head. "*Roma vincit!*" he shouted to the tumultuous applause of 25,000 Romans and the Dara garrison while the Persian phalanx froze in horrified disbelief. Then he lifted the slain father, carried him to the place where his son had fallen, laid him next to the giant, and made the sign of the cross. "May God commend you for your courage today, brothers." Belisarius's stomach heaved at the smell of their blood, and, for a moment, he wished he were anywhere else. Were it not for his promise to his mother, he might have been.

He looked in his hand, beheld the ridiculous weapon he had used to slay his opponent, and wondered how things might have turned out had John not given him his sack of stones. "Fickle fortune reigns," he thought aloud, "and, undiscerning, scatters crowns and chains."

He gathered the reins of the Nisean chargers and mounted one — struggling to hide the pain of his bruises from the admiring eyes of his comrades. He looked again at the Persian line to be sure there were no more challengers but saw only two unarmed young attendants running to retrieve the bodies of their fallen heroes, shouting at him in Persian. He did not understand their words, but their gestures implied that they were furious he had taken their horses. He wondered about a people who seemed more concerned about stolen horses than dead comrades and gave them a disapproving look.

He turned around and, in his best Greek, yelled, "If you want them, come and get them!" then cantered his prizes to the Roman line, where raised swords saluted him. The Persian trumpets blasted for a withdrawal back to Nisibis, and the troops cheered again. "Thank God," he murmured.

As he rode back to the Roman line, John was the first one to greet him. "Did you slay that second Persian with the sack…"

"Yes," Belisarius interrupted with a firmness that conveyed the farcicality of the idea. "Here, you can have them back now." He tried to hand John a blood-soaked sack.

"No, Flavius, I think you should keep it. They seem to have brought you Divine favor. Your return is an answer to many prayers."

Pharas joined them. "A double win is a good omen for us," he said. "What do you need?"

"A bath for me and water for my new horses!" The men around them laughed, and he played along, dismounted, stripped down to his tunic, and headed back to the baths.

"You've earned your bath today," Pharas said as the *medicus*[5] spread ointment on Belisarius's bruises and bandaged his swollen, purple rib cage. "In slaying the giant, you have convinced the army that we can beat them."

Belisarius turned to John. "My biblical history is a bit hazy, John, but *didn't* the Philistines turn and run after David slew their giant?"

John laughed and smirked. "Yes, Flavius. I'm sorry. I'm afraid the Persians may be less acquainted with that story, so you'll have to settle for an orderly retreat."

Belisarius shook his head in humorous disappointment. "Well, that's a good day's work, then."

He then beckoned his secretary Procopius. "Be sure to record that on the day before the battle, a slave to the bath slew two of the best of the Persian army."

Procopius was slight and clean-shaven, with a look of innocence that hid his raw ambition. He had been born in Caesarea in Palestine and was a lawyer by training with an elite Greek education. He lacked experience on the battlefield, but no one knew Herodotus better, and he could recite details from any battle ever recorded by the Greeks or Romans. Belisarius had entrusted him with maintaining a detailed military log of the Persian campaign to be delivered to the Emperor. Pharas had once opined that Procopius harbored an inordinate affection for the general, but Belisarius dismissed the idea.

The *medicus* brought Belisarius into the surgeon's tent, poked and squeezed, then reported to Pharas, Sunicas, and John: "Two, perhaps three, cracked ribs. Nothing serious, but I recommend thirty days of rest and recovery."

"We have a comedian among us," Belisarius said, laughing before wincing from the pain it brought and soberly reminding himself that he was in no condition to pull a bow or swing a sword the following day. He wondered what might happen to him if he were captured, a fate worse than death.

He remembered the life of Valerian, whom the Persians captured in battle almost two centuries before. Then-Shah Shapur ordered the fallen Emperor to serve as a human footstool whenever he mounted his horse. When the proud Emperor could no longer endure the abuse, Shapur ordered him killed by being flayed alive

---

[5] Lat. Field surgeon

and then had Valerian skinned, stuffed with straw, and preserved as a trophy in the main temple in Ctesiphon. Belisarius shivered at the thought.

"The Persians will be back tomorrow morning," he said grimly, "and the entire Persian host will come at us this time."

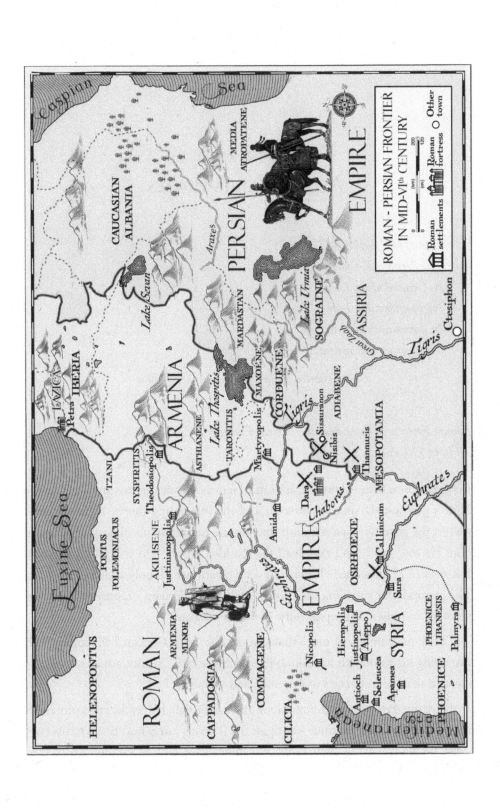

ROMAN - PERSIAN FRONTIER
IN MID-VIᵗʰ CENTURY

Roman settlements

Roman fortress

Other town

# Chapter Three

# All the King's Horses

*"It was for [Justinian] I chased*
*The Persians o'er wild and waste,*
*As General of the East;*
*Night after night I lay*
*In their camps of yesterday;*
*Their forage was my feast."*

— *Belisarius*, Henry Wadsworth Longfellow

*Roman Fortress at Dara near the Persian Frontier*
*28 June 530, A.D.*

In the darkness before dawn, an additional ten-thousand Persians arrived from the Nisibis garrison. Despite his wounds and the impending threat, Belisarius slept well in the governor's palace until the familiar pounding of military boots woke him. He rose slowly and examined the speckled purple skin around his rib cage. His swollen rib cage made him take a deep breath, which only added to the pain. The gratitude for surviving the combat against the Persians suppressed his temptation to complain. Procopius burst in with a message.

"They outnumber us more than two-to-one now, General," Procopius said, massaging his palm with his thumb to relax his nerves. "Constantinus has recommended that we seek terms of surrender and withdraw."

Belisarius gave him an annoyed look and a long sigh; his cracked ribs protested. He wondered if Constantinus was right: the Romans rarely beat the Persians even when the odds were in their favor. His injury gave him an excuse to turn over command to Constantinus, but he knew what that would mean for the residents of Dara, and he would not abandon them. Justinian's orders were clear: check the Persian advance in Syria. Surrender was not in keeping with that order.

He covered himself in gold-plated scale armor, leaving only his neck and calves exposed, then threw a vermilion cloak over his shoulders. Even before the sunrise, it was hot, and he wiped his dripping brow.

When he reached the palace *tablinum*,[6] he found Pharas and John looking grim as they studied the battlefield mock-up, a sand-filled box Procopius had prepared. Belisarius commanded the combined forces of the Roman armies, six hundred mounted archers led by Sunicas, three hundred Herulian cavalrymen led by Pharas, and a heavy cavalry unit commanded by John. The three generals were his most trusted commanders.

But the Persians badly outnumbered them. Belisarius stepped onto the balcony and watched as Sunicas rode up to the villa. Sunicas pulled a chunk of horsemeat from under his saddle, gnawed it like a fox, and washed it down with fermented mare's milk.

From the balcony, he watched John, a man who had saved his life more than once, his swaggering presence reassured Belisarius. He watched the sun rise and reflect off the armor of 50,000 Persians standing shoulder-to-shoulder as far as Belisarius could see. He struggled to conceal his pain as he strode forward to begin his morning briefing. He knew seeing their commander in pain would only add to the somber feeling in the room. As Sunicas and Constantinus joined them in the *tablinum*, Belisarius strutted into the room with the strut of a lion who had just bested a rival.

"Procopius was up all night playing in this little sandbox while all of you were writing nervous letters to your lovers," he said, and guilty laughter eased the tension in the room.

"But now, back to business. The Persians outnumber us only if we believe that a general can command 50,000 troops. I do not think it is possible. Most of their infantry are little more than enslaved people serving masters whom they despise

---

[6] Lat. an office and library in a Roman home that often doubled as a conference room.

more than they fear. They will desert at the first sign of trouble. Their wicker shields and spears no more make them spearmen than flutes would make them snake charmers."

Pharas's laughter surpassed the others, and Belisarius gave him a grateful glance. He could always count on Pharas to laugh at his jokes. His delightful laughter was infectious to all but Constantinus, who remained as dour as a widow at a funeral.

"So, what is your plan, General?" Constantinus asked.

Procopius had made a long groove in the sand to represent the deep trench with multiple narrow drawbridges. He pointed to the mockup. "The fortress at Dara is not large enough to support us, so we'll place ourselves in front of it while the army places itself behind this long trench."

"John, your cavalry will command the right wing. Sunicas, your mounted archers will flank the center." The two commanders nodded their approval of the plan. "Buzes and Pharas, you will cover our left flank, ready to spring into action on the rearguard of the Persian cavalry." Pharas started to say something.

"What is it, Pharas?"

"Flavius, my Herulian light cavalry can remain hidden behind the hills and emerge when the time is right."

*Great thinking.* "Then take that position on the extreme left wing," Belisarius replied.

"What about the *limitanei?*" Constantinus asked. "I fear they will flee."

Belisarius had hastily assembled the *limitanei* from the local garrisons of infantry, mostly unarmored foot archers. "They're not Caesar's legionnaires, I know," Belisarius said, "but they will hold the center ground. They are accustomed to fighting behind the security of high walls, so the redoubt should afford them some protection. The Persian knights will be unable to leap over it and struggle to climb it." He studied Constantinus's skeptical look and added, "Your thoughts, general?"

Constantinus raised his nose in the air, closed his eyes, and shook his head. "Perozes will avoid the trap you have set for him unless he first routes at least one of our flanks."

"True," Belisarius said. "We must confine the Persians to the killing zone where our unmounted archers can play a decisive role. Our cavalry must get behind the Persians. If the flanks fall back a bit, steady them! Treat this battle as an ordinary drill. I'll be waiting with the rearguard reserve in case you decide to cut and run."

His commanders returned feigned scowls, but Constantinus seemed to take affront to the suggestion.

"If we hold them," Belisarius continued, "we can expect an attack on the opposite flank since no general likes to order his troops to march over their comrades' dead or dying bodies, and the sight of dying horses unnerves the chargers, as well. Any questions?"

Most of the commanders shook their heads. Only Constantinus seemed unconvinced.

"What role shall I have?" he asked indignantly.

No one answered until Belisarius started to say something. John quickly cut him off, "You, Constantinus, will be in the rear in case all goes poorly, and we need a general officer to offer terms of surrender."

An awkward silence filled the room until Belisarius spoke, "You have command of the infantry. Once it's clear we have neutralized their cavalry, your men will advance toward the Persian line." Constantinus's hiss and glare indicated his contempt for infantry and his preference to command cavalry. Belisarius had tried cultivating a professional relationship with Constantinus but had largely given up when he suggested that surrender was the best option.

Constantinus tried to lighten the blow to his ego. "I shall inform the Emperor of the folly of this battle and tell him that the human wastage was unnecessary."

"Your apprehension is duly noted," Belisarius said. He turned to his resident expert on the earlier Greco-Persian wars.

"Procopius, surely this is not the first time in history when outnumbered men have stood up to the Persians, is it?"

"No, indeed not, sir," Procopius said. "Spartan King Leonidas used this strategy at the Battle of Thermopylae. The Persians could create a wider front and outflank us with their great numbers, so we limit them by exploiting the hilly terrain."

Constantinus shook his baldhead impatiently. "Thank you for the schoolboy history lesson, Procopius."

"This is a sound plan," Pharas said, "but once launched, our ability to see what Perozes is doing will be extremely limited, and it will be nearly impossible to call back so many men."

Belisarius nodded in relief. He knew that his commanders needed to endorse his plan if he were to gain the confidence of his troops. Yet he wondered if his battle plan were not based more

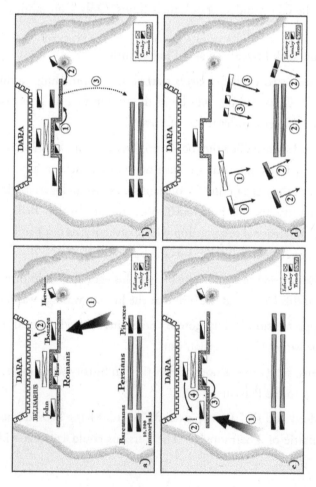

on assumptions and rumors than facts. Much of his intelligence on Perozes's army came from the hearsay of nearby villagers prone to turning every tidbit into a tall tale. The Persians' alleged "mountains" of grain gave him no idea how long Perozes could feed his army without resupplying.

"Pharas is right," Belisarius said. "Keep your men disciplined. Anyone who tends toward brashness should be at the back of the line. Maintain unit cohesion at all costs." He dragged his finger between two steep hills in the sandbox. "This trench extends a mile between the two mountain ridges. We can lower the draw-bridges on the flanking trenches to allow our cavalry to counterattack, but we must not let the Persians cross them. Guard those spots with your strongest and bravest men. The center infantry trench is set a hundred paces back and does not have bridges. Those troops must not venture out until victory is nearly certain. The Persians cannot get around our line, and those two mountain ridges are a day's march away."

He turned to Sunicas. "We have a strong wind at our backs, and our bows are stronger with a longer range. I'm confident we'll get the better of the first contact with the enemy, but we must prevent the Persians from deploying all their troops at once...."

"Or you'll end up like Emperor Valerian on all fours," Procopius said, "serving as Shah Kavad's human footstool."

His commanders laughed at this, but Sunicas glared at Procopius. Belisarius turned to look sympathetically at his adoptive brother and recalled how the Persian shah had enslaved his extended family. "Surrender is not an option," the Hun said.

Belisarius nodded. "If we drive them back, we must pursue them for no more than a mile. If they manage to regroup, they can use their larger numbers to their advantage, envelope us, and snatch victory from the jaws of defeat. If Heaven favors us, we might beat this army today, but don't forget...." He paused for dramatic effect and looked each officer in the eyes. "...we lack the forces to destroy it."

At that moment, General Buzes entered the room. "Sorry I'm late, sir. So, what did you decide? Full frontal assault?" Buzes was an Illyrian famous for his drinking, womanizing, and inability to show up on time. He had big red lips, brown curly hair, and an impulsive spirit.

Constantinus interrupted him. "Like you and your brother Cutzes tried at Thannuris? No, Buzes, we will not attempt another foolish assault!"

"Cutzes died in that...." Buzes yelled and began to charge after Constantinus, who put his hand on the hilt of his sword.

"Gentlemen, please," Belisarius exhorted them, and Buzes backed off. "We're letting the Persians make the first move, Buzes, and there will be no pursuit of the enemy in terrain we have not first surveyed."

A breathless courier arrived, knocking over a stack of lances. "Sir, we have a reply to your peace overture."

"Where is your Persian-speaking colleague?" Belisarius asked.

"The Persians detained him, sir. Perozes claimed that anyone who spoke Persian and worked for the Roman Emperor must be a lying traitor. This box contains his reply."

The general calmly opened it and frowned. "Well, gentlemen, we have our answer." He held up the open box, which contained the translator's tongue.

The senior officers left the palace, mounted their horses, and headed to the front where the Roman army had taken positions in their lines. Belisarius regretted how badly his war council had gone. He preferred to build consensus among his commanders but knew he lacked the standing to do that before this battle. He hoped he had a better standing among the men, but their nervous faces and lowered voices made him wonder if they had doubts about him. Some men prayed desperate acts of contrition to purge their souls of sin, while others fidgeted with their arms or made improvements to the trenches. Hot dust filled every nostril.

Belisarius took his position in the center rear of his long formation with Procopius at his side. The red sun was beginning to beat down on the troops. His escorts, the *bucellarii*, baked under heavy chain mail and scale armor to the knees while their heads cooked in steel helmets and visors, and sweat stung their eyes.

Procopius removed the helmet from his sweaty brow. "When will this battle start anyway?" he asked. "We'll die of hunger and heat stroke if we sit out here much longer!"

*He's right: I need to take care of these men. God help me.*

"Their *clibanarii* and horses are suffering at least as much as we are," Belisarius replied as he watched his men stand at the ready hour after hour. Finally, he rode up to address them, and they saluted him with their swords. His captains gave the order to distribute bread and *garum*, a salted fish paste, ahead of schedule so they would have some sustenance before the battle. As the supernumeraries brought out the food, he suspected it might prompt the Persians to attack.

"Romans! We do not seek a mere victory today. We seek to obliterate the Persian's presumption that they can tread with impunity on land that has been Roman for six centuries."

Belisarius was pleased that the men seemed to forget their private preoccupations and focused on listening to him.

"We did not ask for this war; we did not invade Persia," Belisarius continued confidently. "But I promise you that if you heed the orders of your officers and maintain discipline, we will be victorious today. Pay no attention to their numbers." *Easier said than done!*

"Their cavalrymen seem splendid, but the bulk of their army are idlers who can do little more than undermine walls or plunder the bodies of the slain. For them, fighting means hiding behind their shields. Are you afraid of this?"

"NO!" thundered the reply from the masses as they beat their swords on their shields. Their enthusiastic response cheered him. The thumps on the shields seemed like the army's heartbeat, and he felt a surge of confidence in his men. He forgot about his broken ribs.

"Good, then let's have lunch."

The men laughed and sat down to eat their rations. An infantryman in front of him turned around and yelled, "General Belisarius! Thank you for coming to Dara to lead us." Belisarius gave him a warm smile and a salute.

Belisarius waited with an empty and complaining stomach for his men to finish eating and refit themselves for war before removing his lunch from his saddlebag. As the bread slid down his dry throat into his empty stomach, he heard the blast of a Persian trumpet, and it was not a call to retreat.

Belisarius felt his heartbeat quicken as he tightened the straps and belts on his helmet and armor. The heavily armored Persian *clibanarii*, a tight block in perfect formation, began to walk their steeds about a mile off in the distance. When the mounts were within bowshot of the Roman line, infantry commanders in front of him ordered, "Archers to the ready!"

The Roman infantry archers pulled their bowstrings to their ears and raised them to forty-five degrees. Belisarius spotted the infantryman who had thanked him nervously turn around to ensure that the Roman cavalry was still there. Belisarius gave him a reassuring wave and said to himself, "We're not going anywhere, son." For now, he knew his most important role was to reassure the infantry that the cavalry would not abandon him as they had at Thannuris. He could undoubtedly manage that — for now.

Several more infantry turned around to make sure Belisarius was still there. Embarrassed at their apparent lack of confidence, several gave him forced smiles and awkward nods. Belisarius gently gestured with two fingers for the men to look toward the front. They immediately complied. He reminded himself that the army had assembled most of his infantry from among farmers hoping to protect their homes from Persian raids. Unlike his well-trained cavalry, his infantry archers had minimal training, but they were good and brave men who could turn the battle if well-led. "We have a plan," he said to the men who could not hear him, "just hold steady." He prayed he could follow his counsel.

The Persian horses began to canter in block formation toward the heavy *cataphract* lancers on the Roman left flank, their speed gradually increasing.

"Fire!"

Belisarius watched as ten thousand Roman arrows darkened the sky like a Biblical cloud of locusts. The initial volley unhorsed one-tenth of the cavalry charge, but the Persian lancers kept coming. For every Persian felled by an arrow, another cavalryman ran his army down, making Belisarius wonder if he heard bones shattering in the mix of galloping hooves. In the dust, he could see little but heard the screams of men seemingly silenced by the stampede. He wished again that the Persians had accepted his peace overtures to avoid the loss of life.

The terror of war made him sick; the pure unnecessity of it made him even sicker. He felt the bread he had swallowed come up and spat it out. Procopius gave him a nervous glance. He knew all hell would break loose in a minute and focused his mind on the relative tranquility in the Roman ranks. He tried not to think of the Roman disaster at Thannuris and reminded himself that the Persians were falling into the trenches this time.

"This time, the Persians shall have their battle in the shade," Procopius observed as the arrows darkened the sky. Belisarius thought he was seeking a reassuring word. "You'd think they would have learned the perils archers pose to massed units."

"Yes," Belisarius said curtly, "Let's pray that the archers once again have the better of it."

The Roman cavalry soon aimed their bows up and waited for the order. "Fire at will!" The captains of the Roman left commanded, and the tremendous curved *tromba*[7] echoed his order. Both mounted and unmounted Roman archers unleashed a constant rain of arrows on the enemy. When the third volley of arrows went up, the *clibanarii* were in full gallop, quickly closing the gap. The ground shook under the hooves of ten thousand armored horses, and all but the front row of chargers disappeared in the dust storm that followed them. Buzes's cavalry crossed themselves as they readied for the Persians to slam into their line. Those in front looked nervously behind them and were reassured to see that not a single man fled in terror.

"Here they come," Belisarius whispered. "How can they see through all the dust?"

"How many are there?" Procopius asked.

---

[7] Roman bugle or trumpet

"At least a thousand in the front row, and God only knows how many more are shrouded in the dust storm behind them." Belisarius crossed himself and watched Buzes's cavalry brace themselves for impact. "We have nowhere to go."

Buzes's captains called out, "Launch the *tribuli!*" Trebuchets and foot soldiers tossed thousands of pointed iron tripods in front of the charging Persian cavalry. Each as wide as a human finger, the caltrops scattered on the ground before the charging equestrians permanently lamed any horse that stepped on them.

Belisarius watched the head of the Persian vanguard arrive at the trench and call out to his god, Ahura Mazda. As they came upon the Romans' deep trench, the first wave of horses reared up and tumbled into the ten-foot channel by the stampede behind them. The horses neighed in rebellion at the impossible commands to stop in the middle of a full gallop. Belisarius felt sorry for the poor beasts that carried the cavalrymen into battle. It wasn't their fight, yet they obediently followed their riders into the doom and death.

Men screamed and grunted as they fell, were trampled, and then struck with swords or lances. The clash of swords striking shields, opposing swords, armor, and even bone soon filled the battlefield with a cacophony of madness that excited and terrified Belisarius. He thought that surely the awful noise of this death song must make even the angels in Heaven shutter in horror. Only the Grim Reaper himself could enjoy the beat of axes chopping and the melody of blades singing. The smell of blood, vomit, and feces quickly followed the requiem.

A young, beardless Persian captain, thrown off his horse and impaled on a spike, caught Belisarius's attention. The sound of the stake ripping through his armor and torso made Belisarius shudder. Most of the Persian cavalrymen wore helmets with nose guards and chain mail that protected their cheeks, so he rarely saw the faces of the men killed. The man had lost his helmet, and Belisarius compassionately studied his soft face and rosy cheeks. The man stared at Belisarius in horror as life gradually left his quivering body. A moment later, a second rider was thrown onto the same stake, driving the youth further toward the ground and ending his life. Belisarius gasped. Within minutes, the entire trench was full of men quivering on stakes like helpless fish on a spear.

Mounted and dismounted Persian knights covered in blood, gasping for air, and cursing the Romans facing them, struggled up the soft sandy bank on the Roman side seeking revenge. Many more of the Persians' horses toppled backward from the weight of the armor as they reared up in terror, crushing the bones of their riders. Each fallen rider added to the formidable obstacle. Hundreds of knights fell on sharp stakes at the trench's bottom and screamed as they could not free themselves. The Roman archers above quickly turned these casualties into fatalities.

Belisarius had seen this ghastly scene in Thannuris but took some satisfaction that it was Persians and not Romans this time. He knew that he had given the Romans an unfair advantage but felt no shame. Yet the Persian cavalry kept coming. He looked toward the Persian front: no movement. *That's a good sign.* He turned to Procopius, who looked overwhelmed by the horror of war and ready to flee, more from distress than fear, and smiled.

Belisarius heard a Persian commander scream an order, directing his men around the trench or over the narrow bridges. He wondered if this was the famous Pityaxes. On the other side, the Persians faced the best of the Roman cavalry, but a Persian squadron managed to cross, and Buzes's cavalrymen fell back in good order. He was proud of them. Once a dozen Persians had plotted a path over the trench to the Roman lines, others followed, but the valley of death had reduced the momentous charge to a mere trickle. As the Persian lancers continued to crash into the Romans, they fell back thirty paces. Belisarius watched as the lancers toppled a dozen Romans from their mounts, and he felt his calm depart him.

"Lord, have mercy," Belisarius cried out. "Drop your lances and wield your spathions[8]!" He watched as the Romans unsheathed their longer cavalry swords. The trenches served their purpose, slowing the Persian charge enough to allow the Roman cavalry to make an orderly withdrawal. But the orderly withdrawal was starting to look less orderly.

Belisarius shouted to anyone who could still hear him above the clash of arms and cries of men and horses, "Come... steady! Hold on a little longer, and we can

---

[8] A straight, double-edged sword

envelop them!" Procopius gave him a look of incredulity, and Belisarius stopped chewing the corner of his lip and returned a half-smile.

A moment later, he knew the time had come. "Unleash the Herulians!" He gave a hand signal, and a trumpet sounded to Pharas's cavalry hiding behind the hill. The ax-wielders from Scandza emerged galloping from the hills on the far left of the Roman flank and charged the Persian rear hard.

Belisarius checked the Persian center and left — they had not moved. Pharas's mercenaries emerged and swung their battle-axes into the spines of the enemy's unsuspecting rearguard, who turned to face the Herulians but could not do so in time to save their lives. From a distance, Belisarius watched the muscular Herulians strike their weapons deep into the upper backs of the Persian cavalry, easily penetrating their armor. At Pharas's insistence, Belisarius had once tried the battle-ax but never cared for the weapon because of its difficulty in extraction. He watched as the Herulians struggled to pull their axes out of bodies to horrific effect. The Herulians' proclivity for hitting the spine just below the back of the helmet meant that there were several Persian riders whose heads were attached to bodies only by a few sinews as blood gushed from their necks like fountains. Belisarius knew that the macabre scene must be taking a toll on Persian morale.

"And now it's time to close the noose," Belisarius muttered, turning to Procopius, "Now! Set loose the Huns!"

The signalman raised a second flag. As the Persian rear reached the Roman line, Sunicas maneuvered his cavalry archers into position on the other side. Pityaxes sent a shocked contingent to meet them to avoid becoming surrounded. The unexpected attack on the Persian line's rear had halted their vanguard's advance. His Romans had the Persians almost surrounded. He didn't worry about completely plugging the gap since he usually wanted his enemy to have a narrow escape route if they needed one. An enemy surrounded would fight to the death, and he could not afford to waste his men on vanquishing a foe already beaten.

Belisarius shouted, "Stop yielding ground!" and a trumpet signaled the command for Buzes's cavalry to advance. The Persian column's press was weakening, and they could no longer provide replacements for the rapidly falling knights. Within minutes, the Romans had almost wholly enveloped the Persian right flank.

"They are crowded, confused, and starting to panic," Belisarius said to Procopius. "This is when war becomes slaughter." He considered how much more frightful hand-to-hand combat was than taking missile fire. One had a chance to dodge or deflect an arrow, but every thrust and parry of a sword required an immediate reaction, and if one did that repeatedly for hours, exhausted arms could no longer keep up. When troops combined missile fire and hand-to-hand combat, few units could long maintain cohesion. He watched as one brave Persian, with three arrows in his back, wearily fought on, but after a minute, he was no longer able to raise his sword, and a Hun thrust a lance deep into his belly, disemboweling him when he pulled it out. Belisarius cringed and looked away. He took some relief in knowing that the Persian charge finally seemed to be at its breaking point.

On the far side of the battlefield, he noticed that the Persian infantry had not moved. He returned to the carnage in front of him and saw a Herulian ax split a Persian head in two, and yet the Persian rode on, his confused mount unwitting of his partner's horrible demise. In all his years on the battlefield, Belisarius had never seen such a bloodbath. And why? Because the Emperor refused to send the Shah requisite gold tribute? He loathed the man who had sent these fine cavalrymen to early deaths. The Shah was nowhere near the battlefield.

He looked away from the bloodbath and toward the sun. It was at its maximum height, and he estimated it to be about mid-day. He realized how hot it had become. The surreal scene before him reminded him of depictions of Hell in religious art, but no art could capture the trepidation everyone felt on the battlefield. Blood streams carved little valleys into the trench and flowed down into a giant river. The "islands" of limbs and organs, the screams of men and horses, the simultaneous struggle to survive and yet wanting to die to end the intolerable suffering, the unmistakable stench of death — all these things were beyond the imagination of a man sitting in a palace. Procopius snapped him out of his fear and anger.

"The Persians can't see what's happening," he said. By enveloping the Persian right flank, the Romans had confined the movement of the Persian center, rendering them useless.

Belisarius yelled to the infantry archers, "Concentrate your fire on the interior!"

Belisarius finally recognized the Persian commander by his standard. He watched Pityaxes struggle to find a way to break out of the Roman encirclement. The dead and dying horses littering the battlefield made maneuvering difficult. The wide trench was now ankle-deep in Persian blood, and Belisarius knew the predictable effect agonized cries had on wavering troops. *Pityaxes, get your men out before they all fall.*

He knew what he would do if he had been in Pityaxes's stirrups, and indeed, a moment later, Pityaxes called for his signalman to sound the trumpet for retreat. His men leaped into action, struggling to break through the rear line of Herulians and Huns.

The trap began to break, so Belisarius called out to the Huns, "Pursue them with lances!" Sunicas and his light cavalry were soon plunging their short lances into retreating Persian backs as they tried to break out of the encirclement. Belisarius watched Pityaxes's efforts at an orderly retreat vanish. His entire unit turned their backs on the Roman archers. Buzes saw the opportunity for the Roman cavalry to pursue the retreat and ordered, "Open the bridges!" The bridges dropped, and the Romans pursued the fleeing Persians, who had given up all pretense of fighting as they headed for the safety of their line, desperate to escape a massacre.

Belisarius called out to the infantry archers, "Hold your fire!"

Belisarius tried to follow Pityaxes's movement in the melee. He watched Pityaxes's horse take an arrow in its lightly armored rear and throw him off. He fell hard and desperately looked for a mount while his mounted guards surrounded him.

"Take him out!" Belisarius yelled, knowing no one could hear him. He watched the struggling Pityaxes, but they were all occupied. Suddenly, a lieutenant pulled the Persian general onto his horse, and the pair headed to the Persian line. Several hundred panicked, dismounted Persian knights followed them, shedding their heavy armor as they ran.

Pityaxes tried to pick up the banner when his standard-bearer fell, but as he slowed and bent over to reach it, a Hun lanced his neck and nearly dismounted him. He abandoned it and galloped toward the Persian line with the Roman cavalry close behind.

At the sound of another trumpet blast, the Persian infantry archers launched a volley of arrows into the pursuing Romans so great that it nearly eclipsed the sun, but most fell short of their mark. Watching from the middle of the vast plain, Belisarius ordered the trumpets to signal an end to the countercharge. The Romans began returning to their lines, finishing off the last of the Persians as they did so.

Belisarius considered collecting the Persian wounded but knew he lacked the surgeons to treat them. The Persians were fine cavalrymen, poorly led on this occasion, he thought, but deserving of more than a lance in the chest while lying on their backs. If the battle were over, he would have sent his surgeons to tend their wounds and then sent the Persian prisoners to Constantinople where they would serve the Romans on the Danube frontier. However, he had no such options. He could not spare even a hundred troops to guard Persian prisoners. He needed every available man in the fight. Still, the crunching sound of lances crashing through sternums made him sick. It took years to train a cavalryman to that level, and the Shah had wasted thousands in half a day.

When Pharas, Buzes, and Sunicas were back in the Roman line with their men, Belisarius breathed a heavy sigh of relief. "Well done, men," he said as the cavalrymen resumed their places in the line.

Belisarius's center cavalry, the infantry, and the Roman right flank, which had never moved but had watched the battle in awe, cheered wildly when their returning comrades rejoined the line. It was too early to celebrate as the fighting had only begun. He looked again at the sun high in the sky and wondered what Perozes would do next. He turned to Procopius, "The Persians have ample time to attack again before nightfall."

Once the Roman cavalrymen were back in their original formations, the generals cantered to Belisarius, who remained in his saddle in the center. It was the middle of the afternoon, the hottest part of the day, and the heat cooked the blood, sweat, vomit, and excrement that filled the air. The thrill of victory in the battle's first phase gave way to the realization that the Persians had not yet done their worst. An ominous trumpet blast from the Persians confirmed that.

Pharas, Buzes, and Sunicas were covered in sweat and blood, but smiling. Pharas removed his helmet, revealing a blood stain, not his own. He laughed as he pulled out an arrow that had failed to penetrate his chainmail. Belisarius winced in empathetic pain and said, "Another lucky day, Pharas." The Herulian laughed as he wiped the blood splatters off.

Belisarius saluted the commanders. "Well done, my friends!"

"But the battle is not over, is it?" Buzes asked.

"No," Belisarius said grimly. "There will be more bloodshed before it's over."

"And I shall be happy to drain it from every Persian vein," Sunicas said.

"You hate the Persians, don't you, Sunicas?" Pharas replied.

"I don't fight because I hate the Persians in front of me, but because I love what is behind me." He looked at Belisarius and Pharas, grabbed their hands, and pulled them in close. Belisarius remembered that same handshake when they had liberated the women in their city from the Huns.

Belisarius smiled and said, "Thank you, brother. Now, quickly dress your wounded and prepare for another attack."

The three generals began issuing orders to remove and treat the wounded. While Pharas's and Sunicas's men had few casualties, Buzes's men, who had absorbed the brunt of the attack, had many wounded at the top of the trench. They were placed on gurneys and removed to the field hospital behind the city walls.

"Your men fought well, Buzes. I commend your ability to hold the line."

Buzes nodded gratefully but was distracted by one captain who had lost his arm. "Get a tourniquet on that now before he bleeds out," he ordered angrily.

A figure in black armor strode toward Belisarius from the infantry. "Our left flank is weaker," Constantinus said, observing the medics rushing to clear the dead and wounded. "We should pull reinforcements from the right."

"No, that is what Perozes will expect, and I suspect he'll test our right flank next. The men should hold their current positions so that Perozes will not be able to exploit new gaps in our line. Casualties in Pharas's and Sunicas's units were light, and they are prepared to assist as necessary."

Procopius cantered his horse toward the gathering, "Congratulations, General. You anticipated the Persian movements well so far. The spirits of the men are high, and their confidence in you has grown greater. No one could have better managed the battle."

Belisarius silently agreed but knew that he had merely given orders. Belisarius could see the Persian line a mile off in the distance as the dust settled.

"The credit goes to everyone who followed orders," he said, nodding to Pharas and Sunicas in the distance. "We will see what the Persians do next. They have more fight in them."

For an hour longer, the sun heated the Romans' armor, but they held their lines. Hundreds of supernumeraries[9] emerged from the gates of Dara, pulling carts laden with large urns of water and hurried to quench the thirst of the troops and their horses, returning with Roman casualties on stretchers. The townspeople of Dara invited the wounded into their homes and assisted in tending them. The supernumeraries hurried to collect fatalities before rats appeared as if out of nowhere to make meals of the bodies.

Belisarius noticed several wounded Persians who had escaped the mercy killing of the Roman lances. They moaned in agony and begged for water, but the Persian medics were too far away to hear or offer comfort. Had the Persians asked, he might have allowed them to recover their wounded, but he knew the Romans would benefit from the demoralizing effect that seeing wounded comrades had on enemies who had not yet attacked. Charging through maimed and dismembered comrades at Thannuris had made him hesitate, and it had nearly hindered his escape. He hated being so callous about it, but he reassured himself that there would be ample time for compassion once his men were out of danger. At this moment, he knew his men had to prepare for another attack.

When the water bearers finally arrived, Pharas, Sunicas, and John joined him, and they drank as much water as possible. Belisarius said, "This sun will kill me before the Persians do." A moment later, a providential wind cooled their sweaty backs, and the army erupted into grateful cheers. John removed his steel helmet, and Belisarius laughed at the curious shape of his friend's hair, sculpted by sweat,

---

[9] Non-combatants who provide logistical support to an army in the field

heat, and the heavy helmet. John's energetic laugh lifted his morale and made him grateful for the army's survival.

"That wind will give our archers a decisive advantage when the arrows start flying again," Sunicas said as they watched his Huns pulling arrows from Persian bodies. "Their missiles are a hand's length shorter than ours and lack the range and penetrating power. I've tried using them, but they're too short."

"Save them for close range, then," Belisarius replied.

A courier arrived and handed Belisarius a message. He read the message with a grave look on his face and then looked at the Persian line in the distance.

"What is it?" John asked.

"The Persians are planning to attack again. Spies tell us that you may be facing a charge from the ten-thousand Immortals," Belisarius replied to John. He turned to Sunicas, "Your nemesis Baresmanas will lead the next charge."

Sunicas's eyes and jaws tightened. "I have been waiting for this moment my whole life."

"I know what he did to your family," Belisarius said, "but no matter how much you want to, do not venture out recklessly to avenge them!"

Sunicas smirked. "Much as I might be tempted, I won't break our ranks. But should the opportunity present itself, be assured, I will avenge my family."

Belisarius nodded his assent. His mind wandered back to the young Persian impaled on the stake, and he wished the battle would not continue. He turned to Procopius. "Should we send a second peace delegation? This bloodshed sickens me."

"After what happened to the first? I wouldn't risk the health of another man."

"Well, we must do something to end this. Write to Perozes and say: 'Let us put an end to this needless bloodshed. Return your troops to Persia at once, and let our leaders negotiate peace. Your army has tasted the troubles that befall those who would destroy the peace between our two great empires. If you agree to an armistice now, we will allow the recovery of your dead and wounded and a renewal of the blessings of peace."

Belisarius paused to collect his thoughts, and Procopius suggested, "a prisoner exchange?"

"Yes, tell him as a token of the way he would have us treat them, I respectfully request the immediate release of my negotiator — whose gifted tongue he sent this morning."

Procopius disappeared and returned moments later with a letter tightly wrapped around a long arrow. "Give it to Sunicas. He'll know what to do with it."

Half an hour later, the tortured negotiator rode across the Roman line, slumped over his horse and bleeding from the mouth. Seeing his envoy's distressing condition and the Persians' violation of diplomatic protocol filled Belisarius with rage. He handed a written response from Perozes, which Belisarius read silently and then aloud to his staff. "'General Belisarius, how can we trust you Romans to keep your word? The battle is not over, and I soon intend to take my bath at Dara.' Blah, blah, blah...."

"I am not surprised," Procopius said. "The Persians have wanted revenge on Europeans since Alexander took Syria from them eight centuries ago."

"But they won't have it. Not if I have anything to do with it," Belisarius said emphatically.

By the late afternoon, as a dusty red sun loomed over the horizon, Belisarius and his generals prepared to receive a follow-up attack led by their left flank. The Persian *kus* and *karnay*[10] blasted the call for a second advance, and the Persian cavalry stepped forward to the beat of a hundred drums.

"Officers, to your stations! Pharas, be prepared to support Sunicas on our right flank. God willing, I will see you all for the evening meal." Pharas, Sunicas, and John galloped off toward their men.

Belisarius recognized Baresmanas's standard rise high against his elite armored lancers' line of Persian cavalrymen. Belisarius knew the standard by the description Sunicas had given when he had joined his family as a young boy orphaned by the

---

[10] Persian kettle drum and trumpet

Persian general. It was a red banner with a golden lion wielding a menacing sword and a sun rising behind him.

The thought of facing Baresmanas's Ten-Thousand Immortals filled him with fear and awe. They were the possibly the best cavalry in the world — heirs of the unmounted forebears who defeated three hundred Spartans at Thermopylae nearly a millennium before — and now reconstituted by the Sassanid dynasty to revive Persia's glory days.

As the Immortals advanced toward John and the Roman right flank, Belisarius watched Pharas and Sunicas join John. From his distant vantage point, he saw that the Immortals were covered from head to toe in armor; even their faces were obscured by chain mail. Then his thoughts turned to his adopted brother. He knew the difficulty of killing a man who was so well-armored.

Belisarius watched the Immortals slowly canter their horses, maintaining cohesion, then gradually increase to a full gallop as they reached the missile range of the Roman archers. The ground underneath Belisarius shook as though a steadily more destructive earthquake was ripping the earth apart. The noise was more deafening than thunder. This time it was Belisarius who found himself looking behind him to ensure that the walls of Dara were still there.

The Roman archers launched the arrows high into the air, but the missiles seemed to take down many fewer Persians because of their better armor. Additionally, Belisarius noticed that the Persians had formed staggered lines to avoid colliding with the knights in front of them. Baresmanas's standard led the charge — quite unlike Pityaxes's. He worried about the safety of Pharas, Sunicas, and John.

Belisarius pulled out his bow and fired an arrow at the knight behind Baresmanas's standard-bearer. It sprang off his armor without effect. Baresmanas and his personal guards ran their horses hard. *O Lord Almighty, they're going to leap over the trenches!* One such guard's horse tried to launch itself over the trench but sunk into soft ground and was impaled on a stake. Arrows and caltrops felled several of his guards, but Baresmanas kept charging. When the moment arrived, he leaped up with his horse, and they sailed through the air knocking over half a dozen men at the landing. Soon other riders began jumping the trench, and the Roman cavalry fell back almost to the battlements of Dara, more by force than design. This effect was not an ordered withdrawal nor a retreat, just hundreds of mounted men getting pushed back by the force of a giant wave. Belisarius knew that courage and good order were useless in such circumstances.

Belisarius signaled Pharas's and Sunicas's mounted archers to slip behind the Persians and fire missiles at their backs. Still, they had great difficulty since the Immortals' horses wore armor covering their torsos and upper legs. *Poor Sunicas! Careful!* He had a flashback of the two generals' reckless days as youths. He began to regret his decision to put his friends at such significant risk. John also seemed to struggle to maintain cohesion as the trenches failed to hold back the Persian advance as he had hoped. He wished that he had ordered Sunicas to wear heavier armor. He wondered what would happen if he lost one of them, or two, or all three. A pang of deep sadness and a sense of guilt overcame him.

He glanced at John and saw that two Immortals had surrounded him and were hacking at him with their swords. His retainers struggled to chase them off. It started to seem like the entire Roman right flank was about to collapse. Belisarius began instinctively chewing his lower lip, then reached under his visor to wipe the sweat stinging his eyes.

He glanced forlornly at Procopius. "I'm sorry, friend. I should not have brought you to a battlefield where victory is so uncertain — although I try hard to convey the opposite to my men." Procopius's ordinarily placid face had grown pale with dread, and Belisarius regretted having confided his doubts. He watched as the lawyer from Caesarea pissed himself, his urine running down his leg and making a puddle on the ground.

"Sir, with your permission," an embarrassed Procopius said, "I would like to go and tell the archers on the ramparts to rain arrows on the Immortals."

Belisarius saw it as a valid excuse to dismiss his secretary. He was not a soldier and wanted to be off the battlefield.

"Go!" Belisarius said, and Procopius galloped off toward the city gate.

Belisarius checked his center: it continued to hold, and the infantry archers were showering arrows upon the Immortals. He checked on Buzes and his left flank. Nothing was going on there. The Persian infantry and right flank had not moved. They were waiting, but for what? He wondered for a few minutes if the time had come to send in his reserve force.

Belisarius took a deep breath and gathered himself. He had to focus again, or all would be lost. He turned his attention back to the trenches, which were now a chaotic scene of bodies scrambling in and out. His reserve cavalry had been steadily firing arrows into the Immortals, but he realized that only swords were doing to take them out. *Now is the time for my biscuit-eaters.*

"*Bucellari,* advance along the right flank!" Belisarius shouted out onto the field. A trumpet blast echoed the order, and a line of cavalry pivoted ninety degrees to proceed across the bridges to join John, Pharas, and Sunicas. He followed them as they proudly advanced. They were a new hybrid cavalry that combined the speed and accuracy of the Hunnish mounted archers with the fearsome strength of the Gothic lancers and the heavy armor of the Persian *clibanarii.* As he watched them charge orderly into the melee, he felt some pride that the Romans had finally mastered the art of cavalry warfare after centuries of painful trial and error.

Belisarius turned his attention to his right flank. He gestured for the trumpet to sound again. "Put aside your bows!" he commanded. "Darts!" Behind Belisarius's standard, his cavalry advanced to within throwing distance of the Persians and hurled the armor-piercing, lead-tipped darts they carried on the backs of their shields, taking down hundreds. Then Belisarius shouted, "Charge!" and his *bucellarii* slammed into the side of the Persian column with their lances. The surprised Persians reeled around in confusion and stopped their charge into John's cavalry.

With the tide turning on the battlefield, Belisarius remembered his friend Sunicas and scanned the field for him. The air was thick with the smell of blood, sweat, and the dead. The chorus of male voices grunting and heaving made it impossible to listen for his friend's voice. He remembered that he had ordered Sunicas and his men to go behind the Persians, so he turned his gaze in that direction and spotted the bulk of the Huns attacking the rear, but Sunicas was not there. Then he spotted a handful of Huns attacking the standard-bearer of Baresmanas.

"There you are, brother," he said as he spotted the man in the hat that looked like a yurt and his long hair flowing behind him like a horse's tail. He was attacking a Persian knight in reflective body armor covering his entire body. Belisarius understood Sunicas's determination but grew distressed when he saw that Sunicas and his retainers had separated themselves from the other Huns. "Sunicas, you promised you wouldn't do that!"

Part of him did not want to watch the fight that would inevitably ensue. He was unsure what he would do if he lost his childhood friend today. Despite his fears, he could not keep his eyes off the struggle. Sunicas did not go straight for his enemy, but instead, he struck a lance deep into the standard-bearer's chest, mangling his heart, releasing an explosion of blood, and unhorsing the rider. "That's for my mother," he cried in Persian as another Hun dealt a fatal blow to Baresmanas's last personal guard. Sunicas seized the standard and waved it at the horrified Persians. Belisarius could not help but feel a sense of giddy optimism at this moment of victory that his friend had been pursuing his whole life. Then he noticed that Baresmanas's men were retreating. *They must think that their captain has fallen since we captured the standard!* However, the moment for victory passed quickly as Baresmanas viciously charged at Sunicas.

"Come and get it, you butcher," Sunicas shouted as he turned to charge, leaned forward in his saddle, aimed his lance, and unhorsed him. The Persian struggled to get up off the ground under the weight of his armor. Sunicas looked down at his enemy with no mercy. *This is your moment, friend,* Belisarius thought as he watched his friend spear the belly of the struggling Persian. "And that..." He stared, lifting the lance out of the Persian, "is for my sister!" Sunicas stood there for a while, watching with satisfaction as Baresmanas's guts spilled like maggots from a ruptured fish onto the dusty ground. Relief filled Belisarius's body as he felt his friend's satisfaction in avenging the deaths and enslavement of his family.

Belisarius scanned the rest of the battlefield, hoping to see some resolution. It had been a long day of fighting. He watched as the Immortals began fleeing after seeing their captain fall. Belisarius's *bucellarii* and Sunicas's Huns nearly enveloped the Immortals, cutting them off from the rest of the Persian army.

With Sunicas out of danger, he looked for Pharas and John. Belisarius nervously scanned the battlefield for them, could not find them, and feared for a moment they might have fallen. Then he spotted the Armenian, trying to lead his cavalry in the countercharge. Belisarius called for a signal for John to advance his cavalry on the Roman right flank and watched as the Romans began to recover the ground they had yielded. He then spotted Pharas's Herulians vigorously chopping the backs of Persians like unwanted trees. Belisarius knew that if the Immortals could be fenced in again, they would panic and seek to escape so that victory would come to the Romans.

Belisarius heard the Persian signal for an orderly retreat. He worried that the Persians might lure the Romans to their line, but the floundering Immortals were more interested in escape than victory.

Dismounted Immortals threw aside their heavy armor and fled on foot — only to be stuck in the back by Hunnish arrows. They struggled individually, desperate to avoid the arrows and lance thrusts coming at them from all sides, but Roman and Hunnish cavalry pursued them to the Persian line. Pharas's ax-wielders seemed to make a sport out of swinging their axes at the back of Persian heads and watching their skulls explode like squeezed grapes. His cavalrymen were like dogs chasing a wounded bear in the open field, only now the bear was returning to its laird, and further pursuit would only end badly for the Romans.

The Persian infantry had advanced tentatively so long as the Roman left flank appeared to be breaking. Still, once the Immortals began galloping toward them pell-mell with Roman cavalry in hot pursuit, they turned and ran, becoming easy targets for the *bucellarii*. Belisarius linked up with John as the two rode together in the countercharge toward the Persian line. Belisarius and John slowed their mounts to a canter. Belisarius said, "We have to resist following their retreat."

"Agreed," said John, "we don't know what sort of traps lay in front of that Persian line. We cannot allow Perozes to use that strategy against us again."

"Halt the pursuit!" Belisarius yelled.

He ordered a signalman to sound the trumpet for a final volley of arrows and a return to the Roman line. A minute after the Romans emptied their quivers, Persian reserves fired arrows to cover their comrades' hasty retreat. An arrowhead deflected off a steel epaulet on Belisarius's shoulder, barely missing the gap in his armor near his neck.

Belisarius and John watched his cavalry return to their lines, picking off the wounded as they did so and accepting surrender from those who threw down their arms. When he reached the Roman lines and saw the Roman causalities, he gave orders for their recovery. He looked at the low sun: it would be dark in an hour. Sunicas approached with Baresmanas's captured standard.

"You certainly earned that trophy today, Sunicas," Belisarius said.

"It's a promise kept, Flavius," Sunicas said. "I can finally let my family rest in peace."

Pharas rode up to the group, so covered in blood that he resembled a large organ ripped from a body. Belisarius gave him an amused look. "You look like a vision of Hell, Pharas."

"There is no victory in Hell, Flavius," Pharas said as he wiped some of the gore off his body.

"The day is yours, Flavius," John said as he looked back to the Persians who continued their retreat.

"Indeed, John, the struggle is over, and the battle won."

The four generals resumed their ride to the Roman line.

Crows and vultures descended on the Persian corpses, and hundreds of black rats began gnawing on fingers. The moans of the dying sobered even the most stoic Romans, who surveyed the horrific carnage and realized that they might be corpses themselves in the coming hours. Although the bloodied Persians had been Rome's main enemy for the past century, few troops felt anything but pity for the dying.

For others, the carnage represented an opportunity. Even as Constantinus ordered the infantry archers to move in front of the trenches and collect arrows, caltrops, darts, lances, and swords, they began searching the bodies of the fallen for gold and other objects of value. Belisarius watched them and made no effort to stop it. He thought such were the spoils of war, and so long as the looting did not interfere with the battle or tending the wounded, he did not care.

Belisarius watched one horseless cavalryman limp toward the field hospital. Belisarius dismounted and helped the soldier onto Bucephalus. "You need this more than I do." He gave the man his water, then tore off a piece of his cloak and tied it carefully around the soldier's bleeding leg. The officer gratefully accepted the offer, and Pharas, Sunicas, and John did likewise to other wounded troops.

"Hold on, Flavius," Pharas said with alarm in his voice. "It looks like one of Apollo's arrows struck you," Belisarius said as he remembered the arrow that had bounced off his shoulder. "Your neck is bleeding. An arrow narrowly missed your jugular vein." He tore another piece of Belisarius's cloak and bandaged his neck.

"Lucky Belisarius wins again," John laughed.

Belisarius did feel fortunate, not just for winning his first major battle but for escaping the carnage. He stepped carefully across the field littered with dead bodies, his boots covered in blood and sand. He spotted Constantinus and called to him, but he was too preoccupied riding around collecting Persian arms for his famous dagger collection. Belisarius had never seen a general officer participate in such an ignoble activity, and the generals all shook their heads in contempt.

"This is my favorite part of the battle," Belisarius overheard a Roman infantry captain exclaim as he and the supernumeraries pilfered the dead.

"Wouldn't it be better to take care of your wounded first, captain?" Belisarius asked as disapproving eyebrows arched over his eyes. The captain did not recognize his commander on foot and initially scoffed at him, but upon realizing it was Belisarius, he straightened up and stood at attention.

"Aye, sir. Sorry," the captain said as he looked around, belatedly discovering that there were still wounded on the field. He bowed his head in shame and then loudly upbraided his looting comrades. "I'll scourge any man caught pilfering while our wounded comrades still lie on the field." His men immediately abandoned trade and helped the wounded.

"There is no one more zealous in a cause than a recent convert," Belisarius said to soft chuckles from his staff.

The infantry stripped the Persian prisoners of their armor, tied them, and took them inside the city to be held until the Emperor and the Shah reached a new peace agreement.

The retiring generals rode past Hunnish cooks butchering the dying horses for the evening stew. Belisarius grabbed the reins of a lost horse, looking in vain for his rider, and gently rubbed its nose. "Easy, boy! Your comrades will soon be out of their misery. Let's take you away from this place." He watched the Huns, who valued horses more than any other group, comfort the poor creatures before ending their misery with the stroke of a blade to the neck.

Belisarius walked past a priest walking through the battlefield, hurriedly ministering Last Rites to dying Romans. "How many wounded do we have?"

"A few hundred, perhaps," he replied grimly. "Thank God the Persians are not part of our flock," he added as he looked at their overwhelming numbers. Once stripped of their armor, the Romans grabbed the Persian dead by their feet and dragged them into the trenches — already half-full of the dead — for eventual burial.

Moments earlier, the sounds of steel hitting steel and the screams of victims had filled the field. Now only the weak screams and groans of the wounded stirred the air. It was not a peaceful scene, yet Belisarius found an uneasy peace with how the day had gone.

As Belisarius surveyed the carnage one last time, he saw anxious Persian women emerge from the far hills and begin searching for fallen sons and husbands, heard the wails of mothers and widows, and a melancholy overcame him.

Procopius, wearing a new set of clothes, rejoined the group. "What of the Persian wounded?"

"Our forebears would have walked across the field in a row spiking the wounded, but they are no longer our enemies. They are defenseless brothers-in-arms who fought well today." He turned to the master of surgeons, who was busily attending the injured and said, "Once we have treated our own wounded, dress the wounds of the Persians. We'll send them to our western frontiers if they survive to fight for Rome."

"And the dead?"

"The Persians would want us to leave their dead for the birds to devour, but there are too many of them to respect their tradition," Belisarius said.

"Indeed," John added, "a pestilence could break out in Dara. Better to put them in our trenches."

"Yes," Belisarius agreed, "and if the Persians do not attack us tomorrow, cover the dead in the earth." He noticed the sun drop below the mountains, casting the entire valley in its shadow.

"I would have liked to have charged the general who sent so many young men to a pointless death," Belisarius said to Sunicas, thinking about the victory of Baresmanas, "but Perozes was too far back in the line."

"He is already as good as dead," Procopius said,

"How do you know?"

"That is what Persian shahs do to generals who disappoint them. They remove their fine pearl caps and even their heads to remind the next general of the price of failure."

Belisarius grimaced at the harsh justice practiced by the Persians and chewed his lower lip. "And what do *Roman* emperors do to failed generals?"

"They force them into early retirement, seize their property, and command their scribes to write scathing histories about them," Procopius replied with a smirk.


The next day, as vultures circled the battlefield, a spy entered the governor's palace in Dara to inform Belisarius and his officers that Perozes's arrow count had revealed more than eight thousand dead or missing. "And what of Perozes?" Belisarius asked.

"Perozes is as dead as the Persian hopes for an easy victory. When Shah Kavad's ambassador learned the scale of the disaster, he ordered Pityaxes to ceremoniously strip Perozes of his rank and cut his throat."

Belisarius shook his head. "Every defeat needs a scapegoat."

"True, but that means we'll have the bath to ourselves," Pharas laughed.

# CHAPTER FOUR
# AN ARMY MARCHES ON ITS STOMACH

*Victory has a thousand fathers, but defeat is an orphan.*

— John F. Kennedy

*Callinicum, Roman Syria*
*April 17, 531 A.D.*

Belisarius and his generals were hungry and gathered around a campfire near the Euphrates River. It was Good Friday, near the end of the Lenten Fast, and the men missed their meat and dairy. Sunicas was particularly grumpy that the army chaplain had forbidden him from drinking kumis, his fermented mare's milk. "Milk is forbidden," the priest had reminded him.

"It's no more milk than eggs are meat!" Sunicas retorted to the glare of Belisarius, who shook his head in amused disapproval.

"I'm growing weary of this cat-and-mouse game," Sunicas complained as he spat into the fire. "A year after our great victory at Dara, all we ever do is stand between the Persians and Roman cities. Well, I say we poke them in the eye."

"Our armies will just needlessly bleed each other," Belisarius said. "Our orders are to check the Persian advance into Syria. We are doing that. If we can achieve our goals without spilling blood, so much the better."

"I'm in no shape to fight until we can hunt some game and eat some meat," Pharas said as he felt his once-massive arms and looked at his diminished hulk with alarm.

Constantinus shook his head in disapproval. "Our unwillingness to fight the Persians when we outnumber them has nothing to do with prudence or a meager diet."

The generals waited for him to state the real problem. When it did not come, John asked, "What is it, then?"

"Cowardice, I tell you," Constantinus charged.

Belisarius looked up wearily, "Really?"

"That's what the men say!" Constantinus added.

"Well, the men are wrong, and that's why we have generals," Pharas said.

"The men are just eager to plunder the Persian camp, that's all," John said.

"And so is Constantinus," Pharas added to mocking laughter.

Constantinus put his hand on the hilt of his sword, and Pharas put his on his battle-ax.

"Gentlemen, please," Belisarius said. "The best we could hope for is a draw. I doubt we could beat the Persians badly enough to raid their camp."

"We outnumber them," Constantinus insisted.

"Perhaps, if we can rely on our allies, but that is not certain. Besides, it's never prudent to fight with our backs to a river," Belisarius countered.

"Nevertheless, the men are ready for a fight and will be insisting on one soon," Constantinus said.

At that moment, a captain of the Isaurian[11] cavalry joined the generals. Belisarius was suspicious of his perfect timing.

"What is it?" he asked impatiently.

"The men are clamoring for another fight, sir, and now we have a chance," he said.

"What do you mean?" Belisarius asked. "Aren't your men hungry and weak from the Lenten fast?"

---

[11] Highlanders from south-central Asia Minor

"On the contrary, sir," the Isaurian continued. "The priest has assured us that the Lord would not deny us a victory on the Day of His Resurrection."

Belisarius rolled his eyes. He hated it when monks would get the men's spirit up for a fight based on an ephemeral inspiration rather than sound military judgment.

Constantinus chimed in, "How could the Lord deny men of faith a great victory?"

"Doesn't our faith also teach that war should be a last resort?" Belisarius asked.

"This is our last resort," Constantinus asserted. "They refuse to leave Roman lands and continue to plunder them."

"But they do not advance across the Euphrates, and they have not attacked Antioch," Belisarius said. He turned to Pharas, Sunicas, and John. "What do you think?"

"The Lakhmid Arabs are plundering our territory while the Persians prevent us from attacking them," Pharas said.

"Flavius, I cannot think of a worse time for battle. The Persians currently have the high ground, we have not dug in, and we have no easy retreat if we need to fall back."

Belisarius nodded his agreement, "John?" he asked.

"If we cannot break the Persians, I fear our Ghassanid Arab allies will abandon us," John said. "They only fight with us for plunder and have had no real opportunities in a year."

"Any concerns?"

"Yes, we may outnumber the Persians, but they match us in cavalry," John added.

"Even with Arethas's five-thousand Arab cavalry?"

"They are only lightly armored," John replied, "They wouldn't stand a chance against the Persian cataphracts. Besides, I don't trust them."

"There you have it, Constantinus," Belisarius said.

"I'm afraid it's not that simple," Constantinus continued. "The men took a vote and voted overwhelmingly...."

Belisarius cut him off, "What is this, Athens? That is not how Romans run armies!"

"Perhaps not, but the men are refusing to cross the river and are standing their ground," Constantinus said.

"If the Persians win a decisive victory, they will sack every city in the East," Belisarius replied. He then turned to Pharas, Sunicas, and John and said," Go talk some sense into the men!" He threw his stale biscuit into the fire, went into his tent, and put out the torch, indicating that he did not want to be disturbed.

The following morning, his three friends awoke him at dawn.

"Well? Did you talk some sense into them?"

All three stood there silently, looking at the other two to say something. Finally, John spoke.

"The men will not re-cross the river without a fight. We tried all night to change their minds. They insist we fight tomorrow — on Easter."

Pharas added, "They think we Christians will have an advantage over the fire-worshippers."

Belisarius looked at John, whom he loved and trusted more than anyone, and said, "Very well. Tell them to start digging trenches because the Persian cavalry will try to drive them into the river."

John stood in front of Belisarius awkwardly and added, "Well, Flavius, that's just it. The men have thrown their shovels into the river. They...."

Belisarius flew into a rage and rose quickly out of bed. "What?!"

"The infantry are tired of digging and moving and digging and moving. They just want to fight."

Belisarius took a deep breath. He knew conditions were not suitable for a battle, but if his men were burning for one and his generals could not stop them, it was time to prepare for a fight.

A reluctant Belisarius soon gathered his forces on the field and advanced his forces north along the Euphrates River against Persian general Azarethes. He watched as the Persian cavalry formed a line opposite the Roman line and steadily retreated in good order. Belisarius assigned Pharas to command the infantry on his left flank, placed himself in the center, two small cavalry detachments on his immediate right commanded by Sunicas and Ascan, and the Isaurian infantry on his right flank. On his far-right flank, he placed the Ghassanid Arab light cavalry.

On Easter Sunday morning, his exhausted but eager forces finally caught up to the Persians. Belisarius knew the river prevented the Persians from outflanking him on his left, so he watched for signs that Azarethes might thin his cavalry line and move half his forces to strengthen the Persian right flank. However, the dust kicked up by the Persian horses prevented him from seeing the depth of the Persian line.

As the Persians and the Romans exchanged missile fire, Belisarius turned to John, who sat next to him in a saddle, and asked, "What do you think they are doing?"

"I don't know," John replied, "But I know what I would do."

"What?"

"Move half my heavy cavalry to attack Arethas. His light cavalry can withstand the Lakhmid light cavalry but won't last an hour against Persian heavy cavalry."

An hour later, Belisarius and John watched as his Arab allies fell back when Persian heavy cavalry crashed into them from the hill above the river.

"They're in full flight, Flavius," John observed. They are quitting the battle-field.

The two generals watched in horror, and the Persian attack began to fold the Roman right flank, and his Isaurian infantry began a disorderly retreat toward the river.

"O God, help us," Belisarius cried out. "We need to reorganize the infantry."

Belisarius placed himself between the river and his fleeing infantry. "Form a horseshoe in front of the river. If you run, you'll either be slaughtered on the bank or drown in the river." The Isaurian infantrymen gave him a blank look.

"A bow! Form a bow shape! Make a shield wall!" John yelled.

The infantry archers lined up in the center of the bow with their shields pointing toward the Persian cavalry. The reformed Roman right closed the gap and
butted up against the riverbank. Belisarius realized that the Persians had half-sur-
rounded the Roman line and sought to drive it into the river.

Belisarius yelled desperately to John, "Pull our cavalry into the new line to close
the gap! Have the cavalry dismount and join the infantry behind the shield wall."
As John galloped off, Belisarius watched as an impenetrable wall of thick wooden
shields stopped most of the arrows while the Persians suffered heavy losses from
exposure.

Belisarius called out to Sunicas and Ascan. "Hold off the Persians while we
reform our line, and then get behind the shield wall."

He realized that the Persians had bested him. He wondered if the Persians had
paid off his ally Arethas or if they simply lost courage when unable to stop the
Persian cavalry charge. Either way, he knew the Romans had lost the battle. Now
his only objective was to save his army.

Once the shield wall had formed a solid semi-circle and the horses were inside,
Belisarius called out, "Our backs are to the Euphrates River. We have to hold the
line."

The Isaurian captain, who had been itching for a fight, complained. "That's all
well and good when you cavalrymen have horses upon which to escape. Foot soldiers cannot outrun Persian hooves."

"The cavalry is not going anywhere until the infantry is across the river," Belisarius replied firmly, holding his tongue from chastising the Isaurians who were so
eager to fight.

"Cavalry," Belisarius yelled to reassure the infantry, "fight shoulder-to-shoulder
alongside your infantry brothers. We are retreating as one army."

Belisarius watched as the Persian cavalry launched repeated sallies against his
Roman line. He wanted his cavalry to counter charge but feared that if his shield
wall opened, it might never close again, and the Persians would rush in and surround them.

Casualties mounted, and he watched in dismay as his semi-circle slowly began to contract. He bit his lower lip as he watched the mortally wounded gather in the center of the circle to die in relative peace. Belisarius felt anger — at Constantinus, at the Isaurians, but most of all at himself. Despite his better judgment, he consented to their idiotic schemes. How would he explain this loss to Justinian? And yet, he knew he had more significant worries for now. His only consolation was watching the Persians take casualties as well.

John finally approached him, "We've lost almost eight hundred Romans, Flavius, and thousands more are wounded. I'm not sure how much longer we can hold out."

Belisarius looked at the low sun in the sky, "We have to make it to nightfall."

When the sun began to set, the Persians withdrew to a safe distance, and the Romans made plans to withdraw. He called his generals and laid out his plans. "We must get our men to the other side of the river under cover of darkness."

"If we try to retreat," Constantinus said, shaking his head with his eyes closed and nose in the air, the Persians will pounce upon us and cut us to shreds."

"Not if they don't detect our departure," said Ascan, a trusted cavalry commander.

"And how would you propose we do that?" Constantinus asked.

"Harvest the dry reeds along the river and build massive fires," Ascan said. "They will lead the Persians to believe we are camped here for the night. Make a lot of noise. Sunicas and I will lead our cavalry units on patrols while you lead the infantry across the river."

"I will wait here until all the men are across," Belisarius objected.

"No, Flavius," John said, "that's a bad idea. We need you on the other side to lead the men in case the Persians somehow manage to attack us on that side." Pharas and Sunicas nodded their heads in agreement.

As the last bit of sun dropped below the dusty horizon, the remnants of Belisarius's defeated army crossed the river by swimming, pulling themselves along ropes stretched tightly between the banks. Stripped of their armor, the horses had no difficulty swimming the river's width. Sunicas, Ascan, and their cavalry squadrons spent the night making dust and noise to convince the Persians the Romans would still be there in the morning. To Belisarius's pleasant surprise, the ruse seemed to be working. He quickly formed his men into a semi-circle on the western bank as they waited for the last remnants to join them. However, as the sun peaked above the horizon, Belisarius realized that Sunicas and Ascan were still on the wrong side of the river. Belisarius watched from the opposite bank as the fooled Persians returned to the battlefield to finish the job, only to find most of their enemy gone.

Belisarius looked concerned as Sunicas and his Huns stood at the river's edge.

"What's wrong?" John asked. "Why aren't they crossing?"

"Huns are terrible swimmers; they fear the water," he said.

"What?" John exclaimed. "Then they should have crossed first."

"I know," Belisarius said, his anger at his oversight steadily turning to grief.

"I thought every Roman knew how to swim," John said.

"Sunicas's ancestors grew up in Central Asia, far from any sea or major rivers," Belisarius said pedantically, as though he were re-teaching himself something he knew well. "They just never learned."

Belisarius screamed at them, "Move! Now!" The hesitant Huns entered the water and began swimming across just as a Persian cavalry unit charged toward them. Belisarius watched as several panicked in the water and began to drown.

Belisarius called out to his men, "If you can swim well, go help your Hunnish brothers!"

A hundred Isaurians stripped down and plunged into the water in a race to pull up struggling Huns. Belisarius watched as Sunicas finally went into the water and fared no better, even with the rope as a guide. Belisarius stripped down to his tunic and went in after his adoptive brother. He had learned to swim in the bath near his village and regretted not teaching his brother how to swim.

After swimming hurriedly toward him, he watched Sunicas's little yurt hat drop below the water line again. Belisarius dove frantically after him, and on the third try, hauled up a coughing Sunicas. However, Sunicas instinctively crawled atop

Belisarius's back to keep his head above the water. Belisarius, exhausted from the swim, now struggled to keep his head above the water. He felt himself breathe in water and coughed violently. When Belisarius tried to breathe again, he realized Sunicas was holding him underwater with his legs wrapped around his neck. He could not breathe and struggled unsuccessfully to push Sunicas off him. A vision of his mother flashed before him, "So proud," she said.

Belisarius tried not to panic. He thought: the only way to get this bear off me is to let myself sink. He managed to get his head above the water for a long breath and then let himself sink to the bottom of the river. Sunicas loosened his tight grip as he struggled to get to the surface. Belisarius swam underwater as far as he could to ensure that Sunicas would not try to drown him again when he re-emerged. When he finally got above the water, he caught his breath and looked for Sunicas. His little yurt hat floated past him. Belisarius screamed.

"Sunicas! Sunicas!"

He heard a familiar voice say, "Over here!"

Belisarius turned around and saw Pharas holding Sunicas on his back, with blood oozing out of his wide nose, in a tight headlock and swimming back to shore.

"I've got him, Flavius," Pharas said as Belisarius swam towards him. "He fought me like a pig, so I just knocked him out."

"He's not dead?"

"No, watch!" Pharas lifted his elbow and covered Sunicas's nose and mouth, and the Hun began kicking like a mule. Pharas relaxed his grip and continued to swim to shore. "Easy, brother. I've got you."

After another minute, they reached the western shore and crawled up the bank like rats, coughing up water.

"Flavius," Sunicas said, "I'm sorry. I am not sure what happened out there. I panicked."

"Falling arrows bring you no fear, only deep water," Belisarius laughed, "I understand, Sunicas." He turned to Pharas, "Thank you. You were the only one of us who kept his head."

Belisarius stood up and surveyed the scene. Huns paired with Isaurians were emerging from the water arm-in-arm. The living Huns were running around trying to catch their horses. Several dead Huns floated down the river, but Belisarius realized it could have been worse.

Belisarius looked across at the eastern shoreline and saw Ascan's men trying the get across the water while dodging Persian arrows. Ascan finally dismounted, slapped his ride in the rear, and tried to swim across. Belisarius watched as a hundred Persian archers dismounted and aimed carefully at the last man in the water. He saw an arrow hit Ascan in the shoulder, then a second. The Persians were laughing and seemed to make a sick sport of their shooting as they taunted the Romans trying frantically to swim across. The scene enraged Belisarius. When the third arrow hit, one of Ascan's comrades swam out to bring him in and, a moment later, dragged the cavalry commander onto the bank. Belisarius saw that he had an arrow in each shoulder and one in his lower back.

Belisarius ran over to him and bent over the dying commander. "Get me a *medicus!*"

Several of Ascan's men gathered around him. "We held off the Persians as long as we could, but there were too many of them," one said. "Ascan refused to get into the water until everyone else had."

"Pull him out of the water and put him on his side!" the *medicus* said.

Gaius, the army's most experienced surgeon, quickly ran to the injured man's side and assessed him. After a few seconds of poking and prodding, the man paused and looked up at Belisarius.

"What are you waiting for?" Belisarius yelled, "Help him!"

"I'm sorry, sir, I can do nothing for him. You must call for a priest."

Ascan came to consciousness and coughed up a mixture of blood and water.

"The arrow went through his lung, sir," the medicus said. A priest arrived and began ministering Last Rites.

When he stopped coughing, Ascan said slowly and almost inaudibly, "General, my son Theodosius..." the man struggled to get the words out, "take care of…him." As the words slipped from his mouth, he took several violent deep breaths, gurgling up blood and water.

Belisarius bent his head and leaned on the handsome dead man's chest. He could not stop the tears from falling as he whispered, "I promise I will love him as my own." A moment later, his eyes went vacant, and the light of life escaped Ascan.

After a moment, Belisarius stood and said sternly, "This man saved our army. We all owe him our lives. Let us give him a hero's burial."

There were many burials that night and many more Romans on the other side of the river whose remains went unburied. Belisarius knew they would be plucked by crows and dried by the sun. It made him sick.

After the burials, the Romans set up camp. Belisarius ruminated in the tent quickly set up for him — the only tent in the whole camp since the Persians had taken over the Romans' hastily abandoned camp on the other side of the river. Belisarius was not accustomed to defeat, and it showed on his face. Over several hours, he had developed wrinkles around his eyes, and a feeling of depression overcame him. *God help me,* he thought as he sipped a goblet of wine, half-enjoying one moment of peace by himself. There was no point in making light of the situation. They had barely escaped. If it had not been for Ascan, they would be dead. He was sure of it. That fact reminded Belisarius to send for Ascan's son, Theodosius when he returned to the capital.

Belisarius and his army marched north toward Antioch, encountering no more Persians, and arrived a month later. He loved Antioch even as Justinian tried to rebuild it from the devastating earthquake the year before. Its majestic Greek temples and churches still loomed over the elevated fork in the Orontes River, with bridges everywhere bringing newly cut timber for its reconstruction. Mount Silpius loomed over the city like the sword of Damocles, ready to hurl stones against its thick walls at the next earthquake. The governor of Antioch hosted Belisarius in his palace, which despite a missing roof, still made a stunning impression. As he tried to relax in a real bed, Belisarius suddenly realized that he was no longer alone in his room.

Procopius was standing silently over him. "Yes, what can I do for you?" Belisarius asked, not wanting an answer.

Procopius tried to cheer Belisarius with the news. "Spies tell us that when Shah Kavad learned the Persian casualty figures, he summoned his victorious general and summarily dismissed him. He has instructed his diplomats in Constantinople to negotiate for peace."

Belisarius suddenly remembered what Procopius had said about how the Persians handled their defeated generals. *I lost; what will Justinian do with me?*

Belisarius feigned a smile, "Yes, but what are they saying in Constantinople? And what will the price of peace be when our last battle is a Persian victory?"

"I believe I might have the answer to that general," Constantinus insinuated as he entered the tent uninvited. When Belisarius saw the official imperial seal, he hesitated to open it.

"You know what it says?" Belisarius asked.

"Perhaps, I received an order from the Emperor as well," Constantinus said smugly.

*To Master of Troops in the East: We have learned of your defeat at Callinicum and are deeply troubled. You are to hand over your command to Constantinus and return at once to Constantinople for consultations. Justinian, Emperor.*

Constantinus smiled, "Fortune has a fickle heart and a short memory."

"Thank you, gentlemen; you are dismissed. Please send in Pharas, Sunicas, and John," Belisarius said. The two departed his room, and the three generals entered. He crumpled the letter and threw it into a nearby fire.

Belisarius had never felt so defeated and collapsed in a chair and poured down a cup of wine. He stared blankly at the meal set before him: horse soup and fresh bread. Belisarius thought about what the letter might mean for him and his career.

"Flavius…" Sunicas roughly slapped his friend on the back. "Why so wretched?"

Belisarius suddenly found he lacked the energy and desire to face his friends, no matter how benevolent they were. "What do you think will happen to me?"

"I know what you fear," Sunicas replied, "but it won't come to that."

"How can you be so sure?" *No one can be sure.*

"Flavius, listen…" Pharas said, putting an arm around his friend. "All your commanders, save Constantinus, agree that the defeat at Callinicum came about because our cowardly allies abandoned us."

"Indeed," John said. "And remember, you led the retreat across the river. If you hadn't, we all would have perished."

"Absolutely," Sunicas said. "We will testify to that."

"But will that be enough?" Belisarius asked as he savored the sweet flavor of the wine and wondered if this night would be the last feast he would ever enjoy.

# Chapter Five
# A Bad Moon Rising

*Every man who has in his soul a secret feeling of revolt against any act of the State, of life, or of destiny is on the verge of riot; so soon as it appears, he begins to quiver and feel himself borne away by the whirlwind.*

— Victor Hugo, **Les Misérables**

*Constantinople*
*January 13-14, A.D. 532*

Empress Theodora woke from the most terrifying nightmare she ever had. She rolled over and looked at her husband, who was still sleeping, and then went to the basin opposite her small bathing area. The mosaic pattern on the floor showed two servants setting the hair of a beautiful Empress seated on a chair. But Theodora did not feel beautiful that morning as she examined her pale complexion and thin physique in the mirror. Her curly brown hair matted against her head, and a sweaty film covered her face. She looked weak and vulnerable, and she hated it. Overcome with anger, she visualized herself smashing the mirror to the stone floor. Although the scene was momentarily satisfying, she didn't want to hear the maids whispering about her quick temper yet again.

She had dreamt of violence. Destruction. Burning. Screaming. Angry mobs storming the palace, chasing her down the palace halls and tearing at her clothes. And then there was that utter darkness so black that one wonders whether consciousness is lost. She figured that she must have awakened at that moment. She had had this dream before, but it seemed more real and terrifying each time. She considered discussing this recurring nightmare with Justinian again, but the last time she had, her patronizing husband had just comforted her like a frightened child after a night terror.

Only she knew that the palace was in danger. The month before, a total lunar eclipse had alarmed the people of Constantinople, who called it a blood moon and evil omen. Throughout the night, she stood by the palace window staring at the moon and listening to her detractor shouting angry cries and malicious threats toward the palace. *There is an evil moon rising.* The omen haunted her days and now her nights.

Theodora left her bedchamber and walked gingerly down the corridor, searching for one of the servants. A palace guard stood against a wall, seemingly fast asleep. At her touch, he toppled like a sleeping cow, and his weapons and armor echoed through the cavernous hall as he hit the stone floor. Theodora stared at him contemptuously. She wondered how safe these over-dressed guards kept her.

"You'll be reassigned to Armenia by the end of the day," Theodora hissed as the horrified *excubitor*[12] gathered his pilum[13] and shield off the tiled floor.

At last, she found a maidservant and ordered her to prepare a soothing hot cup of spiced wine, then reclined in a low chair on a balcony overlooking the domes and bell towers and watched the red sun slowly rise over the horizon.

She heard familiar footsteps and watched her husband Justinian walk sleepily towards the *tablinum* where he kept the books he read at all hours by the light of oil lamps. He began his workday before sunrise, but Theodora's former nocturnal life in the brothel had accustomed her to late morning rises, so she preferred to begin work after the midday meal.

She quietly joined him in his sanctuary, silently admiring his pleasantly round face and the soft hands of a man who had the luxury of spending hours reading. He was so absorbed in his books that he did not even notice her. She knew Justinian was a loving and faithful partner, but his obsession with books might as well have been a concubine for how it made her feel.

---

[12] Greek for palace guard.

[13] A Roman javelin.

"Good morning, Your Highness," she said, subtly alluding to the subordination that his obsession made her feel.

Justinian looked up for a moment, gave her an obligatory smile, and grunted something unintelligible that was either "good morning" or "nice hair." She sneered at him and left him in peace with his mistress.

Justinian had lived half a century, and his curly brown hair was beginning to thin at the crown, giving him the look of a tonsured monk. He was studious, temperate, and devout — all traits she admired, but she wondered if he could be the man the Empire required. She scrutinized his simple tunic. Often, he did not bother to don his imperial purple garments, and she worried that he reminded the people of his humble origins. They had both come from sturdy peasant stock, but unlike her, his tastes had not changed. Only a gold signet ring distinguished him from the common merchant.

Justinian's uncle, the late Emperor Justin, had snatched him from the hand of destiny and given his nephew the best education available, grooming him to take his place. Justinian had effectively run the Empire for the last years of Justin's reign, but that mattered little to his enemies. Justinian usually saw trouble coming, but this time, she knew he did not.

On the table, she saw a dusty scroll titled *Leo, Bishop of Rome, On the Two Natures of Christ*. She swept it to the ground and slammed the door behind her. Justinian's head was in the clouds. All week, she had raised her concerns about the growing unrest in the city, but her husband had chosen to ignore her. And now he was reading theological treatises when New Rome was about to burn.

As she continued down the corridor, she saw General Belisarius in full regalia walking toward the *tablinum,* a troubled expression on his face. He stopped at the door, wiped his brows, pulled his thick black hair away from his eyes, put his nose in an underarm, and then reluctantly knocked. Her husband's response was loud and impatient, so unlike his usual gentle tone. When she saw Belisarius enter, she retraced her steps and stood outside the door, hoping to observe and overhear their conversation.

At first, she heard only murmurs, then Justinian slowly raised his voice in the false dramatic tone he used to dress down subordinates.

"What am I to do with you, Flavius?" he thundered.

Theodora smiled. Justinian loved and trusted Belisarius. She couldn't help but move closer to the space between the two great doors that led to her husband's *tablinum*. She had to see him in action.

"Had your last battle been Dara, we would be in a stronger position to negotiate with the Persians. Callinicum undid our advantage, so we must pay for a costly peace. I do not put the blame entirely on your shoulders, but you should have known better than to allow your men to goad you into battle."

The patient general said nothing, irritating Justinian. "Do you have nothing to say for yourself?" he demanded.

Belisarius remained silent until Justinian's raised eyebrows provoked a response. Theodora smiled at her husband's gift for tension and drama but felt sorry for the general. *Like a lamb to the slaughter, he opened not his mouth,* she thought to herself.

Belisarius softly and slowly replied, "We might have succeeded had…."

The smack of a handful of letters Justinian threw onto the desk cut Belisarius off. "I have seen the reports. I recalled you not simply to reprimand you but because I have other plans for you, which we will reveal in due course. For now, know that you retain my favor." The Emperor softened his tone. "Tell me, how is Antonina?"

Their voices lowered to a murmur again, and when Theodora heard clanging armor and footsteps approaching the door, she ducked behind a column. Belisarius emerged, looking chastened but not defeated. As he left the palace, she thought she saw him skip down the stairs like a boy and wondered who had played the better part.

Theodora returned to the imperial reception chamber in the women's wing of the palace. A new selection of gold-threaded silks had just arrived from the Lebanese merchants, and her life-long friend Antonina awaited her there. *After the blood moon and the nightmare, a bit of shopping might be just the thing to cheer me up,* she thought. She pinched her pale cheeks to bring some color to them and stretched the risorius muscles around her face to force her first smile of the morning.

A decade before, Theodora and Antonina had worked together in an upscale brothel in Antioch's theater district after entertaining wealthy clients with their acting, singing, and dancing. Theodora eventually returned to Constantinople to develop more affluent clients in the imperial court. Antonina settled down, got married, and had a child. When the great earthquake leveled Antioch, including Antonina's home, and crushed her husband to death, she too headed for Constantinople, where Theodora, who had worked her way up the social ladder and had successfully courted Emperor Justin's nephew, welcomed her. When Justinian had proposed to her, Theodora had initially refused and insisted on a future decision-making role in imperial policy. Justinian, who adored Theodora and respected her judgment, readily agreed to the demand. When Justinian took the crown from his uncle, he elevated his new bride to the imperial throne, and since then, Justinian's confidence in her had only grown.

Antonina's official appointment in the palace three years before had allowed Antonina to put some distance from her scandalous past and dramatically improved her marriage prospects.

The Empress greeted Antonina with a warm embrace and strained smile. "How are you, friend?"

"I am well," Antonina replied as she pulled back to look closely at Theodora's face. "You look like you've seen a ghost," she said with alarm.

"No," Theodora laughed. "I don't hide stress well, do I? It's just a bad moon rising and nightmares."

"Nightmares about what?"

"About losing everything we have achieved. The city is in an ugly mood, and it has left me unsettled. But we can talk about that later. Please sit down and have some hot wine. I need a distraction from all the intrigue right now."

After sipping her wine, Theodora put her cup down and held lengths of purple silk up to her face. "Tell me, Antonina," she asked. "Which of these suits me better?"

"I would advise you to choose the more subtle Tyrian purple," Antonina replied. The brighter shade gives your complexion a pasty cast, draining the color from your cheeks."

Theodora considered Antonina the most alluring woman in the court and envied her curly auburn hair. Even into her thirties, Antonina used her seductive charm to get almost anything she wanted — especially from men. Theodora knew that her persuasive powers derived almost entirely from her authority as Empress. When they worked at the brothel, Antonina had always fetched the highest fees and attracted the wealthiest clients.

Antonina wrapped herself in the Tyrian purple silk and admired herself in the mirror, the largest of its kind in the world.

"I don't think that color becomes *you*, Antonina," Theodora said, shocked by her friend's audacity. "You are right that it suits me." She turned to the Sidonian silk merchant. "We shall have this one, Phlebas, and we shall require an additional length of silk in the same shade for the Emperor and fabric for the new canopy over the loge[14] at the Hippodrome." Theodora directed her attendant to pay the merchant and dismissed them. A moment later, the servant returned trembling. "What is it now?"

"Your Highness, the merchant is demanding more gold for the silk."

Theodora exploded, "What? Bring that ingrate back here at once!"

When the merchant returned, Theodora had regained her composure. "Tell me, do you have many customers for your purple silk?"

"No, Sovereign Lady," Phlebas replied meekly.

"Then, tell me, what will you do with the fabric you do not sell to me? As you well know, only the royal house is permitted to wear purple. Since you have no other licit customers for purple silk within the empire, I do you a service by purchasing your unneeded surplus. I suggest you take your gold gratefully and ensure that any remaining purple silk is dyed another color or destroyed. Do we understand each other?" She dismissed him with a wave of her hand, and he scurried away.

Reclining on a chaise, her friend's performance amused Antonina. "The bear-keeper's daughter has come a long way."

---

[14] The Emperor's box

"Yes, and won't apologize for it," Theodora said as she joined her. "I have worked relentlessly to get here, and I would sooner be cut to pieces than give it up. I will never again beg for dinner scraps." She gave Antonina an icy look. "Politics is much like stagecraft. We must script every word, costume, and scene so that the audience reacts as we intend."

"And how do you wish them to react?"

"I expect the reverence of the people. It is not love that conquers but fear. I am not like that desperate lover of yours — sharing bathwater and wine with the masses."

"True, my Flavius is far too familiar with his troops, which breeds contempt," Antonina said with a laugh that suggested that she admired this popular trait about him.

Theodora, who was used to directing conversations, resented that every conversation with Antonina seemed to return to her beloved Belisarius. Theodora was ready to talk about the source of her anxiety.

"Justinian and I have been re-writing the protocols for meeting with the Emperor and Empress," Theodora said. "We have decided to do away with the silly old Roman tradition of one-knee genuflection and adopt the Persian tradition of full prostration."

"How have the patricians and Senate received this news?"

"How strange you ask, Antonina, because no one seems to care!" Theodora realized that her friend was not the object of her anger and softened her tone. "They grumble, but they are a voracious crowd. When they are not protesting new palace protocols, they protest the higher taxes imposed on them by that slippery Cappadocian finance minister, or they protest the new laws that undermine their privileges in court. There is no pleasing the landowners, so why bother? It's all a bit much."

Antonina nodded. "They are like children. If we had done as they do, our mothers would have thrown us down the stairs."

Theodora gave her friend an exasperated look. "These patricians think the world would end without them. We could cut down every one of them, and society would hardly notice."

"I agree with you," Antonina said. "Those born into wealth and status will never give us the respect we deserve unless we take it from them. Your reforms undermine their ancient unearned privileges. As much as I detest our chief tax collector, I admire his ruthlessness, forcing these highborn shirkers to pay their fair share. And the justice minister has them squealing like pigs at the slaughter."

"I am glad you understand what is at stake," Theodora said as she reached for a bit of honey-drenched fruit. "Justinian and I are surrounded by grandees who have no appreciation for the radical reforms underway. You are one of the few who comprehend the significance of Justinian's efforts. Establishing greater equality before the law is only the first part of our plan to restore the empire."

"Your beloved Flavius has done a great deal to secure our empire in the East. Justinian also has military plans for the lost western parts, and the two of you could play major roles in carrying them out."

"What do you mean?" Antonina asked. "I thought he was in trouble for losing at Callinicum."

Theodora laughed, "No, of course not. The Iberian War is over. His victory at Dara and Persian bloodletting at Callinicum forced the Shah to sign the Eternal Peace. Justinian has great plans for Flavius."

"Well, someone should have told him that," Antonina said. "He has been in a cold sweat since he learned of his recall to Constantinople. What do you need of me?"

"I need you to keep me informed of Flavius's plans and intentions and advise us if those haughty generals begin to think the Empire should be governed from military barracks again."

"Spy on him? I would never...." Antonina rose to her feet.

Theodora held up her hand. "No, Antonina, sit down. The mob is always looking for a leader. Flavius is a perpetual target for those seeking to replace Justinian and me on the throne. I am asking you, as a friend, to let me know if the circle around Flavius poses a threat to us."

"Of course, I would do that," Antonina replied, "but the Roman Army will never allow a woman in their camps. Would I not serve you better here in Constantinople, where I have many sources among the courtesans of the patricians?"

Theodora felt ready to explode whenever an established custom seemed to supersede one of her orders. She replied in a low, conspiratorial tone that grew louder and more staccato as she spoke. "The army will allow you to enter the camp if I command it." She stood up and walked around the room, searching for eavesdroppers who might be lurking behind the curtains, then sat on the chaise close to Antonina and whispered, "Do not tell anyone about this. Because you were not born into privilege, I can trust you to warn me of threats posed to our reign."

Antonio took her friend's hand. "I know what the people say in the streets. Your courtiers tell you only what they think you wish to hear."

"I am relying on you to give me the unaltered truth, Antonina."

A court attendant entered the room, bringing another golden tray laden with fruit, honey cakes, and sweetmeats covered in syrup. Theodora glared. "Announce yourself before you enter, please."

Antonina quickly chose one of the sweetmeats and licked the sticky syrup from her fingertips. "This is delicious," she said. "What is it?"

"It's the pancreas of a lamb. I don't imagine you ate like this in Antioch," Theodora smiled with pride at the thought of having introduced her friend to the good life.

"No, we ate only bread and vegetables. On special occasions, we had meats and cheeses." Antonina was pleased with Theodora's suggestion of a new role. "The high price of the Eternal Peace has left many wondering whether Justinian knows what he is doing." She paused for effect, popped another sweetmeat into her mouth, and watched the Empress react before continuing.

"When the citizens of Constantinople learned that Justinian had pledged eleven-thousand pounds of gold in exchange for Shah Kavad's assurance that he would not venture into Roman territory, many questioned whether the treasury was being well-spent. Even that ungrateful merchant whom you just upbraided complained of higher taxes."

Theodora looked pleased, "Outstanding; that is precisely the information we need. You are the daughter of one of the empire's greatest charioteers and niece of another. Tell me, what do the chariot factions say of the arrests of their ringleaders for hooliganism?"

"The Green Faction has been unhappy since Emperor Anastasius died, but Justinian's crackdown has increased their discontent. Leaders of the Blue Faction, some of them former lovers of mine, tell me they plan to protest...."

"Protest?" Theodora exclaimed, "Peacefully protest or start a riot?"

"I'm not certain," Antonina said. "They are protesting the arrests. While the Blues normally back Justinian, the two factions plan to jointly present their complaints to the Emperor during the next chariot races."

"That is startling. The Blues and Greens have been killing each other for as long as I can remember. They run rival protection rackets, and any merchant who refuses them risks having his business destroyed or his life taken. It's not safe to walk the streets alone at night."

"Many were dumbfounded by Minister Tribonian's insistence that the laws apply even to supporters of the Emperor. They say that Justinian is ungrateful."

"For example?" Theodora demanded.

"The Blue Faction," Antonina replied. "Their henchmen have long had a free hand, beating, robbing, and even killing. Their livelihoods and leisure time will suffer now that we have revoked their immunity."

"I see," Theodora said. "Justinian's new laws have given Blues and Greens a common enemy."

"Exactly," Antonina agreed. "At the next chariot race, leaders of both factions will insist on clemency for the convicted." Antonina stopped herself when Theodora eyed her suspiciously.

"How do *you* know this?" Theodora asked in an accusing tone that suggested Antonina, whom she had always thought indifferent to politics, might be a co-conspirator.

"My uncle has friends among the Blue charioteers. They told me this in confidence. If you punish them, I fear they will come after me."

Theodora patted Antonina's arm. "I will protect you and your sources but keep me informed. We will need to speak with Narses, the royal chamberlain. Justinian hates surprises but is not as focused on this issue as he should be."

"Of course," Antonina said. "Belisarius plans to attend the races. I'll be at the baths but let me know if there is more to be done."

"Thank you, Antonina. You are a good friend," Theodora said with a genuine smile. "Before you go, I have a gift for you." She went to a table and brought her a gold crucifix brooch studded with gems.

"It's beautiful!" Antonina exclaimed.

"And practical," Theodora said. "Push up on the sapphire."

A tiny door sprang open in the back, and a miniature scroll popped out. "If you need to communicate with me secretly, write your message on a scrap, roll it and insert it in the brooch. The scroll contains codes for key names and places. Memorize them and use them in your correspondence. Write to me whenever you have information that might threaten our reign. I will be sure that your messages reach Justinian."

Antonina embraced the Empress.

"Watch your back," Theodora said gravely. "Military officers are an intriguing lot. They'll cut your throat if they think you stand in the way of their promotion."

CHAPTER SIX

# A NOT-SO-PEACEFUL PROTEST

*A riot is the language of the unheard.*

— Rev. Martin Luther King, Jr.

*Constantinople*
*January 15-18, A.D. 532*

Justinian knew his people were eager to see him at the chariot races at the Hippodrome, but he had work to do. He summoned Tribonian, his Minister of Justice, to the *tablinum*, "Have you executed the ringleaders?"

"There were technical difficulties, Your Majesty."

"What does that mean?"

"The hangman was new to his craft. When the two convicts were to drop from the scaffolding, the ropes broke. The crowd rushed up, overwhelmed the guards, and took the convicts to a church. The priests have reluctantly returned them to us, and we have found a more experienced hangman to carry out the execution ."

Justinian paced the room, trying to control his rage, his hands behind his back, his gaze lowered to the mosaic floor. *I am surrounded by idiots!* "Am I to believe there will be no further problems?"

Tribonian hesitated. "Their leaders are clamoring for mercy, dismayed that the Church so easily surrendered the men whose sentences should have been commuted to spending their lives in service to the faith."

Justinian rolled his eyes. "And they will be raising this issue here?"

Tribonian nodded, shamefaced. Justinian realized that Theodora's warning about the rising red moon and the violent dreams had been an oracle. And now, his reign was in grave danger. The Lord had spoken to his wife in a dream, and instead of taking precautions, he had ignored it. His irritation at himself had him looking for a scapegoat.

"How hard it is to hang a man? Is rope so expensive now we are forced to use an inferior quality? Have you any idea how precarious our situation is becoming?" He threw his crown at Tribonian's head, cutting his forehead. "If you wish to steal my crown, take it, but I will not surrender it to your incompetence!"

Four palace guards, hearing the altercation, hurried in as Tribonian was leaving.

"I'm fine," Justinian shouted. Leave me in peace."


As trumpets sounded and the crowd roared, the Emperor and Empress appeared in the imperial box, Justinian displaying a confidence his wife did not share. She leaned into him and said softly, "Ever since I saw that bad moon rising, I've seen nothing but trouble on the way. We should not be out today, Petrus. It may cost us our lives."

Justinian caressed her leg and gave her his best patronizing smile. "The Blues have always backed us, darling, and the Greens must be pleased that we are enforcing the rule of law. Once Tribonian's executioner succeeds in hanging the two murderers, those who would cause trouble will understand our resolve. And guards at the entrances will prevent them from smuggling weapons into the stadium."

Theodora raised an eyebrow. She was unconvinced.

As crews set up the first race, Justinian raised a hand, acknowledging the crowd, and beckoned Theodora to do the same.

Each of the four factions had entered two chariot teams, but the team leaders had already chosen the winner in most races. Antonina's uncle, Nicholas, would be driving the secondary chariot for the Blue Faction.

Justinian surveyed the vast sea of green tunics. For the first time since his enthronement, they outnumbered the blue ones. He studied the hostile stares of the

Green supporters in the stands. None of them laughed, despite a bear show intended to amuse the crowd. The Emperor gave the signal for the distribution of 100,000 loaves of sweetened bread. *Surely bread and circuses will dull the daggers in their eyes. It always works.*

He examined the faces of his security detail. The *excubitor* on his left sunk his index finger deep into his nostril, pulled something out, curled it into a sticky ball, and flicked it near the Emperor's foot. When he caught the Emperor glaring at him, he clicked his heels and straightened up. The one on his right had his pilum leaning precariously on his body while he gnawed a piece of sweet bread so large that he gasped for breath. The *excubitor* felt the same glare, nodded with a quirky smile as he swallowed the mass, and saluted his sovereign with the remaining bread in his hand. "God help us," Justinian murmured. At least these harmless fellows did not look like they wanted to kill him.

Theodora stuck an elbow into his rib cage. "I am about to start the race." She raised her arms and dropped a wide purple silk scarf. As it floated into the arena, the weights opening the gates fell with a crash. Horse-drawn chariots bolted from the starting block, and the race began. Justinian leaned over, studying each rider, paying particular attention to Antonina's uncle. Nicholas took the inner lane and did not yield it until his Blue partner was behind him, then pulled into a middle lane to allow the designated primary to take his place. At the same time, the rival Green chariot sought to sneak in behind him.

When the Blue primary took the lead in the inner lane, Nicholas closed the opening and nearly collided with the Green charioteer, who pulled back, losing a quarter lap. The secondary Green moved in to take his position. Nicholas pushed him to the outside, and for dramatic effect, as he passed the imperial box, he slammed his wheels into his Green rival, overturning it. The charioteer slammed into the wall and did not get up. Slaves with gurneys rushed out to retrieve him and remove the horses.

With one lap to go, the Blue Faction held both first and second positions. The Green charioteer was less interested in winning the race than in avenging his partner. He rode his chariot straight into Nicholas's wheel, breaking the axel. The chariot somersaulted, detaching the four horses. Justinian covered his cheeks with his hands. Stunts like this had killed Antonina's father, but Nicholas s managed to hold on to the reins as his horses dragged him across the finish line for a respectable fourth place.

"Unbelievable!" Justinian shouted. He took his wife's hand, and she smiled. "This is a providential sign," he said, "signifying that we can overcome insurmountable odds and triumph over our rivals."

"Or perhaps it means we will be dragged to our final destination," she replied.

The Emperor stood and raised his hands above his head until the clamor died down. A herald proclaimed, "Your Emperor offers the noble leaders of our chariot teams an opportunity to speak of an important matter. First, we will hear from the Blue leaders, then the Green. Finally, the Emperor will address their concerns."

The Blue leader walked toward the loge, looked up to the Imperial box, and raised his hands for silence. "Your Imperial Majesty, I should like to call forward my archrival from the Greens." The astonished crowd had rarely seen the two men together, but they stood peacefully, side by side.

"We demand the immediate removal from office of three senior officials — John, Tribonian, and Eudaemon. Your Cappadocian treasurer is corrupt. He has been levying unsustainable taxes on our citizens and imprisoning those unable to pay. He is unworthy of the public trust."

Justinian gave John a sympathetic look. A hoarse voice called from the crowd. "The Cappadocian is a bloodsucker!"

The Blue leader continued. "Tribonian seeks to abolish our ancient rights and privileges so that he may protect the new freedoms and opportunities permitted to his associates and friends. Your Majesty's minister of justice accepts bribes from those who seek to shape the legislation he writes."

"And your City Prefect Eudaemon has imprisoned men without trial, tortured them, and made them disappear."

"Never to be seen again," a Blue Faction member echoed.

"Finally, we demand clemency for Gaius and Lucius, whose lives the Almighty has graciously spared."

A man in a brown cloak rose from his seat, shouting, "Clemency for Gaius and Lucius!"

The Emperor lifted his hand to silence the rising clamor, but the two factions chanted in turn, "Mercy for Blue lives!" "Mercy for Green lives!"

Theodora turned to Justinian in disbelief. He held a gold-bound copy of the Gospel above his head, and his herald proclaimed, "By the Gospel of Our Lord Jesus Christ, your Emperor swears to you that he will investigate these matters. Even now, his courtiers are requesting the resignation of John, Tribonian, and Eudaemon. His scribes are granting amnesty to your comrades."

Justinian looked away from his wife but heard her whisper, "If you yield to these demands, you cede your power to the mob."

"If I do not yield to their demands," he whispered back, "they will seize power without asking for it."

Churls in the crowd yelled, "We don't believe you. Release them now!"

Soon tens of thousands took up the chant.

A Green Faction member pointed at the Emperor, screaming, "Down with Justinian and his whore!"

Theodora's pale complexion turned red with rage.

"What would you have me do?" he asked.

"You are the Emperor. You can do anything! Send agents to pluck them from the crowd. Fill the prisons. Don't sit there like a frog in a boiling kettle while your enemies shout you down."

Justinian stood and raised his hand again for silence, but the crowd had heard enough and chanted in unison, "*Nika! Nika!*" — the Greek word for victory.

Screaming fanatics threw glass bottles at the loge. Justinian ducked, and as the bottle shattered behind him, he sneered contemptuously at the hooligan who had tossed it moments before realizing the gravity of the situation. However, the assailant only howled and pointed at Theodora. He turned around in dread and saw her collapse on the floor, blood rushing from her head. Justinian pointed at the fiend and yelled, "Seize him!" as a half-dozen *excubitors* went after the fleeing villain. He turned to Theodora, grabbed a piece of silk from the loge, and wrapped it tightly around her head. "Oh, my little sweet cake." He picked her up and shouted, "Let's get out of here!"

The remaining imperial guards surrounded the Emperor and Empress with a wall of shields, forming a tortoise shell. Bottle after bottle hit the shields and shattered on the ground.

"Move! Move!" the captain yelled, and the tortoise crawled to a gate that led to the palace through an underground passage.

Several in the mob had mounted the *kathisma*[15] and followed the Emperor's retreat. "Close the gate!" the captain ordered as the first wave surged forward. Two guards remained behind to cover the retreat.

The crowd flooded the grounds surrounding the palace like a tidal wave. A Green Faction leader called out, "Kill the guards, and our problems go away!"

The mob pulled down the gate, struggled to disarm the guards, and pierced them with their weapons. The remaining guards, used to playing a ceremonial role, watched in horror. Justinian tried to ignore the terrified squabbling among the embattled guards.

One young *excubitor* cried, "Are we just going to let this happen?"

Not realizing that the Emperor was within earshot, his comrade replied, "Do you think this Emperor will stand by us if we defend him? He just sacked the three most senior palace officials. What will happen to us if we kill even one of these hooligans? He'll hand us over to the mob leaders, and they will string us up."

A dozen *excubitors* backed off, reducing the *testudo*[16] formation to six. When the remaining guards, all of them Isaurians, arrived at the palace, the household militia met them. "Take the Empress to her bed," Justinian commanded. "Instruct the court physician to clean her wound. Tell him I do not want a scar."

He stared as four guards carried his wife up the staircase to the living quarters, leaving a trail of blood.

---

[15] Imperial throne

[16] A "tortoise formation" formed by troops holding their overlapping shields above their heads.

"Your Majesty," the captain said. "The six men standing before you will stand by you to the end. What are your orders?" Justinian had appointed Tiberius the count of the *excubitors* when his uncle, Justin, had vacated the position to become Emperor. He trusted Tiberius more than anyone save his wife, even if Justinian occasionally resented the count for overruling him on security matters. Justinian knew that Tiberius would lay down his life for the imperial couple and rarely challenged his authority. Tiberius was tall, muscular, and came from tough Isaurian stock who feared nothing so long as they could see a mountain nearby.

For a moment, he did not answer Tiberius, overwhelmed by the shock of the uprising. Justinian considered his prior ignorance of the situation, his wife's futile efforts to warn him, and his inability to grasp the situation. He loathed the person he had been for the past few hours: an arrogant, lazy lout with the courage of a mouse. He needed to prove to himself that he was worthy of the crown on his head.

"Tiberius, tell your men to remove their armor and put on monks' robes. We are going into the city."

"Your Majesty, the mob will tear you limb from limb."

"They will not recognize us," Justinian replied. "I must see the people's mood with my own eyes."

Tiberius and the loyal guards returned looking like Chalcedonian monks with hoods over their heads and short daggers hidden under their robes. They returned to the Hippodrome through another entrance. Justinian surveyed the uneasy monks and wondered if he could trust them. *So long as I do not lead them into great danger.* The Green mob was dismantling the Emperor's loge, removing a wooden column they carried to the gate. Justinian calculated that he was safer disguised as a monk than he would be in the palace.

A voice in the mob cried out, "We have a battering ram!" They broke through the iron palace gate, crushing two guards.

Hundreds of people rushed into the vast corridors, running here and there, searching for the imperial quarters. A senator identified the barracks of the imperial guard, and a mob of angry men shouted, "*Nika! Nika.* They set fire to the administrative wing of the palace, and winds from the Bosporus blew the flames westward.

The false monks watched as a dozen off-duty guards emerged unarmed. They had supposed that the races were louder than usual, but seeing the mob, they hastily retreated toward their barracks, struggling for their weapons. As the remaining guards fled, the mob raided the armory.

"They are armed now," Justinian said fearfully. "We cannot rely on the *excubitors.*"

"Shhh…." Tiberius said, "if the mob hears you, we're finished."

"Now we can defend ourselves," one of the mob shouted, wildly swinging a sword.

Justinian had answered the question that had been gnawing at him: why? *They hate you*, he thought, *and will stop at nothing to kill you.* "We need to get away from here," Justinian said.

He was about to lead his monks back to the palace when he heard several women screaming and fleeing the Baths of Zeuxippos. When they arrived on the scene, they found another insatiable mob, smashing the marble statuary and setting fire to the ceiling. Women, whose husbands had been attending the races, tried in vain to cover their privates as they fled the scene in terror. Justinian watched in shock as rapacious men dragged several women screaming into the various dressing rooms. Their ignored protestations sent a shiver down his spine as he feared the same might happen soon to Theodora.

Two naked women approached them, yelling for help as they fled a group of crazy-eyed young men in green tunics. The younger one grabbed Justinian's robes and begged for protection. The monks formed a circle around them and stared down at the would-be assailants.

"Come on, boys, we're just looking for a little fun," one green said.

"Move along," Justinian demanded.

The men were unwilling to back down until Tiberius showed them his dagger.

The man in the lead stopped the others, saying, "Come on, boys, there are plenty more lasses where they came from," as they headed back toward the baths. The women thanked the monks and fled the scene.

Justinian's eyes followed the savages back to the baths, where he spotted Antonina running off into the baths. He took several steps toward the assailants until the captain put his hand on Justinian's shoulder. "That's Flavius's woman," Justinian said, recalling all the time the two former palace guards had spent together with Antonina and Theodora.

"Let her be," Tiberius cautioned, "we must get you out of here now. It's not safe."

Justinian pulled the hand off his shoulder, "No, we're going. I could never forgive myself if anything happened to her."

"And I could never forgive myself if anything happened to you," the captain insisted, grabbing the Emperor's so hard it felt like a death grip.

Justinian tried his imperial glare, failed to get a reaction, and realized that his security chief would not negotiate the point. "But…"

"Look at her," Tiberius insisted, "she is not afraid. She knows how to deal with such rapacious men and knows all the secret recesses of the baths. If anyone can manage this on her own, it's Antonina."

Justinian recalled how Tiberius's recommendation of Belisarius as his best cavalry officer had prompted him to give him a command position in the East. Tiberius had known Antonina since her arrival in the palace three years before. They watched Antonina flee down the steps to the furnaces.

Justinian reached for the dagger from under his robe, but the captain pushed it back into its scabbard, and, forgetting the requirement for formal address, whispered, "No, Petrus. You might save her, but we'd all be killed."

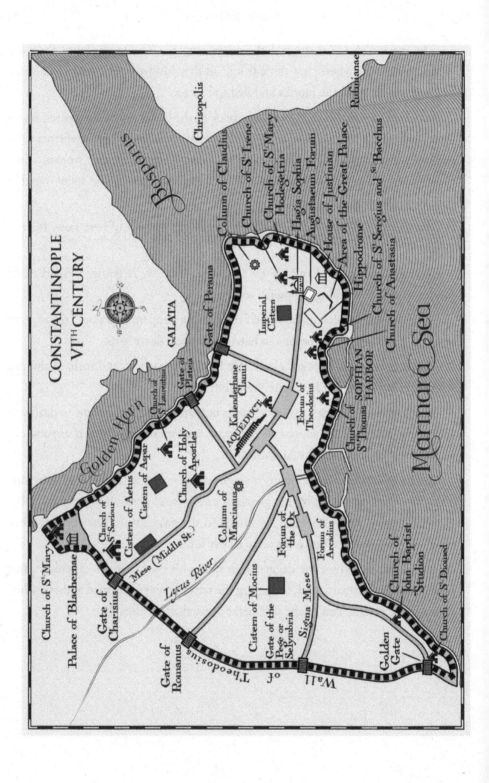

CONSTANTINOPLE
VIᵗʰ CENTURY

Bosporus

GALATA

Golden Horn

Chrisopolis

Rufinianae

Column of Claudius
Church of Sᵗ Irene
Church of Sᵗ Mary Hodegetria
Hagia Sophia
Augustaeum Forum
House of Justinian
Area of the Great Palace
Hippodrome
Church of Sᵗ Sergius and Sᵗ Bacchus
Church of Anastasia

Marmara Sea

Gate of Perama

Imperial Cistern

SOPHIAN HARBOR
Church of Sᵗ Thomas

Gate of Plateia

Church of Sᵗ Laurentius

Kalenderhane Clanii
AQUEDUCT

Forum of Theodosius

Church of Holy Apostles
Cistern of Aspar
Church of Sᵗ Saviour
Cistern of Aetius

Column of Marcianus

Mese (Middle St.)

Lycus River

Forum of the Ox

Forum of Arcadius

Church of Sᵗ Mary
Palace of Blachernae
Gate of Charisius
Gate of Romanus

Cistern of Mocius
Gate of the Pege or Selymbria

Sigma Mese

Church of John Baptist Studion
Church of Sᵗ Dioued

Golden Gate

Wall of Theodosius

# Chapter Seven
# The Fury of the Mob

*We can and must write in a language that sows among the masses hatred, loathing, and scorn toward those who disagree with us.*

— Vladimir Lenin

*Constantinople*
*January 532 A.D.*

In the hellish furnace room, Antonina grabbed a hot poker and waited for one of the ruffians in the mob who had seen her descend the stairs. She backed slowly into the recesses and hid behind a pile of wood fuel, frightened, wearing only a towel. When she had worked in a brothel, she had been in many rough situations and reminded herself that she knew how to handle such men.

"She's in 'ere." She heard a man growl to his companion and watched him descend the steps. Antonina gripped the poker and lifted it over her shoulder, ready to swing.

"Ah, there ye are, my sweet. Ye been waitin' fo' me."

He walked toward her slowly, his creepy smile revealing a row of blackened teeth. As he reached for her, she swung the poker at his head, cracking his skull and causing him to collapse to the floor. Then she stepped out from behind the pile to greet his companion, prepared to attack again.

"Oh, hello! Were you looking for a good time as well? Come and get it! I'm finished with your friend."

The man saw his companion sprawled lifeless in a pool of blood and ran back up the steps. Antonina dragged the body to the oven, struggled to lift it inside, and watched the heat consume it. *Well, now, that's done, and I'm glad it's over.* She caught her breath and fanned herself with one hand while wiping her sweaty brow with the other. She would stay near the furnace until she was sure it was safe to come out. *What would Flavius do?* "Choose your battleground, wait in ambush, and strike first with fury," she said in a deep baritone voice that she used to impersonate him. Her spot-on imitation made her laugh.

She considered the gravity of just having killed a man--again. She wasn't bothered by guilt since his intentions were clear, and he'd certainly had it coming, but she had hoped to leave behind a life of violence when she left Antioch. She recalled her time in the brothel, where a wealthy patron had taken more liberty than she'd been accustomed to. As Antonina found herself in a stranglehold that she was sure would lead to her death, she reached for a dagger under a pillow and thrust it into her assailant's throat. The man bled out on top of her and let out a gargled scream. The busty manager of the brothel, Lupicina, burst into the room, learned what happened, and immediately set all the girls to clean the crime scene and dump the body into the Orontes River.

Constantinople was supposed to be the most civilized place in the world, where someone like her could get a new start. Shortly after her arrival, she found herself almost naked and hiding again from ravenous assailants. She had been victorious again, but did this mean she would never be able to start a new life? Her reflection was cut short by another scream.

Above her, she heard a man's voice shouting, "Stop this madness! These are our wives and daughters," then the sounds of a struggle and a young man tumbling down the stairs. He wore the white toga with purple ribbons of a senator.

She helped him to hide with her behind the woodpile and placed a finger on her lips. Moments later, a dozen men rushed into the furnace room, grabbed pieces of timber, and hurried back up the steps. "Grab an ember and let's burn the palace down," a hooligan shouted.

She wondered where her fiancé was, wished that he were with her, but fearfully realizing that he was unlikely to rescue her, steadfastly resolved to treat any trespassers with the ferocity she'd once directed against unpaying clients.

"This might be the safest place in the city right now," she whispered to the senator. "This is not a day to be dressed in purple."

The workers who had fed the furnace kept a bucket of water there. When she saw it, Antonina drank, offered it to the senator, then spread her damp limbs on a pile of logs as though it were a sauna, closed her eyes, and when it seemed no one else was coming, succumbed to exhaustion.

Justinian watched as his advisors left the palace and rushed towards the docks. With his robed guards, he followed the mob as they trampled and plundered their way through the beautiful city. Plumes of fire bellowed out of the windows of the marble buildings, blackening the white stone. In the chaos of fleeing their burning homes, mothers had been separated from their children, and crying toddlers wandered looking for them. It reminded him of Jeremiah's lamentation over the destruction of Jerusalem: *My eyes are sunken with grief; my stomach churns; my heart is poured out on the ground because of the destruction of my people and because infants and babes languish in the streets of the city.*

One of the monk-guards whispered, "Your Majesty! They're organizing!" and pointed to a large man with broad shoulders, a scruffy grey beard, and blazing eyes who thundered, "To the Hagia Sofia!" He led the mob in green tunics up the grand stairway of the majestic cathedral. A priest stood boldly before the tall bronze doors and said sternly, "The church is closed for divine services."

"Bring the battering ram!" the man shouted, and they began striking the doors within minutes. When they gave way, they crushed several priests who had tried vainly to hold them shut. A lone monk hurried up to the tower and began ringing the church bells madly. He had heard these ominous sounds whenever Huns or Slavs raided his town in Dardania[17] but never expected to hear them warning of troubles in Constantinople. *These people are barbarians, not Romans!*

---

[17] Tauresium, modern Gradište in North Macedonia, ca. 20 kilometers southeast of the capital Skopje

Justinian and his guards followed the mob as a stalwart orthodox priest continued to pray the Divine Liturgy. A ruffian carrying a heavy candlestick came up behind the priest, yelling, "He thinks he's talking to the angels!"

The priest continued to pray, but the ruffian swung the candlestick, striking his head. The priest fell forward, and his skull shattered on a corner of the stone altar. The mob frantically looted precious metal vessels and candlesticks. Two men stripped the dead priest of his jewel-encrusted vestments and *skufia*[18], now dripping with blood. One of them stood at the altar, holding the garments above his head, and shouted, "How much am I bid for this fine vestment?" The mob laughed as though it were a game. A well-founded fear that any effort to stop the mob would also make him a victim tempered Justinian's rage. He made tentative steps to confront the mob.

"No, Your Majesty," his captain said as he restrained the Emperor from rushing forward, "There is nothing we can do."

A priest he knew well mounted the elevated pulpit to exhort the mob. "You will not escape damnation for this sacrilege! The fires of Hell await those who violate the sanctity of the Church and her priests! Your Father's house is not a thief's marketplace! Your forebears spent decades building and embellishing this holy place with the sweat of their brows. Will you now sack it like a pagan temple?"

The priest had said what Justinian wanted to, but his words were all for naught. No one listened. The pillage continued despite the dire warnings. "Do these savages have no fear of God?" Justinian asked his guards.

Tiberius shook his head. "No, so all is permissible."

Men arrived from the furnace room, carrying the torches they had taken and bringing a new wave of destruction. Flames enveloped the wooden timbers of the gold-coffered ceiling, creaking before they began to drop one by one. The heat became so intense that many of the mob retreated with their stolen treasures. Glass shattered down onto the floor, and stones fell from the ceiling, hitting those whose greed exceeded their prudence.

---

[18] A priestly hat

"Your Majesty, we cannot stay here," the captain said as he pulled Justinian away from the conflagration. Justinian and his false monks fled the unbearable heat of the great cathedral as spires of flame filled the sky. Behind them, they heard a thunderous crash as the support beams fell, creating a massive hole in the roof and releasing flames and smoke that billowed into the darkened sky. Justinian coughed violently from the soot and ash.

Justinian knew he had seen and heard enough but wanted to witness more all the same. He wondered why this might be. Perhaps all the violence I have witnessed will eventually inspire actions to correct it. Let my passion animate my will.

Victims of looting, murder, and fire lined the streets. He watched a young man carrying a leg of lamb looted from a local butcher shop. Hardly a single building remained undamaged. Justinian looked at his capitol and his people, wondering how it had come to this. Even the ancient Senate House, the epicenter of organization and civility, was in flames. As the Emperor and his guards continued walking, he stopped when he heard screaming voices whom he recognized coming from the Senate House. He watched in anger as the conflagration consumed the roof and then heard a voice that sent shivers down his spine. An old friend, Marius, cried, "Get out, or you'll be burned alive!"

Justinian watched helplessly as the mob sealed the bronze door with a heavy beam, trapping Marius and his senate colleagues inside. The senators pushed desperately to break it down, but their pounding and screams were useless against the thick beams. The senators tried to smash the high windows to escape, but the effort only ensured more oxygen to fan the flames now engulfing the ceiling. The screams became louder and more intense as the burning beams in the wooden ceiling crashed down on top of them. Then, Marius's tortured voice dropped off, and a moment later, the voices of the other senators became fainter and finally fell silent. The entire ceiling collapsed and shattered the windows, creating a waft of smoke that reeked of pine and human flesh. Justinian moaned the last helpless cry even as the mob laughed and congratulated themselves on having murdered some of his strongest allies. He painfully recalled that his guards had expelled many senators from the palace as a security precaution. Marius's screams haunted him as he realized their expulsion had been tantamount to a death sentence.

The Emperor felt powerless as the crown city of the Eastern Empire, indeed of the entire Christian world, was reduced to a smoldering pile of ash. He sat by a large fountain and wept. Jerusalem, Athens, Carthage, Alexandria, Rome, and now Constantinople. "My people," he cried, "what are you doing?"

They followed the mob from the Senate house to the adjacent great square of the Augustaeum, where there stood a gold column topped with a colossal bronze equestrian statue of Justinian dressed in a muscle cuirass like Achilles, holding an orb and cross and facing the East. Three statues depicting a Vandal, a Goth, and a Persian, knelt in submission at the base. Justinian had repurposed the statue by replacing the face of Emperor Theodosius with his own and crowning it with a plumed helmet of peacock feathers. The city had rededicated it recently, but Justinian knew it would soon be gone as the mob attacked it. His mind fixed on a famous quote of his inscribed at the stone base of the statue: "Keep cool, and you will command everyone." He laughed nervously the way a victim of pain does as a means of coping.

"Your Majesty!" The captain whispered, snapping Justinian back into the moment. "Is it your intention to follow the mob through this accursed city?"

Justinian's rage and despair found a target in his captain, who dared to question his intentions. He lifted the captain by the hood of his robe, shouting, "Who are you to question the motives of your Emperor?"

"Just an *excubitor*, who wants to keep you alive," Tiberius replied.

Justinian knew his captain had a valid point, but he didn't have a good answer. Was he trying to prove his courage to himself or collecting evidence he could later use against his enemies? He did not know--yet. He took a place about a stone's throw from the statue's base.

A sailor pushed through the mob to the column, carrying a rope wound around one shoulder and a battle-ax hanging over the other. He shimmied to the top. He pounded the front legs of the bronze horse until they separated from the statue and shouted, "Bring down the tyrant!" The mob repeated his words, chanting them repeatedly.

The sailor threw down one end of the rope, and a hundred men began pulling on the statue. The sailor began to swing at the horse's hind legs, but as the line grew taut, it separated him from the base of the statue, and he lost his balance. The weight of the ax prevented him from regaining it, and he fell to his death.

After a moment of stunned silence, another sailor grabbed the rope, walked thirty paces with the line in hand, and cried in a powerful voice, "Join me, comrades!"

The narrow legs of the bronze horse creaked as the men pulled and bent it ninety degrees, giving the appearance of rearing up.

Justinian turned to the captain with an uneasy smile, "A fortuitous omen."

Justinian then noticed two men who had been closely observing them since he had overheard Justinian upbraiding Tiberius. He pointed to him, crying, "There he is! Let's get his flesh and blood!"

Justinian froze, realizing that his monk's hood had slipped off, when he looked up to see his statue. The captain grabbed him by the arms and ran with him towards one of the palace gates, but the mob gave chase, howling like hounds on a hunt.

"Open the gates!" Tiberius yelled, but there was no gatekeeper. The five guards encircled Justinian as the captain fumbled with a massive ring of keys. "Saint Peter, keeper of keys, help me," he called to Heaven, inserting a key in the lock. When the gate finally opened, Tiberius pushed Justinian through and pulled it shut behind them. The mob, now armed with daggers, stabbed at the guards who were still standing. The sharp sound of daggers penetrating armor and flesh, the screams of the guards, and the splattering of his robe with blood horrified Justinian, who regretfully realized that his reckless curiosity had compelled their sacrifice. He knew these men, and they were good men. He had commanded them while his uncle was Emperor, and he knew Tiberius would have to relay the tragic news to the widows and orphans. *Lord, forgive my pride.*

Justinian and the captain ran to a more fortified gate and entered the palace ahead of the mob, who had knocked down the first one with the battering ram. Tiberius gave Justinian a stern look. "I hope witnessing all that was worth the lives of those men."

Justinian was too terrified and numb to respond. He regretted needlessly putting their lives at risk and resolved to be an Emperor for whom such sacrifices would be worthwhile.

In the relative safety of Theodora's chamber, he found her lying unconscious with a cut protruding over a purple swelling where the bottle had hit her. The imperial physician and Narses stood nearby with a surgeon.

Justinian took his wife's hand, tapped her on the cheek, and asked, "Theodora, can you hear me?" Her eyes opened slightly, then rolled back, and she regained her senses. Narses brought her water and insisted that she drink it to replenish the fluids in her body after losing so much blood.

"I feared I had lost you, my love," Justinian said. "We must flee the palace — now!"

"What? What just happened? Why am I in my bed?" she demanded.

Justinian ordered domestics to pack Theodora's favorite silks and place Theodora on a stretcher. "The mob out there wants us dead," he said and told her what he had seen. "We must flee while we still can."

Theodora felt the stitches on her forehead and frowned. "What? Are you mad?"

"I will assemble those who still support us and order them to head for the ships," Justinian said as four servants began carrying the Empress in her stretcher to the door.

Theodora looked at him as though he had two heads. "Stop!" she yelled as she tried to understand the panic in the room. The servants put down the stretcher. "Your response to this madness is to summon your advisors?" she asked.

Justinian nodded.

"That is certainly a bold move, sure to hold the mob in check."

They heard more screams, and Justinian ran to a high balcony. "Dear God, what have I done to be so hated?" he cried.

Theodora gave her worried husband a confused look. "You did your job, Petrus. Nothing more! You brought much-needed change," Theodora replied and collapsed into the stretcher again.

Narses said, "People hate change because it makes them realize that our society can be better, that there is more work to be done, and that we are still miles from our destination."

"But that's a good thing," Justinian said as he returned to his wife's side.

When he touched Theodora's face, she sat up, saying, "Not if protecting your ego is more important than promoting the common good." She pushed Justinian's hand away and laid down again with her hand on her head.

The crowd's shouts outside the palace grew even louder, angrier. Justinian returned to the balcony and watched as several men brought scaling ladders and rope. The remaining handful of guards was unable to block their entry. "Time is running out," he yelled to everyone behind him. A loud crash of the collapsing roof of Hagia Sophia was all he needed to realize that his days as Emperor of the East were over.

The grey-bearded mob leader threw back his hood and called up to Justinian's balcony, "Free our imprisoned comrades, or we will do it for you!" Half the mob headed to the Praetorium to release the two charioteers whose bungled hanging had started the riot. Justinian watched from a window as they cut the jailer's throats and set fire to the building.

"I can't watch this any longer," he said as he left his wife's side for the private chapel for some peace while he waited for his advisors. "Take the Empress to the ship!" he yelled behind him. The servants picked up the sleeping Empress and her baggage and headed for the door that led to the port. Justinian was determined to pray for courage and guidance, but his spirit was too troubled, and he could not gaze at the icon of Christ Pantocrator.[19] Outside the palace, more smoke marred the horizon.

With Theodora gone, Justinian grew more despondent. He summoned his ministers and waited impatiently for them in his *tablinum*, but his unsteady nerves left him unable to prepare for the meeting. He paced back and forth, half-expecting the mob to burst through the door at any minute. He looked around the colonnaded room with its mosaics of the heroics of previous emperors and wondered

---

[19] The triumphant Christ seated upon his throne of glory.

if he would be remembered as another fallen Emperor. *What would the mob do to me if they captured me?* History suggested the best-case scenario would be to stick hot needles in both eyes and exile him to a monastery on some far-off island. The worst case was a slow death preceded by days at the mercy of tormenters.

His captain figured the court had about fifteen minutes before the mob penetrated the palace's walls. Justinian took some consolation in knowing that Theodora would be on a ship by then. Walking past another window, he saw the dismembered head of his likeness rolling through the streets.

"Your Majesty?"

Narses, one of his most trusted advisors, appeared at the door.

"Bring in the generals and ministers," Justinian said. "We need to discuss events and determine what we can do."

Narses disappeared but returned after a few minutes looking downcast.

Justinian trusted Narses because he did not look like a leader. His narrow shoulders braced backward as he walked awkwardly, his large gut protruding. His affinity for fancy boots and his fondness for olives made him an object of scorn among the military officers. He was bald, and his protruding forehead and recessed chin made him so ugly a sculptor Justinian hired to create a bust refused the commission, fearing he would incur the wrath of an unhappy subject. But Narses was deferential, glad to be of use, politic, cautious, meticulous, and endowed with a wicked genius for political intrigue.

Justinian often found the man's shrill tone annoying, but he pitied Narses, whose parents had castrated him in hopes that their youngest child would have a career in the court. His absurdity had made him powerful. A eunuch who could never be Emperor posed no threat.

"Your Imperial Majesty," Narses said, "Most of your cabinet has fled the palace hoping to escape the city. Only the generals and their guards remain."

Justinian was not surprised. His best guards had died defending him, and the others had gotten their positions based on political connections rather than merit. Too many were not even fighters. They merely promenaded around the palace like the peacocks in the garden: they were nice to look at but not much use when trouble came. Justinian made a habit of surrounding himself with a few capable men whom he trusted but many more incapable ones who lacked the wits and ambition to overthrow him. Too many emperors had surrounded themselves with brilliant men — only to be struck down by them.

Belisarius and a trickle of generals and advisors streamed into the *tablinum* and gathered around a large table.

"We'll have your cabinet here in another moment, Your Majesty," Narses announced.

"We may not have another moment," Justinian growled. "Well, Narses, let's get started with the remnant we have before the mob joins us."

Justinian asked Narses, who often served as the parliamentarian for cabinet meetings, to officiate at the meeting since his nerves precluded him from doing it.

"Gentlemen," Narses said, "the Emperor asks for your intelligence on the situation so we might explore our options. As you all have noticed, fires are raging through the city. Looters and arsonists have destroyed hundreds of homes — including their own — and most of the churches and public buildings. They have dragged several city leaders into the streets and beaten them to death. The Senate is no more. The horrors that have befallen some women are too terrible to describe."

Justinian looked at Belisarius and wondered about the fate of Antonina. There was no indication that his best general had any idea about what might have happened to his fiancée. *Probably violated and now dead,* he thought.

"Thousands are dead," Narses continued, "and the rioters show no sign of letting up. The Greens are calling for Senator Hypatius to replace the Emperor."

"The former Emperor Anastasius's nephew?" Constantinus asked.

"Indeed," Narses replied, "most of the palace guards who survived the mob's attacks have fled. A small handful are keeping the mob out of the palace compound, but they cannot control this mob much longer. Some of our more reliable sources in the Blue Faction believe we can meet their group's demands without compromising the Empire's integrity. I suggest we agree to dismiss John, Tribonian, and Eudaemon, commute the sentences of the convicted — at least for the time being — and buy off the leaders of the Blue Faction who may have some influence."

Justinian grew impatient with the slow speed of deliberations and figured he now had about ten minutes to get on a ship before the angry mob burst through the door and cut them all down. Nevertheless, he wanted to see what his cabinet recommended before he issued orders to flee the city. Based on their sweaty foreheads, wrinkled brows, and fidgety fingers, he assessed they were ready to join him on the imperial flagship to flee to Asia Minor and assemble an army large enough to take back the city.

"Blackmail only begets more blackmail, Narses," John the Cappadocian snarled. "Are we to believe that the mob will be satisfied once we sacrifice a third of the men in this room?"

*Of course not,* Justinian said to himself. He could always count on his treasurer's practicality.

Mundus, Justinian's Gepid[20] general in Illyricum,[21] stood up. "Narses's hopes are ill-founded. Neither the Emperor's efforts to appease the mob nor the limited punishment we have managed to inflict on them has had an effect. Their numbers grow by the hour. Even now, they are opening the prison gates. Men who hate us lead the mob and are determined to bring us down. We have closed the city's gates to limit the influx of peasants determined to join the ranks. The bodies of the slain litter the streets. The mob has commandeered those who tried to escape. Some are determined to loot the palace and hang Your Imperial Highnesses. I fear we have lost control and lack the resources to regain it. Our only viable option is to flee to the Boucoleon harbor and board a swift ship. We can regroup and try to counterattack when we have massed the forces we need."

"Thank you, General," Justinian said with an approving nod. Mundus's thinking was very much like his own. "Are there any other views on this matter?"

---

[20] An East Germanic/Gothic tribe.

[21] The eastern Adriatic coast; western Balkans.

The officious Cappadocian tax collector stood up to speak. This man's arbitrary laws had helped spark the riots, and Justinian lowered his head to conceal his frown. *Your tax policies have placed us in this predicament,* Justinian thought.

"The Palace treasury will be the mob's primary target, and only lightly armed guards are posted there. We must move the treasury onto ships at once and flee the city. The gold we take with us can be used to raise an army and restore order."

Justinian again nodded his approval.

Procopius spoke next. "Your Majesty, I cannot recall a time in history when the ruling powers were more disadvantaged. You..." he corrected himself, "We, we have lost the support of the people. The legal reforms are unpopular among the wealthy landowners, and the exorbitant tribute paid to Persia has brought accusations that we are squandering the national treasure. I regret to say that I see no alternative but to yield to the protesters' will and abdicate the throne."

Justinian appreciated Procopius's historical perspective but resented the tone of his remarks. *What do you know of governing, you little turd?* "Didn't Emperor Theodosius face a situation like this with a bunch of riotous chariot fanatics in Thessalonica?" Justinian asked.

"Yes," Procopius replied.

"What did he do?" the Emperor asked.

"He ordered the hippodrome sealed up and sent in troops who cut down every rioter inside," Procopius replied.

"Well, that's not an option," Justinian replied. He listened to his advisors with a heavy heart. His military men weighed in with equally grim assessments: flight was the only option. He turned to Belisarius. "Flavius, what do you recommend?"

"My Lord, most of your imperial guards have refused orders to protect the palace. They believe it imprudent to back a government on its way out."

"Tell us something we don't know, Flavius," Justinian grumbled.

Belisarius paused and offered a slight smile. "They are also refusing to back the Greens and Hypatius. You can rely on my household guard of 1600 mounted *bucellarii* and Mundus's Herulian *foederati*[22] who have newly arrived from Illyricum."

Mundus nodded his reluctant agreement. "We have prepared them to assist you immediately in whatever course you decide. The decision is entirely yours, Your Majesty."

"That's where you're wrong, Mundus," a female voice in the back of the *tablinum* called out, "I would like to have a say." Everyone in the *tablinum* turned around and saw Theodora standing in the doorway, assisted by two of her domestics. She wore a purple silk gown and a fashionable hat that hid her hideous wound. A tense unease spread across the room as the uninvited Empress approached the circle of men. Justinian knew his advisors disapproved of her, but their counsel had not impressed him, and he welcomed her point of view.

"Theodora," Justinian said in surprise, "you were supposed to be on the ship by now." He frowned at the domestics who had failed to bring her stretcher to the ship. The servants grabbed the Empress and attempted to remove her from the *tablinum*. Theodora violently shook them off and returned Justinian's look with one of a rebellious adolescent who did not like her husband telling her what to do. Her practiced glare softened Justinian, who rushed to her side and embraced her. "Are you feeling better now, my love?"

John was the first to voice his irritation, "My lady, perhaps it is not fitting...."

Justinian raised his hand to silence him. "I am delighted you are well enough to join us, Theodora. We were just discussing the situation and exploring our options. The consensus has been that flight is the only prudent course available to us. We have lost control of the city; our imperial guards have abandoned their posts. And the mob has taken Hypatius to the Forum of Constantine and proclaimed him Emperor. Only a great deal of bloodshed would restore our reign."

Theodora gave Justinian another look that reminded him that he had told her she would be an equal partner in ruling the Empire. That concession worked well so long as she agreed with him, but now she had gotten off her stretcher and seemed to have other ideas about the best course of action on a crucial matter. He

---

[22] "Barbarian" peoples and cities bound by a treaty (*foedus*) with Rome to render military assistance.

knew she liked to dabble in Church politics, that was fine, and her actions had reduced the tensions between different factions of the Church. Additionally, he had long deferred to her in matters of personal preference since he had no appreciation for pageantry. However, she had never been so brash as to crash his male-dominated Court that had counseled against elevating her to an Empress.

He looked at Theodora and wondered what his cabinet thought of an Emperor who heeded the counsel of his wife when not in the marital bed. At that moment, he did not care — she had been right about the riots when no one else had. He trusted her and regretted the few times he had not. She was the only one in the room whose counsel was not motivated by a desire for a higher position. No matter what his counselors and generals thought of her, he admired her courage and was willing to give her a chance. He owed her that much for what she had endured in the past few hours.

Her purple vestments were blood-stained. She took an empty seat at the table next to Justinian with all the dignity of an Empress. "My lords, the gravity of the present situation prevents me from following the custom that a woman should never speak in a man's council. When extreme danger threatens our interests, the wisest course of action must take precedence over convention."

Skeptical looks greeted her words, but Justinian, Narses, and Belisarius seemed open.

She turned to them. "In my opinion, escape is not the appropriate course — even if it should bring us to safety. It is impossible for mortals to conquer death, but it would be unbearable for an Emperor to concede to the life of a fugitive. May I never see the day when the people do not hail you, Justinian, as their Emperor. They do not know what they are rejecting. If you love your people, may you never let them deprive you of your crown, my Lord."

"If you wish to save your throne, nothing impedes you. We are rich. Over there we have the sea, and yonder the ships. Yet reflect for a moment whether, once you have escaped, you would not gladly exchange safety for death. As for me, I adhere to the adage that royal purple makes a noble burial shroud."

For a time, the room was silent. Justinian saw that Mundus and the Cappadocian were unconvinced but looked at her as though she were Moses descending from Mount Sinai. Belisarius, Procopius, and the others present stood a little straighter. Justinian had suspected that Belisarius might secretly resent the Empress for meddling in the appointment of her sister Comita's husband, Sittas, to replace him as general in the East after the defeat of Callinicum. Still, he heard him whisper to Procopius, "That, my friend, was her finest hour."

Justinian said, "How do we move forward?"

Sensing the political winds had changed, Narses said. "Perhaps by dividing this mob, we can conquer it." He placed several olives into his mouth and chewed them as he spoke, shooting out spittle. "We will never win over the Greens who are set on an unalterable course to make Hypatius Emperor. However, the Blues are divided among themselves."

"This is true," Belisarius said, "Many of them are still loyal to us and may begin to realize that if Hypatius takes the throne, the Greens and their intolerant Monophysite allies will once again have the upper hand."

The Cappadocian treasurer, measuring the mood of his colleagues, conceded, "A distribution of gold may buy their loyalty."

"If we can direct the Blues to eliminate the dissenters among them, the majority will remain loyal to us. Assurances that the law will turn a blind eye should be enough to persuade them. While many opportunists have used the riot as an occasion for pillage, most of the Greens are presently in the Hippodrome acclaiming Hypatius Emperor."

"That isolates them from the more violent faction of the mob," Belisarius said.

Constantinus said, "I served under Hypatius and witnessed his underwhelming performance against the Persians during the Anastasian War. He is a reluctant would-be Emperor whose weeping wife begged him to refuse the throne. Had someone in the palace not..." Constantinus paused to stare at Tiberius. "...expelled him from the palace, he might not have taken refuge with a mob looking for some legitimacy."

Mundus nodded in agreement, "Hypatius is a disastrous strategist."

Narses continued his plan as he used his tongue to strip the fruit off olive pits, his mouth moving bizarrely as though he were toothless, "Once the loyal Blues have been lured from the Hippodrome and warned of the wrath to come, we'll have half as many protestors. The Blues may even assist our efforts to restore order."

Mundus's eyes sparkled. "I can deploy my Herulian escorts to seal off all the exits from the Hippodrome while Flavius's mounted knights rescue the imposter from the crowd."

Belisarius gave Mundus an irritated look. "What does that mean?"

Narses said, "It means, Flavius, that you will pluck Hypatius from the mob and bring him here." Narses pulled several olive pits out of his mouth and dropped them as he pointed emphatically to the floor.

"The Greens will fight. They won't simply allow me to grab him and leave," Belisarius replied.

"Then cut them down," Theodora barked as she removed the bloody bandage from her head and swung it in front of her like a sword lopping off heads.

Justinian looked at his wife as though he hardly knew her. He had never seen this ruthless side of her before. He considered her words, looked at the nasty scar on her forehead, and then recalled the horrors he had witnessed during the riot. What seemed unthinkable earlier in the day now appeared to be the only viable option.

"I'd guess 60,000 people are in the Hippodrome now."

Narses said, "Yes, but we will buy off most of the Blues with gold from the treasury, evacuate them from the Hippodrome, arm them, and give them license to purge the Greens."

"The Greens were unarmed at the start of the races," Mundus said. "They may have pilfered weapons and smuggled them into the Hippodrome, but they are hardly soldiers. They'll be no match for our armored knights."

Belisarius stood up from his seat at the table and began walking about the room. "You are missing the point," he said. "I am not worried about casualties among my *bucellarii*. But what will killing a mostly unarmed mob do to our souls?"

Justinian knew that his old friend had a valid point under normal circumstances, but this occasion warranted a special exception. The loss of life could be much more significant if the riot generated into an all-out civil war.

"Flavius, we are soldiers who kill only because we must," Mundus said as he folded his arms across his chest. "You know this as well as anyone. Nevertheless, to appease your conscience, we can offer them quarter."

Theodora imperiously raised a hand. "Quarter shall neither be offered nor given. Kill them all."

There was a long silence around the table, and all were surprised to see Theodora's hard line on the issue. Justinian was even more surprised that he found himself agreeing with her when moments earlier, he had ruled out the possibility of such a massacre. The massacre of Marius and the other senators had been weighing upon him.

"The prisons were already full," Theodora continued as she drove the point home, "and the mob has burned them to the ground. We cannot accommodate thousands of prisoners; if we were to send them into exile, they would continue to pose a threat."

Justinian nodded his reluctant agreement. "We have no good options. Malevolent action is better than inaction. Bring Hypatius out alive and lock him in the Palace dungeon."

He reached a hand to Theodora, who held it tightly. "Posterity will not remember us for dawdling in the palace while New Rome[23] burned."

Justinian watched his cabinet nod in agreement. "Flavius, your concerns are valid and duly noted, but this is our decision to make, and the blood of the slain will be on *our* hands."

Narses said, "We cannot repeat the failure of the Western Empire."

---

[23] i.e. Constantinople.

"Nor can we stand idly by while an angry mob incinerates all we have accomplished," Justinian argued, "inviting further destruction and invasion. We ascended the throne to restore the Empire's glory, not to stand idly by and watch its destruction."

Belisarius shook his head and sighed, "I will assemble my guard and deploy them immediately." He got up, bowed shallowly, and took his leave without looking at the Emperor or Empress again.

Justinian stood and placed both hands on the table. He looked at the remaining generals before him, hoping this radical solution might resolve the crisis. "You have your orders. God be with you, and God have mercy on us all if we should fail."

# CHAPTER EIGHT
# JUSTINIANUS IMPERATOR

*The limitation of riots, moral questions aside, is that they cannot win, and their
participants know it. Hence, rioting is not revolutionary but reactionary because
it invites defeat. It involves an emotional catharsis, but it must be followed by a
sense of futility.*

— Rev. Martin Luther King, Jr.

*Constantinople*
*January 532 A.D.*

"I am astounded by the sudden change in the bilious Emperor and his court,"
Procopius said as he headed to the barracks with Belisarius and Mundus to address
the *bucellarii* who were awaiting orders.

"That's the power of the Empress over him," Belisarius said as he tried to focus
on the benefits of what he considered an evil task. "Had she not arrived when she
did, I suspect the entire court would be boarding ships by now. Without her appeal, we might all be fugitives without a country. But may God have mercy on us
for what we are about to do."

"Indeed," Mundus agreed, "For the rest of our lives, we will need to atone for
this." Belisarius let out a heavy sigh and nodded his agreement.

Belisarius turned to one of his trusted captains, a handsome youth with thick
red hair. "What's your name, captain?"

"Julius, sir."

"Julius, go and find out where Antonina is. I am concerned that she may have gone to the Baths and gotten mixed up in the troubles there. If you learn anything, inform me right away." The captain saluted and rode off.

Anxiety filled the air at the looted and partially burned stables of the *excubitors* adjacent to the Great Palace, and the troops fidgeted with their horses and armor. The three men rode up, and Belisarius addressed his warriors. "The Emperor has asked us to rescue Hypatius and restore order to this city. Those who would destroy our beloved Empire for vanity will pay in blood.

"We are going to invade the Hippodrome. At Dara, we were outnumbered two-to-one and emerged victorious. Today, the hoodlums outnumber us twenty-to-one, but they are not a trained army. Once they realize why we are there, they will flee like chickens at the sight of a fox. At this moment, Narses is evacuating anyone worth sparing. When that is accomplished, we will block the exits. We have orders to kill the leaders and give no quarter. Once we have recovered Hypatius and subdued anyone who resists, we will turn the place over to armed members of the Blue Faction. You will recognize them by their lapis lazuli facemasks. They will finish what we have started."

Belisarius paused. He was less concerned with what the pending massacre would do to his reputation than what it would to his conscience. Needless loss of life sickened him. "As they fall, remember what these villains did in the Baths today. None of us wants to live in a city without law and order. If they repent their sins and beg for mercy, thank God that their desperate situation has caused them to see reason, but our orders say we are not to spare them. If we take our swords from their breasts, their villainy will return. Are you with me?"

In chorus, the bucellarii cried, "Yes!" and raised their swords to the sky.

His troops, mounted veterans of the Persian campaign, formed a line four men wide that stretched more than a quarter mile. As they rode toward the Hippodrome, the fearsome sight of the magnificent knights compelled random looters and hooligans to stop what they were doing and flee the area. Belisarius knew his *bucellarii's* effect among trained warriors, so he imagined it even more effective among the hooligans. Belisarius observed the sound of thousands of horseshoes hitting the cobblestone streets, combined with the rhythmic clanking of the armor on their horses, filling the rioters with the realization that what had seemed like a foregone conclusion about Justinian's fate was premature.

The *bucellarii* cantered their horses through the pillaged wasteland that was once the jewel of the civilized world. The lacquearia[24] of Hagia Sophia had collapsed entirely, and the stone walls teetered for lack of overhead support. A dozen dead priests had been stripped naked and left at the entrance, their white, mangled flesh contrasting the black ash around them. Wailing women with torn garments fled the Baths for their homes, only to find them ablaze. Theodora's solution seemed less repugnant than it had been only an hour before. He thought of Antonina and looked around for Julius, whom he spotted riding quickly toward him.

"Any word on my fiancée?"

"Yes, sir. The captain of the *excubitors* reported that he had seen her at the Baths about two hours ago. I'm heading over there now, sir." Julius galloped off.

A woman struggled to cover her breasts with a bloodied hand, stood over the body of her assailant, and raised her other hand in a fist, shouting, "Show them the wrath of God!" Her resolve reminded Belisarius of his beloved mother.

Heavy smoke filled the air, mutilated bodies littered the streets, and blood ran thick over the worn cobblestones. The sight of their city in ruins gradually erased the hesitation Belisarius, and his men felt the same way when they received their orders. *This counter-revolution may be the lesser of two evils,* he thought to himself.

As they passed the smoldering barracks of the imperial guards, their stony faces caught his attention. Belisarius said, "Join us, brothers, and the Emperor will forgive your dereliction of duty."

"We're done defending this Emperor," one sentinel replied. "He has lost God's favor."

"God's favor or the mob's?" Belisarius murmured. "Last chance, soldiers. Tomorrow, you may hang for your indifference."

"We will see who hangs from the gallows tomorrow!"

---

[24] A paneled ceiling

As Belisarius's *bucellarii* emerged from the smoke and became visible to the mob in the Hippodrome, the mood changed from revelry to consternation. When they rushed to secure the gate, Belisarius bellowed, "Open this gate in the name of the Emperor!"

The Greens hurriedly placed wooden obstacles in front of the gate and lit them on fire. *Stupid people! You're burning your barricade?* Belisarius held his frightened horse firm and stretched out his hand to push the gate, but the heat burned his palm and forced him back.

He repeated his command as his men brought water forward to douse the fire. They tied one end of a rope to the gate and the other to four heavy horses who galloped away, pulling it off the hinges, and rode into the Hippodrome. The massive stadium looked like it was about a third full, and most of those inside wore green tunics. A few of them smashed wooden chairs and turned them into makeshift clubs. Belisarius admired the mob's determination but turned to Pharas and said, "Never bring a club to a sword fight."

As Narses had predicted, the gold had done its work — at least if the lack of blue tunics in the Hippodrome were any indication. Justinian preferred to buy off his enemies rather than fight them, and most of the time, this was the cheaper solution in the short run.

The Greens had turned a slain nobleman's golden collar into a temporary crown for Hypatius's tiny head and fashioned a ceremonial robe from the purple curtains of the loge. "Romans, behold your new Emperor!"

As he rode into the Hippodrome through the imperial corridor, Belisarius saw the pathetic figure and thought of the scourged Christ standing before the crowd in the Praetorium. The mob blocked the passageway, and the guards refused admittance. Belisarius sent word to the Emperor that he could not enter the Hippodrome. Justinian replied that he should march his troops through the smoldering ruins of the Great Palace to an interior gate that opened into the arena, then seal the gate with heavy timber.

When Belisarius appeared at the head of his *bucellarii*, the guards who had been waving lichen green flags around Hypatius stopped and fell silent. He surveyed the battlefield. The mob had burnt the wooden chairs to ashes. Most of the mob had already fled, and those who remained wore green tunics. A much smaller cluster of Blues huddled at the far end, and they were the first to start scrambling.

Belisarius spotted the reluctant new Emperor standing where the imperial loge had been. The desperation in his face seemed to beg silently for help.

One of the thugs protecting him shouted, "Defend our new Emperor!"

Another screamed, "They'll slaughter us all!"

Screams filled the Hippodrome as the mob retreated from Belisarius and his men. Only the self-appointed praetorian guards surrounding Hypatius stood firm.

Pharas rode up to Belisarius. "Mundus has broken through the southern gate near the substructures."

Belisarius raised his sword, shouting, "Justinianus, Imperator!" And the *bucellarii* swept up the walkways and into the stands. The confining walls of the Hippodrome prevented the mob from overwhelming his smaller forces. The few with lances and swords tried to resist but could not penetrate the knights' heavy armor. One Green with a broken chair charged at Belisarius and smashed it across his face. The act enraged Belisarius more than it injured him since his helmet and face shield protected him. Belisarius laid a heavy downward blow on the villain, completely severing his head from his body.

Underneath him, Belisarius could see dead men whose green tunics were so full of blood that he initially mistook them for the rival Red Faction members. He took out his lance and stabbed the Greens crawling on the ground and trying to avoid fatal blows from the hooves of the warhorses. The screams soon turned into groans, which soon became gasping sounds.

At that moment, it began to snow, and light flakes fell upon the bloody heap of bodies. Once the snow was about ankle-deep, Belisarius noticed that it covered the dead bodies like shallow graves.

After an hour, the remainder of the crowd had surged to the top of the stands. Jumping was the only escape, but no one could survive the four-story fall.

"Those who wait on the Lord will soar on wings like eagles," a Monophysite monk said as he crossed himself and leaped to a bone-shattering death.

Belisarius and his *bucellarii* cut and slashed their way across the arena as Greens hesitated on the walls, preparing to jump. One in ten were pushed off the stands by the stampede behind them. Belisarius ordered his men to charge up the stands and watched as the Greens pushed each other off the heights like the famous lemmings of Scandza to avoid the swords and lances. He always felt that enemy deaths caused by a panicked foe somehow lessened the evil of slaughter. Blood cascaded down the staircases of the Hippodrome and pushed the snow into thick piles of incarnadine slush.

Belisarius saw Justinian's nephews, Boraedes and Justus, on the Emporer's balcony slashing at Hypatius's bodyguards. They dragged the newly proclaimed Emperor from his tenuous throne, tied him up, and hoisted him over a horse with his belly down like a saddlebag.

Belisarius knew what he had to do, but the bloody chaos appalled him. He ordered the *excubitors* outside the Hippodrome to lance anyone trying to escape, then made his way up to the ramparts and looked over the precipice. The scene below reminded him of fishermen spearing their catch in the bottom of a boat. "This is not combat," he thought. "This is slaughter."

He saw the thick, brown wool cloak of a Syrian monk over a fallen body in the stands beside him and bent to look at the dead man. A hand grabbed his sword, and a weak voice said, "Christ will deny mercy in the next life to anyone who denies it to others in this one. Spare these unarmed men. Send us into exile, but do not put us to the sword."

As the monk uttered his last words, one of Mundus's men ran him through with a lance that ran all the way through and protruded out of his shattered chest.

"I didn't like that sermon," the pikeman said.

For a moment, Belisarius felt sick, then wiped the blood off his sword and sheathed it. He dismounted, and nearly slipped on the blood and gore that covered the smooth stone steps of the Hippodrome, shouted, "This is butcher's work. We're finished here!"

Belisarius surveyed the situation one last time. Thousands of Blue faction members were streaming into the Hippodrome through the gates with clubs, knives, and batons to kill their rivals in the officially sanctioned purge. The momentum had turned decisively against the Greens. He decided to leave clean-up operations to the Blues, who turned the event into a violent blood sport. As he and his men headed out through the gate they had come, he stopped by a large public fountain and washed the blood off his hands and arms. His men did likewise; in short order, the water was so polluted with blood that the thirsty horses refused to drink from it.

At that moment, Julius arrived on the scene with a big smile. "I found Antonina, sir. She is safe and well in the furnaces under the Baths. She said she would wait there until you arrive."

"Thank you, Julius." Belisarius quickly remounted and galloped off to the furnaces at the Baths. The short ride was only three minutes, but in that brief span, he saw dead bodies everywhere on the streets. Survivors of the mayhem crawled back to their burning homes or begged for mercy. A handful of nuns from the now-charred ruins of Saint Sampson's Hospital ministered to the wounded, but they had nowhere to bring them to recover. Priests administered Last Rites. Many minimally clothes bathers shivered in the cold and gathered around embers of collapsed buildings to stay warm. Others called out names of lost ones. Belisarius joined their ranks.

A handful of women had gathered in the furnaces to stay warm, and Belisarius asked lingerers where to find Antonina, but there was no information. As he wandered through the furnace area under the complex, he realized he had never noticed how large it was before and cursed himself for not asking Julius for a more precise location. Belisarius was a regular patron of the baths, which served as much of a social function as a hygienic one. He recognized that hundreds of workers must have labored continuously to keep the fires going that heated the bath water throughout the winter.

In a panic after not finding his wife, he began turning over dead bodies that he thought might be Antonina, dreading that he'd find her among them, calling out repeatedly, "Antonina! You can come out." From the bruises on the necks and arms, he could see how the women had struggled, losing their lives while trying to ward off assailants. He had spent a decade fighting on the Persian front but had never seen so much death — all of it senseless. He began to lose hope. *I should have come sooner.*

Then he heard her voice, "Flavius!" And Antonina emerged from the stairwell, the bloodied senator at her side. "Flavius, we're here."

He embraced her bloodstained form. "Are you hurt?"

"No, no harm came to me."

"Thanks be to God." He removed his blood-splattered red cloak and covered her with it as she emerged shivering in the cold. "Thank you, Senator, for protecting Antonina."

"I'm not sure how…" the senator began. Antonina cut him off.

"Flavius, this is Stephanus. He fled the senate house and tried to stop these savages before they struck him and pushed him down the stairs. He needs to see your *medicus*."

Belisarius helped the senator onto his horse and led them to the infirmary.

"Antonina, how did you manage to survive this?" Belisarius asked.

"I know too well the menacing look savages get before they assault women, so they did not catch me off-guard as many others were. I hid in the furnace until you arrived."

"I'm amazed that no one followed you there. I wish I had come to find you sooner. We have been at the Hippodrome, suppressing the mob there. It was a hideous butchery, Antonina, and while we were suppressing the Greens, I feared for your life.

"You cannot be everywhere, Flavius. Over the years, men who have tried to take advantage of me lost the battle. You forget that my father whipped horses for a living, and my mother whipped customers who refused to pay." Belisarius laughed for the first time of the day.

When they arrived at the surgeon's tent, they found Mundus having his gashes stitched.

"Is it over at the Hippodrome?" Belisarius asked as he bandaged his burned hand.

"As I left, Blue gang members finished off the wounded Greens. The Blues are smashing skulls — silencing the moaning wounded and the quiet dead. The moans of the dying and wails of the grieving have replaced the screams of agony. Families are no longer able to recognize the dead. They offer no mercy and seem to enjoy their work."

Belisarius shook his head. "Their blue masks hide their faces but not their shame. They will finish the task Narses gave them within the hour."

After the city's watchmen had quenched the last embers of the conflagration, Theodora and Justinian reclined together in front of a small fire with glasses of wine. Theodora dismissed the attendants. The wind blew through the windows, reeking of smoke and death, and she tried to quell the pungent stench of mortality with a bowl of incense placed on the table beside her. Justinian laid his head on his wife's bare shoulder and closed his eyes as she rubbed his forehead with lavender-scented olive oil.

"Thirty thousand corpses lay rotting in the Hippodrome," Theodora said. "They must be cleared as quickly as possible. It will require at least a week. Old mothers and new widows have recovered some of the bodies, but most are unrecognizable and unclaimed."

Justinian sighed and sat up; the mood broken. "Yes, I've directed Belisarius's men to dig mass graves outside the city walls." He leaned his head on her shoulder again and moved her hands toward his ears. "Massage the temples," he said.

"An eerie peace has settled over the capitol," Theodora murmured.

"Surprisingly, the slaughter has not resulted in unrest," Justinian replied. "I suppose the people are terrified to leave their houses — if they still have houses. Already, the officers of the *excubitors* are on trial, and the renegade guards are boarding ships bound for hardship tours on the eastern front. Loyal members of the Blue Faction who proved their mettle in the Hippodrome will take the place of disloyal palace guards."

"Good," Theodora said, "we should ban chariot races at the Hippodrome until passions cool."

Justinian nodded reluctantly. "Yes, the charioteers are still volatile, and in any case, I have given all the Green horses to the Blues."

Theodora's fingers pressed a little deeper into her husband's temples. "I'd like to preside over the trials of Hypatius and Pompeius," she said.

Justinian's forehead wrinkled under her fingers, "I like Hypatius. He was an unwilling participant. His wife begged him to flee, but he refused, unable to believe the mob would turn so violent."

"I know you think Hypatius was a pawn," Theodora said, "but if you fail to punish him, you will send the wrong signal to future usurpers. Once they are convicted and executed, we should seize their property."

"Very well," Justinian removed her hands from his head. "But I will restore John and Tribonian to their former offices. I need them to build on the unsteady peace that follows times like these."

"I don't believe John served you well when the riots began."

"He did not, but *you* did. Your courage was unmatched, Theo." He turned to face her. "I was so surprised when you interrupted our discussion." He kissed her forehead.

"Let my scar remind you that we must never again depend on one man to protect our crown."

He could hear the anxiety in her voice. He had the same thought.

"Suppose that Belisarius and Mundus had not been available," Theodora said, "Where would we be now? What if, one day, Belisarius is less loyal to you? During the uprising, he might have easily seized the throne. So many of Rome's emperors have died at the hands of their generals."

"I know, I know." He relaxed back onto her bare shoulder and put her hands on his head again. "But for the moment, I trust him. I can only judge the man I know today."

CHAPTER NINE

# HOSEA AND HIS WIFE

*A happy marriage is about three things:*
*Memories of togetherness,*
*forgiveness of mistakes,*
*and a promise to never give up on each other.*

— Surabhi Surendra

*Constantinople*
*Summer 532 A.D.*

Several months after the rebellion, while city workers were still clearing the burned rubble from the streets of Constantinople, Justinian and Theodora encouraged Belisarius to intensify his courtship of Antonina. Although Theodora had played the matchmaker in the relationship, Belisarius had grown fond of Antonina. She was beautiful, intelligent, and witty, but most of all, she expressed an eagerness to endure all the hardships and dangers that wives of military men must endure, and that was unique among the women of his age.

The gardens of Constantinople were reputed to be the most beautiful in the world. Garden paths featured elaborate mosaic designs, formally arrayed and carefully trimmed trees and shrubs, numerous fountains, life-size marble statues, and small shrines. Belisarius loved to walk through them for the peace it brought to him and to steal landscaping ideas for his garden. He looked at his lovely bride-to-be and determined that he would commission a statue of her and that she would be the centerpiece of the garden at his villa.

As they walked through the palace garden in the morning light, he felt the smooth warmth of her hand in his. "You know my past, Flavius. You must be concerned that the palace attendants will have nothing good to say."

"Your past doesn't interest me," he said. "I'm only interested in the present and future. And when have you known me to care what the court thinks?"

"You've never *had* to care," she retorted. "After the chariot race killed my father, I earned my living with the only skills my mother taught me. When I was finally married, I left that behind, but the earthquake in Antioch took that life from me." She stopped walking and pulled her hand from his.

He saw the shame and sorrow in her eyes and wished she knew how deeply he cared for her. He gently took her chin in his hand. He had found inspiration in the example of the Prophet Hosea, who had betrothed a former prostitute in the hopes that he could lead her to a better path.

"All that matters is that you have left your former life and now walk proudly with a man who adores you." He pulled her close, and she fell into his arms.

"Before I married the first time, I attached myself to an army camp in the East and became a favorite among the men. The senior officers, most of whom were married, showed little interest in me. They treated me and all the other supernumeraries with contempt. Only one officer was kind and non-judgmental. That was you, Flavius."

Belisarius laughed.

"I remember it like yesterday," she said as she sat up. "I was negotiating a rate with a young Isaurian when he struck me in the face, called me a whore, and pulled me into his tent by my hair. You were just a young officer without even a man's full beard, but you called out the rogue, dressed him down, took me to your surgeon's tent, and told the *medicus* to reset my nose."

"We recruit these Isaurians for their toughness, not their manners," Belisarius said. "But no man should treat a woman that way."

"You offered me bread and wine. I thought you would use my body in return for your kindness, and I would have gladly agreed."

*Really?* Belisarius thought, turning his eyes away from her to avoid the temptation of wondering what lay beneath her beautifully embroidered dalmatica[25] with depictions of garden flowers. "Instead, you told me that the Empress had converted an estate into a refuge for women who wished to begin new lives. That night, I wept. For the first time in my life, I felt shame and wanted to be a better person — if only to please you. I vowed never to sell my body again, no matter how desperate I became."

Belisarius gently wiped a tear from her cheek and kissed her.

"Never did I dream this kind-eyed young lieutenant would be interested in me."

"Why not?"

"I lacked the pedigree to court a patrician, and I didn't think you would want officers like Constantinus seeing you with a woman who had spent years as a laundress in an army camp."

"You may be right. You were a terrible laundress," Belisarius said.

Antonina slapped his shoulder and laughed. "How would you know? You never gave me your dirty clothes."

"If I had, you might not be walking with me now. My tunic can be quite fragrant after a day under hot armor." Belisarius then grew serious and said, "After you disappeared from the camp, I never expected to see you again."

"Theodora gave me courage. She likes to play the matchmaker. She didn't know that we had met before."

"I never stopped thinking about you," Belisarius said. "And you are so much more beautiful without a swollen nose."

"I never thanked you for your kindness, and here you are, a man in his prime with as many victories in Syria as young Alexander."

"Alexander!" Belisarius roared, "He never had to contend with the intrigue of Byzantium."

---

[25] A robe with wide sleeves.

"Thank you for forgiving me of my past. I have little patience for those who only condemn violations of a single commandment and ignore the other nine."

"We all fall short of the glory of God," Belisarius said, "but in different ways."

"Why have you chosen *me*? You could have any woman in Constantinople."

"Truthfully, Antonina, I have no time to notice women. I'm uncomfortable with most of them and prefer the company of men. But you are different from the court women who spend their days eating, bathing, sleeping, stroking their lap-dogs, or spinning and weaving. You are more like one of my soldiers."

"I'm not sure I expected that answer, General," she said in a deeper voice and laughed.

"Procopius says that you cast a spell on me."

Antonina laughed, "Maybe I did."

"When?"

"A month ago."

"Then it didn't work. Every good witch knows you cannot cast an effective spell during a full moon," Belisarius pointed to the moon. "You'll have to try again."

"You can be sure that I will," she said as she grabbed his cheeks and gave him the most passionate kiss he had ever known.

"That was nice," he said with a smirk and pointed to the moon, "but that didn't work either."

"Then I'll try again in two weeks...."

"I'll be especially on guard during waxing and waning moons."

"Ha! Then I'll cast it while you're asleep."

"You win then," Belisarius said with his hands raised in surrender. "Just promise me you won't cast spells on any of my men."

"I don't have to," she said provocatively before taking a more serious tone. "You should know that I prefer the company of men. Theodora is the exception."

"Why her?"

"We both prefer the company of freethinkers and are unconcerned with what others think of our behavior."

"Can you enjoy the company of men living in squalid army camps?"

"Yes, and more easily than life in the palace."

"I can understand that," Belisarius said, leaning in close to her. "And do you find something appealing in me?" They came to a fountain and stopped to enjoy the cool mist.

"You can be abrupt and formal," she said, "but you're a man of honor. I respect your loyalty to the Emperor and his vision for the Empire. You are disturbingly patient. The prostitutes in the camps were disappointed to learn that your virtue made you inaccessible. You are strong and protective...."

Belisarius looked down, embarrassed at having solicited flattery. Antonina perceived it and changed her track.

"But you have one major fault."

"And what is that?"

"Your naïveté about the duplicity around you. You lack the skill to bend people to your will. But I could help you. We complement each other very well: each is strong where the other is weak."

"I agree," Belisarius said as he looked up, smiled, and gave her another kiss. "Speaking of duplicity, I wanted to apologize for disapproving looks of Procopius and Constantinus. They have not treated you well, and I'm not sure that will change."

"I suppose," Antonina said, "But why does that eunuch hate me so?"

Belisarius laughed, "Procopius might be a misogynist, but he's not a eunuch. He has an archaic Greek view of women's role in society. His ideal is Penelope weaving a burial shroud, faithfully waiting two decades for her husband's return."

"I'm not surprised he is unmarried," Antonina laughed. "What woman would willingly live in his little cage? And what role does General Belisarius imagine his wife will play while he fights a long campaign against the Trojans?"

"I would take her with me," Belisarius said, wondering if Antonina had already had this conversation with Theodora. "The Empress can influence such matters and seemed sympathetic when I broached the issue. She's the most broadminded and ambitious woman since Cleopatra."

"Hmmm. Perhaps being the wife of a soldier would not be so dreary."

"My worry is what the enemy might do to a general's wife if I lost a battle."

"Then, Flavius, don't lose any battles," She patted his cheek. "And what of the children?"

"Army camps are no place for children. They would stay in Constantinople until they reached military age."

Belisarius plucked an Amaranthus and wove it into her hair. He clasped her hands in his "So shall we be wed?"

"We shall," she said and kissed his lips.

"Do you suppose there will be a great scandal?"

"I certainly hope so," she said with a laugh. "You mustn't trouble yourself. Theodora's time in the brothel did not prevent her from becoming Empress."

"Yes, I was the only advisor to Justinian who did not counsel against the marriage," Belisarius said. "Even the former Empress Euphemia preferred that Justinian wed Amalasuntha, the beautiful, widowed queen of the Goths in Italy."

"And you won much favor from Theodora for that," Antonina replied. "She renounced her former life. She deserves a second chance."

"After their scandalous marriage, most of society was prudent enough to keep their judgments to themselves," Belisarius said.


On the wedding day, Antonina knelt in the church, repenting her life of polyamory and resolving to lead a chaste and monogamous life. Belisarius, who was waiting outside, was glad of her genuine remorse.

As she emerged, the priest said, "The Lord spoke more harshly to those who neglected the poor than those who committed sins of the flesh. Your sins are forgiven. Now go and be worthy of the man you are about to marry."

"You look as though he lifted a heavy yoke from your shoulders," Belisarius said.

"You have no idea how happy I am today," she replied, kissing his cheek.

Belisarius had been Constantinople's most eligible bachelor for years, and some wondered how the former prostitute had managed to woo the princeling — until they saw her.

They were married at the parish church in Rufinianae,[26] which offered a view across the Bosporus to the Great Palace and the Hagia Sophia. Wearing a gold-trimmed silk gown, carrying a bouquet of purple vitex, her auburn hair glowing in the sun, she was as graceful as a swan descending slowly onto a lake.

Theodora and John the Armenian witnessed their vows.

"You'll love marriage, Flavius," John whispered as he signed a document attesting to his witness of the marriage. "We do. It teaches you to love another more than yourself."

Belisarius smiled. He knew his friend hoped marriage might finally cure him of his self-absorbed fits of depression. As they left the church, bells rang in celebration, and the wives of the *bucellarii* scattered rose petals. Their path from the church to Belisarius's villa was lined with sixteen hundred *bucellarii* who raised their swords to form a canopy as they passed.

The aroma of roasting lamb and peppered pork filled the air, and the guests sipped wine brought by vintners from all over Asia Minor. Not since the Emperor married Theodora eight years before had there been such a lavish reception. Belisarius's estate, a large villa complex in traditional Roman style, was well-equipped to handle more than two thousand guests. The gardens, while dwarfed by the Emperor's garden in Constantinople, were large enough to fill a racetrack and were full of flowers from seeds and bulbs that Belisarius had collected all over Asia Minor, Armenia, and Persia. His favorites were the tulips he had collected during his service on the Roman-Persian border, which he thought resembled the turbans some Persians wore.

Belisarius encouraged his guests to walk around the garden since the villa could not hold everyone. His domestics offered the guests goblets of wine and trays of cheese and bread. A small crowd gathered around a large gift that the Emperor's

---

[26] Rufinianae is a small city in the Constantinople suburb of Chalcedon in western Asia Minor.

staff was unpacking in the statuary around the garden that featured heroes from Roman Antiquity and Christian martyrs. Justinian had given him as a wedding gift a life-size marble statue of Saint Sebastian, pierced by several bronze arrows and lying on the ground dying.

"Why did you pick this particular statue as a gift?" Belisarius asked as he, the Emperor, the Empress, and Antonina watched the domestics uncrate it.

"Because I admire the courage of Sebastian, a Praetorian guard, who, after facing a firing squad of archers and miraculously recovering from his many painful wounds, confronted Emperor Diocletian for his cruelties," Justinian said. "I hope you will never be afraid to speak truth to your Emperor, Flavius."

"And I hope you will never club me to death if I do!" The two former palace guards laughed together.

Suddenly, the growling of a ferocious beast interrupted the moment's tranquility, scattered the guests in every direction, and caused several trays of wine and cheese to crash to the ground. Theodora laughed as she took the leash from a domestic, reined in the beast, and settled it down. "My wedding gift to you is this guard dog. My father bred mastiffs to attack bears. At the Hippodrome, the father of this dog took down the largest bear I've ever seen." She patted the dog's head, put her face next to it, and let him lick her lips. "He is very affectionate but will protect you at all costs."

"Does he have a name?" Belisarius asked.

Theodora laughed. "Argos. My father gave all his dogs the same name. He couldn't allow himself to become attached to creatures who fought bears to the death every week."

The two couples formed a reception line and cordially greeted their guests. The imperial couple relaxed court protocols so guests in their best clothes would not have to fall to the ground in homage. Belisarius dismissed Procopius's suggestion that the Emperor was trying to upstage him. He knew that many had come to the reception as much to meet the Emperor as to congratulate him. He and Antonina affectionately locked hands whenever they were not greeting their guests.

Several of Antonina's former consorts from the East joined the reception. The day before, when Belisarius met the tall, middle-aged woman who still managed the brothel in Antioch, he'd made her swear she wouldn't allow her girls to solicit business at the wedding and found her promise unconvincing.

Courtiers from the palace offered their congratulations and were followed by all the senior military officers in the area. Antonina seemed bored, but she came to life after seeing her former colleagues from the brothel.

Belisarius nudged his bride and whispered, "Who are the provocatively attired women?"

She turned her face away. "Oh, they're former colleagues."

The busty brothel manager pushed two younger women forward, "Hello, I'm Lupicina. This handsome man must be the most esteemed Belisarius, former general of the armies of the East. We are so proud of our Antonina for turning her life around and making such a catch."

"Most of us have been trying to escape since we came of age," a blonde woman said.

The other woman had a face covered with white flour and heavily rouged cheeks. "I want to meet a wealthy client, who will fall in love and marry me so I can have a settled life," she said in terrible Greek.

"That rarely happens, of course," Lupicina interrupted. "Most of us remain in the profession until old age robs us of our beauty and income."

Antonina laughed and said, "You're still beautiful."

Belisarius noticed the Emperor and Constantinus talking nearby and became uncomfortable with the women's vulgar banter. *Must they be so loud?* He felt like he was being judged for his wife's past, and the companions of Constantinus gave him a harsh look. Belisarius blushed with embarrassment and put his finger to his lip to get them to speak more softly.

The rouged woman momentarily spoke more softly but soon resumed her voluble tone. "If we cannot find a proper husband — and not many respectable men are willing to marry us — we try to amass enough money to start a business before we reach middle age."

"Antonina is very fortunate, and we all envy her success," the blonde said. "Thank you, General."

"Antonina squeezed his hand. "They are wonderful women. I almost wish you knew them better."

"I think one encounter will suffice," he said stiffly and then laughed at his awkwardness. He would not allow the stares of people like Constantinus to ruin his wedding day.

As the sun was falling in the midday sky, the most distinguished among the guests came into the great room, where a feast had been prepared. The meal was prepared by the family of Peranius, an Iberian[27] prince who had fled Persian oppression, settled in Constantinople, joined the Roman army, and served with Belisarius on the Persian front.

Byzantine hospitality required that food and wine flow abundantly until the guests departed. Peranius served fire-roasted chunks of salted pork and onion, chicken covered in garlic, herbs, walnut paste, bread oozing with hot cheese, spicy lamb-filled dumplings, bean soup, and fresh and dried fruits throughout the evening.

The wine was kept cool in subterranean terracotta containers and poured frequently. A lengthy toast preceded every sip, and every toast required that the guest finish the cup.

As Belisarius put down his eighth cup, he excused himself. He was beginning to lose his wits. He whispered to Peranius, "Add water to the wine, or we'll all be dead soon."

Peranius signaled the wine steward. "At this point, I'm not sure anyone will know the difference."

"Come, let's dance!" Antonina pulled at her husband's arm. Her face shone bright with drink.

"Belisarius staggered to his feet. He had a roaring headache but danced around with his guests. He was not much of a dancer but enjoyed the joyful comradery.

---

[27] Eastern Roman province in the Caucasus Mountains.

He disapproved of the wild revelries of his inebriated guests. Procopius, usually quick to criticize Belisarius's choice of company, settled into conversation with the women from Antioch. *In vino veritas,* Belisarius thought.

When a band of women came to take Antonina away, Belisarius attended to his guests, directing those serving to withhold the watered-down wine from anyone who had lost their wits or the contents of their stomachs.

The guests formed a line to walk in a circle around the atrium. The dancing was solemn and formal. The dancers' torsos remained decorous while the hands and arms moved around gracefully. However, Antonina's Antioch friends added provocative movements of the hips and legs, which they'd learned in the East. Belisarius enjoyed watching his wife's hips gyrate rhythmically, but the sight of Constantinus, who stood next to some monks with their arms folded across their chests, deflated him. *I suppose Antonina's new status in court should preclude that sort of dancing.*

Later, some lower-ranking officers were tipping the Antiochene women in exchange for dances. Belisarius made a familiar hand gesture, pointing with two fingers to his eyes and then one to his men, and the women moved on.

Belisarius and his guests sang and danced through the sculpture gardens and fountains as the evening ended. The place made Belisarius feel like a true Roman. As they followed the ladies of Antioch in an enjoyable dance around the garden paths, he recalled his happy wanderings through the forested grasslands near his hometown as a child. Whenever he wanted to get his troubled mind away from palace intrigue and war planning, he wandered for hours under the canopy of the tall trees, admiring the flowers, watching the birds build nests, and taking in the energy of the wildlife.

The guests carried the couple in an oversized chair to the consummation suite. Belisarius loved these people and their spirit, but he was grateful that the wine had finally run out and their guests began returning to their homes.

He fell onto his couch and watched his beautiful new wife undress, preparing for what would come next. The light of the oil lamps shone through her white linen gown, revealing the silhouette of her body. She wound flowers into her hair, perfumed herself with rose water, and rouged her lips. The yellow copper light of the fire reflected in her gold wedding band, reminding Belisarius that an Egyptian once told him the vein of love ran from the heart to the fourth finger on the left hand. He thought she was the most perfect woman he had ever seen, so beautiful he could hardly believe she was his.

Like a hungry lioness, Antonina crawled onto the couch beside him. She was the temptress, the experienced lover, who devoured his mouth with hers. An ocean of passion washed over him, and she moaned as he grazed her neck with his lips and caressed her.

Afterward, she swung her legs across the bed and sat up. Belisarius admired the beauty of her unclothed body as she moved across the room. Her skin was smooth, her frame slender.

"Why are you looking at me?" she asked.

"I'm enjoying the show."

"Did you enjoy our wedding celebration?"

"Yes, of course. What do you mean?"

"I noticed your disapproval of my friends from Antioch. They traveled for two months, and you greeted them with awkward embarrassment and dagger eyes. Without them, what a dull celebration we might have had. Your military friends are so stiff."

Belisarius pulled on his tunic and stood before her.

"Antonina, some of your friends offered private dances to my men — for a fee." He strutted around the room with his arms clasped behind his back. "I had hoped they would have behaved more appropriately."

Antonina gave him a stern look.

"And you! Dancing like Salome for Herod," Belisarius said. "I hope this is not a sign of things to come."

Antonina's body slumped. "I will take my leave," she said softly.

"What? Why?"

"Good night, husband."

She threw a cloak over her shoulders and sought out the inn where her friends were staying.

Belisarius sat up in his bed, wishing his wedding night had turned out differently, but feeling justified in his rebuke. He had worked hard for his good reputation and didn't need it tarnished by the shady ladies from Antioch. He got up, poured himself a goblet of wine, swallowed its entire contents in a few seconds, and went to the *caldarium*.[28]

He stepped into the hot water, laid back, and soon found the wine and water taking him into the deep recesses of memory and dream. He envisioned a ten-year-old boy with his family at the public bath. As he floated in the air above watching the scene, a satyr flirted with a young woman managing the bath. He watched as the satyr's hand slid down the partially exposed back of a playful female attendant, who welcomed the caress with a coy smile. Belisarius scorned the domestic's wanton encouragement and stared at the satyr's cloven feet — until the sound of sobbing diverted his attention.

As he tried to make sense of the dream and moved toward the satyr for a closer look, Belisarius recognized the face of the satyr: it was his father, and the source of the weeping was his mother. A burning rage deep inside him disturbed his sleep so much that it nearly awoke him, and he wondered about its meaning. As he dozed off again, he was astounded to see that his mother said nothing. Other women in the bath stared at Belisarius's father with stern looks of disapproval and murmured.

Young Belisarius moved toward his mother, sat next to her, and wiped away her tears. Then he stood up and marched over toward his father. "Stop it, Father!" He pulled his father's hand off the female attendant, who discreetly slipped away.

"Hands off me, boy!" His father violently pushed him into the deep water and stormed after the bath attendant. As Belisarius the dreamer slipped below the surface of the bathwater and began coughing, young Belisarius of the dream struggled to swim to the edge of his bath. As his head emerged above the water, his father's

---

[28] Lat. room with a hot bath.

cleft feet chased desperately after the nymph, each step echoing loudly on the stone floor.

Belisarius recalled how his father's pushing away shocked and deeply wounded him. The bitter memory had long served as a metaphor for the growing distance between him and his father. Before that moment, he had admired his father more than anyone else in the whole world. The shove felt like a betrayal not only to him but to his mother. Belisarius emerged from the water in tears and returned to the loving arms of his mother. She comforted him with a tender kiss and dried the tears on his face with a cloth. This was the day he began obeying his father out of fear rather than respect.

"Why do you put up with that, Mother?"

She looked at him with a steady smile as she vigorously rubbed the cloth into his scalp, "Because I have you, Flavius," she tapped the end of his nose.

He looked at her with a bewildered look. "What do you mean?"

His mother took a more serious tone. "Your father's actions are inappropriate, Flavius, but I've found I can't change his behavior with confrontation, only love."

"But he's humiliating you, Mother."

"He's humiliating himself, Flavius, though we all have to share in it."

"How long will you put up with it, Mother?"

"As long as it takes, Flavius." His mother perfumed herself and began fixing her hair into a tutu.[29] "You know that love always wins in the end, right?"

"Yes, Mother, but I can see he's hurting you."

His mother kissed him on the forehead. "Love bears all things, Flavius, and I hope you remember this when you have a wife of your own. Marriage is hard and sometimes full of pain, but you just keep loving people through it all. It's not the pain that matters, Flavius, it's what you learn from it and what you do with it." She gave her son a warm embrace, "You're going to be a great husband to your wife, aren't you, Flavius?"

"Yes, Mother," young Belisarius said as he embraced his mother.

---

[29] Lat. a hairstyle worn by married women that featured a high, cone-shaped bun frequently embellished with jewelry.

# Chapter Ten

# The Rival

*To conquer with arms is to make only a temporary conquest; to conquer the world by earning its esteem is to make a permanent conquest.*

— Woodrow Wilson

*Constantinople*
*June 533 A.D.*

Sweat streamed down Antonina's face as her body convulsed. It was a hot day, and Antonina was in labor with her third child. The contractions were coming too quickly for the midwives, and the baby had turned the wrong way in the womb. "I can't do this!" Antonina screamed, gripping the older midwife's hand. A younger midwife reached for a surgical knife in case the child had to enter the world the way Caesar had. Antonina looked around the room at the oil lamps underneath an icon of Saint Monica, the patient mother of Saint Augustine. The younger midwife noticed her gazing at the icon.

"'Whoever loves does all things without suffering, or, suffering, loves her suffering.' That's what Augustine would say," the midwife said calmly and with a smile.

Antonina's eyes filled with rage. "I don't need..." she didn't finish the sentence but screamed out, "Bah!" The younger midwife fell backward in fright, knocking over a bowl of warm water. A domestic ran out to fill it again. A nervous Belisarius peaked his head around the corner and asked, "Hey, how's it going in there?"

A second later, the domestic arrived with a new bowl and slammed the door again.

The older midwife remained calm and felt Antonina's belly. "She's trying to spin into position but needs help." The midwife pushed Antonina hard on one side of her abdomen, and Antonina watched as the creature inside her did a somersault. Antonina screamed again.

The older midwife felt Antonina again and said calmly, "We won't need the knife. She's in position. All you need to do is push."

Antonina took a deep breath, concentrated her strength, and pushed until she could feel the head.

"One more push, and she's out!"

Antonina pushed again with all her might, and a tiny head emerged. "It's blue," the older midwife said with some alarm. "Antonina, you must push her out the rest of the way now!" Antonina screamed a third time, and the baby leapt out. Antonina waited for the anticipated first cry, but it didn't come.

The older midwife quickly unwrapped the umbilical cord from the baby's neck and clamped the cord with a string as the younger midwife cut the cord with the knife. She then held the baby by its feet and gave it a little thump on the back. The baby cried out, announcing its violent entrance to the world.

"You have a healthy baby girl!" the older midwife announced as she handed the baby to her mother. The younger midwife cleaned the baby while the older one took care of Antonina. Within minutes, the baby was nursing on Antonina's breast.

"Are you ready for your husband?" the older midwife asked.

"In a few minutes," Antonina replied as she put a cold rag on her face.

The midwives called for Belisarius, and Antonina passed him the bundle wrapped in soft linen.

He delicately rubbed her face with the back of his fingers. "Thank you, wife. She is beautiful. I heard so much screaming I was tempted to come into the room with my sword drawn."

"That is what women suffer to give birth," Antonina said. "Perhaps it is no worse than pulling arrows from your body after a battle. Do your men scream?"

"Not the brave…"

"Husband, do *not* finish that sentence until you have been injured. Why must birth be so painful?"

"It's the sin of Eve," Belisarius said, trying not to laugh. "It seems a just punishment for all the misery your fondness for forbidden fruit has brought."

"You're incorrigible," Antonina laughed. "I suspect you half believe that."

Belisarius held his daughter above his head, then pulled her towards his face and kissed her forehead. Belisarius gently returned her to her mother's breast.

"You know," he said, "This child puts everything in perspective. As a father, it will be easier for me to invest in the Empire's future fully. It adds a nobler purpose to the struggle."

Antonina pulled him close and kissed him. *Perhaps this will herald a new beginning,* she thought.


The following week, the child was baptized at the church in Rufinianae, and the Emperor and Empress served as her godparents. She was christened Joannina Nino in honor of John and his wife, and they hosted a small reception.

Belisarius's villa was a square building of red Roman brick and tile surrounded by umbrella pines, Mediterranean cypress, and orchards. The herbs used in Roman cuisine grew in abundance, perfuming the air. Belisarius called his home "a glimpse of paradise before the fall."

White marble columns lined the inner courtyard, where flowers bloomed nine months of the year. A shallow *impluvium*, a pool that served to collect rainwater and provided a habitat for a chorus of frogs, allowed light and fresh air to circulate through the villa. The mosaic floors depicted hunting scenes, plants, and animals native to the region.

Belisarius's *tablinum*, his library alcove between the atrium and the peristyle, was filled with scrolls on natural science, which he hoped would someday interest his daughter.

The large formal dining room, the *triclinium*,[30] was furnished with a horseshoe-shaped table that allowed servants to serve food and wine and made it possible for all the guests to see and converse with each other.

Every room had at least one small window and walls decorated with scenic landscapes and mythological images, a throwback to pre-Christian beliefs. When sanctimonious guests looked askance, Belisarius reminded them, "We're never far from our pagan roots."

Belisarius welcomed his guests to the table. The guests included many senior officers from the Persian expedition, Archelaus, the admiral of the Roman fleet, and Phlebas, a Phoenician silk merchant. The latter had provided the baptismal gown for Joannina. Archelaus's gift was a stuffed animal shaped like Porphyrius, a legendary great white whale infamous for attacking Byzantine fishing vessels. Archelaus poked Joannina with the soft toy and made her laugh. Belisarius gave the admiral a sharp look.

"Isn't that a man-eating beast?"

"Not necessarily," Archelaus replied. "I hope Joannina can get along with nature better than our fleet."

Belisarius passed around his daughter and showed the awkward, childless officers how to support a newborn's wobbly head without snapping it.

"A year ago, I was a bachelor, and the army was my family. Today, I have a wife and a daughter, and I have adopted Antonina's two children."

The honored guests at the table all responded with a resounding "Hear! Hear!"

"Being a father of three is a great honor and responsibility, and it has given my military service new purpose. I want to give my children a stronger empire."

He looked proudly at Antonina's adolescent son, whom he had begun to train in the arts of cavalry warfare, archery, and strategy. Photius was still awkward, trying to find his way in the world. His fuzzy beard and scars from childhood pox gave him a rough appearance, but his loyalty endeared him to his adoptive father.

---

[30] A dining room with couches along three sides.

His mother, who treasured beauty more than character, rarely looked at her son lest he see her shudder at his sight.

"I have not been a good mother to Photius," Antonina whispered to her husband. "I hope you can assist in parenting him because I don't know what to do with him. Ever since his father died in the earthquake in Antioch four years ago, he has been very detached."

"I'll do what I can," Belisarius promised.

As domestics served guests traditional Thracian pork and vegetable stew from a large clay pot, Antonina leaned her head close to her husband. "Thank you for bringing them into the family," she said.

"I'm happy to share this big house," he said. "It was far too quiet here."

Belisarius looked at his wife and saw her choking up about something.

"What is it?" he asked.

"Seeing Archelaus and Phlebas just reminded me of the worst period of my life, which seems so distant from where I am today," Antonina said.

"What do you mean?" Belisarius asked.

"This is neither the time nor place," Antonina insisted.

"Please, tell me."

"I've never told you this before," she whispered, "but when I was on the cargo ship that carried Photius and me to Constantinople, I stood on the ship's bow with the anchor in my arms one night and considered jumping overboard."

Belisarius gasped and took her hand. "I am glad you didn't."

"A kind silk merchant named Phlebas saw how desperate I was and approached me. 'You haven't jumped yet,' he said. 'I suspect your fear of death follows from your fear of life. Once you have lived fully, you'll be ready to die.'"

"We owe Phlebas a debt of gratitude," Belisarius said as he eyed the quiet silk merchant. "And I recall that you later gave birth on the deck?"

"Yes, the ship's captain, Archelaus, chased the crew away so I could suffer the pains in privacy. Three days later, we arrived in Constantinople."

A servant had been nervously waiting, afraid to disturb their intimate conversation. Belisarius beckoned him.

"General, your guest of honor has arrived."

"Invite him to wash his hands, then bring him to me."

"Who is this guest of honor?" Antonina asked. "I don't like surprises."

"Theodosius, the son of my friend Ascan, the officer who covered our retreat after the battle of Callinicum."

"Why is *he* the guest of honor?"

"Because I would like him to join our family, as well."

"Will he live with us?"

"Yes, if you agree. Theo is a bright but reckless youth who will lose his way without a strong family."

A moment later, a handsome, beardless youth galumphed into the room and stood before them. His open-mouthed smile, legs and arms spread wide, seemed to say, "Here I am!" His face resembled sculptures of Emperor Caligula, and the flamboyant red tunic he wore enhanced his ruddy complexion and full lips.

Antonina stared at him and began fanning herself. "He shall certainly stay," she said with a smile that seemed too eager. "Let me introduce myself. I am Antonina Belisaria."

Theodosius made an awkward bow, and Antonina gave him a formal embrace.

"Yes, Theodosius, this is my wife," Belisarius said as he walked over to greet the youth and then announced to his guests, "Theodosius will be joining our family as a true son. His father has asked me to look after him." He embraced the youth and walked him over the Antonina, who took the boy's hand.

"Don't think of me as your mother; think of me as your friend."

Theodosius smiled nervously and thanked her. She introduced him to her son Photius whose scowl suggested he resented the attention this arriviste brought to himself.

Theodosius unwittingly sat in the chair of the toastmaster, which had been reserved for Belisarius. The General ordered servants to bring another chair to the table.

Procopius, seated between Belisarius and Photius, said, "It looks as though the two of you have a rival for Antonina's affection."

That evening, after the guests departed, the family relaxed in the *triclinium* and enjoyed another luxurious meal celebrating their growing household. Belisarius smiled as he watched Theodosius, who already seemed comfortable with them. Everyone enjoyed the boy's charm, especially Antonina, who moments earlier had been struggling with horrible memories, was never so full of laughter.

"Have you heard the latest joke about the Greek and the Roman?" Theodosius asked.

"No, Theo, tell us," Antonina begged.

"An old Greek and Roman soldier are arguing at the tavern."

Belisarius watched as the shy youth came out of his shell like a crab. "The Greek says, 'We Greeks invented everything for which the Romans undeservedly take credit. The Roman counters, 'Yes, but we Romans improved on them and made them more useful.'"

Belisarius, a proud Roman, laughed, "It's true!"

"The Greek says, 'Athens invented democracy.' "And the Roman replies, 'Yes, but Rome realized the perils of making every civic decision a matter for a plebiscite, and invented representative democracy in the Senate.'

"The Greek says, 'Yes, but we created beautiful architecture like the Parthenon.' The Roman says, 'And we improved your building techniques and used them to create practical structures like aqueducts and bridges.'

"The Greek, growing frustrated, finally says, 'Ah, of course. But, you know, the Greeks invented *sex*.' The Roman laughs. 'That may be true, but *we* introduced it to women!'"

The entire room erupted into boisterous laughter, and Antonina laughed longer than anyone else. "Theodosius," she said, "you are delightful. I'm so glad you've come to us."

Belisarius always delighted in his wife's melodic laughter that struck him like a ripple of sunshine. He was grateful for the entertainment but yawned. "It's time to retire for the evening."

Antonina showed the villa to Theodosius while Belisarius waited for her in their bedchamber. He heard them laughing together and then drifted off to sleep.

Antonina woke him as she slipped onto the couch beside him. "I think I like Theodosius."

"Yes, I thought you might."

"Please forgive my earlier hostility. I didn't want anything to distract you from our other children."

"It is you whom he has distracted," Belisarius said.

Eighteen months after the riot, Justinian convened a secret council of his ministers and generals at his *tablinum* in the Great Palace. Before the meeting, he studied a large mosaic map on the wall depicting the Roman Empire's height under Emperor Trajan. The map revealed terrain, rivers, mountains, and the web of 200,000 miles of roads that spanned the vast empire. And it depicted caricatures of the various races that inhabited each area.

In the Eastern Empire, well-dressed, urbane people stood beside the great churches: the Mother of God in Jerusalem, the church of St. John in Ephesus, and Hagia Sophia in Constantinople. In the Western Empire, long-bearded savages wearing animal skins and wielding ferocious weapons stood beside ruins of once-great cities. The bright sun illuminated the gold mosaic tiles in the eastern half, but the western half featured dark tiles, except for a large, unnamed island northwest of Hibernia[31] made of many red and orange tiles. A casual observer might have mistaken it for Hell. *It's the perfect backdrop for the meeting,* Justinian thought.

---

[31] Latin name for modern Ireland. Northwest of it is modern Iceland.

The *tablinum* also served as Justinian's library, where he maintained a thousand scrolls of theology, philosophy, history, science, mathematics, architecture, and Greek and Roman literature. To prevent the smell of the moldy pages from overwhelming him, he fumigated the room with incense, which he claimed also repelled paper worms.

As Justinian waited for his cabinet, he considered the first six years of his reign. The most memorable event had been the judicial reforms, and he was genuinely proud of them. However, he also suspected that the average person associated his short reign with the Nika riots and the subsequent massacre. *Not much of a legacy,* he thought. He wanted to be ranked among the great emperors, and to do that, he knew that he would need to build and conquer. *I will be the Emperor who restores the lost western provinces to the Roman Empire,* he thought as he stared at the map.

Belisarius arrived first, wearing a simple white woolen tunic rather than the more formal toga that was his prerogative as a general. *This is the man who will bring me greatness,* Justinian thought.

"Flavius!" The Emperor roared.

"Petrus!" Belisarius roared back. He walked toward his old peer in the imperial guards and gave him a warm embrace, but Justinian did not reciprocate.

"Flavius," the Emperor said sternly, "As I mentioned earlier, the old days of congenial informality must end. You know I favor you over my other generals, but I must appear impartial at war council meetings. Understood?"

"Yes, Your Majesty."

The Emperor noticed the pained reaction on his old friend's face and sought to distance himself from the policy by adding, "Theodora wants this, but you know that Antonina's intimacy with her gives you a great deal of influence in the court."

Belisarius nodded.

His ministers entered the room: John of Cappadocia — restored to his position as finance minister, Narses — his grand chamberlain, Epiphanius — the Patriarch of Constantinople, Admiral Archelaus, and several senior commanders, each lavishly dressed in long, wide-sleeved embroidered silk tunics called dalmatics. He had great confidence in all these men, especially in Belisarius. His concern, however, was that young, ambitious men like Belisarius and John might someday use their talents against him. Only Narses and Epiphanius posed no threat, but only because Roman law precluded eunuchs and patriarchs from wearing the purple.

Domestics had placed enough wine, cheese, bread, fruit, and meats on the table to keep the meeting going into the night. Justinian planned to sell his ministers and generals on his dream of a reunited empire. He stood and began to address the council.

"The events of last year have taught us the importance of maintaining the initiative of the empire. After the Nika Riots, we became the laughingstock of the world. It is time to reclaim our place as the world's premier empire. From now on, this council will set a course for the empire's restoration."

He watched his counselor's attentions turn from delight at the array of refreshments to a mix of skepticism and excitement.

"What about the bloody Persians?" Mundus asked.

"We have finally secured an Eternal Peace with Persia and are positioned to reduce the number of our forces there."

"So, where do we start?" Narses asked.

"In Africa. The Vandals have recently given us just cause for war by dethroning our friend and ally King Hilderic and replacing him with the usurper Gelimer. Our Roman brothers are suffering under the heavy weight of his tyranny, and our spies say the Romans in Africa would welcome a chance to be part of the empire again."

"What about the Goths?" Belisarius asked.

"Our new alliance with Ostrogoth Queen Amalasutha in Italy makes the reconquest of North Africa a realistic objective. Since King Hilderic murdered Amalasuntha's sister, the former Vandal queen, the Goths have renounced the Vandals. Hilderic massacred six-thousand Gothic guards, and in doing so, destroyed the long alliance between Vandals and Goths."

Procopius, who had long complained to anyone who would listen that the Vandals constantly preyed upon his family shipping business, was the most enthusiastic about the prospect. He added, "For a hundred years, these barbarians have preyed on our ships like Leviathan."

Archelaus, admiral of the Roman fleet, echoed these thoughts, "Their pirates have plundered our ships, stolen our food, burned our ports, and enslaved our citizens. Their sack of Rome seventy-five years ago set that great city into a decline from which she has never recovered."

Epiphanius, the Patriarch of Constantinople, said, "We must not forget that these Vandals are Arian heretics who believe Christ is a creature not of the same substance as the Father. They have persecuted the one true Church by exiling priests and confiscating our houses of worship."

A chorus of amens and cheers went up as those gathered agreed the time had come to end the Vandal threat.

"The Patriarch is right. We can no longer tolerate this. Well, gentlemen, the tide is about to turn," Justinian said.

John the Cappadocian had been quietly watching his colleagues. "Your Majesty, the city of Carthage lies more than three months' journey from our capital. Even if your army is successful, it will be a year before we hear about it." John, the man who had to come up with ways to pay for Justinian's dreams, had the habit of challenging collective thinking during imperial cabinet meetings. Everyone but the admiral grumbled under their breaths at his skepticism.

The admiral, who knew the time it took to sail to various ports in the Mediterranean, nodded in agreement.

"If the expedition fails," John continued, "it will ruin the Empire financially. The last attempt to reconquer Africa ruined the empire. And even if we succeed, we will never be able to hold it without first taking Italy and Sicily from the Ostrogoths. These plans will escalate our costs and ruin the empire. The reconquest of the West is too ambitious for one Emperor."

Justinian looked at his finance minister in exasperation. "Only an hour ago, you agreed to support this initiative. And now you are making your Emperor look like a fool?"

Justinian raised his hand to silence the room. He had heard enough. "The plan that never starts takes the longest to complete. The public treasury is full, and we intend to use it to invest in a campaign to retake Carthage." He patted John on the back. "We appreciate your concern that this expedition will bankrupt the treasury, but...."

Narses came to the Emperor's defense. "The wealth the Vandals have stolen over the past century will certainly cover our costs, and we can use these recovered treasures to rebuild our city from the ashes of the failed uprising."

"Indeed, it's a brave new world," the Emperor said. "Have a little faith, John."

He turned to Belisarius. "This will be different from the expedition our illustrious predecessor Leo and his appropriately uncelebrated General Basiliscus launched, ending in disaster at Cape Bon."

"You speak of the expedition that drained the treasury of 130,000 pounds of gold and killed a hundred-thousand Romans," John said.

*Basiliscus was a fool. Belisarius is a proven leader,* Justinian thought as he decided to ignore John. "Flavius, you will lead our army."

Belisarius nodded and bowed in gratitude.

Archelaus said, "We have secured five hundred ships and hired twenty-thousand sailors, mostly from Egypt and Asia Minor. We can transport ten-thousand infantrymen and five thousand cavalrymen. We will stop in Sicily to secure horses for your cavalry, water, and additional supplies. My biggest concern is the Vandal navy, which destroyed Basiliscus's expedition before they landed."

Belisarius said, "When we arrive on the African coast south of Carthage, our army will need to make a quick landing to ensure that the Vandal Navy does not overcome our fleet. Once our feet are on the ground, we will have overcome the greatest obstacle."

*See that you don't make a fool out of me, Flavius. The Empire will not get a third chance to reconquer Africa.*

"Good thinking, Flavius!" Justinian said, "You will endeavor to win the local population's support to ensure your landing is well-received and provisioned. We are the rightful heirs of that great land, and we shall reclaim it for the empire and the Church."

Belisarius nodded, adding, "That will be critical to maintaining control of the region."

Justinian suspected that some of his generals hoped to line their coffers with the spoils of war. *Greed is the root of all evil and will undermine everything we do,* he reminded himself. "Our conquest there will not give us the freedom to do as we *like* but as we *ought.*"

Narses said, "As an added precaution, we have supported insurrectionists in Sardinia and Libya, which we hope will divert the attention of Gelimer and cause him to divide his forces. This distraction should reduce the number of Vandal ships and deplete their army."

"I hope it works," Belisarius said. "Facing the full force of the Vandal army will diminish our chances of success."

Of course, it will work, Flavius. Gelimer cannot ignore insurrections, or his entire empire will collapse. Let me focus on the grand strategy; you focus on Africa. Justinian concluded, "I leave the conquest of Africa to you, Flavius."

CHAPTER ELEVEN

# LEDA AND THE SWAN

*A sudden blow: the great wings beating still*
*Above the staggering girl, her thighs caressed*
*By the dark webs, her nape caught in his bill,*
*He holds her helpless breast upon his breast.*

— *Leda and the Swan*, W.B. Yeats

*Constantinople*
*Summer 533 A.D.*

Theodora tried to relax as her lady-in-waiting dressed her hair for the day. She admired the mosaic on the wall of her bedchamber depicting the beautiful maiden Leda with Zeus, who had transformed himself into a swan to seduce and ultimately assault her. *It's a beautiful work of art,* she thought, *but I wonder if it ever occurred to the artist that it depicts an act of rape. Probably not.*

A servant announced, "Your Highness, the Lady Antonina is here to see you at your request."

Antonina entered, and her eyes followed Theodora's. "Leda is usually depicted having lowered her garments and seduced the swan. This mosaic is much more violent."

"I always thought the union was non-consensual," Theodora said.

"I had heard that you performed this scene when you were a young actress at the Hippodrome," Antonina said. "Is that why you have chosen it for your bedchamber?"

"No, it came with the palace," Theodora laughed. "I kept it only because Justinian hates it so."

"So, how did you and the swan…." Antonina asked in a tone of bemused wonder.

Theodora did not like to be reminded of the episode in her life when she had been an erotic dancer. "That is best left veiled in the obscurity of history."

"Oh, please, a hundred thousand people saw it, and you can't tell your best friend?"

Theodora hesitated and then blushed, "First, they starved the swan. Then I was made to lay down, wearing almost nothing, and they sprinkled grain on me. The hungry swan beat its wings to get to the grain, and I pushed it away, but it could not get enough of me. Do you know what I did the last time I performed that scene?"

"Do tell."

"After the swan's assault, I stood up, grabbed its narrow neck, and broke it in half."

Antonina put her hands to her mouth, "Ahh! The poor creature! Why?"

"The swan's neck was only a symbol of the 100,000 male gawkers in the Hippodrome who saw the rape of Leda as a joke."

"And then?"

"They were stunned and silent for a long time. You could have heard a coin drop, and then, to everyone's astonishment, Emperor Anastasius's wife, Ariadne, stood up, and slowly began clapping. The Emperor clapped with her, and soon the whole Hippodrome applauded, not because they liked my show, but out of respect for the Empress. That's when I realized the power an Empress could wield."

"I see," Antonina said.

"That is why this mosaic remains on the wall."

"And is that why the Emperor hates it?" Antonina asked.

Theodora laughed, "No, he's just a bit of a prude. Do you remember who was conceived because of that union of Leda and the swan?"

"Remind me."

"Helen of Troy," Theodora said. "That's what the girls in the brothel used to call you."

Antonina laughed, "I was much younger then."

"Yes, but you dazzle men." Theodora retorted, trying not to sound too jealous. An awkward silence hung in the room as both women looked away.

"Well, I've got other things to do today, so I should get to why I summoned you."

"Yes, please do."

"I know you have just given birth, and I'm sure you are eager to spend time with your daughter, but, as we discussed, I wanted to confirm that you are still willing to join your husband on the African expedition to keep me informed of developments."

"You still don't trust the men?"

"Not at all. Too often, the men tell us what they think we want to hear or what will assist them in their next promotion. I need information from various reliable sources without Procopius and all those self-congratulating generals contorting the facts to serve their ambitions. Can you do that for me?"

"I will try but can a woman...." Antonina replied.

"No buts. Times are changing, Antonina. Since the Nika Riots, Justinian has consulted me, a woman, on every policy in the Empire, especially decisions about the Church in the East. We plan to abolish many of the old Roman laws that gave preferential treatment to men over women."

"For instance?" Antonina asked.

"We are ending the so-called honor killings of allegedly unfaithful women. How many times have you heard of those?" Theodora asked.

"Too many," Antonina replied. "I almost became a victim of that law when a rival for my first husband's affections unjustly accused me of adultery. What of the divorce law?"

"Divorce will no longer require a husband's consent, so abusers who refuse to release their wives will no longer have the power to reject her appeal."

"Do you remember poor Macedonia? Her husband beat her unconscious," Antonina said.

"I had her in mind when I wrote this," Theodora said. "You'll like this one: We're going to close all the brothels managed by Empire officials."

"We lost most of our wages to those villains, and they did nothing to protect us," Antonina said. "That explains why John the Cappadocian hates you so much. He profits a great deal from that."

"Indeed. But here is my favorite: We will end the practice of forcing women to abort their children." Theodora welled up and touched Antonina's arm. "I don't know how often those villains forced me to undergo that awful procedure so my panderer wouldn't lose revenue during my pregnancy and maternity."

Theodora tried to regain her composure, but her sadness turned to anger. "We'll prosecute those savages who kidnap girls and turn them into sex slaves."

"Our friends in Antioch will be proud of you," Antonina said. "What else?"

"Thank you! We will end the law that prevents women from inheriting property and obtaining full custody of their children after the death of their husbands." Theodora stopped, remembering why she had so passionately advocated for this change. "You know that I… lost custody of my only son in Antioch because the court ruled that my former occupation made me an unfit mother."

"I know." Antonina sat beside Theodora and put her arm around her. "I hope you and John are reunited someday."

"We'd have to be discreet. Justinian knows nothing."

Antonina put a finger to her lips. "What else have you planned?"

"I'm setting up shelters for our girls in the brothel and creating dowries so they can be married. And we'll lock up the panderers who try to put them back on the streets."

Antonina clapped her hands and smiled, "And what of the swans?"

"We will make rape a capital offense," Theodora said. She looked at the mosaic again and turned her thumbs up while snapping her tongue.

"That would have solved my problems years ago," Antonina said. "But haven't the men tried to oppose you?"

"Of course. Let them. You know, we inherited very unjust laws from the Greeks...."

"And the Roman pagans who hated women. We are only now infusing the law with the Gospel."

"I'm not sure the theologians would agree with you," Antonina said.

"Christ never said that men are the heads of the households or the sole decision-makers. That was Saint Paul, who was subject to the old Roman laws. They would have beheaded him long before they did if he had railed against slavery or the patriarchy."

Antonina nodded. "Theology makes my head hurt. I hope your campaign succeeds."

"It will, but it will take years before people embrace this vision. Laws are easy to change, hearts less so. We need women willing to challenge men's thinking about our place in the world, and you are ideally suited to the task."

"Do you suppose these new laws will make it easier for me to live among the troops?"

"Not at once, but in the long run, yes."

"Even women leading men into battle?"

"Antonina, they will listen to you because you are my friend and the wife of Flavius. But they will respect you because you will think of things they do not, such as caring for war refugees."

"I'm not so sure. The men want me silent."

"They wanted me silent as they prepared to leave the city to a mob. Your silence won't help you. Say what you need to say. Be brave. I have faith in you."


A week later, Belisarius arrived at the docks in the harbor near the Imperial Palace. It was a perfect day: the sun shone brightly, and there was just enough wind to ensure the ships got out of the harbor without much effort. The sight of hundreds of ships in the area filled Belisarius with hope and pride. *The Empire's best days are still in front of her.*

He watched as his stepson Photius and adopted son Theodosius boarded his flagship. Archelaus, the former Praetorian Praefect, now Paymaster of the Forces who also served as *de facto* admiral of the fleet, greeted them. Procopius accompanied the general with instructions to keep the Court fully informed of military developments. Antonina was the last passenger to arrive.

Belisarius had been surprised at how easily she left their infant daughter. He had hoped that she would be more attached to their child than she'd been to her other two children, but he was pleased to have her company for what promised to be an exhausting and challenging campaign.

He watched his wife and an absurd number of porters make their way to the ship with her luggage. "Ah, Antonina, there you are!" he said as he helped her up the gangplank. "Where is the face to launch a thousand ships?"

Antonina smiled. She had kept the fleet waiting for more than an hour. "A thousand ships? There are only six hundred so far, so until your remaining *four* hundred arrive, I am *early*." She shouted orders at the stevedores who loaded chest after chest of her personal effects.

Procopius gave Belisarius a sympathetic look. "Don't worry," Belisarius told him. "This is a five-hundred-ton ship; her baggage will not sink us."

"You should have checked with Procopius," he told Antonina. "He might have helped you decide what to bring. He is our resident expert on all things African." Procopius returned a look that suggested he wanted as little to do with Antonina as possible.

"She has no business here, General," he grumbled. Belisarius knew that Antonina, who had grown up on the racetrack with little opportunity for formal education, had little appreciation of Procopius's scholarship and rarely valued information that did not come from her circle of trusted women.

"You will have to take that up with the Empress, Procopius," Belisarius laughed. "The ships are full of ears, but I know I can trust my wife not to betray me."

Antonina took his hand. "Welcome aboard, my love," he said. "I am so pleased that you are with us."

As his wife supervised the storage of her cargo, Belisarius inspected the ship. He leaned over the deck, rubbed the solid oak siding, inspected the tightness of the joints, and gazed proudly at the high mast. His flagship was a masterpiece of Roman engineering. The crimson sails were magnificent in the early morning sun.

"She's a design much improved from the ships of the Late Republic," Archelaus said. "The Romans knew little of shipbuilding until they captured a Carthaginian quinquereme[32] at Messina, took it apart, and built a hundred. That fleet defeated the Phoenicians at the battle of Mylae."

"I am particularly pleased with the red sails of the chief galleys," Belisarius said. "Our sailors will have no difficulty distinguishing Roman ships from Vandals."

"Yes," Archelaus agreed, "The inability to distinguish friend from foe on the high seas contributed to the Vandal victory over the Roman fleet almost a century ago."

"Do we have enough oil to light all the lanterns on the galley sterns at night?" Belisarius asked.

"Yes, General. Don't worry, we have thought of everything."

Belisarius laughed, "Admiral, no one thinks of everything. Something always plagues an undertaking of this size."

Several thousand onlookers had gathered on the docks to see off their fathers, brothers, sons, husbands, and lovers. Belisarius wondered how much they knew. He smiled as several in the crowd recognized him and hailed the Empire's greatest general. He waved before going below deck, with Procopius following behind. "If we lose the element of surprise," Belisarius said, "and the Vandal fleet is waiting for us, we are doomed. I know land warfare but know nothing about seafaring. I share the troop's anxieties about our vulnerability to a naval attack or storms at

---

[32] An ancient galley propelled by five banks of oars.

sea. The sooner we land, the better. Three months on this ship may be the death of me."

Justinian, with Theodora by his side, boarded the ship. "The hopeful dreams of every Roman lie with you, Flavius," he said. "Bring glory to Rome and bring King Gelimer and the Vandal treasury to me."

Belisarius bowed gratefully and smiled.

The Empress said, "The flagship on which you sail is the same ship the Emperor and I would have taken had we decided to flee from the Nika Riot mob."

"A much better use of the ship, Your Highness," Belisarius replied.

"See that you succeed, Flavius. We have no room for failure on our watch."

## CHAPTER TWELVE
# THE WHITE WHALE

*There are certain queer times and occasions in this strange mixed affair we call life when a man takes this whole universe for a vast practical joke, though the wit thereof he but dimly discerns, and more than suspects that the joke is at nobody's expense but his own.*

— *Moby Dick*, Herman Melville

*Sea of Marmara*
*A.D. 533*

The ropes were let loose from the docks. A gentle breeze from the north filled the sails and slowly pushed the flagship dromone out of Constantinople's harbor. It was a single-masted, single-banked bireme[33] with a roof and pavisade of shields to protect the rowers on the upper deck from missile fire. If it stood upon its bow, the ship would reach the height of a ten-story building. It was rigged with the new single, triangular lateen sail rather than quadrilateral sails, making it swifter and more reliable at catching the wind.

One hundred and fifty sweaty Egyptian sailors rowed the flagship out of port. Belisarius cast one last wistful glance at the great city where he had spent so many happy years and wondered if he would ever return to see it. As it bumped the pier, Belisarius, standing next to Antonina on the bow's deck, lost his balance and grabbed Antonina. "Hold on tight."

---

[33] An ancient ship with two levels of oars on each side; the primary late Roman war galley.

Belisarius hated the sea and worried that his thalassophobia would cause his wife and men to disrespect him, so he worked hard to hide it. He was a land man and, had the long march along the eastern coast of the Mediterranean Sea toward Carthage been a viable option, he would have preferred it. But now, he was on this ship at the mercy of the winds, the sea, and whatever other evils lurked on the water, ready to devour him. Belisarius tried to relax by listening to the steady cadence of the undulating waves beating like a drum against the side of the dromone.

A strong wind filled the fleet's sails, and a loud cheer erupted from the crowd as the ship sailed from the port to join hundreds more anchored nearby. As the captain shouted commands to weatherworn sailors wearing little more than loincloths, the most beautiful city in the world became little more than a speck on the horizon. Belisarius turned to Antonina. "Will you regret leaving a comfortable court life to share living space with sailors and soldiers?"

"I have spent more of my life smelling the sweat of men than the perfume of eunuchs," she said. "I was accustomed to rough company when I lived with my mother in the brothel. These are my people."

"Well, we're all happy you've come along," he said. "The oarsmen love you and smile whenever you watch them — at least until I show up. I need someone I can trust to help with all the details I manage. Don't worry about Joannina; our daughter is safe. With luck, we'll be home again before she's walking." Belisarius kissed his wife's forehead.

"I think you are more worried than I am, husband," Antonina said.

As the ship left the harbor, the wind yanked the sail and pulled the ship into choppier water, and the ship began lurching violently up and down. The captain let out a hearty cheer while Belisarius groaned.

"How is it that you're unafraid on the battlefield and yet fear the sea?" Antonina asked.

"My worst day in the army was not Callinicum but sailing to Seleucia Pieria," Belisarius said grimly.

"What happened?"

"We hit a squall, lost control of the ship, and hit some rocks. The ship sank, and I and only a handful of the crew survived."

"Oh my. That explains it." Antonina said, looking like she was trying to suppress a grin.

"I'll take a slow death by sword to a cold and lonely death on the sea."

Antonina kissed her husband, looked up to the sky, closed her eyes, and raised her hands like a seeress. "Flavius, I see a death in bed at a ripe old age after being stabbed by a jealous lover."

Belisarius laughed and kissed his wife. She took his hands and firmly planted her thumbs into his wrists, just below his palm. "Put pressure here; this will help." She then went below deck and re-emerged a few moments later with a small sack. She pulled out a small yellow tuber and said, "Take a bite of this and chew it for a long time."

"What is it?"

"It's allium[34] from India. It should reduce the nausea."

Belisarius took a bite and chewed it. "Nasty. You really are a witch, aren't you?"

Antonina laughed. "Every sailor's wife knows about allium. Phlebas introduced it to me. His wife even cooks with it. It's expensive though."

"Thank you, wife."

After only two days at sea, the fleet had barely reached the end of the Sea of Marmara when Belisarius noted trouble ahead. *The Vandal fleet already?* Belisarius wondered. The ships in the lead had all let their sails slacken; the ones behind them were forming into a line across the Dardanelles Strait.

"What is it, Flavius?" Antonina asked.

"I'm not sure, but it's probably safer for you to be below deck for now." Antonina hurriedly disappeared. The admiral ordered the captain to bring the ship to the front of the fleet. As they neared the front of the three lines of ships, Belisarius gasped in horror as his worst fear materialized when he saw the shattered timbers of a transport vessel with dozens of sailors and soldiers in the water clinging to the

---

[34] Equivalent to modern garlic

flotsam as they struggled to stay above the water. He felt his heart racing but worked hard to project calm by casually taking another bite of the allium and pinching his inner wrists. Belisarius looked at the admiral and captain, who, while concerned, did not seem to be overly surprised by the wreckage. He wondered how the fleet would ever make it to Africa when they had not even made it to the Aegean and had already lost a ship. *This is a catastrophe! Will the fleet suffer the fate of Basiliscus's fleet and lose its men at sea?* Belisarius nervously looked around: there was no sign of an enemy anywhere. *What is going on?*

"Let's get these men out of the water!" the captain yelled.

The sailors dropped their oars, formed a human chain, and pulled up the drowning men. Several sailors dove into the water to reach those who could not swim toward the ship. Within minutes, the ship was full of dozens of terrified, wet men vomiting seawater and struggling to talk. A trumpet blast followed, and several ships joined the flagship to pull their comrades from the wreckage. Several dead bodies floated on the surface, and one of them was missing both legs. Belisarius had joined one of the human chains and reached down to grab the last panicking sailor to pluck him onto the deck.

Antonina emerged from below deck with several blankets and fresh water and began helping the rescued soldiers. A *medicus* began tending to a sailor with part of an oar piercing his stomach. A pool of blood gathered underneath his wound as sailors tried to stem the blood loss. He screamed hysterically, "Porphyrius! Porphyrius!" Another rescued sailor did the same. *Who is Porphyrius?* A look of dread filled the eyes of the Egyptian sailors on the flagship, and they looked up to Heaven and began muttering incomprehensible prayers.

Belisarius gave him a confused look and approached the one sailor who seemed to have recovered his wits and asked, "What in Heaven's name happened here, sailor?"

The man struggled to cough seawater out of his lungs and turned his head in time to avoid vomiting on his commander. Once he caught his breath, he gasped, "Sorry, sir. It was Porphyrius!"

"Who?"

"Porphyrius, at least that's what we sailors call him. He's a great white whale who has been wreaking havoc on the fishing fleet of Byzantium for years now."

"Is this a joke?"

"No, General."

As the flagship's crew brought on board another dozen men from another wreckage, the captain yelled, "Get these men some dry clothes."

The fleet admiral approached Belisarius, "General, we have spotted Porphyrius about a mile ahead. The other ships refuse to move as Porphyrius seems to be guarding the straits."

Belisarius gave the admiral a skeptical look, "You mean to tell me that this fish is stopping the fleet of the Romans?"

"He's no fish, General," the Admiral said, "he's a monster! They say he's thirty cubits[35] long!"

"Half the length of this ship?" Belisarius asked.

"Aye, sir," the wet sailor affirmed as he accepted a warm blanket. "He came right underneath and cracked the hull." The man shivered bitterly, and his teeth rattled, despite the water not being cold, and Belisarius concluded that the man's shaking was from fear. "Then he headed straight for us and hit the port side. Half the men fell into the water. And then…"

The sailor paused as his eyes filled with terror, and his voice went shrill. "He started eating us!" The man crossed himself. "The Lord does not want us to head out to sea. Just like the Prophet Job…"

Belisarius put his hand on the man, "Relax; you're safe now."

"We must turn back," the man said as though struck with delirium.

Belisarius watched as his crew pulled up another screaming, legless sailor. The whale had stopped the entire fleet in the water, and ships began crashing into one another as they tried to pull the victims out of the water. Waves clubbed the sailors bobbing in the water as they struggled to grab one of the ship's oars. Suddenly, a dark cloud obfuscated the sun, and a flash of lightning struck the mast of a nearby

---

[35] Ca. 45 feet

ship, shattering it into bits and causing the crew to collapse on the deck. Belisarius felt his nausea coming on again and took another bite of the allium he had in the sleeve of his tunic. *Not now!*

"Heaven have mercy on us," Belisarius cried out. "*Medicus! Medicus,* get over here!" A rush of men attended the poor soul. *There's another man, lost.* Belisarius turned back to the admiral, "How have you faced this monster before?"

"We haven't; we just race back to the shallows."

"Flight is not an option," Belisarius said.

"I will not have my fleet destroyed by this creature," the admiral barked.

"Where is this creature now?" the captain shouted.

"We don't know, sir," came the reply from several men.

"We saw Porphyrius headed in the direction of your bow, sir, perhaps a mile ahead," another sailor reckoned.

"If we dally here, Admiral, the Vandals will learn of our fleet and destroy it on the sea," Belisarius retorted. He looked around on the deck and pointed to a large ballista[36] on the ship's bow. "I've seen missiles from those split trees and rocks. Surely it can take out a whale."

The hostile faces that met that suggestion suggested to Belisarius that they thought he was crazy."

"You cannot kill the creature!" one sailor yelled.

"We can kill anything with a heart, sailor. Does it have one of those?"

"I don't know, sir, but it does bleed."

"Then it has a heart."

"Perhaps if you can get a straight shot," the admiral said. "But that will not be easy with these waves. Shooting a moving object on a moving platform is no easy task."

"Take us to the beast, Admiral!" Belisarius said.

---

[36] Bolt thrower

The sailors shook their heads in disapproval and looked at the captain, who in turn looked at the admiral.

"Sailors, to your stations! Now! We're going to war against Porphyrius!"

The sailors didn't move and grumbled among themselves. The captain took out a short whip and cracked it. "You heard the order! Man your oars, or I will rip the hide off your backs."

The crew hustled to their places, and within three minutes, what had looked like a hospital on the verge of mutiny again looked like a tightly run warship. The rescued sailors, realizing they were on their own now, tended to each other. The ship's drummer beat a rhythm with a kettle drum to which the oarsmen rowed with increased intensity. The ship, no longer motionless on the waves, crashed through them like a war elephant charging through infantry. Belisarius went to the bow of the ship and leaned into the wind.

Despite the tossing waves, Belisarius forgot about his nausea and focused his mind on this unseen threat to the fleet. He was pleasantly surprised that the admiral followed his guidance since he did not command sailors. *The navy is only here to support the army. My jurisdiction starts when we encounter the enemy,* he reminded himself, *and the enemy had attacked.* He knew little about Porphyrius, but like any first encounter with an enemy, he reasoned, it knew nothing about him.

Belisarius felt his confidence coming back, turned to Antonina, and yelled, "Witch, your potions are working."

The crew groaned upon hearing the news and gave Belisarius looks mixed with admiration and contempt. The crew watched as the man with the missing leg expired on the deck in a pool of blood. The first man saw this, got a fierce look, and yelled, "Kill the devil!"

Belisarius nodded his approval and watched as the soldier turned the crew's mood.

"General, I request the honor of operating the ballista in this quest," he said.

"Do you know how to operate it?" Belisarius asked.

"Aye, sir," he said with a proud smile, "ballistae are my specialty."

"Then I have a gold aureus if you can land a fatal missile in his skull." He reached into a sack, pulled out the precious coins, and nailed it to the ship's mast.

Every man on the ship glowed. As Belisarius watched most of his men rally behind his words, he turned to the admiral and said, "This is my favorite part of the job." The murmurers held their tongues and took a wait-and-see approach.

"Rallies are only as good as the victories that follow them," Archelaus replied sourly. He turned to his men and yelled, "Oarsmen, return to your stations. Captain, set a course for the breaching whale yonder," he pointed to Porphyrius, who jumped completely out of the water at that moment.

"Dear God," one sailor murmured, "he's coming straight for us!"

The ship's chaplain yelled, "God save these mariners from the fiend that plagues us so!"

The captain yelled out, "Full speed ahead. We have ourselves a whale to hunt."

A drummer began beating the drums to set the rowing pace for the oarsmen. The ship was moving at full speed upon the water within a minute. Belisarius thought that it must have been like this for the Romans attacking the Carthaginians at Mylae, and the thrill of that thought caused him to forget his fear. The warship passed the other ships that had stopped either out of fear or to save drowning comrades.

Someone yelled from one of the other ships, "Send that devil back to Hell, General Belisarius!"

Belisarius smiled with pride at how his men had rallied the murmurers in the face of fear. Belisarius went to the bow of the ship and stood just above the figurehead of the ship, a gold-plated wooden statue of Saint Nicholas, the patron saint of sailors, in red liturgical vestments with his right fist raised as though poised to strike the heretic, Arius. Belisarius pointed to the spout of water about a quarter mile ahead. He turned to the soldier operating the ballista.

"Are you ready to save the Roman fleet today?"

"Aye, sir," he replied as he set the missile in the ballista and checked the torsion springs and the oil in the slide.

"How close do you need to be?"

"For a fatal shot on a moving target, no more than the ship's length, but it has the range to hit him now."

A squad of infantrymen with pila and another of Hunnish archers gathered around Belisarius. The whale disappeared every few seconds but reappeared and, upon noticing the flagship treading upon his territory, increased its speed. The flagship passed another ship taking on water after Porphyrius had cracked it. The admiral signaled a ship behind them to come to their aid.

"The damned beast is still coming for us," the captain yelled.

"You've got one shot, men, so make it count," Belisarius said.

As Porphyrius approached, archers drew their bows back, and crossbowmen inserted missiles. Belisarius held his hand in the air to hold their eager fire. "Wait... wait... wait! Now!"

The missile catapulted from the ballista with a loud "thwap." A second later, the Huns unloosed a dozen arrows. Most hit their target, but the whale kept coming.

"Pila! Throw them now." Belisarius yelled over the sound of the great monster splashing and thrashing about in the depths. The infantry threw them, and three stuck into the back of the whale, accompanied by a low melodic moan. "You've done it!" Belisarius shouted. "You've..."

All at once, Porphyrius dove under the water and disappeared. "Where did he go?" the sailors asked one another.

"He's going to come up from underneath the ship and try to tip us!" a sailor yelled, ending the premature celebratory mood. The crew looked at Belisarius with looks of horror and anger in their eyes.

"The General's just pissed him off!" one of the murmurers cried out.

Belisarius felt dagger eyes from half the crew. As he was about to offer words of encouragement, Porphyrius's tale hit the bottom of the boat, knocking everyone on the deck off his feet. As the ship's bow rose above the water's surface, men rolled down the deck like scree down a hill. When the bow crashed down upon the water, the oars knocked the rowers off their seats, and cries of pain echoed on the deck.

Porphyrius then re-emerged, came out of the water, and struck the ship's bow again, breaking off the wooden hand of Saint Nicholas, abruptly stopping the ship, and throwing Belisarius and several of the whale's assailants into the water with loud splashes. Belisarius grabbed one of the oars in the water to stay afloat and helped some of the others grab onto oars.

"Pull the General out of the water," the captain yelled. Several rowers abandoned their stations and ran to assist their comrades.

The captain yelled again, "he's coming back!"

Belisarius, a good swimmer, helped two Huns in the water grab oars and crawl up on the side of the ship using the oar holes. As Belisarius scrambled to get out of the water himself, he saw Porphyrius, bloodied, with his back riddled with missiles and a pilum stuck just above his evil eye, looking straight at him.

"Archers ready?" he yelled, but as he was about to yell "fire," Porphyrius slammed his head into the side of the ship, knocking over the archers, and his tail thrashed down upon the oars, catapulting more oarsmen into the water. A giant wave rushed onto the ship's deck and swept more sailors into the water.

Belisarius felt himself pulled underneath the ship by the waves and felt several oars hit him in the head. *This is no way for a cavalryman to die*, he thought to himself as he struggled to get his head above the water. He thought he was about to surface several times, but each time hit the bottom of the ship or an oar. He swallowed a large amount of water and took some into his lungs. He frantically dived deeply, hoping to emerge somewhere that would let him get a breath of air. When he came up, he bumped into something soft and fleshy: it was Porphyrius. He tried to open his eyes, but all he saw under the water was darkness and blood. Terror seized him, and he felt himself panicking for lack of air. He tried to think, but fear of drowning consumed him.

He swam underwater as far as he could one more time, and this time his head emerged from the sea. He took a deep breath, coughed the seawater out of his lungs, and rubbed his burning eyes to restore his vision. He desperately tried to discern where he was while he caught his breath. He saw that he was about a good spear's throw from the ship and swam towards it. He didn't care if it was under attack from Porphyrius: he knew he could not afford to be separated from the ship.

He kept his head above the surface as he swam and watched as the sailors threw spear after spear into the whale — all without seeming effect, though in thrashing from side to side, Porphyrius had rolled onto his back.

Belisarius shouted to whoever might hear him, but all hands on deck were focused on killing Porphyrius. He was grateful that the whale was not coming after him for the moment. He could think again and wondered how they would kill the creature. He realized that no one would know precisely where the heart might be in such a mysterious creature. *His heart must be as tall as a man and weigh twice as much! Surely, we can find it.* As he arrived at the ship, he caught his breath, climbed the oar holes, and ran across the deck to the ballista operator. "Shoot him in the heart!"

Belisarius pushed aside the ballista operator, took careful aim, and fired a missile that sunk deep into the creature's belly. The whale groaned from the shot, rolled onto his back again, and blew out a massive fountain of blood from his spout-hole, covering Belisarius in a shower of sticky, red gore. Belisarius watched as each respiration became more and more agonized. Belisarius looked Porphyrius in the eye again; this time, he did not fear but pitied him. He had seen the look before in men just before their hearts burst from exhaustion.

All at once, the whale dove into the water and emerged seconds later as he heaved himself into the air and crashed down upon the side of the ship, cracking the deck and splintering oars. As one oar came down, Belisarius felt something hit him in the head. He felt dizzy as a streak of warm blood ran down his face, and his vision began to fail him.

He awoke on the deck an hour later with a splitting headache. He rubbed his eyes and felt his sight return. He smelled some fish cooking. He gently touched the source of his headache and felt stitches there. *Is this the afterlife? No, it hurts too much.* He turned to his side and vomited red seawater.

"Oh no," he said.

"You're fine," the *medicus* said, "the blood is not yours."

He noticed Antonina seated by his side in the bed of the captain's quarters.

"Flavius, we thought we'd lost you," she said as she caressed his bandaged head.

"Ouch!"

"O Flavius! Flavius, you could have died out there! You need to be more careful. This army needs you. I need you!"

"What?"

"You have a nice goose egg there," she said. "You're lucky that Archelaus was able to pull you out. Good thing you weren't wearing your armor, or you'd be at the bottom of the sea."

"What happened?"

"When Porphyrius struck the ship again, the troops put so many arrows and pila into him that he looked like a porcupine and swam away! But you may have delivered the coup de grâce!"

"He's still alive?" Belisarius said as he sat up in surprise and terror.

"Perhaps, despite the missile from the ballista in his lung," its proud operator informed.

"Where is Porphyrius now?" Belisarius asked.

"He fled to the safety of the Sea of Marmara again. I don't see how he can survive his wounds," Archelaus pronounced.

"Unlike you, General," the medicus said. "But you must rest."

"Did we lose any men?" Belisarius asked, ignoring the *medicus.*

"Yes, from our ship, the whale swallowed two of the Huns forthwith, while another drowned when he went overboard," Archelaus announced. "In the whole fleet, who knows?"

"I hate the sea," Belisarius announced. "How is the ship?"

"Fine, General. Saint Nicholas lost an arm, and we lost several oars, but no whale is going to sink this ship. It's the finest in the fleet."

"Were any others sunk?"

"Two, and a third is undergoing repairs. However, the entire fleet is sailing once again."

"Good," Belisarius replied as his eyes began to close.

"You made the right call, General," Archelaus said. "You'll be the toast of Byzantium's fishermen."

"Indeed," the captain said, "I think the only danger to the fleet now is your breath!"

Belisarius laughed as he sought to find his allium, but it was gone, and within minutes, the victor at Dara felt himself slipping into a long sleep.

# CHAPTER THIRTEEN
# BISCUITS AND WATER

*It is easier to find men who will volunteer to die than to find those who are willing to endure pain with patience.*

— Julius Caesar

*Aegean Sea*
*A.D. 533*

Days later, the southbound fleet stopped at Heraclea on the Thracian coast, where they remained for five days, taking on a plentiful supply of cavalry horses before continuing south. At Abydos, the winds stilled, and they remained at port for an extended stay.

Belisarius and Antonina took up residence in the palace of the local prefect. As they were enjoying a meal, General Constantinus rushed into the *triclinium* at the governor's palace to announce that two Hephthalite Hun confederates involved in a drunken brawl had killed one of their comrades.

"Let Sunicas handle it," Belisarius said.

"Sunicas has done nothing," Constantinus replied. "He insists that the fellow had it coming and has demanded only blood payment for the family."

Belisarius calmly took another bite of his lamb.

"General," Constantinus said, "Either this is a Roman army governed by Roman law, or it's a Hunnish one. If their own traditions govern every allied tribe, how can we enforce military discipline?"

Belisarius spoke without looking up from his plate. "Thank you, Constantinus. Please send for Sunicas. You are dismissed."

Constantinus sulked out of the room, and a few moments later, Sunicas appeared.

"My friend," Belisarius said, "we can have no tolerance for cultural traditions that conflict with army discipline. Your compatriots' intemperance exacerbates their crime rather than excuses it."

"I understand," Sunicas replied, "but this death is a purely Hunnish affair and does not fall under the purview of Roman authority."

Belisarius shook his head. "I cannot command drunkards. The tradition of the self-governing *foederati*[37] ended when the ships launched. I need every man in the army sober and alert lest our enemies get the better of us."

"What would you have me do then?"

"If a Roman committed the capital offense, the punishment would be the same. Hang the culprits."

Sunicas swallowed hard. "Flavius…" Belisarius gave him a look that said he didn't want to argue the matter. "I won't miss those two troublemakers, but this decision will be unpopular in our ranks."

"We don't need to be popular, Sunicas. We need to be obeyed."

An hour later, Sunicas reported, "You sent a powerful message that we will not tolerate such license, but most of the troops believe you overreacted."

"The object of life, Sunicas, is not to be on the side of the majority but to avoid joining the ranks of the insane."


As the fleet headed into the Aegean Sea, Belisarius stood on the deck with Antonina and noticed the admiral had a dark look on his face as he spoke with the captain. *What is it now?* He and Antonina approached the pair on the deck and asked, "What is it, Archelaus?"

---

[37] Treaty-bound allied mercenaries of the Empire.

"Red suns in the morning are a bad portent," he said grimly. "We may see a storm this afternoon. I hope you have sea legs."

Belisarius swallowed hard, and Antonina squeezed his hand. He remembered how sick he got during his first time on a ship and how the sailors would joke that whenever so much as a ripple touched their boat, he would gag. "Perhaps we should stay closer to the shoreline then." Archelaus nodded have gave him an amused look. He considered the merits of staying below deck to reduce the effects of the sea sickness but knew his men could not see him cowering like a rat in the ship's bowels.

Within two hours, a cold gust fell upon the sails of the Roman fleet, the sky darkened, and waves became so high that water came pouring in over the side, prompting the captain to order several of the rowers to begin bailing. Antonina sought comfort by leaning on her husband, but he knew that his own anxiety about the storm offered her no reassurance. Procopius, apparently unbothered by the waves since he came from a long family of sturdy seafarers, approached the apprehensive couple.

"The first time that the Romans tried to take Carthage, they lost an entire fleet — bigger than ours — to storms," Procopius said with a mischievous look.

*This man has a gift for presenting interesting historical facts at the most inopportune moments.* Belisarius frowned and said, "Procopius, tell us a story about a fleet that safely reached shore."

As waves tossed the fleet up and down, Belisarius noticed that many smaller transport ships struggled to stay afloat. Belisarius watched as the mast of one ship snapped in half because of the high wind and left its crew helpless on the water. Soon heavy rains began to fall, and the large raindrops stung as they crashed into the faces of the passengers. A loud crack of thunder struck the mast of a nearby ship and started the sail on fire. The noise made the whole crew jump, and Belisarius nervously approached the admiral as they watched the crew rush to extinguish the fire. Belisarius found himself hoping for the seemingly remote possibility of a dull day at sea.

"Admiral, I think it's time that we sought safe harbor for the fleet, or we may not survive the day," Belisarius said.

The admiral and captain both gave the terrestrial commander an irritated look, "General," the admiral said, "The shoreline has several rocky promontories that will shatter our ships if we get anywhere near them."

"Agreed," the captain said, "We have to ride out the storm."

"How long will it last?" Belisarius asked.

"Not as long as the ship, General," the admiral said. "Rest assured; this ship is unsinkable."

"Unsinkable?" Antonina gasped. "Nothing is unsinkable."

"This ship is. She is built of sturdy oak by the best craftsmen in the Empire. I tell you, not even Noah could have built something stronger." The admiral laughed, but his confidence did not settle Belisarius even a bit.

From his perch on the poop deck, Belisarius watched the dark cloud with interior lightning flashes approach the Roman fleet even as growing waves prevented them from trying to escape. By the early afternoon, the waves were higher than the masts of the ships, and three nearby ships in the fleet succumbed to the waves, while three others began to head toward the shore. Water flooded the deck, while those below deck worked hard to bail it out. *Even if we survive the storm, it will so scatter our fleet that we will be easy prey for the Vandal navy.*

"No!" the admiral screamed as though his mighty voice might be heard amidst the crackling thunder and crashing waves. "The land will be your death!" Realizing the ships had mistaken a shepherd's fire in a cave to be a lighthouse offering safe harbor, the admiral ordered the captain to hoist a flag that signaled those ships should not attempt a landing at this point.

But the admiral's commands were lost in the wind and the growing darkness. Belisarius watched tragically as one ship after another crashed into the rocks that penetrated the ships' hulls, reminding him of battering rams breaking through heavy doors during a siege. The sound of timber shattering on rocks and men screaming as they lurched into the water filled Belisarius with dread.

"God help us!" Belisarius cried as two anxious rowers agreed to begin praying aloud.

"You pray to Christ," the first said.

The other replied, "I'll pray to Poseidon."

As flotsam from the wrecks slammed into the flagship, the crew worked to pull in survivors. The crew of the ship struck by lightning abandoned their burning vessel, jumped into the water and swam to the flagship. The admiral gave Belisarius a stern look, "See? What did I tell you? Men who follow orders will always fare better than ones who do not."

Belisarius nodded his agreement. "I leave the fleet's survival to your more capable hands."

Antonina joined her husband in watching the ships shatter on the rocks as sailors and horses scrambled desperately to get out of the water before debris smashing into the jagged rocks crushed them. Men screamed for help as they tried frantically to cling to something that would keep their heads above water. Very few succeeded. As Belisarius helped shipwrecked sailors onto the deck, he wondered if he too might soon be in the water seeking to cheat death yet again. He wondered whether Justinian fully appreciated these sailors' sacrifices to bring his army to Carthage.

"Admiral," Belisarius said with tremors in his voice, "What can we do for these men?"

"Had they followed their captain's orders, they would not be in the current situation," the admiral said with rage and sadness. "They missed their chances to save themselves when they steered their rudders into the rocks. Any ship trying to help them will likely end up in the same situation. I will not waste my pity on fools."

Belisarius knew from experience that the admiral was right. He had lost many men who, had they followed orders, would still be alive today. However, the response still seemed cold as they sailed past sailors too close to the rocks to rescue. He was relieved to see that errant captains who had been heading for shore turned their ships back out to sea.

The admiral forced a smile. "It sometimes takes a tragedy to make men come to their senses."

Belisarius counted a half-dozen ships destroyed. He stared at the shipwrecked corpses bobbing up and down with the waves and then looked up at the hostile sky as lightning flashed around him. "Lord, take these souls into your care. Please spare your army more losses. You know that losing two or three hundred men can be enough to cost your Empire a battle." Cold raindrops stung his face as they struck, and he wondered when the storm would pass. The admiral seemed to anticipate his thoughts.

"The storm came to us from the west," Archelaus said as he pointed toward the shore. "Look beyond that dark cloud."

Belisarius squinted to keep the rain out of his eyes. Beyond the dark cloud, he could see the evening sun desperately trying to break through the clouds.

"I would say another hour of this, and we'll be complaining about the sun's heat."

"The sun?" Belisarius asked confusedly, "I thought it was evening."

The admiral laughed, "No, just darkness from storm clouds." Indeed, an hour later, the clouds almost miraculously parted, and the sun came out. In the east, Belisarius could see a rainbow forming where the storm was slowly petering out. The men on the ship let out a big cheer as a giant sunbeam moved across the water and landed on the ship's deck.

"Praise be to God," the crew yelled and spontaneously broke into a *Stella Maris*[38] hymn. Belisarius joined in the Latin sailor's song and was surprised that even the Egyptians seemed to know it well. He laughed at how the bawdy, yet magnificent baritone voices put the entire ship at ease.

*Give us a pure life, Lord,*
*And prepare a safe endeavor*
*So that we may see Jesus*
*And rejoice with Him forever.*

A loud clap of thunder briefly shattered the second verse, but it slowly faded into a soft rumble. *Is this a sign of divine favor or more wrath to come?* The crew fell silent, and Belisarius wondered whether the storm might return when the wind direction changed. The ship's chaplain, whom Belisarius and the men relied upon to interpret such signs, yelled out, "The voice of the Lord is on the waters. The

---

[38] Star of the Sea

God of Glory thunders," and the whole crew erupted into another loud cheer and resumed their singing.

Belisarius pulled his wife close to him and said gratefully, "The tempest is over."

The captain and admiral laughed uproariously when they overheard Belisarius, who gave them a puzzled look.

"It's never over, General," the captain said. "We just lurch from one crisis to the next. Enjoy the peace while it lasts."

The peace lasted three days. Belisarius watched the sun rise on the ship's deck as he tasted his morning *bucellatum*.[39] He smelled it. It was spoiled. He threw it into the sea, and an albatross scooped it up midair, then opened its beak and let it fall. "Too nasty even for you?" he asked.

Soon the whole ship was full of sailors retching the spoiled biscuit.

Admiral Archelaus approached Belisarius, a gelatinous mass oozing between his fingers, "How are we to survive on this? I've seen it before. This biscuit should be double baked to resist mildew."

The ship *medicus* agreed with the admiral, "Our sailors are suffering from food poisoning and bloody diarrhea, and they are severely dehydrated."

Belisarius told the *medicus,* "The fleet will have to re-provision in southern Greece."

"It's the Cappadocian's fault!" roared the admiral.

"What do you mean?" Belisarius asked, reluctant to question one of Justinian's most trusted advisors. "Before you start...."

"The Finance Minister must have decided to save some gold by using the heat from the furnaces of the public baths to bake the bread rather than dedicated ovens," the admiral said. "He's done this before."

"Indeed, John was concerned about cutting costs," Belisarius reflected, "Now our army is paying the price."

Archelaus signaled the other ships to approach his. They needed to know the extent of the damage to their food supply, and what they found out was grim.

---

[39] Biscuit after which the *bucellarii* (the biscuit-eaters) derived their name.

"Now we have no food," Constantinus cried as Belisarius stood by while the crew tossed the remaining biscuit overboard."

"How long till we put into a port?" Belisarius asked.

"Fair winds permitting, not for several days," the admiral replied grimly.

"By then, the whole fleet will be sick," Constantinus murmured to anyone who would listen.

Belisarius turned to Procopius. "Inform the Emperor of John's negligence. This tragedy should never have happened. And send a sample of the biscuits to John."

Belisarius went below deck to see how the rowers of the flagship were faring. They looked green or famished.

"I didn't eat any," one half-starved sailor bragged, "and I'm glad of it."

The man seated next to him, covered in vomit, admitted, "I was too hungry."

He checked on Antonina. "I didn't eat that rancid stuff. It smelled fermented. Did you eat it?"

Belisarius realized that he had but had not noticed that it was bad. "Yes, but I'm used it."

"Are you? You look pale."

Belisarius went to find the chamber pots, but there was a long line. He noticed several sailors leaning over the deck rail with their tunics up and defecating violently into the sea. One was so weak that he fell in. The ship behind them pulled the wretched soul out of the water. He then felt his stomach retching, ran to the edge of the deck, and heaved his breakfast into the sea.

"It's the bread of death," the chaplain said, "whosoever eats it shall die."

"Not yet, I hope," Belisarius replied.

Belisarius knew that his sickness was mild compared to others and helped the sailors sew men into body bags and drop them into the sea as the chaplain commended their souls to God. As Antonina sewed the opposite end of a body bag, her eyes filled with tears of rage.

"Flavius, I swear to you, I will not rest until I have seen John the Cappadocian reduced to the condition of your men today."

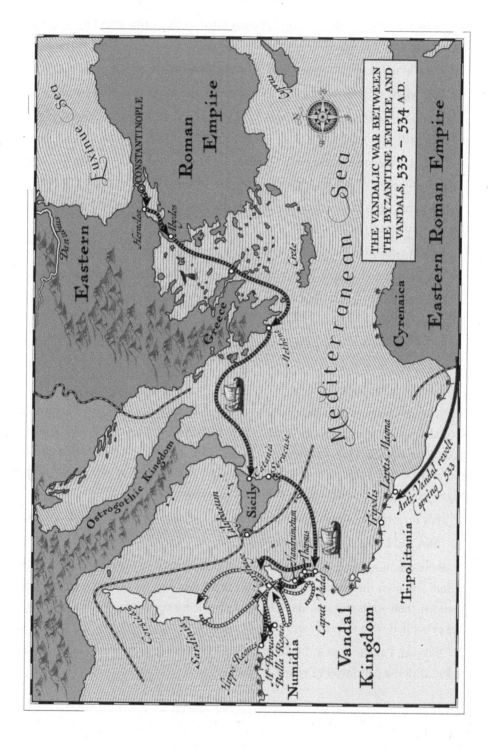

182                    ROBERT BRUTON

When they arrived at Methone, Belisarius went to see the surviving troops. The pungent aroma of death and vomit nearly overcame him, but it felt good to be on land again. The healthier troops washed and practiced fighting techniques, but most of the army rested on the beach.

"Are you feeling better, soldier, now that you have edible food in your belly?" Belisarius asked one soldier with sunken eyes and tight pale skin.

"No, sir," the Isaurian replied.

Belisarius wiped the soldier's sweaty forehead and put a cup of water to his mouth. "Keep eating and drinking as much as you can. You're burning up."

"Yes, sir." The soldiers obediently took a big gulp and immediately vomited.

Belisarius beckoned the *medicus*, "How bad is it? Will they recover?"

"Those who keep food down may live, but most don't want to eat."

Antonina arrived and knelt beside the soldier. She gave him a small sip of the water. Belisarius waited for him to retch it up, but he did not. "Just drink a little bit at a time, but *all* the time."

"Thank you, Lady Antonina."

Belisarius looked with approval at his wife's ability to nurse so many men back to health. He walked around the beach, surveying the emaciated troops. Many of the bodies thrown overboard had washed ashore and required burial.

Admiral Archelaus approached him, "We've lost five hundred men. We can't save those who have died, but as soon as we land in Africa, we will gather up all the provisions of fresh and dried fruit and bread we can find to help the recovery of those who may have to fight." The admiral's empty stomach gurgled loudly, "Sounds like I'm having trouble managing protests in the lower ranks."

"If it's not the seasickness, it's the hunger. What else could go wrong?" Belisarius asked.

"Plenty," the admiral replied.


The fleet disembarked from the southern end of the Peloponnesian peninsula north for Zacynthus before turning west to cross the Ionian Sea towards Sicily.

As they approached Catania, Belisarius heard a rumble in his stomach, and a sudden high wave hit the side of the boat, causing him to lose his meal. He gave the admiral a desperate look. "Does one ever get used to this?"

"It takes years," Archelaus replied, but the waves may not be the cause of your nausea. I fear our water supply has spoiled. Follow me."

They descended into the ship's bowels, inspected the barrels of drinking water, then brought a cup above deck to examine in the morning sun.

"It's full of algae," Belisarius said.

He walked among the rowers. The deck smelled of vomit and feces. They were lethargic again, and their captain had taken several off their oars.

Back on the main deck, Belisarius saw that his godson, Theodosius, was entertaining Antonina with an impersonation of the Emperor. He had perfected Justinian's gait and the peculiar accent of his rustic Greek. They were trying to distract a nauseous crew with their singing and dancing, but the sailors were too ill to be amused this time. Bilious and thirsty, Belisarius approached his wife with his hand on his stomach, "How is it, dear, that the ravages of the contaminated water have spared you?"

Antonina smiled and whispered, "I brought a personal water supply." She took his hand and led him below deck. She had stored several trunks filled with hundreds of glass bottles of limpid water nestled in damp sand. "My previous sea travels have taught me not to trust the ship's water supply. Try one, husband," she said using the lilting voice of a courtesan schooled in the art of seduction.

Belisarius uncorked the bottle, smelled it, and then guzzled the entire bottle. "I brought extra if you'd like some, but I'll first need an apology for the contemptuous look you gave me when the porters brought these trunks on board. Did you suppose I brought nothing but silks and shoes?"

Belisarius shrugged as though convicted.

"Feel free to share some with the admiral and that Philistine pettifogger of yours," she said.

Belisarius apologized. "How many bottles are there?"

"Plenty."

He grabbed a bottle each for Procopius, Archelaus, and Photius and discreetly delivered them. "Not a word of this to the other ships, or we shall have a mutiny in the fleet. We have enough clean water to see us through to Sicily. My commanders must be healthy." The commanders asked no questions about the source.

Guilt and remorse overcame Belisarius. When he rejoined Antonina, he said, "I cannot in good conscience drink more while our crew is wasting away. Wife, you must be generous to them."

Antonina gave him a sour look. "Very well, but there is not enough for the entire ship."

"I understand, but we can help the sickest crew members. Give them each one ladle."

Theodosius looked on in horror as common sailors consumed the clean water. He uncorked a bottle and pranced around the deck, drinking it in front of the rowers. Belisarius was appalled. These suffering men were sailing into a battle that might end in their deaths.

"Theodosius," he barked, "we brought you on this expedition to learn something of the art of war. Show these men some respect."

Theodosius feigned surprise. "Perhaps your troops need a distraction from the trials that await them."

On the fourteenth day, as the red sun rose above the horizon, Belisarius heard a shout from the top of the main sail, "Sicily! Sicily ahead!" Belisarius led the crew in hurrahs and prayers of thanksgiving. When the fleet finally dropped their anchors in the harbor of Catania, the crew was dehydrated and thirsty, but they had survived.

The admiral approached him. "We're missing a dozen ships."

Belisarius sighed. "We're almost there. Justinian has brokered a deal with Queen Amalasuntha to get us fresh water, food, and horses here. Once our Gothic allies have loaded the ships, we'll be off."

Celebration and joy were in the air as towers with compound pullies hoisted crates with fresh supplies onto the ships. They were finally able to thrive, even on the open sea. Belisarius knew that sufficient wind would have them in Africa in two weeks, but he required information before they could set sail again.

He summoned Procopius to the deck. "While we provision the ships, I want you to sail ahead to Syracuse to gather intelligence on the status of the Vandal fleet and army."

Procopius considered the risks and started to voice his concerns about the Vandals catching him and hanging him for being a Roman spy. Belisarius noticed his hesitance and put his hands on his shoulders, "Procopius, wars are fought in mystery, but the more facts we have, the more successful we'll be."

Procopius nodded his agreement, adding, "I'll tell the Syracusans that I'm working for my family's shipping trade and learn what I can."

"Thank you, friend."

The reluctant spy returned a few days later with a wide grin. "General, I have great news: Gelimer fell for the Emperor's ruse. The bulk of the Vandal fleet and five thousand of his best troops have departed to put down the rebellion Narses instigated in Sardinia."

"Good work, Procopius! Inform the troops. They'll be encouraged by the news. Who is your source?"

"A childhood friend called Phlebas, an honest and reliable man who conducts a silk trade with my family in Caesarea. Three days ago, he returned from Carthage, where the Vandals had recently dispatched their fleet. Gelimer's brother Tzazon is leading the expedition."

"That suggests Gelimer doesn't know we're coming," Belisarius said. "Thanks be to God. Despite all the talk at the ports and delays, we have somehow maintained the element of surprise."

With renewed confidence, full bellies, and fresh drinking water, Belisarius and his men were ready to finish the last leg of their journey. A short stopover in Malta allowed them to practice quick disembarkation so they would be ready to meet the Vandals upon arrival. Belisarius leaned over the outer deck railing and let the sea motion lull him into a calm stupor. He was getting used to the constant motion of the ship. When he closed his eyes, he saw another distant shore, one he had never visited, North Africa.

## CHAPTER FOURTEEN
# OUT OF AFRICA: ALWAYS SOMETHING NEW

*For [Justinian], with sails of red,*
*And torches at masthead,*
*Piloting the great fleet,*
*I swept the Afric coasts*
*And scattered the Vandal hosts,*
*Like dust in a windy street.*

— *Belisarius*, Henry Wadsworth Longfellow

*September 533 A.D.*
*Caput Vada, North African Coast*

"Land ho!" the captain called to the admiral. "Africa is in sight!" Within an hour, the green coast of North Africa emerged clearly into view, and the smell of fresh vegetation filled the salty nostrils of the hungry horses who were eager to jump overboard and head toward the verdant hills. The weary fleet cheered and groaned, eager to be on land again.

When they landed on the beach, Belisarius, John, Pharas, and Sunicas joined the crew, both Christians and pagans, in falling to their knees, kissing the ground, and offering prayers of gratitude to Saint Nicholas or Poseidon for delivering them back to *terra firma*. The viridity of the hills renewed their hope of success. Belisarius observed several Pharas's cavalrymen dancing around an image of Thor. Belisarius gave Pharas a puzzled look and said, "I thought your Herulians were Christians."

"They are."

"Then why are they worshipping pagan gods?"

"Because their fathers did."

Belisarius gave him another bewildered look. "But they don't believe in them, do they?"

"Of course not," Pharas said in a defensive tone. "Maybe Thor hasn't done much for us recently, but he's still our god."

Belisarius shook his head and laughed.

They were at Caput Vada, about one hundred and thirty miles or nine days' march south of Carthage, the Vandal capital. Unarmored cataphracts disembarked first with only their swords. Finally, the famished horses were offloaded and compelled to swim to shore, where they soon found happy grazing grounds.

"We survived the most vulnerable part of the expedition," Archelaus said as he joined Belisarius and his cavalry on the beach.

"I know," Belisarius responded as he supervised the building of trenches and placing spikes for a military encampment, "Let's waste no time in deploying our infantry and archers into formations." Belisarius issued orders to John, Pharas, and Sunicas, who quickly dispatched light cavalry scouts to begin surveying the landscape north, south, and west of the landing zone and determine whether the Vandals were aware of their presence. Belisarius smiled at the resilience of his men who had survived the long and wretched journey. Pride for his men filled his heart as he watched them silently take a position.

"My one hundred dromones will patrol around the transports lest the Vandal navy appears," Archelaus said, "but there is not an enemy ship within a day's voyage now."

"I believe we have achieved tactical surprise," Belisarius replied, astounded at his good fortune. *Now it's time to plan and take advantage of our luck.* He watched the sweat run off the backs of his men as they furiously dug their trenches for the camp. He wasn't sure if it was Roman discipline, fear of the Vandals, or perhaps a combination of the two. He thought of Rome's disastrous effort to retake North Africa a century before and how the Vandals had tricked General Basiliscus into letting his guard down. He was determined not to make the same mistakes. *These*

*Vandals had beat an overwhelming force because the Romans were sure of their victory. Don't appear too confident, or your men will get lazy.*

He paced around the camp as a demonstration for the diggers, who watched him nervously. Their work pace picked up whenever their general's watchful eyes fell upon them. Satisfied that the work was getting done, Belisarius convened army and navy officers to a war council under a date grove not far from the beach. Officers who had survived on little more than stale biscuit and salted fish for months ravenously consumed the fresh and sweet fruits.

"Enjoy them, men," Belisarius said. "They were given to us by a local Roman farmer who welcomed us to his land. He assured me that the nearby residents would generously support our campaign but also asked for assurances that our army would not descend like locusts upon their land. I gave him those assurances, so make sure that your men respect the property of the Roman population. They should be willing to pay for it if they want to supplement their rations with local produce." The officers nodded their agreement.

Admiral Archelaus, Belisarius's second-in-command and financier of the expedition, opened the discussion. "The first matter to consider is where to harbor the fleet. All deep harbors are under Vandal control, yet if we leave the fleet at sea, the Vandal Navy or sudden storms could dash it to pieces. I propose mooring the fleet in a harbor six miles south of their capital and launching our attack from there."

John, Pharas, Sunicas, and several officers offered similar concerns. The consensus was to move the fleet into the Carthaginian port. *Perhaps they have fonder memories of being on ships than I do. Is no one worried about the Vandal navy?* Belisarius quietly heard them all, then said, "For three months, we have dreaded the possibility that the Vandals would discover our fleet and sink it before we even arrived in Africa. Having put to shore, we have overcome the first threat to our success, and I propose that we do not tempt fate by putting out to sea again. If we try to take Carthage by sea and are unable to land our fleet, we will have lost the crucial element of surprise."

Belisarius paused to assess his fellow officers' reactions. John nodded his head in agreement. Pharas, whose Herulian ancestors loved the sea, was neutral. Sunicas, who felt vulnerable whenever not on his horse and even more vulnerable when not on land, quipped, "I would rather dig trenches with a spoon than get back on that cursed ship."

All laughed save Constantinus. "The bulk of their navy is either in Sardinia or Libya. We should sail the fleet to Carthage and launch an amphibious landing there."

"Have you seen the walls of Carthage, or the heavy chain strung across the entrance to its harbor?" Belisarius asked.

"No, but..."

"I won't attack a fortified defensive position unless compelled. And that chain will rip the rudder off every Roman ship that manages to get across it. No, we will not attack Carthage."

John, Pharas, and Sunicas nodded their heads in adamant agreement. "Our advantage is our superior cavalry," John said.

"We cannot deploy our horses against the walls of Carthage," Pharas added.

"And we have no siege equipment," Sunicas reminded Constantinus.

Seeing signs of assent beginning to emerge, Belisarius continued. "I propose we entrench our camp in the Roman manner and begin an overland march towards Carthage, with the fleet following as closely as possible."

The officers discussed Belisarius's proposal, and eventually, even Constantinus agreed to his plan. Belisarius smiled. He tried to build consensus among his senior officers whenever the situation would allow it. "Alright," he said, "let's get to work."

The Roman infantrymen were familiar with the process of building a camp. They dug a long square trench and erected stakes at forty-five-degree angles to create an effective barrier against a charging enemy. Belisarius stripped down, grabbed a spade, and joined the foot soldiers in the arduous effort. After digging for an hour, he struck a hidden spring in the dry land, filling the trench with fresh water, a good omen.

"Lucky Belisarius," an infantryman proclaimed, and the moniker stuck.

"I'd rather be a lucky commander than a good one," Belisarius said.

The men cheered and began collecting freshwater in their skins. Once they had filled them, hundreds of thirsty horses moved in and lapped the water out of the trench.

Belisarius dictated a simple letter to the Emperor.

"Your Majesty, our landing in Africa was unopposed. Your army and navy are safe. Flavius."


Despite Belisarius's earlier warnings to his general staff about the need to respect the property of the local landowners, a handful of soldiers set their eyes on the dewy orchards and helped themselves to the fruit. Belisarius promptly had the men arrested and brought to his tent.

"What are your names?" he asked from behind his desk in his newly erected tent in the center of the Roman camp. The two men appeared to be brothers of average height with light brown hair and hazel eyes. Dressed in filthy, sweat-soaked clothing, they were as thin as rakes and looked as if they had barely escaped starvation during the dreadful voyage.

"Uliaris and Ulysses," they replied.

"Do you two understand that what you have done is an offense and insult to the Empire's honor?"

They both nodded their heads in shame.

"Our control of these lands depends on winning the hearts and minds of the local population. Despite their Vandal overlords, most of them are Roman and speak our Latin tongue. If we come as conquerors set to plunder the fruits of their labor, we will incite the same rebellion that now distracts Gelimer. But if we come as liberators and treat them as fellow citizens, we will win their respect and loyalty. They will welcome our occupation, allowing us to return to our homes before long."

The two marauders lowered their heads even further.

"Soldiers, you have broken the first rule of hospitality, which is sacred in this part of the world. If you want fresh fruit, bargain for it, and pay for it. The army pays you for such wants, so there is no need to steal."

Belisarius turned to the head of his military police, a bald and brutish man. "Ultor, give them one lash for every fruit plucked from a tree without permission or payment."

Ultor escorted them to an open space in the middle of the camp, tied them to posts, and ripped the shirts from their backs, "How many for you, mate?"

"I ate four pears," Uliaris confessed, and Ultor administered four lashes.

"And you, mate?"

"I ate three bunches of grapes," Ulysses confessed. Ultor turned toward Belisarius and gave him a confused look as if to say, how many grapes are in a bunch?

Belisarius offered a weary smile and held up three fingers. Many of his troops were watching in astonishment at his severity. "Let the stripes on their backs be an example to anyone with the temerity to act like Vandals," he said. "Moreover, in keeping with the Empire's new laws, I will hang any man found guilty of rape or murder. We are Romans and Christians and will act accordingly or pay the price for our disregard of divine providence."


The North African countryside was a lush and fertile plain with rising slopes from which streams and rivers flowed. As the army marched toward Carthage, Latin-speaking inhabitants met them with warm receptions. The army's discipline and fraternity soon overcame local anxieties about the new occupier. The Romans offered to exchange trinkets from Constantinople for food. Despite the distractions, the Romans still managed to march a dozen miles a day. Young boys marched alongside them, imitating their stride and pretending to be auxiliaries in the force. Occasionally, cavalrymen hoisted eager young women onto their horses.

Constantinus observed this casual attitude with disapproval. "You're letting discipline slip," he told Belisarius as they rode their horses' side by side in the long march to Carthage. "What will become of these civilians if the Vandals attack us now?"

"So long as the march is maintained, I don't mind these distractions," Belisarius replied. "It reminds our men and the locals what we are fighting for."

As they approached a church, a village priest stopped his service to bless the troops. "Free at last," he said, and his congregation watched the day-long parade of 15,000 Romans.

The Roman governors of Leptis[40] and Hadrumetum[41] intercepted Belisarius, who embraced them. "Governors, thank you for the keys to your cities and for offering to provide our troops with food and water. Your liberation is at hand, and we are happy to welcome you back into the Empire like lost brothers returning from a long exile."

Fifty miles from Carthage, the army arrived at the country palace of the Vandal kings, a traditional Roman villa they had seized from a once-prominent family. The enslaved descendants of that family and the Roman governor stood on the dramatic front staircase of the villa and greeted Belisarius's marching army. A domed edifice with arches and columns crowned the top of the staircase. White marble statues of Roman gods flanked the assembly, and the area was lush with flowers in full bloom.

"General, please encourage your men to help themselves," the governor said. "We would rather feed Romans our produce than hand it over to our Vandal over-lords."

Belisarius permitted the troops to help themselves to the orchard's fruit, while the governor invited the officers to the villa for lunch under the dome. The villa's red brick façade and white stone columns reminded him of his estate in Rufini-anae. As they entered, a life-size statue of Roman General Publius Cornelius Scipio Africanus greeted the visitors. Belisarius bowed and stood in front of the statue, recalling his study of the battle of Zama while at the military academy.

As he looked pensively to the west, he turned to John and said, "It was a few days' march from here where Scipio's three legions attacked Hannibal's Carthaginian forces. The Carthaginians fought bravely but were routed, surrounded, and massacred. Moorish women stripped them of their tunics, swords, and lances, and

---

[40] Just east of modern Tripoli, Libya. See map.
[41] South of modern Tunis

the dead soldiers lay naked in the sun. Seven hundred years ago. I see it so clearly; it is almost as if I were there. "

John laughed and raised a skeptic's eyebrow.

"You don't believe me, do you, John?"

John shook his head, "No, Flavius, I don't."

"Sometimes it just seems like we're all different actors in the same drama," Belisarius said, "and I know I won't be the last."

The governor joined the conversation and said, "Scipio defeated Hannibal on the superior discipline of his men and the strength of his cavalry, the same way you will."

"How do you know we Romans are better disciplined than the Vandals?" Belisarius asked.

The governor, an ancient fellow with an old man's head, mounted sturdily on a muscular youth's physique, laughed, "I see these Vandals lying about in the hot sun all day. While they still practice their military drills, the easy life we Romans have given them has made them lazy. Their hands are soft, and they've grown too accustomed to luxury. They have struggled to contain even the Moors."

"I hope you're right," Belisarius said. "Where are the Vandals now?"

"They fled upon hearing of your arrival. We've waited a long time for your return. Welcome back!"

This reception was precisely the sort of news Belisarius hoped to hear, and he didn't mind the comparisons to his childhood hero, Scipio. "Thank you for waiting." He turned to John and said, "See? This old Roman remembers me from Zama!"

John just shook his head, "Flavius, Flavius."

Belisarius, Antonina, and the Roman officers decided to stay the night at the villa and regain some of the vitality they lost at sea. Their Roman hosts ensured that Belisarius's army was provided with supplies for their long march to Carthage and generously supplied the cooks with local produce for the large banquet.

After digging a trench around the entire estate, the army settled down to their finest meal since their deployment began. The banquet for the officers was held in the great hall of the villa and consisted of every sort of meat and fruit one could imagine. Belisarius had not seen so much food since his wedding. Several of the infantry gathered outside the villa commented that they hadn't eaten so well in their entire lives. The Romans were especially fond of the abundant bread and wine.

"Our masters gave us orders to kill our herds and cut down the orchards lest the food wind up in your bellies, but that seemed extravagantly wasteful," the old Roman said. "So now it's yours to enjoy."

Belisarius sat at the head of the table next to John and Sunicas, toasted the Romans, and promised them he would generously reward their lavish hospitality.

As they ate, Archelaus turned to Belisarius and whispered, "There has been no sign of the Vandal Navy. We have unconfirmed reports that they may try to land troops behind ours and attack our rearguard, but it is unclear how large that force might be. I have ordered the fleet to follow the army's northward march up the coast."

"Good, the navy will be in sight until we have to turn west away from the coast."

Belisarius turned to his beloved friend, John. "Your cavalry scouts will be the vanguard force. Lead them three miles ahead of our troops and regularly inform us of the enemy's location. If you can defeat him in an engagement, do so, but keep in contact with the main body."

John nodded and passed the word to a captain who left the villa and sought out his three hundred cavalrymen.

Belisarius turned to Sunicas, "Keep your Hunnish cavalrymen three miles west of our main party. Scout out the Vandals and cover our left flank. Engage if you can but avoid direct contact. The Vandals have never encountered mounted archers, so you should be able to inflict great damage on them if you avoid close contact."

"Yes, Flavius," Sunicas answered, chewing the remnants of pork ribs since horseflesh was not available. "It will be like the battle of the abducted mothers," Sunicas joked. "And I presume you will keep your distance so you can properly manage us?"

"Of course, Sunicas, you know the drill." They laughed together. "That's where Gelimer is most likely to aggress if spies have apprised him of our landing, so I will lead the rearguard and the infantry."

Pharas, sitting next to Sunicas, asked with a sparkle in his eye, "And my Herulians, Flavius, are we to protect our right flank from attackers from the sea like Porphyrius?"

"No, Pharas, when the time comes, you will track down Gelimer." Belisarius slapped his old playmate's armored shoulders. "You know better than anyone what it takes to get a prince to abandon his home and reside in Constantinople. Whoever does that will ensure our victory." He raised his glass and hoped with all his heart that the Empire would win this campaign.

# CHAPTER FIFTEEN
# IT'S GOOD TO BE KING

*There were times we regretted*
*The summer palaces on slopes, the terraces,*
*And the silken girls bringing sherbet.*

— *Journey of the Magi*, T.S. Eliot

*Carthage, North Africa*
*A.D. 533*

Although he had a gnawing toothache, it was an otherwise perfect morning in late summer for Gelimer, King of the Vandals. From his luxurious palace in Carthage, he could admire the fertile rolling hills beyond the city walls and watch as the red sun rose over the Mediterranean Sea, casting a crimson glow.

As the morning breeze gently stroked his bronzed, unwrinkled face, he turned toward the east to escape a gust of strong wind, which hurled his long golden locks over his face and obstructed his vision.

From his majestic vantage point on a high balcony, King Gelimer reveled in his magnificent city of 400,000 souls and his pirate fleet anchored in the harbor. He beheld the magnificent Cathedral of St. Cyprian, the hippodrome, the amphitheater, the public baths, the large parks, and the flower gardens. How different it was from his ancestors' cold, barren wilderness. Deposing his cousin Hilderic had been a nasty business but a small price for becoming master of all this.

Beside him, his twin brother, Ammatas, said, "It's good to be king, isn't it?"

"And of such a glorious place," Gelimer said without turning his blue eyes from his glorious city. "To think that our great-grandfather scraped a living by pulling sea trout from the frozen Baltic. How pleased he would be to see how easy life has become for us." The delicate and smooth silk of his translucent morning gown caressed his skin.

"Are you ready for the day's entertainment?" Ammatas asked.

"What have you arranged for us today, dear brother?"

"We have wenches captured on the Greek islands and dancers from Egypt. And as the ice in the cellar is nearly melted, we should finish the sherbet." He snapped his fingers, and an older Vandal domestic pushed two young girls toward the twins.

"Come, ladies," Ammatas said, beckoning them.

Reluctant, the Vandal woman gave them another little push, and the smaller one began to whimper. The woman whispered something to her, and she stiffened, then stepped forward.

"Don't be afraid," Ammatas said. "We have treats." Gelimer held out a tempting tray of sweets and smiled, revealing rotten teeth.

A Roman slave appeared with a silver tray of sweetcakes, fresh fruits, and cheeses that the famished girls reached for and quickly finished off. The Vandal woman poked them in the back with a stick.

Ammatas snapped his fingers again, and the girls dressed in silks brought trays of sherbet, hesitantly moving their hips to the rhythm of a lyre.

"Their heart doesn't seem to be in this," Gelimer said sadly.

"We'll see about that," Ammatas said as he reclined on his divan and beckoned the girls to join him. The Vandal woman gave them a final push and then left.

As one of the girls shyly sat beside Ammatas, there was a loud commotion at the large double bronze doors. The guards had failed to prevent a young man from bursting into the room.

Gelimer waved the guards away. "What is it, nephew?" he asked Gibamundus.

"The Romans have just landed at Caput Vada and are headed for Carthage!"

"Are you sure?"

"Yes, uncle, a thousand ships have landed."

"Who is your source?" King Gelimer asked.

"A Vandal who managed your orchards near there said that the Romans descended like locusts. He estimates 25,000 Romans, nearly a third of them cavalry."

"Leave us!" Gelimer yelled at the girls, pushing them out of the room. "Sorry to spoil the party, brother. I was so looking forward to it, but I am afraid we have a war on our hands. Gibamundus, call up the army. They must prepare to march by first light tomorrow. I think it's time we paid a visit to the former king."

The twins descended to the palace dungeon. A skeletal figure, wearing only a loincloth, was chained to the wall.

"Hilderic, dear cousin," Gelimer said, "I have good news and bad news. Your rescue team has arrived, but they will never reach you."

He turned and made a subtle gesture, which his brother easily registered. Ammatas stepped forward and plunged a dagger deep into Hilderic's belly. The chained prisoner gasped and slumped forward, struggling for breath.

"Your old boy Justinian will be disappointed to learn of your early demise," Ammatas said.

"You...fools!" Hilderic said, gasping for air and spitting blood from his mouth. Gelimer and Ammatas jumped back. Hilderic grinned, and with a final bout of determination, he continued, "With no legitimate Vandal on the throne...," Hilderic struggled to catch his breath, "you have made our kingdom ripe for the picking by the Romans."

Ammatas plunged the dagger into Hilderic again and turned it upward until his heart exploded, spraying a shower of blood all over the two brothers. Hilderic gasped in pain and then expired. Gelimer wiped his face and watched in horror as the blood ran down Ammatas's hand and dripped off his elbow. Ammatas wiped his dagger on Hilderic's loincloth and sheathed it, then put both hands into Hilderic's open wound and rubbed them on his face as he stuck out his curled tongue. "Brother," he said, "Hilderic has joined our warrior fathers in Valhalla."[42]

"I think you enjoy murder too much," Gelimer said, disgusted by the gore and his brother's proclivity to treat dead men like slain animals.

---

[42] The great hall of the dead in Norse mythology where heroes slain in battle are received.

Ammatas scowled. "Someone has to do your dirty work. The Arian missionaries who persuaded you to follow the soft ways of the dead Jewish preacher did you no favors. No blood, no glory! Tomorrow, a committee will receive the Romans, and I will be the first to greet them."

"You're not afraid, brother?" Gelimer tugged nervously on the braids of his beard.

"We have beaten the Romans twice before and can do it again. Before the first frost, I promise you we will be in the palace having our way with those two girls."

"Hilderic's family will support the Romans and open the city's gates," Gelimer said.

"I think not, brother. Gibamundus and I will be sure every one of them is dead by nightfall."


When Gelimer returned to his chambers, he was surprised to find that the two girls had returned and were eating his sherbet. They looked at him in terror and looked for the nearest exit.

Gelimer screamed at them in his Vandal tongue and feigned a chase, and they disappeared through the servants' door. He kicked the silver platter across the room, shattering the dishes into a hundred pieces, then went to the palace kitchens, sat on the wet ice blocks, removed the crown from his head, and devoured sherbet until his stomach could hold no more.


Early the following day, the two brothers met on the parade grounds in the center of Carthage that served as a muster point for the Vandal cavalry and infantry. The sun shone brightly, and the army basked in its glow and eager anticipation for their generation's chance to kill some Romans. The sight of several thousand splendidly arrayed soldiers gathered before Gelimer filled him with hopeful confidence that had died with the last breath of Hilderic. He knew he needed to keep his apprehensions about the upcoming battle to himself. He had heard reports about Belisarius's surprising victory at Dara against the Persians and wondered if this was the same army the Vandals had been beating on land and sea for a century.

Gelimer was huddled with Ammatas, Gibamundus, and two cousins, both generals, their arms on each other's shoulders, as he instructed them in his plan to defeat the Romans.

"Brother," Gelimer said, "I am putting six-thousand men under your command to observe the Roman vanguard, which is now a day's march south of Carthage. Your mission is to distract their army and deceive them into believing we will attack them from the front. Only you and your men stand between the Romans and our capital city. Keep the lines of communication open."

"Gibamundus, you will have two-thousand men under your command. Your orders are similar: monitor the movements of the Roman left wing and engage it if the outcome promises to be favorable. I will sail east of Caput Vada, disembark, and attack the Roman rearguard with the largest part of our force."

"Brother, that is brilliant," Ammatas said, "They will never expect us to attack the rearguard. They are looking to encounter us with their vanguard while marching toward Carthage."

"Indeed," Gelimer said, "together, we will drive the Romans into the sea. And now, I must pray."

"We need warriors today, not saints, brother," Ammatas said.

After the others left him, Gelimer returned to the palace, grabbed his armor, headed for his small private chapel next to his bedchamber, and knelt to pray. He stared at the mosaic of Cyprian, the city's former bishop, above the high altar and did not like the stern look the saint gave him. Gelimer had seen the bishop as a harmless relic, but now, he seemed to stand in judgment over his actions as king. *You begin your reign with the murder of a cousin who trusted you, and now you seek God's favor?* the saint seemed ask. He tried to silence these unhelpful thoughts by uttering a retinue of pre-battle prayers as he donned his armor.

"Lord, prepare me for battle. I put on the armor of God: the girdle of truth, the breastplate of righteousness, the shield of faith, and the helmet of salvation." He looked at Cyprian again, who seemed to say: *this armor does not fit you, brother.* Even more loudly, Gelimer said, "Lord, I wield the sword of the Spirit. He picked up his sword and twirled it through the air. Cyprian's gaze showed strong disapproval. *Sheath your sword, for it belongs not to the Spirit.* Gelimer pointed the sword menacingly at the icon and said, "I am king and shall do as I please."

Gelimer left the chapel fully dressed for battle but still feeling unready. He tried to comfort himself by thinking of Ammatas, who was sure of their impending victory. *Ammatas is an optimist*, but Gelimer did not share his brother's optimism. His ancestors had defeated the Romans, and there was no reason to believe these upstarts would not meet the same fate. However, hesitancy lay at the bottom of his stomach. He could not go to battle in this state and needed a place to think without the judgment of dead men.

He went to the royal reception room and sat on his lonely throne, gripping the golden arms, thinking of all that had transpired since he had deposed Hilderic. His life had become too complicated, and the crown weighed heavily on his small head. Being king helped him make new friends, meet girls, and marry the most beautiful woman in the realm, but the stress it brought him made him wonder whether it was all worth it. *Mosaics of dead men in churches do not haunt the average peasant.* He wished his nobles had offered the throne to Ammatas. He had protested when they put him on the throne, but no one trusted his brother.

He loved Ammatas more than anyone, including his wife, formerly an enslaved lover. As boys in the Vandal court, they had played and trained for war together. Their kin had lobbied in support of Gelimer against their more prudent cousin Hilderic and unseated him, accusing him of lacking martial virtue. However, for them, Ammatas was a rash man with too much martial virtue. The rivalry between the two brothers took on a new intensity after Gelimer eclipsed his twin by assuming the throne. Ammatas was a tempestuous youth whose countenance was only distinguishable from his brother's by the elaborate tattoo on his face and neck. The mark was a punishment his father had forced upon him when he was twelve for blaming his mischief on his identical twin, "Now we'll be able to tell which of you is the rogue," he'd said.

After Ammatas and Gibamundus left Carthage, Gelimer met with his advisors in the palace *tablinum,* which the Vandals used as a war room. The mosaics reminded all inside of the great naval victory over the Romans a century before. A general named Genseric, a grandson of the Vandal king who had sacked Rome, walked to a bust of his forebear and said, "Your generals all strongly advise against putting Ammatas in a leadership position. He might try to turn the battle single-handedly. We should mount a coordinated attack to use our superior numbers to full effect."

Their mother burst into the room. "I must speak with you, Gelimer — and alone."

When he excused himself, she whispered, "I had a terrible dream about the coming battle. None of the palace treasures will mean anything if I lose a son. We may bring the wrath of God upon us. You sent your brother to destroy Hilderic's kin, but they are my beloved cousins and childhood playmates."

"We can no longer trust them."

"I beg you, Gelimer," she grabbed his hands and fell to her knees, "don't destroy the people I love. Keep your brother close. I fear his vanity and rashness will end his life prematurely, as it has nearly done so many times. Even as boys, you two were rivals, and that has worsened since you took the throne."

"Mother, he is one of the few generals I can still trust, and you know I could never control him. Please go back to your sewing and allow us to plan this war."

## CHAPTER SIXTEEN
# FIELD OF WRATH

*Of all the nations, the Vandal Kingdom was the most luxurious. They indulged in daily baths and enjoyed banquets abounding in the sweetest and the best that the earth and sea produced. They wore gold and silk and passed their time in theaters and hippodromes. They had dancers, mimes, and music, and all sexual pleasures were in great vogue among them.*

— *History of the Wars*, Procopius of Caesarea

*Ad Decimum, North Africa*
*September 13-14, 533 A.D.*

John the Armenian watched from behind the slope of a ridge as two thousand Vandal cavalrymen ventured out on the dusty road leading south from Carthage. John loved ridges and knew how to use them to hide his cavalry movements from the enemy even as he tracked their movements. The gentle hills still offered green grass to his horses and abundant fruit trees on abandoned orchards. His horses and men had been waiting for the Vandal garrison to emerge from the roads leading to Carthage. After several hours of hiding under the tree canopy from the dehydrating heat, the Vandals finally appeared.

They were a magnificent host: tall, handsome men with long, flowing blond hair wearing spotless armor that sparkled in the morning sun. John looked at the armor of his men. It was shiny but speckled with rust from three months on the humid sea. He thought about how easy it must be to maintain armor in a dry climate. Then he smiled to himself. *Yes, how easy.* He looked at his knuckles, rough and callused from rubbing sand onto the rust spots of his helmet and wondered how the hands of the Vandals looked. *Probably soft, like their women's.* He laughed at his smug vanity.

"Dear God," Uliaris cried, "Look at them all! Does Belisarius expect the three hundred of us to stop them?"

John snapped out of the gaze on his rough hands and gave Uliaris a stern look. Uliaris had the same Germanic blood as the Vandals, but it must have been bred out of him. He had a large aquiline nose, dark curly hair, and skin reddened by the sun. A veteran of the Persian War, he had known nothing but combat for half his life, and he was as ready a soldier as Rome could fashion so long as he was sober.

"Perhaps not stop them, but slow them down and warn him," John replied steadily.

"It's a suicide mission."

"You underestimate the element of surprise," John said.

"Yes, we'll surprise them when they wonder why such an inferior force would attack them."

"No, Uliaris, we will surprise them when they encounter, for the first time, mounted archers who kill them before their lances can reach us. These Vandals have no bows. It took us a hundred years to understand how to defeat the Hunnish mounted archers. The Vandals won't figure out how to do it in a single battle." John smiled and winked at Uliaris.

John waited until the Vandals were in perfect position, then he signaled his men to show themselves at the top of the ridge. There was a commotion in the Vandal ranks as they yelled enthusiastically about the possibility of a morning skirmish. Their leader rode to the front of their ranks and made a hand signal that caused their double line of men to fall into four lines. A knight in golden armor prompted his magnificent horse into a full gallop, breaking away from his unit. John ordered his men down the ridge in a horseshoe pattern to receive the charging Vandal lancers at a safe distance. When the Vandals were within a hundred paces, he gave the "loose" command, and three hundred archers launched their arrows. The golden knight moved before the rest, lowered his lance, and headed straight for John.

"Kill the golden lancer!" John yelled as he put away his bow and took out his shield and lance. He realized that his gilded armor had singled him out.

The Roman cavalry archers loosed a second flurry of arrows at the target, most of them missing, some lancing off the knight's armor, but three managed to penetrate. They launched a third barrage against the men who appeared to guard the golden knight and felled several of them. Still, the golden knight, now pricked with arrows, made straight for John. *Is this a man or a demon on this steed?*

The golden knight's lance thrust slammed into John's small shield and threw him violently to the ground. John's hand stretched out in front of him in a failed effort to brace his fall. As his hand hit the rocky ground underneath him, he held on to his sword and tried to stand up to confront his assailant and show his men that, though dismounted, he was still in fighting condition. However, he was unable. He felt a throbbing in his shoulder that concerned him but would have to wait until after the battle to address. The golden knight dropped his lance and began slashing and cutting the Roman knights gathered around their fallen commander.

John watched from the ground as his guards threw *plumbatae*[43], fired arrows, and finally began hacking at the bloody gap in the neck between the armor and helmet of the golden knight. As the horse hooves stomped around him, kicking dust into his face, he had difficulty seeing what was happening, but every few seconds, he would feel a burst of liquid on his face. John did not know if it was human blood or horse piss, perhaps a combination of both, but he soon found himself covered in it. Something hard hit him in the face, and after recovering from the blow, he realized it was a man's severed arm. He looked above him as its owner hosed him down in more blood before falling on top of him.

He struggled to stand and raise his small shield to strike something before realizing that the fall had dislocated his left shoulder. As the shield dropped from his useless arm, he looked for his horse, but it was nowhere to be seen. He knew he was an infantryman now, and the prospect made him feel like a dwarf among gi-

---

[43] Lead-weighted throwing darts

ants. He joined his guards trying to bring down the golden knight and those surrounding him. The golden knight and his guards hacked to death a dozen of John's men before Uliaris, the scourged pear thief, got behind him and struck him with a hard blow of his sword to the throat. The knight fell to the ground, and his bodyguards panicked.

John looked at the sight of the dead knight, lying amid blood, hacked limbs, and intestines, and it seemed surreal. He had seen depictions of Hell in church artwork, and it all seemed too fantastic — until now. The damned dead were not naked — yet — and no monsters or flames shot up from cracks on the ground, but otherwise, it was a horrifying vision.

When the Vandals saw the golden knight go down, his two-thousand-man unit began to falter. *Thanks be to God,* John thought as he looked for deliverance from the horror around him. Roman arrows felled most of them well before they reached the Roman line. When half of them were either dead or wounded, they realized they were no match for the mounted archers and began a hasty retreat. *He thought it must have been like this for the Romans who first encountered the Hunnish mounted archers.*

Uliaris helped John to recover his horse and remount.

"Pursue them!" John shouted. "Shoot at them until your arrows run out, and then charge them with lances!" John found his horse, carefully remounted it, and followed his cavalry as they slew the Vandals who fell behind in the retreat.

As the Romans chased the fleeing Vandals and approached the walls of Carthage, the Vandal garrison showered them with arrows. John heard two arrows bounce off his helmet and raised his sword to call for a retreat. "Halt! Fall back!"

He watched as the gates of Carthage opened to the retreating Vandals. "Return to our starting point. Gather the wounded along the way."

When John and his men returned to the hilltop ridge, they found dead Vandals everywhere, but only a few dead Romans. A *medicus* tended to the Roman wounded until he saw John, leaning to the left like a tree ready to fall. John, who had forgotten his injury in the heat of the battle, groaned again when he lifted his shoulder. The *medicus* examined John's shoulder and said, "You know what I need to do."

John nodded and braced himself as the *medicus* grabbed his back and shoulder, snapped the joint into its proper place, and put his arm in a sling. John cried out in pain, and medicus stepped back, afraid that John might strike him.

The golden knight's body had enough arrows to fill a small quiver. John pulled the helmet from the face, partially tearing off part of the skin on his smashed-in cheek.

Uliaris said, "He fought like a demon. Even with six arrows in his chest. Who was he?"

"I don't know," John said, wiping blood off the face of the warrior. "Somebody's dead son or brother."

Uliaris leaned closer for a good look and said, "Look at that tattoo."

"Is that a pitchfork?" John asked.

"No, I think it's a runic letter symbolizing fortune and protection."

"It didn't work very well for him."

"No," Uliaris agreed, "tattoos are poor substitutes for common sense."

Belisarius worried as he wondered what had become of John. It had been several hours since a courier had delivered news that a sizeable Vandal cavalry force had departed from Carthage. *John must have attacked it.* No news, however, was usually bad news, so he sent a courier out to learn of John's status. His army was blind in the vanguard with John's forces not reporting. If John had attacked, it must not have been the main force since John's three hundred cavalrymen would have been overwhelmed. He found comfort in that analysis but wondered if it meant that Gelimer's main force had somehow managed to get behind him and attack his rear. *That is what I would do.* He gave orders to reinforce his rearguard and pull stragglers up immediately.

The main Roman force-marched west along the coast toward the ten-mile mark from the Vandal capital of Carthage. A courier soon after arrived and reported that John's unit had engaged a superior number of Vandal cavalry, soundly defeated them, and chased them back to Carthage. Hours later, they arrived where John had engaged the golden knight and the garrison from Carthage. They waited for word of the location of the enemy's main forces.

Belisarius surveyed the carnage. "What happened here, John?"

"The Vandal lancers charged in a disorderly manner, designed to instill fear rather than break our ranks. We took out their leader, and they faltered."

"And then you chased them back to Carthage?"

"Exactly."

"Good. Let us hope they stay there. Well done, John," he said as he slapped him on the shoulder to a loud groan. "Trouble with that shoulder again?" John nodded with a grimace.

As they spoke, Sunicas arrived. "We spotted a Vandal scouting party on a hill." He shook his head and laughed, "These Vandals had never seen what Hunnish mounted archers could do. They charged, and we feigned a retreat. Then we formed two lines and did loops around them while shooting arrows into their ranks. Several Vandals tried to pursue us but could not catch us, rendering their lances useless. By the third lap around the Vandals, they ordered a retreat into the salt pan."

"Did you pursue them?" Belisarius asked.

"Yes, until we ran out of arrows. The Vandals left several hundred dead and wounded, including a golden knight. We lanced the wounded Vandal stragglers."

"Well done, Sunicas," Belisarius said. "Now, we need to find the main Vandal force."

"If I had to guess, I would say it's hidden behind the main force, or our scouts would have spotted them by now," Sunicas said.

"The two main forces have not yet met, and only a fraction of our forces has engaged in skirmishes, but it seems the momentum of the battle may be turning in our favor," Belisarius said. He walked through the corpse-littered battlefield, kicking away black rats that swarmed over the dead. The rats had chewed off part of the face of the man in the golden armor, exposing his skull. "I hate rats," Belisarius said.

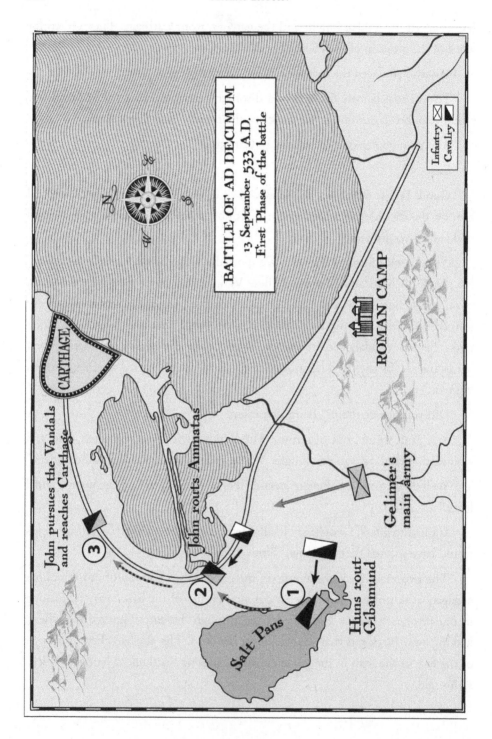

BATTLE OF AD DECIMUM
13 September 533 A.D.
First Phase of the battle

Infantry
Cavalry

ROMAN CAMP

Gelimer's
main army

CARTHAGE

John pursues the Vandals
and reaches Carthage

John routs Ammatas

③

②

①

Salt Pans

Huns rout
Gibamund

From the crest of the hill, he looked south at a large cloud of dust chasing a smaller one. "We should be getting more messages from the couriers. Where are they?"

"Several couriers are arriving now," Procopius replied. "Should I gather the general staff?"

Belisarius nodded, and the mounted generals gathered around him.

The first courier from the Roman rearguard rode up, "General, the main force has been spotted, and the rearguard is now engaged in an orderly retreat."

"That's all you have for me?" Belisarius asked. The courier nodded.

A few minutes later, a second courier arrived. "I'm not sure how long they'll hold on," he reported. "They're vastly outnumbered."

"Is it Gelimer?" Belisarius asked.

His generals shrugged, except for Constantinus. "More than likely. He's about five miles out and headed straight for us."

"From the south. Quite clever. I might have expected that."

"How did he get behind us?" Constantinus asked.

"We saw the Vandal navy land a force to the east of Caput Vada," the courier reported. They have been paralleling the movement of our main force about five miles south — just on the south side of that ridge. Shortly after we spotted Gelimer's standard, Vandal scouts gave chase, intercepting us and eventually putting us to rout. I may be the only survivor from my unit. What are we going to do, sir?"

Belisarius bit his lower lip. "We're going to continue advancing another mile north and prepare for battle."

Constantinus stepped forward. "No, General, we should prepare to engage them here."

Belisarius gave his haughty general a weary look. "We would miss an incredible opportunity if we did that. Signalman, sound the horn! We will assemble and march north."

"General, this is insane," Constantinus protested.

Belisarius took a deep breath and sought the assistance of providence to deal with the officer who seemed to question every command. "Constantinus, go join your men and proceed north at once."

After they had marched a mile, with the sea on their right and rolling green hills on their left, Belisarius ordered his men to halt and fall into battle formation. The infantry quickly dug trenches and put stakes in front of their positions to prepare for a Vandal charge. Belisarius took a place with his generals by his side and watched with pride how diligently the Roman infantry performed their task. He knew they hated spade work, but they knew that an infantry unit behind trenches and stakes was nearly impenetrable, and now was as good a time as any to take camp building seriously. The news of the cavalry's successes had buoyed spirits, and the infantrymen were eager to have a chance to prove themselves in battle.

The Vandals closed in and occupied the ground less than a mile away. Belisarius took a position in the center of the main force and waited for the approaching dust cloud.

Within minutes, the frenzied remnants of the Roman rearguard crashed into the main Roman force and quickly found their places in the infantry square. Their proximity with the larger Roman force restored their confidence. The Romans faced their enemy to the south and waited, and waited, and waited.

From his slightly elevated vantage point, Belisarius could see a mounted Vandal in gilded armor arrive at the spot where the first golden knight had fallen. Dust climbed up to meet the Vandal, who surveyed the dead, dismounted from his steed, and dropped to his knees in apparent distress. Then Belisarius heard a primordial scream from the man, which he knew he would not soon forget.

"Is that Gelimer?" Uliaris wondered aloud.

"Perhaps," John said. "And is rat face his twin brother?"

They heard another anguished cry as the man they suspected to be King Gelimer beheld his brother's partially consumed and lifeless body. The wretched man rocked the corpse back and forth in his arms and wailed. He stripped off his armor and began beating himself on the head in a show of inconsolable grief. After a while, he stared in the direction of the Roman army.

"What's he doing?" Procopius asked just as Belisarius's best scout, Squintus, arrived.

"He's grieving," Squintus said. "That knight must have been his twin Ammatas. I've heard they were close."

"But we're in the middle of a battle," Procopius protested and then paused. "Is that why we retreated? So we could demoralize him just before the battle?"

"Exactly," Belisarius said, looking at Constantinus. "Military history should have taught you that the best time to attack is when your enemy doesn't want to fight."

"You're lucky he hasn't attacked while we gather our forces and dig trenches," Constantinus said as he took a cloth and wiped the dust off his black armor and helmet.

Gelimer's commanders gathered around him, seemingly waiting for orders from their king and expecting his rage to fill him with a new determination. The captain of the scouts spoke to Gelimer, who rose and engaged him in conversation.

"What do you suppose he's saying?" Procopius asked.

"I suspect he's recommending that the Vandals attack now before we've consolidated all our forces," Belisarius replied. "Are our scouting parties assembled?"

Pharas nodded, "All but a few scattered units."

"And what do you suppose Gelimer is saying?" Procopius asked.

The Vandals carried the body of the fallen golden knight behind their front line and disappeared. "Gelimer has been undone by the sight of the rats feeding on his brother. He will want to mourn and bury him."

"Has he lost his senses?" Procopius asked. "No one buries their dead in the middle of a battle."

"Procopius, when you're the king, you do as you like," Belisarius replied, "even if that means the entire Vandal host joins in a requiem mass and prays on the battlefield for his deceased brother."

In front of his men, Belisarius always tried to sound confident, but he wanted to be sure. He called his scouts to debrief them on Gelimer's movements.

General Solomon, his third in command, told him, "You will be surprised to learn that, according to a half-Roman defector, the Vandals are assembling to pray for the repose of Ammatas's soul."

"How much time of mourning must we give the grieving monarch before we attack?" Belisarius asked with a grin.

"If you were to wait for the final benediction, that would be very generous."

"Ten minutes then? The trenches are nearly complete, and Sunicas's Huns should be in position in Gelimer's rear by then."

"Yes, if the liturgy of these Arian heretics is anything like ours," Solomon replied.

"Sound the advance trumpet! Officers, take your positions."

At the sound of the trumpet, every man ran about into position and tightened the buckles of his armor. Belisarius called the commander of his infantry forward, "I am counting on you to ensure their discipline and focus on the task — not on the prospects for enriching themselves by pilfering from the slain enemy. Too many battles are lost because the infantry forgot why they came to the field."

"We learned our lesson in Persia, General!" The commander was unable to look Belisarius in the eye. He had a history of failing to focus his men on the battle.

"Make sure of that, or this will be your last command," Belisarius replied.

From his position at the center of the Roman line, Belisarius watched the armored men march south in perfect unison toward Gelimer's main force, like the formidable Roman legions of old, advancing across the plain to the beat of the drums. He surveyed the open field before him, covered in dried grass and dotted with piles of sheep manure. As 45,000 men marched on the fragile turf, the air tasted like the dust of the Sahara. Belisarius licked his dry lips and put a finger to his ears to remove the dust. He had not had a proper bath in three months and longed for the fertile plains of his native Thrace.[44]

---

[44] Area west of Constantinople

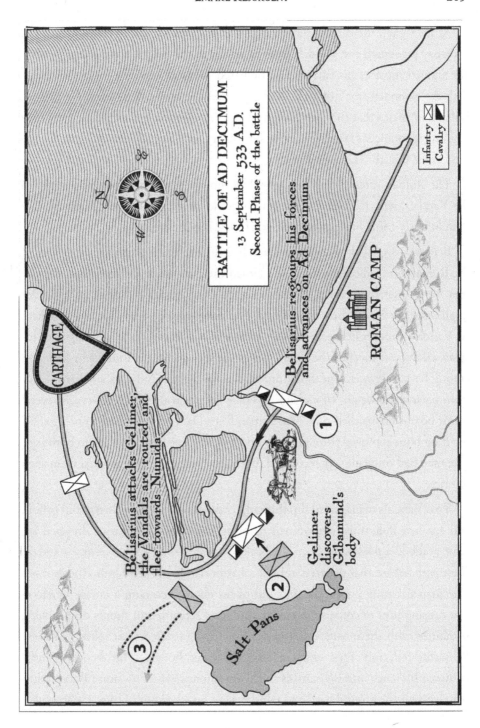

BATTLE OF AD DECIMUM
13 September 533 A.D.
Second Phase of the battle

Infantry
Cavalry

CARTHAGE

ROMAN CAMP

1 Belisarius regroups his forces
and advances on Ad Decimum

2 Geliner discovers
Gibamund's body

3 Belisarius attacks Geliner,
the Vandals are routed and
flee towards Numida

Salt Pans

At his signal, the cavalry moved slightly ahead on the flanks. Behind them, a wide bay prevented the Vandals from attacking at the rear. Belisarius had personally trained most of his cavalry and prepared them to assault a force unfamiliar with the extended reach of archers using composite bows. Were these Vandals so isolated in Africa that they were unaware of the evolution of warfare, or were they feigning ignorance? Had the first two skirmishes been ruses? Belisarius spat out the dust in his mouth. "Let's find out."

The Roman mounted archers launched thousands of arrows into the ranks of the Vandals, who fell before their lancers could close the distance. Then the Roman infantry came into range and added their missile fire.

Belisarius signaled his *bucellarii* to advance with the infantry in the center of the Roman line. The Roman cavalry aimed their arrows at the front line because they were closer and because there was a good chance that a falling horse and rider might take out two or three other horses and riders whose paths were now blocked. As Vandals counter-charged, Roman arrows flew into the sky like a plague of locusts, taking out most of the riders. Belisarius thought of the injuries he had seen among his cavalrymen: the worst ones were not from sword cuts and arrows but from having the weight of a charging horse fall upon the man and crush several major bones. He recalled one infantryman from Dara who had had a horse's shattered leg bone removed from his skull and had all three bones broken in both legs. The man had miraculously recovered, but many others never recovered from such injuries.

Two Vandals managed to slip through, crashed into the *bucellarii* at full gallop, and reached Belisarius, determined to bring him down. Belisarius dropped his bow, grabbed a *plumbatae* from the back of his shield, and threw it at a Vandal's chest with a force that penetrated his steel armor and knocked him to the ground. The man defiantly pulled the dart out of his chest, loosening a deluge of blood and causing him to collapse. A steady throng of screams and shouts of the living combined with the moans and groans of the dying created a cacophony of noise Belisarius felt only Hell could exceed for sheer horror. The second Vandal slammed his lance into Belisarius's shield and threw him off his horse Bucephalus. Belisarius hit the ground hard and felt the wind knocked out of him. He struggled to catch his breath and examined his shield arm: sore but unbroken. As Belisarius struggled to get up, his retainers surrounded him and helped him remount. Furious, Belisarius made straight for the Vandal, who was hacking one of his guards, striking him in the back of the neck with his sword. Blood spouted from the Vandal's severed neck like a fountain, and only tendons kept his bobbing head attached to the body. Belisarius nervously grinned at the bodyguards. The Vandal's horse turned and galloped back to the line with a nearly headless rider — horrifying the second wave of attacking Vandals.

The Roman centerline continued to advance and repel most of the Vandal charges. Belisarius took his bow and aimed at a Vandal lancer riding toward him from forty paces off. He released the string, and as the arrow struck the knight in the throat, he somersaulted backward from his horse. The horse stopped, hindering the advance of the knight behind him. Belisarius watched as blood came gargling up from the man's lungs, and he began to drown in his blood.

Belisarius heard the swoosh of hundreds of arrows speeding through the air behind him and watched knight after Vandal knight fall before reaching the Roman line. The few who made it through were so riddled with arrows they had no strength to fight. Still, new human waves kept coming, and Belisarius wondered how many more were ahead.

He knew the Vandals outnumbered his army, but the dust of the battle prevented him from assessing the size of Gelimer's army. Fear of the unknown began to work on him. How were his flanks holding? Had Sunicas's archers been able to attack the Vandal rear? He looked at the dead young Vandals lying about him and wondered what made them rush into certain death. *Is it the zeal of older men telling Horaces's old lie? "It is sweet and fitting to die for the fatherland." Yet how much sweeter still to live for the fatherland? They will never know now.*

He looked behind him and saw no sign of the Vandals neither in the rear nor the flanks, but as he rode closer to the Vandal line, he realized that Gelimer's army was completely inundated with unreturned missile fire. His men had fought bravely and wisely. The Vandals were losing their cohesion, dispersing to the west in fear of John's vanguard to the north. Belisarius kicked his horse and ordered his cavalry to pursue them in full gallop. He worried that it had been too easy, that the Vandals were luring him into a feigned withdrawal. He spotted John and called out desperately, "Find Gelimer!"

He was wary of being drawn into *terra incognita*, where Gelimer had been trying to rally his fence-sitting Moorish allies. If his vanguard advanced any further, they would become disconnected from the infantry who had barely engaged in battle and struggled to keep up with the galloping equestrians.

John rode up. "Gelimer is gone. We won't catch him before dark. Further pursuit is too dangerous."

"I'll make that call," Belisarius said. One remaining golden knight, Gelimer's household guard, and his swiftest cavalry had managed to escape the melee, but most of the Vandals had been cut down or surrendered. He realized that his hopes for a single, decisive battle to defeat the Vandals were unattainable. Without any further direction, John resumed his search for Gelimer.

Mutilated and bleeding corpses littered the ground as far as the eye could see. He gave the nod, and his foot soldiers rummaged through the pockets of the dead. The sight of this had bothered Belisarius when he was younger, but he was more pragmatic now. *Dead soldiers do not need their gold, and living ones are underpaid.* He also knew that if his men did not perform the task, plenty of others would.

Sunicas slapped Belisarius on the shoulders. "The day is yours, Flavius. These Vandals were fighting yesterday's war."

"This day belongs to the Devil," Belisarius said as he surveyed the death around him. "Nevertheless, your men performed brilliantly today, Sunicas." He wiped the sweat off his brow and caught his breath.

Procopius rode up. "We estimate the Vandal casualties at 20,000."

Belisarius shook his head in sad disbelief. As the sun slowly began to set, he watched distraught Vandal prisoners forced to dig trenches to bury their comrades. Vandal wives and mothers appeared on the battlefield and wandered about with torches, weeping, in search of the bodies of their husbands, fathers, and sons. A wailing woman crawled into the burial trench and turned the heads of the dead, dreading the sight of a familiar face. Vandal gravediggers stopped to help her, but their new Roman overlords confronted them. The Roman guards pointed to the still-hot setting sun and the scavengers circling overhead, but Belisarius gave them a stern look.

The victorious generals somberly rode their horses around the battlefield as the infantry rounded up lightly wounded Vandal prisoners. The Huns collected their arrows from the field and pulled them from Vandal corpses as though they had more value than the lives of the men they had taken. A Hunnish archer gleefully yanked an arrow from a dying Vandal, its barbs catching on his organs and ribs as he screamed and writhed in pain, then lay lifeless.

Under the eyes of Belisarius and their captains, the infantry stripped the chain-mail from the dead Vandals and stacked it in carts. "The Empire will improve our infantry equipment today," one captain said, laughing.

Belisarius gave the captain a somber glance as another cart stacked with dead Vandals arrived at a mass grave. *Suffer the hardness with good cheer.* The words of Horace reminded him but failed to convince him.

As he rode about the field, littered with the wounded, Belisarius recognized several of his *bucellarii,* including Arzes. An arrow had stuck Arzes between the nose and right eye, penetrating almost to the back of the neck. He watched in amazement as the missile bounced up and down as the cavalryman, paying no heed to his wound, continued to ride.

"Soldier, see the *medicus* at once." Obediently, Arzes followed Belisarius to his Greek surgeon's tent. Upon seeing the general, he stood up from his seated position beside another patient and attended him. "What can I do for you...?"

"My man..."

"Oh...yes, sit down, boy." The doctor took hold of the man's neck.

"The barb is just below the skin," the doctor said. "Miraculously, you will lose neither your eye nor your life." He cut off the shaft of the arrow. "Close your eyes." Belisarius could only guess what was coming next and was all at once grateful that the sight of blood and guts did not cause him to faint. Then the surgeon took a knife to the soldier's neck. The man let out a furious shriek at the pain of the incision. "Hold him down!" The surgeon instructed. Belisarius complied and pressed down firmly on the soldier's shoulders. Within seconds, the doctor care-fully removed the barb and the remaining part of the shaft, sanitized the wound with wine, and stitched it up.

"You can let go of him now, General." Belisarius breathed a sigh of relief and released his man. Arzes opened his eyes, and a small, tired smile formed on his mouth. *Thank God!* Feeling like he needed to reward the man's bravery, he handed something to the man. "I have a gift for you." It was Ammatas's helmet and visor. "This will hide the nasty scar."

The soldier started to laugh but stopped almost immediately due to the pain. "It pains me."

"I'll whip any man who tries to make you laugh," Belisarius grinned, gripping the man's knee in solidarity.

After being reassured that the man would receive all the care he needed, Beli-sarius rode to where the once-formidable Vandal line stood. Most of the dead had received arrows in their backs as they tried to flee the Roman archers. *What a waste of life*, he thought.

General Solomon rode alongside him. "Gelimer is fleeing south toward Nu-midia[45] — probably hoping to reunite the remnants of his forces. Our spies tell us that Tzazon has brutally put down the rebellion in Sardinia and is making his way back to Africa."

"So, the Vandals are not yet defeated. We will need to repeat this slaughter," Belisarius said, wiping the sweat from his brow. "I had hoped to destroy the Vandal Kingdom in a single battle. Where is John?"

"He is near the gates of Carthage, General," Solomon replied. "Don't worry."

When Belisarius and his generals reached John and his scouts, John rode up close and reported, "Tzazon is bringing five thousand of the best Vandal warriors with him from Sardinia. He could land within the week."

"And they have proven themselves in battle," Belisarius said.

---

[45] Area in North Africa west of Carthage

When the city gates were in sight, Belisarius ordered his troops to bivouac on a nearby hill for the night to avoid risking an ambush from the city in the dark. His men quickly made camp with trenches and pikes around the perimeter. He knew he didn't need Vandals coming like wolves in the night and stealing the victory." *What treachery will the night bring,* he asked himself.

The following day, Belisarius was amazed as they approached the outer city walls of Carthage. Never in his wildest dreams had he imagined that the citizens would line the streets waving palm fronds and tossing flower petals at the feet of the conquering heroes. The Carthaginians offered his men loaves of bread and goblets of wine as the liberating heroes rode through the city. The Latin-speaking Roman residents of Carthage hailed Belisarius as the new Africanus, a compliment he could not begin to accept.

Constantinus's murmurs helped Belisarius keep perspective. "Gelimer is no Hannibal, and you are no Scipio. If Gelimer had charged before we had gathered all our forces, or if he had cut off John and destroyed our fleet, we'd all be dead."

From atop his broad warhorse, Belisarius could see the hidden citizens, Carthaginian women easily distinguished from the Romans by their dispositions, their anxiety on display for any who cared to look, their misery heightened by the sight of Vandal captives harnessed together like a long train of horses. He scanned the faces of the crowd, trying to decipher the people's genuine sentiments. He saw Romans waving their fists in the air and shouting encouragement. Many women were dressed in fine silken stolas and offered the soldiers affectionate embraces and kisses.

As Belisarius rode down the streets, a Vandal woman with a child in each hand called out, "What will become of us?"

A woman with six young children huddled around her asked, "Where are you taking our men?"

And a third cried, "We have taken sacred vows to our husbands. You, a Christian, cannot take them from us!"

Others inquired about the future of their property and children. *I have no interest in governing these people. I need to find someone who does.* He watched as Solomon, one of his less able generals, began competently addressing the crowd's concerns. *He will do.*

When they arrived at the former Roman governor's palace, which Belisarius had designated as his military headquarters, Antonina greeted him with a relieved embrace and warm kiss at the entrance of the *tablinum.*

"Flavius, what will you do with the women? They have been hovering at the palace gates for days now, shouting at me!"

"Nothing," he responded dryly.

"What do you mean? What will become of them if you deport their men and confiscate their property?"

"They'll have to seek new arrangements."

"New arrangements? Are you so cold?"

"I have my orders. What do you want me to do? I cannot leave them here! They'll revolt."

"If you take away their men and property, they will either be forced to prostitute themselves or break their wedding vows and take up Roman lovers."

Belisarius refused to look at her. He was weary from battle and wanted to wash the blood off his face. He knew his talents were on the battlefield, not in the courtroom. *Why is my wife obsessed with everyone's concerns but mine?* "Antonina, these decisions are beyond my control."

"No, they are not. Write to Justinian and Theodora. Explain what will happen. Ask for a policy that does not penalize the women for the wrongdoings of their men."

Done with the conversation, Belisarius turned on his wife and shouted, "I have no influence over such matters, wife!" By the look of dismay on her face, he was not surprised when she stormed out of the room.

# CHAPTER SEVENTEEN
# UNHAPPY WOMEN

*A woman is fully capable of being faithful. Temptation is not her weakness. All she wants is love, attention, honesty, and loyalty. Before she cheats, she will whine, cry, and complain about everything that makes her unhappy. It's a warning before destruction. Pay attention.... Never make her feel single, or she will act as such.*

— Anonymous

*North Africa*
*Fall A.D. 533*

Antonina was restless and upset. She had not seen her husband in weeks. The lonely wife knew he was coordinating mop-up operations of remnants of Vandal forces but wondered why his work so often precluded him from joining her for dinner or sharing her bed. She knew he had a hundred things to do but could not understand why seeing his wife was not one of them. She wished she had stayed at home in Constantinople with her daughter like the other officers' wives. A domestic brought her a tray of fresh fruit and cheese. She feigned a grateful smile.

She walked over to a desk and sat down in the *tablinum* of Gelimer's palace to write a letter to the Empress. She stared at a happy marble statue of Eros with an arrow pointed at her. She glowered at it and hissed, "Aim your useless weapon at my husband, fool!" She regretted that all her female friends were so far away. Whenever she found herself at variance with her husband, she wrote to Theodora. Not that the practice granted her any comfort or reprieve, as she knew it took at least six months for her friend's reply to reach her. She was lonely and realized that coming on the campaign had been a mistake. She was not doing her friend any favors since Flavius only consulted her when he needed her to plan a special meal.

After an hour of carefully writing a letter with her best penmanship, the sounds of laughing outside the door interrupted her silent brooding and raised her spirits slightly. Theodosius burst into the room wearing a pointed white hat, white knitted socks, and a short, multi-colored tunic stuffed with padding in the middle to make him appear absurdly fat. He had whitened his face and painted a silly red grimace nearly reaching his ears.

Antonina looked up and, despite not wanting to, laughed. "Stupidus!"[46] she cried, trying to conceal her delight while wiping a tear from her eyes that fell on her letter, smearing the ink and ruining it. She crumpled the paper and threw it at him, feigning anger. She half-expected him to run out of the room at her jeering response to his uninvited arrival. But instead, Theodosius pranced around her, mimicking her, tossing the paper in a ridiculous, child-like manner. *This foolishness is just what I need,* she thought to herself.

Theodosius's ocean green eyes did not leave hers. Antonina quickly wiped her face clean of any makeup that her tears had smudged and resettled her long flowing cream-colored tunic across her lap. Part of her wondered why he was even there, but another part was happy that he was. Antonina bit her lip to restrain a moan from leaving her lips. The unrestrained side of her wanted to rip his ridiculous clothes off to reveal his true form. *What a clown. He knows how beautiful he is.* But to think, much less do, such a thing would be a betrayal. *Would it be worth it, though?* Not wanting her thoughts to be too obvious, she turned away from him. He gently rested his hands on her shoulders and began to massage them. The motion caused her body to relax and her mind to forget that he shouldn't be there with her, alone. "What is a beautiful woman like you doing crying by herself?"

*He thinks I'm beautiful?* The thought made her body quiver with desire. She shook her head violently, loosening the tight bun expected of an honorable lady. *I cannot be thinking these things! No! Be rude; it's better that way.*

She brushed his hands off her shoulders and turned to face him.

---

[46] A famous Roman clown known to play the mimic fools and mock people thought to be too serious.

"A man would never understand. You're all alike."

"Try me." She had to think of what to tell this boy. She did not intend to share her marital grief with him.

"What will happen when all the Vandal men in Carthage are deported to Persia, leaving the women with no one?"

"The birth rate will drop." He suggested, smiling broadly.

Antonina tried to resist a smile but couldn't. "Oh, Theodosius, you always know how to cheer me." She looked at his ludicrous attire and laughed before trying hard to be serious again. "There will be an insurrection. We women are not powerless. An unhappy woman makes an unhappy home. There will be riots in the streets."

"Have you spoken with my godfather?" Theodosius said as he removed his hat and the padding inside his tunic.

"If he is ever around, he dismisses everything I say."

"Perhaps you might approach the Empress. You have far more influence with her than he has with the Emperor."

"That's exactly what I was trying to do when you burst in here and caused me to ruin my letter." Antonina's face softened when she saw the hurt on Theodosius's face. "But thank you for listening."

As he left the room, her eyes followed the man under the red tunic, watching the movement of his tight muscular calves as he glided out the door. He knew how to keep a woman's eye.

Belisarius walked alone through the streets of Carthage. The city had taken on a carnival atmosphere since its emancipation, as the people celebrated in the streets. Almost every house had lit a candle in the window to welcome the liberators. Bells rang triumphantly as Vandal refugees sought sanctuary in the churches. *No man is without honor except in his own home*, Belisarius thought. His army had done more than conquer Carthage. They had won the hearts of its Roman population, as well.

As he rode to Gelimer's palace, a clown with a familiar face passed him, but the face paint prevented recognition. As he dismounted, he surveyed the anxious staff and assured them their lives were not in danger. A clever, elderly gentleman appeared to head the royal staff and welcomed him in perfect Latin. "General Belisarius, we have prepared a feast for the victor. While you and your men are not the guests we originally expected, we ought not waste this luscious food."

Belisarius smiled and invited his officers into the banquet hall. Men who hadn't had a decent meal in four months sat before a heavenly feast of peppered steak served on silver plates and poured wine in gold goblets. Belisarius motioned for his reluctant men to sit at the table. They followed orders with weary eyes, but none would partake of the feast. Procopius, speaking for many of the officers gathered, turned to Belisarius and whispered, "General, having slain our foes on the battlefield, are we now to die of poison at the table?"

Frustrated, Belisarius slapped his scribe roughly on the shoulders and stood up. "Is this why you sit there and refuse to dine? Pick up your knives and eat! Our hosts were slaves, most Roman, and we have liberated them. Now that they are free, they won't risk their lives with the sort of dishonorable deed we have so often seen in Constantinople!"

He signaled the chief of the royal staff, removed two goblets from the head of the table, and politely asked him to fill them with wine. He looked around the room at the domestics to gauge their disposition, then handed one cup to the majordomo[47] and took the other for himself. "A toast to your liberator, the Roman Emperor." He raised his cup, and the majordomo did likewise. Procopius moved to slap the cup from his hand, but Belisarius restrained him, tipped it back, and drank down the wine. His officers nervously waited for him to fall over dead, but he did not. After a moment, the servant drank the wine, and a moment later, when their general was still standing, the officers breathed a collective sigh of relief. "There! Now eat!" The men roared their acceptance and happily followed orders.

Belisarius began to enjoy the delicacies before him. As he reached for a string of plump grapes, two beautiful young girls approached him, fell to their knees, and smothered his hands with kisses. They were draped in the classical attire of Greek

---

[47] The chief steward of a large household.

sculptures, and their wide, dark brown eyes were moist. Their dramatic gesture moved him, and he smiled and brought them to their feet.

"General Belisarius, we would speak with you," they said in Greek. The sorrow in their eyes and the innocence in their faces made it impossible to deny them. "Yes, speak."

"We are Roman citizens from Crete. A month ago, Vandal pirates raided our village, captured all the young women, and brought them here. We beg you; please find a way to bring us home."

Belisarius studied them and kissed their hands in return. *This is precisely why we came here*, he thought. He remembered the time as a teenager when he, Pharas, and Sunicas had freed the young women whom Bulgarian Huns had carried off to enslave. He thought of his mother, killed in the escape attempt. He thought of her last words to him, "Keep our people safe," and smiled, knowing he had fulfilled his promise.

"We shall send a ship there tomorrow," he said. "And thank you, young ladies. For me, this is the best part of the job."

The girls jumped up and down in glee and clapped their hands. "General," one said, "a few days ago, we would have leaped from a palace window to save our honor. We will never forget your kindness." Belisarius introduced them to the ship's captain, who took them to the docks, and then the general returned to his meal.

His mind was so full of the satisfaction of helping them and the tenderness of their soft hands holding his that he barely noticed his wife's arms or the sweetness of her breath upon his neck. He turned around, kissed her, and wondered whether his previous attention had touched a jealous nerve. He gently kissed her hand and then turned to the guests seated beside him. The men at the long table seemed to be enjoying themselves. They were eating, drinking enthusiastically, laughing, and telling fireside military life stories. Procopius alone refused the refreshments.

"Surely something must suit your fancy," Belisarius said.

"Of course, but...."

"Yet you see that I have not been poisoned."

Procopius smiled and downed a goblet of wine.

Belisarius stood and addressed his officers. "Today is the Feast of Saint Cyprian, a bishop of this great city and a martyr of the Faith. When this war is over and we are safely home, remember with pride what you have accomplished here! On the vigil of this day, invite your neighbors to your table and say, 'These wounds I had on Cyprian's Eve.'"

Several injured officers stripped their sleeves and showed their freshly stitched scars.

"Recall how you overcame both fear of the sea and the vast Vandal army." Turning to his generals, he said, "Tomorrow, we will also begin repairs of the city walls. Gelimer has let them fall into disrepair and knows where they are weakest. We should expect him to strike as soon as he has gathered all his men for a counterattack. Sleep well tonight, but tomorrow, we must find Gelimer and the remnants of his army and pursue them until they surrender or perish. Put every uninjured Vandal to work repairing the walls and watchtowers. Dig a deep trench around the entire city and place stakes."

"What if the Vandals refuse?" Pharas asked.

"Then lock them up," Belisarius said. "It's high time these soft-handed barbarians built something with their own hands." With that, Belisarius took Antonina's hand and said to Pharas, "Excuse me, I need some rest time with my wife."

Antonina smiled and walked with her arms locked around Belisarius's. *Good, she is not angry with me,* he thought, seeing love in her eyes as he escorted her from the room. As they departed the banquet hall, the officers whistled and made catcalls. Belisarius turned around, winked at them, and gave Antonina a quick pat on the rear. She scurried quickly to the bedchamber and prepared herself for her first night in four months in a proper bed with her husband.

The royal bedchamber was the most magnificent room Belisarius had ever slept in. Marble and Roman frescoes covered the walls, and large glass windows let in the early evening sun. Silk sheets draped across the bed, and Belisarius fell back into its soft cushions like a boy falling into the water.

Antonina looked at her husband's filthy sandals and said, "You *are* going to wash your feet, aren't you?"

"Yes, of course, dear," Belisarius said, immediately removing his sandals and washing his feet. "You look beautiful already, darling. Come to bed."

"I'll be right there," she replied. "I've been waiting for you all week. You can wait a few minutes for me."

"Please hurry," Belisarius begged her. "I've missed you."

As she prepared herself in an adjacent room, Antonina said, "You know, you need to learn how to delegate more of these problems to your subordinates and walk away. You have forgotten how to relax. You work too hard."

Belisarius waited as she brushed her hair, applied perfume, and lit several oil lamps, but exhaustion and the dinner's potent wine soon got the better of him, and the victor of Carthage slipped into a dream.


Belisarius woke to the smell of his wife's rose and orange peel-scented hair. As the warm morning sunbeams burst through the window, he smiled and watched her breathe in and out. At that moment, he was overwhelmed with love and pride. *She is my wife! How?* He leaned closer to her soft cheeks and kissed her gently but did not wake her.

The night's revelry had ended late for all in the city except the general. He had made sure that his troops impressed every military-age Vandal male into reconstructing the city's walls, so Gelimer had little opportunity to recruit a new army. He realized that his forces wouldn't manage to hold Carthage if Gelimer attacked it with the battered remnants of his army and Tzazon's reinforcements.

The task before him was to ensure loyalty, peace, and prosperity in the city. His soldiers heeded his demands for respect for the women and children. Still, he was concerned that sending Vandal prisoners to Persia might permanently break up families. He remembered his father once told him in his old age, "When you kill a man, you steal not only a life, you rob his wife of her right to her husband and his children to their father." Deportation to Persia would have the same dispossessing effect as death.

As he looked out the window of the palace balcony, he was pleased to see that commerce among the Romans in the city had resumed as though the regime change had been nothing more than a minor distraction.

He put on his armor, grabbed a small loaf of bread for breakfast, and headed out to inspect progress on the rebuilding of the city's defenses. The sounds of shovels assaulting the earth around the walls and mauls pounding stakes into the ground made it difficult to converse. Pharas's hulking figure met him at the door, taking half the loaf himself.

"If we can defend these walls," Belisarius thundered as they arrived at the city's main gate, "we will always have a fortified base to fall back upon — no matter what happens on the battlefield."

Pharas nodded his agreement. "Any word on Gelimer's whereabouts?"

"Not yet."

As the sun reached its full arc in the sky, Belisarius supervised the wall's reconstruction and even assisted in much of the menial work. Sweat poured down his face, and he wondered what possessed him to wear his armor. As he used his knife to sharpen a stake in the ground, a group of Vandal women seeking clemency for their men accosted him. Pharas tried to push them aside, but Belisarius motioned for them to approach.

"We are widows either by death or by the Emperor's deportation orders," a woman with five small children surrounding her said. "Are you to punish the innocent with the guilty?"

"Indeed," said another, "What have the children done to deserve poverty and starvation? We need food."

"Is this Justinian's idea of a just new society?" a third Vandal woman asked and then spat on the ground at Belisarius's feet.

Belisarius sent them to a nearby church but realized that the widows had a valid point, and the church did not have the resources to feed all the widows and orphans. Pharas gave him a sympathetic look.

"There are always winners and losers in war, Flavius. This problem doesn't fall on you," Pharas said as they watched desperate Vandal women approach his soldiers repairing the wall and offering laundry and cooking services.

"You know it's all a pretext for hooking up with our troops, don't you?" Pharas asked. "Just watch them." Pharas pointed to an Isaurian infantryman who dropped his pickax and discreetly slipped away with an attractive Vandal woman. Belisarius and Pharas followed him at a distance and watched him enter her home.

"What goes on in there?" Belisarius asked.

"First, the kids set to washing his clothes while the woman bathes him. When he is all cleaned up, well, you know the rest of the story," Pharas said with a wink.

"How common is this?" Belisarius asked.

"It's going on all over the city," Pharas said. "Can you blame our troops? Look at those women! They're beautiful and desperate to find a Roman who can offer them security and perhaps a means to support their families."

"I had no idea," Belisarius said. "We must wrap up this war before these distractions make our men forget why they are here."

"They know why they are here," Pharas laughed. "It's their generals who are clueless."

Belisarius gave him a playful scowl and shook his head. As the two generals walked back toward the mending wall, they ran into Procopius, who was shaking his head in disapproval at all the violations of the non-fraternization protocols.

"General, the Emperor has decreed...."

"You know, these Vandal women are right," Belisarius interrupted and continued his conversation with Pharas. "Antonina said the same to me last night. What am I supposed to do?"

Procopius replied, "Part of me echoes the Republican Roman Senator Marcus Porcius Cato in his view that '*Carthago delenda est.*'"

"Carthage must be destroyed?" Belisarius asked and gave him a weary look, "Procopius, you're of no value to me today." As they passed by Constantinus, supervising reconstruction on another section of the wall, Belisarius dropped his voice to a whisper. "The best we can hope for is that those women who have lost everything can attach themselves to Romans."

"There are too many widows and not enough men for that," Procopius said. "We're courting disaster here."

"If I were the Emperor, I might do things differently," Belisarius said impatiently, then realized that Constantinus was within earshot and returned to a whisper. "But I'm not, nor do I aspire to be."

Constantinus puckered his lips, squinted his eyes, and shook his patrician head at Belisarius. Belisarius knew the resentful look of disapproval well from his years as a younger officer advancing quickly in the ranks of the army while Constantinus's military career stagnated, and the look still made him feel uncomfortable.

"Regardless," Procopius insisted, "this has to...."

Belisarius cut him off. "Procopius, we're done discussing this. I can't listen to this anymore."

Belisarius left his scribe by the gate near the Forum and headed towards the cathedral, where he sought refuge from his critics. As he entered the church, he blessed himself with holy water, bowed before the high altar, and then knelt to pray for perspective before an altar devoted to Saint Cyprian. He closed his eyes, took a deep breath, and murmured, "Lord, give me the wisdom to govern this city justly."

A moment later, he felt a gentle tap on the shoulder. A Roman wearing a miter and embroidered silk vestments interrupted his solitude. "Welcome to our church, General. You know, a century ago, Vandal heretics turned this cathedral into a stable for their steeds. Over there," he pointed at the high altar, "they scourged our priests and seized or destroyed the adornments. They emptied the reliquary of our beloved Cyprian's bones into the street, scattered and trampled on them. It's time to make things right."

Belisarius crossed himself, stood up slowly, and looked at him wearily. *I just want to pray! Can I not have but a moment's peace?*

"Tomorrow, I know you will rededicate this place to Cyprian's honor and fulfill the promise for justice that the saint made to his disciples in visions after the

Vandals sacked their city. Nevertheless, I hope you take Cyprian's pleas for unity in the Church to heart."

"Unity requires that the Church regain all the properties that the Vandal Arians have seized," the bishop insisted.

"And the Vandal clergy? What about…."

The bishop interrupted him, "General, four ecumenical councils, particularly at Chalcedon, have affirmed the co-eternity of Christ with God the Father. The Vandal Church denies the equality of this Trinitarian formula and asserts that Christ was a mere creature whom the Father later divinized."

"I thought Hilderic had been relatively tolerant of the orthodox creed-"

"Perhaps, but Gelimer persecuted us…."

"I hope that with the tables turned, we can avoid ugly payback. We would like to keep the peace here."

The bishop gave him a sour look. "The Emperor has granted the Church full authority to judge these matters, and his letter to us indicates that you are to defer to the bishops in ecclesial affairs." He handed Belisarius a letter with the imperial seal.

"I fear that your seizure of every church will do more to exacerbate the problem than solve it," Belisarius said. "Vandals remain a sizable part of the population. If you disenfranchise them, you risk civil unrest…."

Before he could finish, the bishop snorted and started to walk away, then turned back and said, "Oh, and General, we would be grateful if you would refrain from wearing your sword while praying. It makes some uncomfortable."

Belisarius bowed, nodded politely, and left the church. *Men wearing swords shouldn't pray? God help this place.*

He had not eaten since that morning. When the smell of some roasting chicken overtook him, Belisarius went in search of it. In the great square outside the cathedral, he saw Pharas waiting for him in a queue outside a thermopolium[48] and decided to join him. The fair-skinned blonde woman selling the spiced chicken was a Vandal.

Belisarius reached into the small purse under his armor to grab some coin but realized he had none. Pharas laughed, "The wealthier the man, the less money he has in his purse," he said, and passed the woman two Roman coins.

"Thank you," she said as she eyed the plumes on their helmets. "It has been difficult for us since you Romans arrived. You are deporting my husband to Persia, and I don't know how I'll survive."

"You seem to be making a good living," Belisarius said.

"True, but at the end of the week, I will be forced to leave my home and the kitchen where I prepare the chicken," she said. "After that, I will be on the street with my three children. Sure, Gelimer had a heavy boot on our necks, and now we have traded a Vandal tyrant for one in Constantinople."

Belisarius didn't like hearing Justinian equated with Gelimer, but he knew the woman was partly right. He took a ravenous bite of chicken and turned to the crowd of curiosity seekers around him. "We will be kind and generous to the people here so that when our army departs, the Empire will need to leave nothing behind except a minor garrison. Any Roman soldier who violates the hospitality the Carthaginian people have shown us will be flogged or hung."

The outspoken Vandal woman raised an eyebrow and gave him a skeptical look. "Your vision of this new just society is a dream for you Romans and a nightmare for us."

Not knowing what to think of that, Belisarius ignored her. "If we are to reconstitute the Empire and Church here, Christian ideals of fraternity will have to replace pagan models of conquest. My troops will not forget this. We don't want you, citizens of Carthage, to open the gates to Gelimer if he ever returns."

---

[48] The Roman equivalent of a food truck.

"They may not reopen the gates to Gelimer," the woman said, "but I promise you, the whole of Africa will cry to heaven for justice. Our men will eventually come back to us and revolt."

Realizing that this woman could not be comforted by his intentions, Belisarius motioned for Pharas to escape the brazen woman. Still hungry, they instinctively followed the next delicious smell that overtook them. They walked up to the fish-grilling stall and ordered two. As Belisarius took his first bite, the fishmonger started to yell.

"Aren't you that general, Belisarius?"

"Yes..."

"Well, a captain in your navy plundered our shops after we allowed your fleet into our harbor. Didn't you promise us that Roman property would be respected, yet this captain," he pointed toward a man on the nearby docks, "and his crew has requisitioned everything from my shop! And other peoples' too!"

Belisarius ordered Pharas to summon the captain to explain himself and called out to Ultor, who was lashing any Vandal slackers rebuilding the walls, to join them. A short while later, Pharas returned with a nervous Egyptian, who made no effort to deny the theft in front of so many angry witnesses.

Belisarius turned impatiently toward the captain and his crew and said, "After your punishment today, you will return everything you have stolen." Belisarius turned to his enforcer and said, "Ultor, give him thirty lashes." He was a military man, he thought, not a judge.

As Ultor tied the captain to a pier on the docks, Belisarius grabbed the whip from Ultor's hand, grasped the captain's collar, ripped his tunic from top to bottom, then pulled his arm back, with a loud snap, delivered the hardest lash he could. The crowd watched in horror as the whip lacerated the skin on the captain's back and left him screaming in agony. "That's for making a hypocrite out of me!" he shouted. He handed the whip back to Ultor. "Twenty-nine more, and don't be soft. Make an example of him."

A crowd of Roman Carthaginians gathered to watch the flogging in the shadow of Cyprian's cathedral. Belisarius turned to address them as Ultor administered the remaining lashes. As Ultor administered the last lash, the captain lost consciousness. The skin on his back hung in bloody shreds.

"For centuries," Belisarius told the crowd, "many like Saint Augustine have asked whether Christians should fight or turn the other cheek. I leave that question to the theologians. Today, the question is whether soldiers should act like Christians." He watched as the nearly unconscious captain was cut down and carried away by four terrified marines who knew they might soon receive a similar sentence. "Our answer says something about the world we choose to live in.

The once-skeptical shop owners thanked him and applauded as Ultor tied the next marine to the pier for a flogging. "Pharas, get me away from here," Belisarius said. "I'm sick at heart. We have over-promised and under-delivered."

"Don't take this personally, Flavius," Pharas said.

"Let's get out of here, Pharas."

Belisarius and Pharas mounted their horses and returned to Gelimer's palace, where Belisarius found Antonina at her desk. He could not think of a time when he had been happier to be at home with his wife and away from the administrative problems associated with the occupation. He missed his quiet villa and vineyards at Rufinianae.

"I'm sorry I was so drowsy last night," he said, kissing her head. He glanced at the half-dozen scrolls laid out and ready for the courier to take to Constantinople.

"It's nothing," she said unconvincingly. "How is your little war coming along?"

*Little war?* "We haven't fully won the war yet. But we're already losing the peace. Every malcontent in the city accosted me, begging for something."

Belisarius walked around to the far side of their bedchamber and felt his body sink onto the bed.

"Oh, you poor thing." Antonina put her pen back into the ink jar and fell on the bed next to him. "I wrote a letter to the Empress today. Perhaps we can include some of the things you've dealt with today." Antonina offered, stroking her husband's forehead. Belisarius could feel the tension in his body dissipate at her gentle touch. *She has a way....*

"No, she'll just sow more strife.

"Okay, well, if that won't work...." Her smiling eyes danced as she subtly tip-toed her soft fingers down his chest to his core. He could feel his body responding to such touches but did not have the mental stamina for such exertions.

Closing his eyes, he took her hand and raised it to his mouth. "I'm sorry, wife. I'm just too burdened." Disappointment replaced the once-sensual look in her eyes. Without a word, she stood and walked away from him.

After his body had taken a mid-day break from the heat, he ventured out into the city to inspect his men's progress on restoring the city walls. He did all he could to avoid the desperate glares of the women standing in the streets and the priests loudly arguing amongst themselves on the staircases of the cathedrals. He had one task in mind for that afternoon: to consolidate their victory so they could depart knowing their conquest would hold. Only one man he knew could carry out what he had in mind: John. He found his Armenian friend with his kinsmen, practicing maneuvers on the field of Mars.

"John!" he yelled to get his attention. He immediately looked in Belisarius's direction, said something to his men, and then joined the general on the ramparts. "John," he said, "we must find Gelimer — soon."

"I know," John replied. "I've been waiting for some instruction on that count. With your leave, I'll lead my three hundred scouts to establish his whereabouts and find the Vandal treasure."

"Good," Belisarius said. "Justinian is counting on it to help finance this expedition."

"Finding it will be a challenge," John said. "The Vandals claim that Gelimer took it with him when he met the Roman army, thinking he might need to purchase allies among the Moors and Visigoths."

"Good! If we find Gelimer, we find his treasure."

As the sun began to set near an oasis in the Numidian desert, Belisarius and John rode out of the city to meet with Moorish chiefs. The Moors offered the best hospitality a tent could afford, although the Romans found it very primitive and rough. The tents smelled of camels and urine, forcing a sneeze out of John. Belisarius hoped that with the defeat of the Vandals, he might persuade the Moors to join the Roman side.

"Greetings, General Belisarius," the Moorish chieftain said in imperfect Latin. "You are most welcome. We wish to offer an alliance so our peoples can live in peace." The Moor placed a tray in front of them with crackers, meats, and dates. Belisarius obligingly selected a cracker and bit into it. It left a bitter taste in his mouth. The Moor offered him a drink.

"Try this," he said. "It's from the old Roman city of Ceret in southern Hispania."

Belisarius took a drink, and to his surprise, it was intense and sweet — very different from the watered-down, dry wines he usually consumed. It went a long way toward rinsing his mouth of the bitter cracker. "This is great. What is it?"

"We call it sherish[49], and we cannot agree to peace terms without a toast with sherish." He handed him a bottle of the beverage.

"Thank you," Belisarius said. "And we have brought a gift for you as well."

John emerged and presented the chief with a chest with fifty pounds of gold aurei.

"Thank you, General Belisarius," he said, taking the chest. "We have lived with the Vandals for a century, yet they have never offered us anything so generous. You have our promise of eternal friendship."

"The Emperor is grateful for your support," Belisarius said. "Now tell me, ally, have you any knowledge of King Gelimer's whereabouts?"

The Moor smiled, "Yes, of course."

Belisarius waited a moment for him to volunteer more information, but it did not come. He nodded to John, who disappeared from the tent and emerged a moment later with another small chest. He withdrew a magnificent dalmatic of a Byzantine noble, which he presented to the chief, then offered several more to the chief's attendants.

---

[49] Modern sherry

The Moor smiled and bowed graciously, then stripped to a loincloth, donned the garment, and nodded in grateful approval. "You will find your fugitive king in Numidia, but you will not recognize him. You do not need to seek him out. He will come to you. Gelimer is assembling the remnants of his forces."

"When?" Belisarius asked.

"Within the week, he plans to march on Carthage and expects us to join him. In the meantime, he has offered gold to African peasants who attack you."

"Only our stragglers and marauders will fall victim," Belisarius said.

"Indeed," Pharas added, "The operation has merely tightened Roman discipline and ensured greater vigilance."

"Gelimer's lack of strategic vision once caused him to kill Hilderic and thereby gave us a *casus belli*[50]," Belisarius added. "Every action Gelimer takes undermines his royal authority."

"The Vandal captives are murmuring the way they did before Hilderic was deposed," Pharas said. "If this is a misinformation campaign, Gelimer is fooling no one."

"Tell me," Belisarius asked, "will you join his forces?"

"Of course, "the Moor replied, "we will *join* him on the battlefield, but...."

"But what?"

"How shall I say this? We are not eager to join the losing side. If you show us that you can defeat Gelimer, we will have no reason to fight and will quit the battlefield."

"Do I have your word?"

"General, we are a practical people, more interested in plunder than war. Please do not chase us off the field after the battle ends."

"Agreed. Thank you for meeting with us." Belisarius lifted himself to his feet, bowed, and turned to leave. John followed closely behind.

---

[50] An act or situation provoking or justifying war.

As they left, John said, "That was a successful diplomatic effort. I never thought you could so easily obtain eternal friendship."

"Ha!" Belisarius barked. "We have not bought peace. Perhaps neutrality."

"True, and now we know where Gelimer is."

"Indeed."

# CHAPTER EIGHTEEN

# FROM SHERBET TO MILLET

*Noticing that Belisarius came suddenly toward him with his infantry and the rest of his army, Gelimer jumped onto his horse, neither saying nor ordering anything, and fled to Numidia. And his kinsmen and a few of his servants followed him, panic-stricken and silent about the event.*

— History of the Wars, Procopius of Caesarea

*North Africa*
*A.D. 534*

Gelimer sat in his dark, dank cave, staring aimlessly into the dull fire while poking a stick at it until a sudden wind blew noxious smoke into his face. He choked, coughed, and stood up quickly to get fresh air. As he stood, a stalactite hanging from the cave ceiling clubbed him on the top of the head. Gelimer screamed a curse, grabbed his longsword, and struck the rock several times with his blade before his assailant fell to the ground and shattered. Gelimer felt a trickle of blood running down his forehead and into his eye, blinding him and causing him to run into another stalactite. This one knocked him to the ground. His household domestics rushed into the cave to see what had happened. As one tried to put a bandage on his forehead, he pushed them away.

"How many more weeks will we be confined in this wretched place?" he screamed out to his servants, knowing that no one dared answer. He had been in a foul mood since losing the battle, and he knew he had become an irritable old cuss as well as anyone else. His generals avoided his company unless they had good news, and none had arrived since the defeat. He called over the servant whom he now allowed to bandage his forehead. *Where is my brother? Didn't he get my message recalling him from Sardinia?*

An excited courier entered Gelimer's cave and happily announced the news that all had been waiting for: "Tzazon is here! Tzazon is here!" The courier then ran out to share the news with the other Vandals. Gelimer summoned him back.

"Tell me more."

"Tzazon successfully destroyed the rebellion of the Gothic governor Godas in Sardinia."

Gelimer's staff let out a loud cheer, but Gelimer sulked, "And while he was gone, we lost all of Africa!" The courier went out to talk to those who welcomed his news. Gelimer had resolved that no good news would make up for the disaster that had befallen his kingdom a month ago. He had been hiding in a cave on a mountain in the Numidian desert, trying to avoid the Roman scouts prowling about the desert seeking to destroy him. He looked at his scrawny arms and legs and loathed himself for the weakness he felt. He knew that he was safe in his cave that had once been home to thousands of happy, well-fed bats. The cliffs jutting up from the open plain surrounding him ensured that no Roman army could reach the highly defensible position except at a very high cost. Still, the guano stench overwhelmed him almost as much as the pesky flies that buzzed around his head. He no longer bothered to slap the annoying insects off his dry lips.

A few moments later, Gelimer scowled as he heard cheers: his victorious brother had returned and was now visiting his new realm. He embraced his brother, then stood back and hung his head. "Ammatas and Gibamundus are dead," he said, "and while we mourned their loss, we lost our kingdom." Tzazon acknowledged that he had heard the tragic news. "Your absence in Sardinia guaranteed the overthrow of our place as masters of Africa. I am so glad you have come home."

Tzazon looked around at the barren cave, the guano-covered floor covered with a shabby rug, and his brother's distressed appearance. His dirty, half-naked appearance and protruding ribs disguised his once regal, athletic appearance. Dehydration had hollowed Gelimer's once handsome features, and incessant weeping had made his eyes swollen and red. A cloud of despair hung over him.

Tzazon cried, "Do not lose heart, brother. The war is not over."

"It is from where I sit."

Together, the two brothers left the cave and wandered through the sad multitudes of Vandal exiles living in makeshift tents in the desert highlands. Their survival depended on Gelimer's diminished resources. As the two walked through the refugee camp, the sight of Tzazon lifted the spirits of everyone except Gelimer. The king had expected to be cheered by his victorious brother's arrival, but now he found that his vanity made him resent the messianic figure who had just arrived. He tried to put on a happy face, but the rankness of the human feces all over the refugee camp and the wretchedness of children begging for food scraps overwhelmed him with grief. A long line of women waiting their turn for a chance to drip their buckets into the muddy and slightly brackish water suddenly made him thirsty.

When they returned to the cave, Tzazon said, "Your troops have ceased practicing their military drills." Gelimer nodded but said nothing as he returned to his perch on the small stool and resumed his daily routine of poking at the fire with his stick. "Your army has all the *esprit de corps* of men shipwrecked on a deserted island," Tzazon said before realizing his words only caused his brother's mood to worsen. Gelimer did not respond.

Tzazon pointed to the bloody bandage on Gelimer's head and said, "At least you fought honorably and offered your blood for our people."

Gelimer was amazed to find he no longer cared about his now sullied reputation. "I was attacked by one of these cursed stalactites."

His taller brother laughed for a moment and then became deadly serious. "We need to get this army back into fighting shape again," Tzazon said. "And you must behave like a king."

Gelimer looked up slowly and brushed away the flies from his lips. "I am the king of the flies and am behaving accordingly." Tzazon gave him an astonished look. Gelimer added, "Is it mealtime yet?" Tzazon ignored him, but Gelimer could see he was trying his brother's patience. Tzazon took a deep breath and asked calmly, "How many troops do you have?"

"I don't know...." Gelimer snarled. "A few thousand, perhaps."

"That's all we need, brother," Tzazon said as he slapped Gelimer on the shoulder. "They are still loyal to you."

"They are tired and hungry and despise me," Gelimer replied as he scornfully threw his favorite stick into the fire. "We barely escaped with our lives."

Tzazon paused and stared. "You really are broken, brother. I can see it in your eyes."

"Yes," Gelimer sighed as silent tears cut white lines through the dirt on his face.

"Perhaps for the moment," Tzazon said reluctantly, "I could take charge of the troops."

Gelimer felt the weight of the heavy crown lifted from his head. He knew this was not another coup attempt but an effort to lighten the load of one who could bear no more. He trusted Tzazon. He smiled gratefully and nodded his agreement.

"Rest, brother. I will organize what remains of your forces and integrate them into my troops. Tomorrow we will recapture our beloved city."

"I would like that very much," Gelimer said, poking the fire again with a new stick.

"We must join forces and recruit the western Moorish tribes," Tzazon said. "My spies tell me that Belisarius's Hunnish mercenaries have been complaining to General Sunicas about the rigors of Roman justice, the length of their African expedition, and the distance of the campaign from their homeland. We may be able to persuade those homesick boys to fight with us."

Gelimer almost smiled again. "We could lure Sunicas's deputies and mounted archers with promises of spoils and use them to attack the Roman rear."

Tzazon laughed, "Indeed." He looked Gelimer up and down and took away his new fire stick. "The most powerful weapon on earth is a human soul on fire." He held the ember to his mouth and blew on it until it burst into a flame. "You're going to need to snap out of your slump if we're going to defeat the Romans."

The next day, the Hunnish rebels tentatively agreed to Gelimer's proposal.

Belisarius rode Bucephalus to the fountain in the middle of the city to give the thirsty beast a drink. As he removed the bridle, he noticed it was dry. A Roman woman with an empty bucket said, "Those cursed Vandals cut the aqueducts. We have no water."

Two months had gone by slowly, with little recent progress toward a final Roman victory. The Romans had repaired the defensive walls, but the Vandals refused to attack. Despite having a rough idea of where the Vandals were hiding, John could not locate either the king or the Vandal treasure.

As Belisarius looked for a place to water his horse, he heard a shout at the palace gates that interrupted the relative peace. A flustered man stood at the gate requesting immediate entry. Belisarius could hear the guard trying to refuse him given the morning hour, but the man was insistent.

"Let him pass, sentry," Belisarius said.

"General, we found Gelimer. He's assembling his army near the village of Tricamarum, a two-day march from the city."

Confident that a mere five hundred troops could hold the city's rebuilt defenses, Belisarius ordered a trumpet call to muster. Within two hours, he had assembled his entire army and led it out to meet the Vandals. Antonina met her husband at the city gates and bade him an affectionate farewell.

"How long will you be gone this time, husband?" she asked coolly.

"Long enough to miss you, darling." He leaned over his saddle to kiss her forehead, then led his troops to find Gelimer. A priest standing over the arch at the city gate blessed the Roman troops as they passed underneath him. Roman citizens lined up to cheer the army as they marched toward the remnants of Gelimer's army. Roman women threw rose petals and blew kisses while vendors offered the troops additional provisions for the march. The sun shone happily above them, and a cool wind from the north provided relief from the worst of the heat.

The soldiers, especially the Hunnish mounted archers, were eager to deal them a final blow so they could return home in time for the spring planting. Belisarius knew he had to finish what he'd started and to capture or kill Gelimer. Subsequent couriers had reported that Tzazon commanded the Vandal center, and Belisarius determined to focus his attack there. He had already seen how Gelimer crumbled on the battlefield when he lost a brother.

Belisarius assembled his generals and discussed his plan. As always, he sought input from his staff and then made the final decision: to start the attack with mounted archers, check the Vandal cavalry, and then attack the center infantry. Belisarius ordered his cavalry to halt briefly at a creek to water the horses as they rode on horseback to meet the Vandals.

Among Belisarius's officers, only Constantinus objected to the plan. "General, they outnumber us three to one," he protested. "It would be far more prudent to fight defensively behind the city walls."

Belisarius let out a barely audible sigh, and Pharas, Sunicas, and John gave him a sympathetic glance and smiled.

"Constantinus, the city will be out of water in two weeks," Pharas explained. "We are not provisioned for a long siege."

"If we wait for Gelimer, I'm not sure we'll be able to rely upon my Huns," Sunicas added.

John gave Constantinus a stern look and added, "Men like Gelimer, who are famous for their cruelty, are also known for their cowardice. If we sow fear in his mind, it will prey upon him. The Vandals celebrate Gelimer's brutality, but never his courage."

Constantinus was silent and let the other generals ride ahead.

"Keep your eyes on the Moors in their rearguard," Belisarius said. "Their chief has committed to remain neutral until our victory is assured and should remove themselves from the field if the Vandal center does not hold."

After the horror of the massacre at the Hippodrome, Belisarius had resolved to refrain from taking the lives of defeated men whenever possible, but that day, he made an exception. He looked his generals in the eyes and said, "We must destroy the Vandal army in this battle. If we do not, they will continue to regroup and attack us. The Empire cannot afford a prolonged war. Cut down every Vandal warrior who refuses to surrender. Allow no one to escape."

After two days of hard marching, scouts reported sighting Gelimer's army. The field before them was brown and dry except for a creek that separated the Romans from the Vandals. Belisarius and his mounted knights sat in the rear of the Roman center between two flanks of cavalry. Fifty thousand Vandals waited to repel the attack on the other side of the creek.

"Look," John said, "the Vandals have dropped their lances and are fighting only with swords." Belisarius smiled.

The Vandals positioned their forces in front of a circle of wagons where they set their women, children, and personal belongings. Belisarius looked sympathetically at the ragged lot that had fled their homes to seek the safety of the Vandal army.

"I have seen this sad sight before," John said as they watched nervous mothers huddling their children under the wagons and covering their eyes with blankets. "It reminds me of what happened to us in Armenia when the Persians last came through. You think you have a home, then a foreign army comes, and suddenly, you don't. And then you worry that you'll be enslaved."

Belisarius, who had left Antonina at the governor's palace in Carthage, asked, "What sort of warrior brings his family to a battlefield?"

John shrugged his shoulders. "Risking the lives of women and children is madness."

"Gelimer is placing the burden of protecting those innocents on our shoulders," Belisarius said as his armor began to seem heavier.

His spies in the Vandal camp had reported that the women had reminded their men that they would be victorious if they maintained their sangfroid and courage because they were bigger and stronger than the soldiers from Byzantium. Even Gelimer's wife, who had endured the grief and shame of her husband's earlier defeat at Ad Decimum, had shouted, "Return with your shield or on it!"

A trumpet signaled John's cavalry to advance from the center of the line. They launched their arrows, drew their lances, and rode at the Vandal line with reckless thunder, but it was not enough to break the formation. Belisarius gave the command, and John's men returned, then charged again. The lancers crashed through the Vandal line, taking out hundreds, but failed to break its cohesion.

Belisarius recalled John's men to the front of the Roman line. "Are you making progress?" he asked. "I see nothing but dust."

"We nearly have them," John replied. "The first time, they held their ground. The second time, those in the back broke ranks, and those in the front panicked. A third charge will break them."

"Then make it so."

John's cataphracts charged the Vandal line at full gallop. So long as they were not slowed or stopped, their armor protected them. Their lances pierced very few men, but their armored horses stampeded the Vandal lines and shattered them.

With the Vandal line reeling, Belisarius ordered his *bucellarii* forward and then his infantry. As his cavalry advanced, Belisarius recognized the red standard of Tzazon. Tzazon rode a great black steed surrounded by five retainers, but Belisarius noticed a vulnerability in Tzazon's ranks. He knew if his army eliminated Tzazon, it might spell the end of the faltering Vandal army. However, as Belisarius charged forward, he realized that Tzazon's were guards counter-charging his white standard, were locked on him, and determined to prevent him from reaching them.

Belisarius called for a courier. "Tell John to have his battalion in the center attack Tzazon's standard at once. Go!" He watched John masterfully slash through a crowd of attackers and overwhelm Tzazon's retainers, leaving the Vandal general defenseless. John cut downward on Tzazon's wrist and severed his sword hand through the bone. Tzazon's sword fell to the ground with the bloody fisted hand still attached. Tzazon let out a horrified shriek and tried to retreat. Blood pulsed through the open stump, and his retainers desperately tried to surround their leader. But it was all for naught. Before they could, John struck Tzazon in the chest with his sword. As the Vandal fell from his horse, dead, a panicked scream arose from the Vandal retainers, and their resolve to fight faded. Wounded screeches, sounding more animal than human, rose from the Vandal line as it slowly melted away.

Belisarius ordered his left and right flanks to swing around and attack the ends of the Vandal line. He watched Gelimer's yellow standard turn and head toward the Vandal camp. John had dispersed the Vandal center, which was reeling from the three assaults and the collapse of their infantry line. The line began to shorten as John's troops moved to fill the gaps.

Off on a distant hill overlooking the battlefield, the Vandals' Moorish allies stood by, discreetly watching the collapse of the Vandal front without showing the full force of their light cavalry. Belisarius watched with apprehension, wondering if the Moors would charge and rescue their allies now that Roman cohesion was breaking in pursuit of the Vandals. *A decisive counterattack might dislodge us.* As John's men worked to widen the hole they had created in the Vandal center, Belisarius ordered his advancing infantry to launch missiles into the unbroken section of the line, and the Vandal defense began to collapse. He watched the crest of the hill; the Moors had not moved. The chief had kept his word — so far. *It's time to finish this battle.*

"For Rome!" Belisarius shouted, raising his sword toward the sky as thousands of missiles whistled through the air. The men echoed his cheer and marched in double time towards the Vandals with their swords raised in the air.

Belisarius then remembered his Hunnish problem. Sunicas had told him before the battle that he was confident that his Huns would remain loyal to Rome. Still, Belisarius knew that the execution of the drunken brawler had cost him some popularity among the Huns. He looked at Sunicas's men, who had remained on the flanks waiting for the trumpet sound to advance. *Will they advance?* With fear and trepidation, Belisarius signaled the trumpet to charge. A trumpet blared. They're not moving.

"Blow it again! Louder this time!" Belisarius roared.

Another blast flowed, and this time, Sunicas raised his hand and directed his mounted archers toward the Vandal rear. Belisarius breathed a sigh of relief. Sunicas had truly persuaded his rebel Hunnish cavalry chiefs to see the war to its conclusion.

When the Moorish chiefs saw the terrifying Hunnish archers descending on the Vandal rearguard in a cloud of dust, they turned their horses around and led their light lancers off the battlefield. Sunicas saluted the Moors and directed his Huns to avoid pursuit and direct their fire at the backs of the few Vandals who had stood firm in the onslaught. When these, too, finally began to flee, the Huns charged with their lances.

There was no stopping the skimble-skamble flight. The entire Vandal army, which outnumbered the Romans almost three-to-one, reeled in disorder. The slain Vandals numbered about eight hundred, while the Romans had lost only fifty men.

The *bucellarii* scattered the remnants of the Vandal line as Vandal officers tried vainly to halt the retreat. "You cowards! If you run now, your former lives will be lost forever."

"Tell that to our chicken king!" one Vandal replied in full flight.

Gelimer's royal standard lay on the ground, but there was no sign of the tyrant. The Romans enveloped the few brave Vandals who remained on the battlefield, forcing them to drop their weapons in surrender. Several retreating Vandal officers shouted, "Back to your wives, men!"

"We might have captured Gelimer had he not feared the wrath of his wife more than Roman swords," Procopius said.

The officers laughed, and Belisarius shook his head as they watched Gelimer and his retainers run from the field, leaving his wife and children behind.

As the Romans pursued the fleeing Vandals to their wagon-encircled camp, many threw down their weapons and shielded their wives and children. Others sought refuge from the missiles under the wagons, but the Romans dipped their arrows in pitch and rained hellfire upon them. Soon, their cover was an inferno, and the women and children screamed for their men to surrender.

"General Belisarius, you must come quickly!" A lowly officer bowed hesitantly.

Belisarius rode to John, who had not left the battlefront for a moment. Five Vandal commanders assembled to parley with the Romans about twenty paces from the line.

"Speak!" Belisarius shouted.

"We will surrender our weapons in exchange for a promise of security for our lives and property."

"Unacceptable!" John shouted.

"What are your terms then?" the Vandal official replied.

"We'll spare your lives — and nothing more," Belisarius shouted. "Your king has abandoned you. We grant you two hours to determine the fate of your surviving comrades and the women and children behind you."

Belisarius took to the shelter of his private tent for the full two hours, cleaning his weapons and stripping himself of his heavy armor. The skin underneath his clothes was blood-stained and raw. He took a cloth from the basin of water that his servants had supplied him and cleansed himself of the mud, blood, and gore of the battle. But nothing could rid him of the haunting sound of those women and children screaming for their men to surrender. The image of those vagabonds on the battlefield would be burned into his heart and mind forever; he was sure of it. "Reckless fools," he murmured of the cowardly Vandals.

After cleaning himself thoroughly, he ripped the tent door open and saw that the sun had dropped toward the horizon. It had been two hours. And, just as he was wondering about the courier, a man on horseback bolted up the straight towards his tent. Seeing this, his associates made their way to his tent and stood by to receive the courier, who jumped off his horse and handed the general a scroll, "We accept your terms, General."

"Bind the men and take them to the port," Belisarius told John. "They have decided to live." Once the Romans accomplished this, a long line of wailing women and children followed their bound husbands and fathers back to their former capital.

The bay of Carthage was alive with the bustle of thousands of men moving provisions from warehouses to ships as the Romans worked to maintain trade with their Carthaginian partners.

"Are the transport ships ready?" Belisarius asked.

"Yes, we have lined up the men on the docks," John replied.

"I'd like to see them before they board."

Belisarius made his way to the edge of the docks, where six prisoners of war were kneeling with their hands tied behind their backs, their necks attached to adjoining poles, and their heads bowed. He stopped in front of the Vandal commander, Genseric, a grandson of the first Vandal king, and tilted the man's chin upwards to look into his eyes. He saw an empty pool of sorrow, the look of the defeated.

"What is to become of us?" the commander asked.

"Choose to join the ranks of the Emperor's army in Persia or pledge your allegiance to me and serve the Empire under my banner."

"And our wives and children?"

"Your wives will also begin new lives. Your children will either remain with them or become charges of the Empire. The Empire will return all stolen property to the rightful owners and release your Roman slaves from bondage."

"And our king?"

Belisarius was amused. "He will either die in depravity in the Sahara or be sent to Constantinople to serve at the Emperor's pleasure."

Genseric and his men resigned themselves to their fate and quietly admitted that Belisarius had offered them better terms than those they had offered the Romans over the past century. He turned to his son, bound beside him. "Gelimer would have cut them all down. Save your rendezvous with death for another day."

# CHAPTER NINETEEN
## STOPPING FOR DEATH

*"Because I could not stop for Death —*
*He kindly stopped for me —*
*The carriage held but just ourselves —*
*And Immortality."*

— Emily Dickinson

*North Africa*
*A.D. 534*

Belisarius was in Gelimer's palace enjoying a hot breakfast with Antonina when the bells of the church of Saint Cyprian began ringing. The sound of the bells had an ominous ring — almost as though it were in another key. It reminded him of the chants he'd heard at solemn liturgies to remember the dead. He looked at Antonina, and she seemed to have the same reaction.

"Does the key of that bell seem particularly ominous?" he asked.

"Yes, it does."

"That's no way to start with morning praises," Belisarius said.

The bells had unnerved him, forcing him to get up from the table. He walked over to the palace's balcony and looked at the rising sun. It was as red as blood, and though the sky was clear, a black cloud formed over the palace complex and began to rain. Belisarius put his hands out in disbelief as he felt the heavy drops on his palms.

"Have you ever seen the rain coming down on a sunny day?"

"It happens," Antonina said. "What's wrong, Flavius? You look troubled."

"I don't know. Something doesn't feel right about today."

The bells stopped ringing, and the city fell silent again. Belisarius and Antonina resumed their breakfast. A moment later, Sunicas appeared at the door with a look that he had not seen since his adopted mother died after the raid by Huns. The epicanthal fold of Sunicas's eyelids prevented Belisarius from seeing his brown eyes until a torrent of tears flowed from them all at once. Belisarius and Antonina stood up suddenly from the table.

Sunicas tried to speak but was unable.

"What is it, Sunicas?" Antonina asked.

Sunicas took a deep breath, said, "John..." and then burst into tears.

Belisarius waited patiently while he waited for his adoptive brother to put together an intelligible sentence. The ominous feeling that had sunk his soul earlier in the day returned.

"What are you talking about?" Belisarius asked when his patience had come to an end.

Sunicas nodded and took a deep breath, and then another. "John has been mortally wounded," Sunicas finally said, choking on his own words.

Belisarius embraced Sunicas for a long time. He recalled the first time he met John when the two were young *excubitors* and eventually left to join the army. The two had worked together to create the Roman cataphract that combined the best parts of the Persian armored cavalry, the Gothic mounted spearmen, and the Hunnish mounted archers. After years of training together, they had mastered the art of cataphract warfare and had beaten Persians, Goths, and Huns at their own game. He could never have done it without John's encouragement and support. And now, his friend was mortally wounded. Belisarius felt as though he had just lost his right arm.

Belisarius fell to his knees as though he had been sucker-punched and put his face in his hands. He felt alone in the world until Antonina joined him on the floor and embraced him, stroking his hair. He felt sick at heart and numb and refused to believe it. After all, John had been like a brother to him. The two had been virtually inseparable in every battle, and a sense of guilt plagued him that his best friend had been wounded in the field while he was enjoying the good life in Gelimer's palace. Then he wondered whether someone had let John die by some act of negligence or cowardice.

He could not imagine a world without the man who had introduced him to Antonina, been his best man, and godfather to his only child. He recalled the Armenian's hearty laugh, his unsurpassed courage in battle, and his devotion to his family. He recalled the way the sun reflected off his smiling face and how he would dance, as though in a wedding, with his arms outstretched, whenever he entered the bath. He felt as though the music had died, and all joy in life had been taken from him.

He had freed John from Persian captivity in Armenia during the Iberian War, and in gratitude, John had sworn his loyalty and had been the most loyal friend he'd ever known. He remembered his wedding reception, where John, noticing his inattention to Antonina, said, "Better to neglect the whole world than your wife." He thought of John's wife, Nino, whose life was forever changed.

"How did it happen?" Belisarius finally asked.

"He was overtaking Gelimer in Numidia when he spotted several drunken Roman troops who had taken a jug of wine from a captured Vandal wagon," Sunicas said.

"Oh, didn't I tell you that a drunken army was a danger to itself?" Belisarius growled in frustration, recalling his harsh treatment of the Hunnish murderer. "What happened?"

"John went to chastise them for inebriation while the enemy was still lurking about," Sunicas continued slowly, "when an arrow struck him in the nape of his neck."

"What?" Belisarius roared. He had expected a mortal blow from the enemy, not friendly fire. He grabbed Sunicas by his tunic and shook him. "No! No! This cannot be happening!"

"I'm sorry, Flavius," Sunicas said, "he was a friend to us all..."

"Tell me who did this!"

Sunicas hesitated, stammered, and then fell silent.

"Who?" Belisarius thundered again.

"Uliaris!" Sunicas confessed.

"Uliaris?"

"Yes, the pear thief, whom you scourged. He fired an arrow at a crow but missed his target and did not see John further down range."

*Drunkenness always leads to debauchery.*

"Take me to John at once," Belisarius ran out of the palace and quickly mounted Bucephalus. Antonina waited by the door for a farewell kiss, but Belisarius did not notice and flew past her.

He and Sunicas rode hard all day into the Numidian wilderness, commandeering new horses to maximize their speed. As the sun set, they arrived in a temperate valley, and not a moment too soon, finding the place. Underneath an oak grove, they found John, attended by his retainers who had gathered around him. He saw a broken Uliaris kicking an empty wineskin, but he disappeared when he saw Belisarius.

Belisarius quickly dismounted his exhausted horse, which collapsed after riding for hours. Belisarius ran over to John and stopped when he saw him lying on the ground.

"Flavius," John said in a weak whisper, "it seems the Grim Reaper has come for me." He laughed a quiet, weak laugh.

John had a blood-soaked bandage around his neck and looked as white as a sheet. He was seated on the ground with a large oak serving as a backrest. One look at his friend, and Belisarius knew his chances for recovery were slim. He looked at the *medicus* attending to John, and the surgeon just shook his head sadly.

"John," Belisarius said as he knelt next to him and touched his shoulder. He found he could not say anything more.

"Flavius, I'm sorry." John struggled to speak, half-delirious from the loss of blood and the injury to his throat.

Belisarius wanted to do something but knew there was nothing he could do that the *medicus* had not already tried. He assessed from the injury that John was probably unable to drink. Belisarius tried to hold back tears. "We have come too far to…" but could not finish the sentence.

Belisarius's sadness briefly turned to rage as he looked beyond the grove for the man who had done this. He saw Uliaris pacing back and forth, kicking the empty wineskin, asking himself repeatedly: "O God, what have I done?" Uliaris sobbed like a child who had lost a parent. John had been like a father to his men — many Armenians orphaned in the bloody wars with Persia.

John's throat gurgled with blood as he cried, "Flavius, do not punish Uliaris… an accident. He will grieve my death for the rest of his life."

Belisarius wept as he held John in his arms, and the red blood spot continued to grow on his bandage. The light rain continued despite the sun's radiance and a clear sky. He looked at the sky and saw several swallows swooping down on a crow. Belisarius wondered what he would tell John's widow and their children. *Better not to mention the senselessness of the death.* As he took his last breath, a serene look appeared on John's face. He gazed at the sky and said, "Lord, now let your servant go in peace."

Sorrow and rage welled up in Belisarius. He was torn between wanting to punish the drunkard who had killed his friend and John's request to spare him. He looked at Uliaris's fallen face and said sadly, "I would rather have lost my right arm than this noble soul. Be sure John's death has not been in vain."

Without raising his head, Uliaris said softly, "My own death would have been more fitting."

"At the last wish of a dying friend, I won't have you flogged, Uliaris, but see that you put your life in order. Spend your remaining days making up for the good you have stolen from the world today. And pray that everyone who loved John as much as I can forgive you. Now leave me."

As Uliaris slipped away, Belisarius gently placed John's body on his horse and rode slowly back to Carthage. He arrived as the sun rose the next day and took his friend's remains to a hill just outside the walls of Carthage. There he summoned a priest and the remnants of John's cavalry unit, mostly Roman Armenians. Under a wide oak, they wept and prayed, then wrote personal messages on pieces of cloth torn from their sleeves and tied them to the branches of the tree. Belisarius wrote,

"To the bravest man I ever knew, may the Lord reward you for your courage and kindness. Until we meet again, Flavius." He tied the cloth to the tree, took a shovel, and threw the first mound of dirt onto his friend's body.

After the burial, Belisarius untied the sack of five smooth stones from his belt and placed them atop the soft earth mound in a pentagonal pattern. He recalled how John had given them to him just before his duel with the Persian giant before the battle of Dara. With his voice choked by tears, he whispered to the mound, "I cannot carry them with me anymore, John, for I fear that they have become too heavy." As priests and cantors chanted a *Dies Irae*,[51] Belisarius could no longer endure the sight of John's grave and remounted Bucephalus and returned to the palace.

When he arrived at the palace in the late morning, he sat at a desk in the *tablinum* and wrote to John's wife, who was caring for his daughter, Joannina. Belisarius greeted Antonina and his staff at the door and asked for a moment to write a letter to John's family.

Dear Nino, I am at a complete loss for words in my hope to console you for the death of your beloved John. I have lost my dearest friend and most loyal lieutenant, but you have lost a devoted husband and the doting father of your seven children. I can only hope that you might find solace in the gratitude of the Empire he died to restore, and in the resurrection, promised to those who faithfully serve Our Lord. Take pride in knowing that he offered so costly a sacrifice at the altar of glory. I pray that our Heavenly Father may ease your sorrow and leave you only a cherished memory. Respectfully, Flavius.

When Belisarius put down the stylus and sealed the letter, Antonina embraced her husband. "I know how much you loved him."

Belisarius began to speak, but when his quivering voice failed, he stopped and pushed at his eyes with his fingers to prevent tears. He took a deep breath and said, "How was your day?"

---

[51] A prayer for mercy on Judgment Day.

Antonina hesitated, then realized that he needed a diversion. "I went to the Cathedral of Saint Cyprian today just as an Isaurian was dragging a beautiful Vandal woman from under the altar by her blond hair."

"What did you do?"

"I screamed at him, and the rogue and his compatriots fled, recognizing me as your wife. The terrified woman and several with her followed me out of the church."

"What can I do?"

"Give orders for a lieutenant to guard them and arrest anyone who tries to violate them.

"Consider it done."

"Hundreds of women are in the palace seeking your protection."

"We will do what we can for them. Have you had word from the Empress?"

"Not yet, but our army must not view the women as possessions of the Vandals they have slain."

Pharas stood in the doorway and knocked. "I heard the news, Flavius. I am so sorry. John was like a brother to us all." He entered the room and embraced Belisarius. "There is something I need to tell you, but it can wait until later if you'd prefer." Antonina started to object, but Belisarius cut her off.

"No, I could use a distraction. What is it?"

"John's cavalry chased Gelimer to a cave at the top of Mount Papua, but the steep terrain prevented them from successfully assaulting the hill. We may have to starve him out."

"We cannot wait for that," Belisarius said. "If we cannot take Gelimer by force, we will negotiate and persuade him to surrender voluntarily without further loss of life."

"How will we do that?"

"Wine, women, and song."

The next day, while Belisarius managed clean-up operations and arranged for a stone to mark John's grave, Antonina found herself alone and bored — again. She took a leisurely bath, brushed her hair, perfumed herself, and put on some eyeliner and cheek rouge. She took some powdered mouse brains mixed with crushed eggshells, brushed her teeth until they were white, and walked over to look at herself in the mirror. She smiled, reminded herself that she looked pretty good, and wished someone would tell her he noticed.

She called Macedonia. "Teach me that fun board game with the little chariots you are always playing with the other domestics."

Macedonia returned a few moments later with a board and a pair of dice and proceeded to play. "I'm blue," Antonina declared. Although it was her first time playing, she won handily. "Did you let me win?"

"No, my lady. You beat me by deceiving me about your intentions. It won't happen again," she said provocatively as she spat on the dice for good luck, rolled them, and gave her green charioteer a commanding lead. This time, Macedonia detected Antonina's guile, blocked her passageways, and beat the blue charioteer to the end of the miniature hippodrome.

"Well-played, Macedonia. I underestimated you."

"Thank you," Macedonia said. "Anytime you're ready to be beaten again. Let me know," she said with a smirk. Macedonia turned to leave the room.

"Please stay with me," Antonina said. "I could use some company, and my husband is never around. "Let's go for a walk in Gelimer's garden."

They walked for several hours, talking about men and their tendency to over-promise and under-deliver. "Is there someone in your life?" Antonina asked.

"There was a man in Constantinople, but no one here," she said with a frown.

"Then you're in the same boat I am," Antonina laughed.

"No, my lady. You have General Belisarius, the noblest man in the Empire."

"Flavius may be the noblest Roman, but he is not mine."

"The war will end soon, and you will get him back."

"I hope you're right."

They returned to the palace, and Antonina stood on a balcony overlooking a courtyard as her husband rode in. She watched her husband dismount and gently stroke his horse's mane.

She yelled to him, "You spend more time talking to that foul-smelling beast than your wife."

"I'm sorry; I have neglected you."

Belisarius ran up the stairs and gave her a friendly kiss. Then he removed a scroll from his sack and began reading it. Procopius arrived a moment later, and Belisarius began dictating to him. Antonina realized that she had lost her husband almost as soon as she had gotten him back.

She returned to her bedroom, dropped herself on the bed, and stared at the frescoes on the coffered ceiling depicting the Vandals' sack of Rome. She had left her infant daughter behind, and to what end? She'd followed her husband into battle at the Empress's request and because her husband ostensibly needed her, but he'd ignored her. As she often did when she was bored and felt forgotten by her husband, she wrote another letter to Theodora. She admired her friend's ability to find a way to have influence in the court beyond the role of the Emperor's wife. Perhaps the Empress could advise her on navigating a man's world. She told Theodora how much she loved her husband, how neglected she'd felt. Soon, she was sobbing and crumpling the letter.

Theodosius came in and smoothed the letter. He sniffed it as though testing it for hints of perfume and then said, "Oh, what is this? Is it a love letter for me?"

Antonina detested Theodosius's presumption. *You think the world revolves around you.* "No! Don't you dare read words meant only for the eyes of the Empress."

Theodosius laughed, and Antonina grabbed the paper, tearing half of it from his hand, but he refused to surrender the other half and ran about holding it over her head.

"Hand it over now, your rogue, or I'll have you...."

"That's exactly what I had in mind." Theodosius laughed and surrendered the scrap he was holding.

Antonina threw it into the oil lamp. "How dare you speak to me like that!"

"I'm sorry," he said.

"You have trouble with boundaries, Theodosius."

He nodded. "Father has charged me with your security...."

"Yes, but not that type. You should be grateful to him that you are not on the front lines."

"He told me not to take my eyes away from you and to be a companion to you whenever he is out...."

"Listen, godson; it is time for my bath. You need to leave at once."

"I'll accompany you. It is my duty."

Antonina found his audacity both troubling and amusing. She missed having company and increasingly realized that a friend who was a thousand miles away might as well not exist. She needed another person in her life. *Should I trust this rogue?*

"I am the wife of the general."

"I am your companion," Theodosius replied as he tenderly touched her cheek.

All at once, Antonina freed herself from his grasp and walked towards the double doors of her private chamber. "Ladies, I will take my bath now. Please prepare it." She called Macedonia, who was waiting for her directions from the hallway. Antonina returned to her room, half expecting her unabashed godson to have left by the hidden door.

Nevertheless, he remained, bold and stubborn. And by the inviting look in his eyes, she knew what he was requesting of her. Looking into those piercing, admiring eyes and surveying the way the light reflected off his bronzed skin, the muscular frame that always beckoned her from beneath his clothes, she was finding it harder and harder to resist him.

*This behavior is inappropriate*, she thought to herself.

He walked towards her, his strong hands reaching out for her. "And yet, you stand here, thinking about it. Thinking about us...." By now, his hungry advance had brought him face to face with her, so close that she could almost feel his plump lips begging to touch hers. *No, no!*

Antonina turned her back to him and rushed out to the hall, not stopping for a minute. "Macedonia, I am ready."

Antonina spent the next few weeks doing very little, her mind filled with the rejection that she constantly felt from her distracted and hard-working husband and the flattery and evident desire that Theodosius had for her. She could not help but compare them. To one, she was merely a companion; to the other, she was incredible, someone desirable, lovable, and attractive. She had not realized how she had missed feeling beautiful. Theodosius fulfilled this need in her every day. On one sweltering summer day, Antonina told Macedonia and her other servants to rest in the cool of their quarters with the intent to spend her afternoon naked in the quiet peace of her private bathhouse. After ensuring her servants had left, she disrobed and walked back and forth before a mirror, admiring the beauty of her figure, even at her age. *Well, he does have reason to admire me. I will say that.* She walked nude down the hall and into her bathhouse with a broad smile spread across her face. She felt beautiful and alive.

Perceiving that there was no one around, she took her time to immerse herself in the pool, dipping her toes in first and slowly walking down the three stairs into the shallow end of the pool. She dipped her head into the water for a moment and then immerged, breathless. Her vision slowly refocused to reveal a ruggedly handsome man standing completely naked above her on the walkway of the bath. It was Theodosius.

"What a dazzling show you have put on."

"Theodosius!" Antonina yelled, immersing herself completely in the water, hoping that would hide her form.

"Oh, no need for that. I've seen every inch of you now. And may I just say you are delectable."

She could not help but laugh at his audacity. *The boy does not take a hint.* But she couldn't ignore that he seemed willing to do anything and everything to be with her.

"You really want me, don't you?"

"With every fiber of my being."

"Then let it be so."


Days turned into weeks, and Antonina began to wonder why she had not agreed to succumb to his desires much earlier. He was a vivacious lover and a diligent friend. He became active in every area of her life: dressing, eating, and bathing. Her daily routine became livelier and more fun. She no longer felt the need to have her servants around her for the company and often dismissed them when Theodosius entered the room. Theodosius entertained her with impersonations of eccentrics on Belisarius's general staff and in the palace. He made her laugh, and it helped pass the time.

After some time, it came about that as Macedonia and two other servants were preparing her daily bath, they accidentally came upon Antonina in the bath and in the arms of Theodosius. They quickly bolted out of the room. Antonina panicked: her discreet affair was no longer a secret. She wondered if she could trust them not to reveal her indiscretions. *She reminded herself that they were bound to secrecy*, so she was not worried about Flavius. Though a loving husband, he wasn't attentive enough to care what she did with her time anyway. After the discovery, she dismissed Macedonia and the other domestics from the royal bath chamber. "Theodosius will comb my hair today," she said. She watched as Macedonia walked away with a disapproving look on her face. *Don't judge me.*

Having watched Macedonia perform the task for so long, Theodosius had no trouble. "Has anyone told you how beautiful your hair is?" he asked.

"Not recently, but Flavius raves about Bucephlalus's silky mane."

He selected the clothes she wore that day and for many days after that. He helped her select silks from the East. He applied powder to her face, rouged her cheeks, and lined her eyes in the Egyptian style.

"Don't you prefer younger women?" she asked.

"Not at all! You are the sun that eclipses all the other stars." He said, caressing her neck and kissing it with his soft voluptuous mouth.

She came to love his poetic streak, which was absent in her relationship with Belisarius. In the evenings, Theodosius read Ovid to improve it. Gradually, he made Belisarius the primary target of his ridicule. At first, she refused to laugh, but her barriers came down over time. Late one evening, Theodosius regaled her with a spot-on imitation of her husband, perfectly capturing his high military bearing, Thracian-accented Latin, and his dramatic oratorical gestures. Antonina initially recoiled at his mocking tone but eventually laughed so hard that she began to cry. Theodosius tenderly wiped her tears and then hesitantly kissed her lips. Stunned, she forcefully pushed him away. "I am *not* the woman I used to be."

"No, now you are my woman!" He said smiling and kissing her lips.

*Your woman?* She thought to herself, wondering what she was doing and knowing it wasn't good.

Many nights in her empty bed, she wrestled with guilt, resolving to end her tryst with Theodosius. She desperately missed his company, wanted to see, kiss, lie with him, but he wasn't there. She looked at the spot beside her where Flavius should have been, and a deep bitterness welled up.

One night, a storm arose. The wind howled, and the trees moaned like bent masts on a ship pulled hard by a sail. Antonina awoke in fear and reached out her hand confidently across her bed to find her husband, whispering his name on her lips. But Flavius was not there, and the pain in her heart overwhelmed her. She called out his name into an empty, aching room, but he did not respond. *He's probably sleeping in a tent by a campfire near his horse and men somewhere in Numidia.* An inner voice told her she was atoning for all the times she had forgotten him.

Antonina closed her eyes and tried to remember when they had laughed together. The lighthearted fun she had with Theodosius had long since replaced them. She realized what Theodosius had become to her: he fulfilled her needs in a way the busy general no longer did. She still loved her absent husband and did not want to hurt him or sully his reputation. If Flavius never found out, what harm could come from a bit of romance on the side? But what if he did find out?

The next day, however, Belisarius returned to her late in the evening after a week of riding out to talk to Moors and spies about Gelimer's possible whereabouts. Exhausted, he came to bed without a bath and smelled of horse and sweat. It repulsed her, and she kept her distance even though she had been looking forward to his company. In the morning, as Belisarius strapped on his armor and prepared to mount Bucephalus to begin his military duties, Antonina approached him. "Husband, will you not join me for breakfast? I made some fresh bread."

"Sorry, darling," he replied, "No time for such luxuries." He slapped his ration sack and said, "Just a biscuit today."

Antonina held her head in disappointment, and Belisarius embraced her and kissed her softly. "Flavius, I'd like to speak to you about something important when you have a moment."

"What is it?" he asked impatiently as he swung a leg over Bucephalus.

"It requires your full attention. Let's talk later when you have some time."

"Tonight," Belisarius said firmly. "Have a blessed day, dear." He clicked his mouth, and Bucephalus started off toward the city gate.

Antonina spent the entire day preparing for the special dinner she would share with her husband that night. She told Theodosius to leave her alone that day, wondering if she should end the affair immediately. *Oh, what a wretch I am,* she thought as she gave specific orders on setting the table and selecting the wine. She was grateful that Theodosius did listen and gave her the space she needed to think. She needed a romantic evening with her husband to remind her that he loved her.

But Belisarius did not make it home, and as the sun set, she sat in the palace by herself, waiting for her husband to come to enjoy the special dinner she had made: his favorite Thracian stew and fresh bread. After watching the steam cease to rise from the two bowls, she picked them up and threw them across the room. "See you tonight," she said mockingly in a deep military voice that sought to imitate her husband's. "Tonight — just like every other night." Macedonia heard the crash, ran into the dining room, and gave her a sympathetic glance. "I'm sorry, my lady," as she cleaned up the mess.

The next day, Antonina awoke and found herself alone in her bed again. Looking at the space beside her, she knew she could not be happy with a life where she did not feel beautiful or desired. She would look elsewhere if she could not get such attention from her husband.

As she prepared to take her daily bath, Theodosius stood nearby and pointedly ignored her. She went to him and let her undergarment fall to the ground. "Theodosius, I'm sorry I sent you away. Come, join me in the bath." She took his hand and jerked it back when he tried to pull it away. She removed his tunic, escorted him into the bath, put her arms around him, and fervently kissed him in a way she had once reserved for her husband.

After the bath, as he dried her body, she took his face in her hands and locked her eyes with his. "Theodosius, we have carried on like fools. We cannot let anyone else know of what we are doing."

"You mean to put me aside?"

No, my dear. I mean only that Flavius must never learn of this. It would break his heart and, perhaps, mine, too. If he does learn of it, I will deny it, and you will likely be in grave danger. You would have to request sanctuary at a monastery to show the world how much you regret seducing the General's wife. If that happens, you must leave Carthage immediately and put on a good show of penitence until his wrath has abated. Understood?"

Theodosius nodded, "Do you think he's noticed anything?"

Antonina laughed. "He wouldn't notice if I shaved my head…."

"What of Macedonia and the domestics?"

"They know that if they cross me, I'll ruin their lives, and Flavius will never believe them if I deny it. But be discreet. He permits me the sort of flirtatious behavior other husbands wouldn't tolerate, but you may not receive the same deference. Flavius will give people the benefit of the doubt; it's his greatest flaw. Take care you don't test his patience."

"What if I do?"

Antonina thought for a moment. "The Empress would support us, and Flavius needs her support."

"It won't come to that," Theodosius said. "My godfather adores me."

## CHAPTER TWENTY
# BRING ME A LIAR

*The road back to God is a road of moral effort, of trying harder and harder. But in another sense, it is not trying that is ever going to bring us home. All this trying leads up to the vital moment at which you turn to God and say, 'You must do this. I can't.'*

— *Mere Christianity*, C.S. Lewis

*Carthage, North Africa*
*534 A.D.*

Water dripped from the walls and the ceiling of the dark wine cellar in Gelimer's palace. If Belisarius had not been reluctant to trust the servants to choose a good wine, he never would have ventured there. He used his torch to light the oil lamps as he made his way down the passage. Belisarius heard a voice from the upper doorway behind him, then footsteps. He quietly unsheathed his sword and hid in the shadows.

A shadowy figure appeared on the stairs. "Who goes there?" he demanded, pointing his sword at the man's throat.

"Flavius, it is I. Pharas."

Belisarius lowered his sword. "You ought to know the dangers of sneaking up on me!"

"Aye, General."

"What are you doing down here?"

"I'm thirsty. And I'm still uneasy with the servants."

As Belisarius moved into the cellar, he caught sight of lovers twisting and moaning, and he wavered between looking away and scolding them.

"Get up! You ought to be ashamed …" And then his breath left him. As the two disengaged from their passionate embrace, he recognized the faces of Theodosius and his wife. He rubbed his eyes in disbelief as rage filled his heart. He took his sword out of his scabbard and considered cutting down his ungrateful godson, but prudence born of a broken heart soon overcame him, and he dumbfoundedly sheathed his sword again.

Theodosius lept up and rushed up the stairs past him as he fastened his belt. Antonina straightened her gown and stood before her husband without a trace of shame on her face.

"O Flavius! Theodosius was carrying down some of the spoils from the Vandal treasury. Have you seen this marvelous chalice?" She handed him a golden vessel, then, without saying another word, mounted the staircase and disappeared. He stood there holding the chalice, considering what he had just lost rather than what he had just gained.

Sorrow and rage paralyzed Belisarius's heart. He stared at the chalice, wondering if he had been naïve to believe Antonina could be a faithful wife. *That is my wife, the woman who vowed to be true to me.* Pharas put a sympathetic hand on his shoulder, but Belisarius shrugged it off. He turned to the shelves, chose a bottle of red wine, and handed it to Pharas. "Take this and a fresh loaf from the kitchens on your way up the stairs. I'll join you later."

As Pharas departed, he grabbed another bottle, opened it, poured the contents into the Vandal chalice, and drank deeply. He reminded himself that he had married a former courtesan and wondered if that had been a mistake. *No, she promised to be true.* It had worked out in the end for the Prophet Hosea, but would his Antonina give him as much heartache as Gomer gave Hosea? He asked himself why this was happening and knew the supernatural answer but didn't like it. *Surely there must be an easier way to learn patience.* How was he to confront his wife about this? He loved a good fight, but not with his wife.

Belisarius sank into a depression as he wondered what Theodosius offered that he did not, where his marriage had gone wrong, and whether he could save it. He slumped down onto the cold floor of the cellar, poured the remainder of the wine into the chalice, and put it to his lips, but after only a sip, he threw the vessel against the wall only to have it bounce back onto his lap.

Belisarius stared off into nothingness, and his imagination, stimulated by the wine, brought him to a scene of domesticity involving his mother once again. It was early in the evening as the sun went down on the family villa. A gentle breeze waved the family laundry like battle standards. His mother was heavy with a child whom Belisarius would never meet and hanging tunics to dry. His father emerged naked from the villa bath, smelling like a perfumed eunuch, and pulled a clean tunic off the clothesline. Putting it over his shoulders, he discreetly slipped away without so much as a goodbye. His mother gave his father a strong look of disapproval. *Shirker,* Belisarius thought to himself, but knowing full well that his father's unwillingness to help with chores was not his mother's primary concern.

As his father walked down the road leading toward the town of Germania, his mother snapped her fingers, and a young female domestic who had just brought another basket of clean, wet laundry, approached her.

"I'll finish up here," his mother said as she joined young Flavius to hang up the laundry. "Follow my husband at a distance. Ensure he doesn't see you. Report to me what he's up to."

Belisarius's eyes followed the domestic, who discreetly followed his father off the estate, and returned an hour later — after Flavius and his mother had eaten their evening meal.

"It's the same woman and the same place," the domestic reported.

A few moments later, her husband returned, and walked past his family, this time smelling of lavender. He began washing the perfumed sweat from his face and hands.

"I made a wonderful stew," she said, "but Flavius and I have already eaten. I left some for you in the pot in the oven."

His father nodded his gratitude, headed into the kitchen, and served himself a bowl.

"Flavius, I think it's time you and I sheared the sheep," his mother said as she headed out to the barn and grabbed some shears.

His mother's fast, deliberate pace told him she was on the warpath and not to be diverted from her course. She muttered angrily to herself, and Belisarius only heard brief snippets of her vitriol. He knew not to interrupt but occasionally did just to try to ease her heartache.

"All these years, I have turned a blind eye, hoping if I loved him more, he would love only me. Was that too much to ask? Was it? But I was never enough...."

"Mother, you're a great wife, and..."

"I made his meals, washed his clothes, and cleaned his villa..."

"Father doesn't know how good...."

"Your father has pushed me to the breaking point, Flavius. I have given him the benefit of a doubt every time, and to what end?" She stared at him for an answer, but he bit his lips in prudent silence.

Suddenly, she stopped. The brisk pace was too vigorous for a woman in her final month. Belisarius worried that she might go into labor right there. She caught her breath and massaged her protruding belly.

"Are you alright, Mother?"

She said nothing but resumed her walk.

"There comes a point, Flavius, when enough is enough. The philandering stops today!"

Belisarius nodded his approval. He resented his father for the pain his duplicity brought to his mother and for his weakness for other, lesser women. She had talked about what they would do if she caught her husband cheating again, but he never believed she had it in her--until now.

They arrived in the village and found the place: a small but satisfactory house with a thatched roof and a candle in the window. They stood in front of the door.

"You remember what we discussed, Flavius?" his mother asked.

Young Belisarius took a deep breath, nodded, and knocked on the door. His mother stepped back from the door.

A beautiful sylph with flowing golden locks and rouged cheeks and lips answered the door. The potent fragrance of a lavender perfume filled his nostrils. She greeted Belisarius's whiskerless face with an eager smile, looked him up and down, grabbed his hairless chin, and said, "You're a little young for this sort of thing, aren't you?"

"Yes, ma'am," Flavius said coyly, returning a smile. "This is my first time."

As she reached out a hand to welcome him inside, Belisarius grabbed it, jerked it behind her back, pushed his free arm hard into her scapular, and slammed her face down onto the bed. The woman started to scream and tried to resist, but Belisarius knelt on her back, gagged her, tied her hands behind her back, and then tied her feet with the efficiency of an experienced shepherd. At that moment, his mother emerged in the doorway.

"Do you know who I am?" his mother asked the woman.

The blonde looked at her and nodded in terrified cognition. She struggled to break free, but Belisarius only pressed his knee harder into the middle of her back.

His mother examined the young woman closely, as though inspecting a sheep, and nodded her head in ironic approval. "He certainly has fine taste, but I'm afraid, my lady, that your last customer is a married man, and we can't have him running around like a lusty ram leaving his seed everywhere."

His mother removed the shears from her apron and sat on the bed by the woman's head. The young woman began shaking her head violently, but Belisarius had her firmly under his control.

"Don't worry, my lovely shearling, no harm will come to you so long as you never, ever return to Germania." The young woman sobbed and nodded her head in vehement agreement.

His mother put the shears close to the young woman's neck and made a cut and then another and another. The woman's long, luxuriant hair fell to the floor, and after a few moments, she had the close shave of a sheared sheep.

His mother examined the young woman's bald head and nodded her approval. "What do you think, Flavius? Do you think your father will still be interested in this sheared ewe?"

"Not nearly so much, Mother," Flavius said with a grin.

His mother collected the lavender-scented hair and put it into a bag. A moment later, a monk appeared at the door.

"Oh, Father, your timing is perfect," his mother said. "I have just recruited a young woman for your new convent. She is all prepared and ready to go."

The priest nodded, and Flavius followed him out the door carrying the young woman and put her on the back of a mule like a sack of grain. The woman struggled until she fell off behind the mule, who kicked her hard in the back. Resigned to her fate, she offered no further resistance when young Flavius placed her on the mule again. The monk took out a rag and roughly wiped the rouge of the woman's lips and cheeks. A moment later, the monk began walking the loaded mule up the road toward a dock on the river. "Don't worry, daughter, soon enough you will look back on this moment as the day when you came into the light."

His mother took the candle by the window and lit the dry thatch on the roof on fire. Within a few minutes, the entire house was engulfed in flame, as the package on the back of the mule looked on in despair. Belisarius looked on in proud approval.

As the beams of the structure collapsed into the ground and smoldered, his mother turned to Flavius and said, "Well, it's time we returned to your father. I've made some fine cheese *globos*[52] that he will enjoy.

The vindicated pair returned to their villa, greeted the man of the house with a kiss, served him the *globos*, and then returned to the barn together. She took the bag of lavender-scented blonde hair and braided it into the black tail of her husband's favorite horse as young Flavius watched.

"What have you learned from all this, Flavius?"

"Never to cross you, Mother," her son said with a smirk.

"What else?"

Belisarius's long silence prompted his mother to answer the question. He shared his mother's rage at his father's wanton behavior, though he wondered if

---

[52] Lat. Roman equivalent of donut holes.

justice had been dealt to the right person. Still, he was immensely proud of his mother's strength and decisiveness.

"The most effective way to deal with infidelity is to remove the cause of it," she said calmly. "Confronting your father would only have pushed him away, but now, I shall have his undivided attention." She gave her son a long embrace. He was astonished that she could still love his father after all his philandering. "You have to protect the honor of your family — at any price."

Belisarius awoke from the dream and tried to make sense of it all. He recalled his resolution to protect his family from scandal. He smiled and chuckled as he recalled that his father, upon learning of his former paramour's fate, fell to his knees and begged forgiveness from his mother. It was gratefully granted. Indeed, this purging had been the last time his mother caught his father philandering, but he wasn't sure if it was because his father had had a genuine change of heart or because the local women knew what might happen to them if they disrespected his mother. It was all the same in the end.


Several days later, Uliaris approached Belisarius in the palace, followed by four servants carrying a heavy sack. He was drinking not from the chalice but straight from the bottle. "What is it?" he angrily barked, frightening a swallow away.

Uliaris stepped back and stuttered but managed to say, "I have finished the stone obelisk for John's gravesite. I thought you might want to see it before we erect it."

Belisarius froze. In his heartache and self-indulgence over Antonina's infidelity, he had forgotten entirely about his grief over his best friend's death. He put the bottle of wine on a nearby table, put his hands to his eyes, and squeezed out the tears before anyone could see them. Regaining his composure, he said, "Thank you, Uliaris. Show it to me."

The four servants removed the sack to reveal a white marble obelisk the height of a man that read: O gracious Lord, who commended the Roman centurion for his faith, receive your faithful servant John into eternal life.

"That's very fitting," Belisarius said. "Thank you for arranging that." He put his hands on the obelisk, then his forehead on his hands, and wept. *John, John, John: what am I to do?*

"We will leave you now, General." Uliaris took the bottle and said somberly to Belisarius, "This will not help you, brother." Uliaris's attention was diverted by the return of the swallow. As he looked at it, he said, "A swallow will drop dead of starvation before ever having felt sorry for itself."

Belisarius nodded his agreement as the five departed the palace.

As he rode to Gelimer's cave in the desert of Numidia, Pharas encountered the fallen king's bodyguards. "I seek an audience with your king," he said.

Recognizing the Roman general, the guard replied. "Leave your weapons here and follow me."

Pharas dismounted his horse and handed his sword to his lieutenant. He walked more than a mile, then climbed the cliff that had been impossible to ascend in full armor. At the top, his heart was moved by the sad sight of Gelimer and his two nephews in rags, huddled around a smoldering fire.

The king, who had once reclined on divans covered in silk, was squatting on a dirt floor, waiting anxiously for a foul-smelling biscuit to cook in the fire. His eyes were sunken with grief, and the skin on his face was so tight that he resembled a mummy more than a man.

His young nephews and bodyguards looked no better. A Moorish woman, swarming with vermin and smelling like a camel, waited on the pathetic remnants of the royal court.

"Your Majesty," Pharas announced in the most respectful tone he could muster for one who seemed more like the Lord of Flies, "General Belisarius has sent me to offer you generous terms for surrender."

Gelimer gave him a brief empty stare and poked at the fire.

"The Roman navy has captured your royal treasure fleet. You have no means to finance another army. The remainder of your Vandal army has surrendered, and they are onboard ships headed for Constantinople."

"My Visigoth allies in Hispania[53] will not desert me," Gelimer said weakly.

"They have already renounced you and will not offer you sanctuary. You no longer have allies. Roman ships have seized all their major ports. Vandal ports at Septem and the Pillars of Hercules[54] in southern Hispania will soon surrender. We have sent our fleet and expeditionary forces to Corsica and Sardinia with Tzazon's head as proof that Vandal rule will soon end there. You have lost the province of Tripolitania and the coast of Libya to revolts."

Gelimer poked furiously at the embers.

"Your kingdom, except for this mound of rocks, is utterly lost, brother," Pharas concluded.

"That's all very well, but I am not interested." The king's eyes remained on the fire. "I am a free man here." He pointed his smoldering stick around the cave's walls as if demonstrating the extent of his kingdom. "The circumstances are difficult, but I have my liberty. I will not become Justinian's slave. One day, the tide may turn against your Emperor who has so unjustly attacked me."

Gelimer finally looked up, his expression defiant. Pharas realized that the fallen king was determined to punish himself and his family for his incompetence and cowardice.

"I'll give you time to consider the offer. In the meantime, General Belisarius has instructed me to ask you if there is anything you need."

Gelimer laughed. "Anything I need? I need my kingdom. I need my two brothers and my nephew. I need my soft bed and my wife. I need sherbet and dancing girls. I need my mother, clean clothes, music, fresh bread, and a bath." He spat out the coarse biscuit, and bits clung to his rotten teeth and dried lips. The tough old Moorish woman who had prepared it glared at him. "I cannot subsist on birdseed."

Pharas turned to leave. *As a dog returns to its vomit, so a fool repeats his folly,* he thought.

---

[53] Modern Spain and Portugal.

[54] The Roman name for two promontories on either side of the Strait of Gibraltar.

Gelimer's nephew Thrasamund, an emaciated lad, suffered from an intestinal worm. The day before, a Moorish doctor had nearly enticed it from his body and wrapped it around a stick when it broke in two, and the lucky half crawled back inside the boy's rectum. He had been watching the weathered woman prepare a crushed millet paste with the eagerness only famine brings. He reached into the fire, grabbed the hot biscuit from the ash-covered potsherd, shoved it into his mouth whole, and chewed it with his mouth wide open to prevent it from burning his tongue.

The woman struck him hard on the temple with the palm of her hand, sending him rolling across the ground, and began beating him with her long spatula, then pried his mouth open, pulled the still steaming morsel out, and fed it to her famished son. Gelimer awakened from his stupor as fury consumed him. He drove the woman from the cave, poking his hot stick at her forehead.

"Be gone, devil woman. How dare you? This boy is a prince!" He consoled his sobbing nephew with an embrace and gently rubbed the bruises on his bloodied head. He felt the boy's tiny ribs, and uncle and nephew wept together.

The next day, Pharas ascended the mountain with a pack on his back. If Gelimer surrendered, the war would end. Lives would be spared.

At the cave, he sat on one of the low stools around the fire and opened the pack. "Your Majesty, General Belisarius and I wish to convey our sorrow over the loss of your brothers and nephew. They fought bravely in battle, as did all your men. General Belisarius has instructed me to advise you that he lacks the authority to restore your kingdom and is woefully short of dancing girls. However, he has sent you these."

Pharas unrolled a carpet and placed a lyre, a loaf of Roman wheat bread, and a sponge on it. Then he pulled out a bottle of wine and smiled. "The wine is from your palace cellar, and the General tells me it is the finest vintage he has ever tasted."

Pharas poured a cup of wine and offered it to Gelimer, who eyed it suspiciously until Pharas poured one for himself and drank it all. Gelimer began to weep. He tore at the Roman loaf and shared it with his nephews, who devoured it like starving wolves.

"Like yourself," he said, "I'm an illiterate barbarian, but I speak the language of common sense and have an honest heart. Why do you persist in your stubbornness? Will you bring further ruin to yourself, your kin, and your guards?"

"For the love of freedom and an abhorrence of slavery."

"Alas! My dear king, are you not already the most wretched of slaves starving with only these vile Moors as companions?"

Gelimer looked at his nephews and nodded.

"Would it not be better to surrender and pay your obeisance to Justinian in Constantinople than to live in penury, the undisputed monarch of a cave?"

Gelimer poked at the fire and took another bite of bread.

"Justinian himself is said to be enslaved by the Empress," Pharas laughed. "That generous prince will grant you a rich bounty of lands, a seat in the Senate, and the rank of Patrician. Such are his gracious intentions, and you may depend on the good word of Belisarius. So long as heaven has condemned us to suffer, patience is a virtue. But patience degenerates into blind and stupid despair if we reject the proffered deliverance."

Gelimer looked at Pharas and then at his fatherless nephews. He took the sponge Pharas had placed on the carpet, silently dipped it into a water bowl, and dabbed his tear-swollen eyes. A faint spark glistened in his piercing blue eyes. He plucked a few strings of the lyre and, in a tremulous voice, began to sing the eighty-ninth psalm:

*Lord, why have you rejected your anointed one*
*And tossed his crown into the dust?*
*All who pass by have plundered him;*
*He has become the scorn of his neighbors.*
*You have exalted the right hand of his foes;*
*You have made all his enemies rejoice.*
*Indeed, you have turned back the edge of his sword*
*And have not supported him in battle.*

*You have put an end to his splendor*
*And cast his throne to the ground.*
*You have cut short the days of his youth;*
*You have covered him with a mantle of shame.*

The stoic Pharas felt a tear threaten to escape his eye, and Gelimer's nephew Thrasamund began to weep.

Pharas placed a hand on Gelimer's shoulder, and after a moment, the fallen king's weeping turned to laughter, and his nephews laughed with him.

"This is too absurd," Gelimer said. "My vanity has prevented me from accepting your offer, but I accept it now."

When the news of Gelimer's approach reached Belisarius, the general was making a pleasant visit to John's gravesite under an old oak tree just a few miles from Carthage, where Uliaris's newly erected stone marked John's final resting place. Belisarius went down on one knee, put his head on the obelisk, and bid his old friend farewell.

"Your wife Nino and I have something in common: we have both lost a spouse — her to death and me to infidelity. I will keep your family in my prayers and ensure they are never in want. And John, help me bear this burden, help keep Antonina faithful, and, if possible, help make Theodosius a better man." He laid down a bouquet of purple vitex flowers he had gathered from a nearby shrub and asked, "What would you do in my place, John?"

Belisarius waited, but no answer came, only a gentle breeze. He walked over to a small fire nearby where a shepherd was warming himself. He greeted him and stared into hot coals.

The shepherd said, "The man in that grave was a friend of yours?"

Belisarius nodded but said nothing as though he did not want to interrupt something John might say.

"I saw you speaking to him. What did you ask?"

Belisarius was reluctant to open himself to a stranger, particularly since he was still choked up.

"Help for a lost sheep?" the shepherd replied as two lambs came up to him and began bleating. He fed them with a handful of something taken out of his handbag.

Belisarius nodded again and made a heavy sigh.

"Just feed them what they need, and they will return to you," the shepherd said.

Belisarius considered the shepherd's words, thanked him, mounted Bucephalus, and headed back to Carthage. He wondered if John had somehow found a voice in the shepherd. *What did that mean? Love her even more?* He resolved to do that but was still unready to discuss the delicate matter with his wife.

Belisarius had expected Theodosius to disappear after his shameful revelation. He was surprised to find him in front of the mirror in the palace bath, combing olive oil through his hair. *Look at him: preening himself like a peacock!* Belisarius tried to resist the temptation to approach Theodosius as he feared his anger might get the better of him. His instincts were right. As he walked past his godson, he suddenly found himself charging at the half-naked youth and knocking over the mirror he was using to admire himself. It came down with a crash and shattered into a thousand pieces. Theodosius fell back.

"You ungrateful swine." He pinned Theodosius against the wall, ripping the loincloth off his waist. He put his face in Theodosius's, grabbed the youth's manhood, and squeezed them almost to bursting. "The next time you touch my wife, I'll have your testicles removed." Theodosius gasped for air but was unable to say or do anything. Belisarius threw Theodosius to the marble floor littered with broken glass and said as he scrambled to get away, "I'll be watching you."

Belisarius washed his hands and departed the palace. He rarely succumbed to anger but strongly felt that, in this instance, he was justified. He reminded himself that he could not afford to treat his wife that way. He took a deep breath as he remembered the words of the shepherd. "I have done nothing more than driven off a wolf," he murmured as if the shepherd had seen the altercation.

Belisarius summoned the Roman leaders of Carthage outside the palace walls and asked them to refrain from shouting insults at the defeated Vandal soldiers when they marched through the city. Vandal citizens who had still harbored dreams of restoration lost all hope and began wailing at the sight of the ragged tyrant walking down the street with a chain around his neck.

Despite his loss of fortune, Gelimer marched through the streets at the side of Belisarius with a calm countenance. The general had finally completed the mission with which Justinian charged him, but he was not a happy man. He considered Aristotle's counsel that happiness was the consequence of a virtuous life, but he was still miserable despite his efforts to lead a virtuous life. As he returned to the palace, he saw his wife standing on a balcony, smiling at him and waving. He wondered how she held him in so little regard even as other women acclaimed his success. *Nothing good can come from this line of thought.*

He glared at her, and she turned away dejectedly. His anger pivoted back to sadness as he recalled his conversation with John on his wedding night: *do not let the sun go down on your wrath.* He reflected on how the passions undermined his enemies on the battlefield and knew that it was no different in love. He grew frustrated at the inability of his mind and heart to work together.

But he put his pain aside and graciously received Gelimer and his household into his old home, inviting them to bathe and offering them fine garments. Belisarius checked on the defeated monarch as he made dinner arrangements. He watched Gelimer spend two hours washing and marveled enviously at the simple joy bathing brought him. Gelimer laughed and played in the water with his nephews, recalling regretfully that he had never before found an opportunity to do this as king. It occurred to Belisarius the servants must be wondering which of the two had been defeated: the grim Roman or the now worry-free Vandal.

The household assembled at *cena*[55] for a feast in Gelimer's honor. Belisarius resolved to have a pleasant evening in the company of his Vandal captives who, despite their unfortunate circumstances, seemed to have far fewer worries than he did.

Gelimer's palace was a classical Roman structure with arched windows, columns, and mosaics. Gold ornaments filled the room. The mosaic on the floor of the great hall depicted the Roman destruction of the Carthaginian city after its

---

[55] The main meal, usually eaten at mid-day.

conquest and the deportation of its population into slavery. Belisarius watched as Gelimer stared at it as though for the first time, seeming to wonder what his fate would be, and yet not seeming to care one way or the other. Despite his diminished frame, Gelimer no longer looked like a beggar and was again wearing attire befitting his former rank.

Everyone, except Belisarius himself, seemed relieved that the war was over, and peace reigned again in the city. At first, Belisarius thought he would pity the man who had lost his kingdom and two brothers, but the only person in the room he pitied was himself in his broken marriage. He watched forlornly as his wife flirtatiously poured wine into the goblets of his generals and Gelimer's household while his chalice remained empty.

He was astounded to see Theodosius at the table. He had a grim look and refused to look at Belisarius. *The audacity of this wretch knows no limits!* Belisarius stared at the bottom of the empty vessel until Gelimer called one of the servants over and asked her to fill it. Belisarius considered excusing himself from the table, but military protocols precluded that.

"General, thank you for your hospitality," Gelimer said as he and his household sat at the table next to Belisarius and his general staff. "I feared you might decimate our city. The first time you Romans conquered it, there was hardly a stone left upon a stone."

All at the table, save Belisarius, laughed. He tried to snap out of his daze and rage against Theodosius, forced a smile and laugh, and tried to remember what Gelimer had just said. Several guests gave him sympathetic and worried looks, and Antonina pointed to the mosaic on the floor, triggering his memory. "Uh, yes, those were different times, indeed. I am glad you and your family have joined me and my wife... Antonina." He wondered why he had forgotten her name for a moment. "I know that you have had a difficult journey. Please enjoy the meal, which I trust you will prefer to the simpler cuisine of the Moors." All in the room laughed, and Belisarius felt his distracted mind trying to rejoin the group.

"You have quite a place here," Belisarius said, rotating his head to admire the extravagant wealth cluttering the dining area but knowing it would soon adorn Justinian's palace.

"Account no man happy before his death," Gelimer replied, harkening the warning to Lydia's overthrown King Croesus.

Belisarius gave him an ironic smile and raised a wide-mouthed chalice filled with wine. "We recovered this chalice..." He remembered the awful moment before Antonina had handed it to him in the cellar.

Gelimer gave Belisarius a surprised look. "Where did you get that?"

"We recovered this chalice and the six-branched golden candelabra on our table from the treasure chests loaded onto your ships headed for Hispania, which we captured off the coast of Hippo Regius when unfavorable winds blew it back to Africa."

"You have captured my prized possession. Congratulations. It's a fitting reward for you." Gelimer said.

Belisarius was surprised by the sycophantic remark.

"Your people stole much wealth and angered the entire Roman world," Procopius said, out of step with the jovial mood and unwitting of Belisarius's request to keep the conversation free of animosity. "When your Vandal forebears descended from northern Europe through Gaul,[56] Hispania, and North Africa, they sacked every city in their wake, enslaved the people, and filled their wagons with loot."

Belisarius glared at Procopius, worried that he might offend Gelimer and end the efforts at reconciliation. He recalled that the Vandals had preyed upon Procopius's family, all sea merchants, for generations. Gelimer simply responded, "I know the history of my people."

"Once the Vandals had spent that treasure," Procopius continued, oblivious to Belisarius's frown, "they turned the captured Roman navy in Carthage into a formidable pirate fleet. It went from port to port along the Italian coast, sacking and burning cities and monasteries and leaving local economies in ruin."

Belisarius pinched his lips in a gesture to Procopius to stop talking. He watched for a sign of offense from Gelimer, but the king seemed more interested in the food on the table than in Procopius's attempts at defamation.

---

[56] Modern France

"Your sack of Rome a century ago exceeded even the depravity of the Gothic sack a generation earlier," Procopius added. "It marked the end of the great city of Rome."

"That's enough, Procopius," Belisarius said sternly.

Gelimer paused from gnawing on a roasted lamb rib and responded to Procopius without looking at him. "You may be interested to know that among the treasures my grandfather Genseric hauled away was this golden menorah before us. You Romans seized it after destroying the Temple in Jerusalem, then commemorated the glory of its theft on the Arch of Titus." He and his fellow Vandals laughed. Gelimer looked at Belisarius and added, "As you reap, brother, so shall you sow."

Belisarius thought the man had a valid point. He lifted the chalice. "Is it true that Joseph of Arimathea drank from this?"

Gelimer smiled. "I am not certain, but the chalice, menorah, thuribles[57], trumpets, and showbread table are so exquisitely crafted I cannot believe they could have come from any other place."

Belisarius studied the chalice and menorah carefully and nodded in agreement.

"So, you will send these treasures to Constantinople?"

Belisarius nodded.

"I recommend you advise the Emperor to return the menorah to Jerusalem. It has brought nothing but doom and misery to every city where it has been kept since it was taken from its rightful home. A Carthaginian Jew forewarned us of this, and our failure to heed him now puts you at the head of my table."

Belisarius smiled. "I will relay your concern to the Justinian. The Emperor intends to build a great new church near the ruins of the temple in Jerusalem, and it would be a fine adornment."

He stood and lifted the chalice. "To peace in the Empire." Those around the table tipped their cups and emptied them.

---

[57] A container used to burn incense.

As they finished their meal, Belisarius received a scroll from a courier, read it to himself, and then made a scowl. He turned to Gelimer and whispered, "Justinian has recalled me to Constantinople, and Antonina and I will accompany you and your family on our flagship. Upon arrival, the Empire may see its first triumphal parade in many years." Belisarius wondered if the true purpose of the recall was to honor him or an indication of trouble. Too often, victorious generals had returned to the capital only to be blinded or executed. "I am afraid that you and the Vandal treasure will be the main attraction."

Gelimer laughed. "I am sure it will be a glorious day for you, General Belisarius, but don't get too acquainted with such honors. I have found them to be very fleeting."

"Indeed, all glory is fleeting, isn't it?" Belisarius replied as he watched his wife at the other end of the table laughing with Theodosius and looking in his direction. *Much like a happy marriage,* he thought to himself. Unable to watch the spectacle any longer, Belisarius excused himself from the table and went to bed.

The following morning, Belisarius and Pharas arrived at the port of Carthage to oversee the packing of the Vandal treasures bound for Constantinople. A dark cloud obscured the sun and flashed with bolts of lightning. The ships bounced up and down on the waves and crashed violently into the docks. Stevedores worked quickly to try to finish before the rain came. Belisarius's mood felt as dark and ominous as the weather. A sudden gust pelted his face with hail, and he sought cover in the bowels of his flagship. It reminded him of the scene wine cellar again. Antonina approached him with a joyful skip in her step that only enraged Belisarius even more.

"Husband, I have news I must share with you," she said with a smile.

*Woman, you are simply going to pretend that I did not see what I saw, aren't you? If you refuse to bring this up, I will.*

"The only news I want from you is an explanation of what Pharas and I saw in the cellar. It is better to know the worst than to wonder."

Antonina gave him an astonished and innocent look. "As I told you, we were selecting items from the Vandal treasure to help finance your *bucellarii*. You know they don't come cheaply."

"And you were making this selection in a state of undress?"

"It was hot. Theodosius removed some of his garments to ease the heavy lifting."

Belisarius stared at her. "Antonina, my eyes were not deceived."

"You actually think I could do that to you?"

"Well, yes! And should I see such a scene again, I will cut the stones off the man involved."

"Are you threatening your godson?"

"I threaten no one; I merely promise to make eunuchs..."

"Flavius," Antonina gently interrupted, "Such talk is unworthy of you."

Belisarius studied his wife's feigned innocence and tendency to rub her right palm with her left thumb whenever she became uncomfortable with a conversation. He finally got a reaction from her and laughed cynically, "And adultery is unworthy of you, wife."

Antonina stormed out of the cabin and off the ship. Belisarius made no effort to follow her.

Pharas boarded the ship and gave Belisarius a sympathetic look. "A discussion about the wine cellar?" Pharas asked.

"Yes."

"Has she apologized?"

"Not at all. She has denied that anything untoward happened."

"Oooh," Pharas groaned. "I don't envy you."

"What did we see, Pharas? Did we let our imaginations run wild?"

"My imagination is always running wild; don't ask me," Pharas said with a smirk.

"What should I do?"

"There is only one thing you can do."

"What's that?"

"Castration of the rogue."

"I've considered that already, but I meant about Antonina."

"You need a chastity belt for her."

Belisarius rolled his eyes. "She would never agree to that."

"I don't know what else to tell you, Flavius," Pharas said. "You're a good husband, so I'm not sure there's much you can do other than forgive her. The rest is up to her."

"Thanks, Pharas."


That evening, Belisarius gave the matter more consideration in the palace. The storm had passed and delayed their departure until the next day. The tension over the cellar scene only added to the estrangement in their marriage, and he desperately wanted to put it behind them.

He approached his wife in her bedchamber. She gave him an apprehensive look and braced herself for more confrontation. Belisarius spoke slowly and softly. "I will forgive you this transgression but see to it that you keep your sacred vows in the future."

Antonina flattened a wrinkle in her husband's tunic, then cupped a hand around his ear and whispered, "Your eyes deceived you, Flavius, but I thank you for your generosity. Our marriage ought not flounder on a misperception."

He stepped away from her and was silent for a time. Then, without looking at her, he said. "I love you, Antonina, but your actions have caused me great pain."

An attendant knocked on the door and announced, "General Solomon is here to see you, sir."

Solomon awkwardly entered the room, and Antonina took a step back and assumed a formal pose.

"My regrets, General. Am I intruding?" Solomon asked as he entered the room.

"As a matter of fact, yes," Belisarius said. "We were...."

"No, of course not," Antonina interrupted. "Solomon, please come in. We were just finishing our conversation. Hold your tongue for one moment as I have some important news for my husband."

"Of course, My Lady," Solomon said as he waited by the door with his hands together.

Belisarius gave Antonina an impatient look at her gift for avoiding uncomfortable conversations. "Antonina, another time."

"Husband, this cannot wait," she said stiffly. "This morning, I came to you to warn you General Constantinus and other envious rivals have sent a secret message to Justinian alleging that you covet his imperial diadem and plan to make yourself the king of Africa. One of the courtiers in my service provided me with a copy." She handed it to him.

The shocking letter filled Belisarius with despair and a sense that nothing seemed to be going right. "My officers conspire against me," he murmured even as he wondered if this urgent news was only a ruse to distract his attention from Theodosius. "Constantinus chafed at being my subordinate, but...."

"He despises people like us," Antonina said, "and constantly disparages us to his fellow officers. He claims to have descended from Emperor Constantine the Great, which may be true. He has the same wide eyes, aquiline nose, and cleft chin."

"He does," Belisarius acknowledged as he began to believe the veracity of the conspiracy.

"I see his contempt for you in the way he closes his eyes and lifts his nose whenever he speaks with you or anyone else he deems inferior. He holds himself erect as though posing for a sculptor. I have written to the Empress, assuring her that this allegation is a fabrication and that we will return to Constantinople immediately so the Emperor can see that you harbor no pretensions to his throne. If we delay, the allegations may sway the court."

"We'll depart at once," Belisarius said and kissed his wife's forehead, then turned to Solomon. "I trust you to safeguard the goodwill of the people of Carthage in my place and maintain the peace."

# CHAPTER TWENTY-ONE
## VANITY OF VANITIES

*Vanity of vanities! All is vanity.*
*What do people gain from all the toil*
*At which they toil under the sun?*
*I saw all the deeds that are done under the sun;*
*And see, all is vanity and a chasing after wind.*

— Ecclesiastes 1: 2-3, 14

*Constantinople*
*534 A.D.*

The Roman fleet of three hundred ships sailed from Carthage the following day. Antonina joined her husband on the flagship even as Belisarius had Theodosius assigned to the ricketiest vessel in the fleet and one manned by Egyptian sailors so that Theodosius had no one with a common tongue to speak. The lack of privacy on the ship precluded the couples from having a candid conversation about Theodosius for the entire voyage. Belisarius found himself wishing the small ship would capsize or suffer from another whale attack to rid him of Theodosius. Every time he tried to bring up the issue of Theodosius, Antonina changed the subject or walked away.

Unfavorable winds caused the flagship's journey back to the port of Constantinople to be two weeks longer than the outbound voyage. As the flagship arrived on the docks in mid-summer, thousands gathered to acclaim the great conqueror and catch a glimpse of the Vandal captives who had wreaked havoc on the Empire for a century. Women threw flower petals at his feet and waved palm branches, and he wished that his wife had similar affections for him. Boys ran up to him to touch his sword and armor as though they had magical powers. It was Belisarius's first experience with such adulation. While he had dreamed of it as a young man, it presently all seemed a bit much for a man who only felt he had simply responded to his military duties.

The admiration of the crowd was a welcome distraction from his brooding about his ungrateful godson. Theodosius's treachery worked on his mind even as he assisted the court in planning for the triumph. *I fed that boy and gave him the finest tutors in Constantinople, and he repays me by seducing my wife?* Antonina seemed distant and inquired, to Belisarius's silent fury, about when the fleet expected Theodosius's ship to pull into the port.

Empress Theodora arranged a version of the traditional Roman triumphal parade to remind the people of the fortune that had come to the Golden Horn since Justinian's ascension to the throne. The destruction of the Nika Riots only two years before had caused many to wonder whether the Lord had cursed Justinian's reign. Now, Belisarius's victories over the Vandals in Africa offered a compelling case that the Empire's best days were yet to come. After three centuries under siege, the Roman Empire was emerging from its long slumber and had recaptured its lost energy. The Emperor and Empress made plans to honor Belisarius like no other Roman had been honored in many generations. Considering his many other problems, he tried to focus his attention on the coming accolades.

Warm sunlight filled the air as thousands of Roman cavalry and infantry marched to the Hippodrome of Constantinople. Trumpets heralded the arrival of Rome's new Caesar. Unlike previous conquerors, who rode in chariots pulled by a team of white horses, Belisarius walked the streets followed by his army, King Gelimer, a throng of disheartened Vandal captives, and dozens of Vandal treasure wagons. Giraffes and elephants captured in Africa and not seen there in centuries joined the parade, raising wild cheers from the crowds. Belisarius would have preferred a less pretentious procession, but Theodora had insisted that he present his conquests to the Emperor and bow before him to receive his blessing.

Belisarius wore a white cape over golden ceremonial armor, and a white plume sprouted from his helmet. Gelimer was permitted to dress in the imperial purple one last time, but Theodora insisted that he also wear golden chains around his wrists, symbolizing his surrender.

Tens of thousands of people lined the city streets, cheering and waving banners. Belisarius saw their elated faces and heard their uplifting chants, all the while wondering if he was worth all of this.

"Look at the size and muscular physiques of these warriors!"

"What sort of general could have beaten such a sturdy lot?"

Even Gelimer had recovered his statuesque physique after ten weeks of generous sea biscuit and African produce.

Behind the Vandal captives, Roman infantry officers marched in lockstep, creating a rhythmic cadence with their clanging armor as their nail-studded sandals, marching in perfect maniple formations, created a hypnotic sound that conveyed power and promise. Everywhere, the white standard of Belisarius hung from poles topped with Roman golden eagles. Belisarius's elite guards marched through the Forum of Constantine before turning and heading toward the Hippodrome, which had seen few large crowds since the Nika Riot. He entered the Hippodrome through the starting gate for the horses and stopped to address his men.

"The citizens of Constantinople expect a good show," Belisarius told Pharas. "This city hasn't seen an infantry march since the Goths defeated the Romans at the disastrous Battle of Adrianople a century and a half ago." While the Empress had ostensibly orchestrated the triumph to pay tribute to the army, Belisarius knew that she wanted to ensure its primary aim was to honor the Emperor.

Belisarius led his troops around the Hippodrome and stopped before the reconstructed imperial stage. When trumpets announced that the Emperor was ready to receive them, Belisarius and Gelimer climbed the steps to the imperial thrones, where Justinian sat wearing a crown of golden laurels and holding a scepter.

"Your Imperial Highnesses," Belisarius proclaimed in a dramatic baritone, "I give you Gelimer, King of the Vandals."

The crowd cheered as Belisarius presented the manacled monarch to Justinian and Theodora.

Narses walked behind Gelimer and ceremoniously stripped the royal purple cloak from his shoulders, saying, "Prostrate yourself before the Emperor and Empress."

The deposed king, the tallest man in Constantinople, measured the dwarfish chamberlain with his eyes. Belisarius got a worried look. *Are you going to try some publicity stunt to embarrass the Emperor?* Seeing Gelimer hesitate, Belisarius removed his plumed helmet and cape and prostrated himself. Narses ceremonially laid the deposed king's purple robe at the imperial feet, and Theodora placed one foot on it.

Gelimer, entirely unimpressed by the solemnity of the occasion, snickered and murmured the words of King Solomon, "Vanity of vanities. All is vanity."

In the clamor, only Belisarius heard him and whispered, "Please, allow them this," and Gelimer prostrated himself. Theodora smiled at his humiliation, but Justinian ordered him to stand and embraced him.

Belisarius thought that the obligation to prostrate brought dishonor to the imperial couple given the more egalitarian traditions of simple genuflection that separated Romans from the ridiculous pomp and groveling that Persian shahs required of their vassals. He had once been Justinian's closest friend and an equal in the imperial guards, but their informality had ended at Theodora's insistence. Belisarius missed his old drinking buddy even as he was happy for Justinian's success. *Power is the ultimate barrier in friendship,* he thought.

Since the Nika Riots, Theodora required all subjects, particularly patricians, generals, and senators, to prostrate themselves and kiss the feet of both Emperor and Empress. He knew that Theodora might construe his failure to abase himself as a sign of disloyalty, so he obliged her.

The Emperor instructed Belisarius and Gelimer to turn and face the people. He stood and raised Belisarius's hand while Narses made a dramatic gesture that signaled the crowd to cheer, and after long applause, signaled silence.

"My fellow citizens of Rome," Justinian declared, "today, we celebrate the return of our victorious armies from Africa. Our reign also marks the beginning of the restoration of the Empire to its former glory. Long gone are the days when barbarians overran our Empire and brought nothing but death and destruction.

From this day forward, our enemies will feel the full might of our power and tremble before us."

Narses gestured again, and the crowd went wild again with cheers. Belisarius looked into the adoring crowd and saw his wife, standing next to Theodosius and having a conversation as though they were only people in the Hippodrome. *Damn! His ship came in.* Belisarius stared at the rogue as though his glare might put a lance through Theodosius's heart, but his godson never even noticed. Belisarius felt like a bull in a cage wanting to charge out but constrained by the necessity of decorum. All he managed to do was snort and stomp his foot. Gelimer, standing next to him, gave him a puzzled look.

Justinian continued, "Today, the deposed king of the Vandals stands before you. In our great mercy, we have decided to pardon this rebel and spare him the just punishment for the murder of Hilderic. He is now an ordinary man and will live a life not dissimilar from your own. For the Lord has done a great deed for us. He casts down the mighty from their thrones. He fills the hungry with good things."

At that, Narses gave a signal, and courtiers tossed gold, silver, and copper coins into the frenzied crowd.

"What a bunch of lickspittles," Gelimer murmured, staring at the Empress and her courtiers. "The former Hippodrome comedienne must have enjoyed watching a successor to Genseric prostrate himself before her."

As the crowd dispersed, Belisarius escorted Gelimer to the imperial *tablinum* to meet with Justinian and Theodora. "As General Belisarius promised, we have arranged to bestow on you a handsome estate," Justinian said, "and will offer you the rank of patrician once you renounce your heretical Arian beliefs."

"I have no wish for your rank," Gelimer replied. "Such worldly glory is transitory." And he turned his back on the Emperor and left without bowing. Narses was enraged, but Justinian waved him off.

The following day, Belisarius accompanied Gelimer to a ship that would take him to a magnificent estate in Galatia, which John the Cappadocian seized from a Roman patrician who had failed to pay his taxes.

"May we meet one day again," he said, then turned to Gelimer's nephew, Thrasamund, and presented him with a small ceremonial knife from Lazica,[58] saying, "Use this the next time you need to pluck hot bread from the oven."

"Truly, Flavius," Gelimer said, "no friend has surpassed you in kindness and no enemy in clemency." He embraced Belisarius and, holding his shoulders, said, "I hope someday you find happiness since, to my surprise, this day does not seem to have brought you any."

Belisarius gave him a puzzled look. "It's that obvious?" he asked.

Gelimer laughed. "Yes, and not just to me." He let go of Belisarius and said, "In my experience, it's often harder to manage a single person than a whole army, but I know you'll find a way."

When he returned to the Great Palace, Belisarius found Justinian in the treasury with Narses and John inspecting the vast Vandal hoard. "Narses, ship the menorah from Herod's temple to the Mother of God Church we are constructing in Jerusalem. Let us hope it brings peace to its new home."

"John, I have ordered the striking of a gold coin with the image of our best general and the words: 'Belisarius, the glory of the Romans'." He patted the general's shoulders. "Well done, Flavius. This is a prototype of the coin." Belisarius saw a likeness of himself mounted on Bucephalus, like a Roman general of old.

"Thank you, Your Majesty, you are too generous. This was not necessary."

"Oh, but it was," Justinian said. "When you succeed, we succeed."

The following day, the people filled the Hippodrome again as Justinian called Belisarius to the imperial stage. "General Belisarius, in recognition of your outstanding achievements in bringing peace with Persia and conquering the Vandal nation, we hereby name you consul of the Empire for the coming year, ranking second only to the Emperor and Empress."

The crowd cheered the new Caesar, although most knew the title no longer carried the significance it held during the Republic. "Belisarius! Belisarius!" they

---

[58] Eastern Black Sea coast; modern Republic of Georgia

chanted as the Empress fidgeted uneasily. Belisarius spun around and acknowledged their acclaim.

The Vandal captives inducted into his elite guards hoisted him onto a curule chair. As his attendants distributed silver plates, golden goblets, and other treasures from Gelimer's palace, Constantinus questioned the wisdom of his liberality.

Belisarius replied, "The only wealth we keep is what we give away."

His guards carried him through the streets of Constantinople to the cheers of a hundred thousand enthusiastic admirers. The people's joy filled him with such gratitude that, for a moment, he judged this the happiest day in his long military career. And then he saw them together again: Antonina and Theodosius walking amidst the crowd. He tossed several coins in their general direction, and the people around them fell to the ground to pick up as many little treasures as they could. Antonina and Theodosius, engrossed in a lively conversation, never even noticed.

Belisarius knew that Antonina had kept some of the Vandal treasure to help him cover the vast expenses of his ever-expanding household guards, which now included many Vandal warriors. All that Belisarius kept for himself was the Arimathean's chalice. Once his devotees returned him to the quiet of his apartment in the Great Palace, he held the chalice up to the light of an oil lamp and admired its unadorned simplicity and purity. To him, it symbolized the unattainable perfection toward which he must strive.

Later, as he relaxed on a balcony, still glowing in the popular adulation he had received, Antonina reminded him that many in the palace resented his success.

"Yesterday," she said, "after Justinian announced your consulship, Theodora warned me of a conversation in which Narses warned that the people love you too much. She thinks that Justinian has created a potential rival and that you might opt to redeem that popularity someday."

"If this is true, what will they do to prevent it?" Belisarius asked.

"Narses advised against appointing new consuls. He recommended you be sent from the city and kept fully engaged on faraway battlefields."

"Giving me armies would seem to undermine their concerns about me marching them against the Emperor," Belisarius said.

"Not if he gives you him a negligible force." Antonina countered.

"Is there talk of that?" Belisarius asked.

"Yes, even giving you only a quarter of the strength you need to succeed in your next campaign."

"That would be setting me up for failure," Belisarius said.

"Narses didn't care. He has spies watching you."

Belisarius felt his heart sink into his stomach. "How does depriving me of success benefit anyone?"

"O husband, you don't understand the power of envy, do you?"

Belisarius stared at the chalice for a long time, then filled it with wine from Gelimer's cellar and swallowed a long, slow drink. He hoped the unique flavor of the African vintage would bring him back to the glorious moment when he rode into Carthage to the cheers of liberated Romans.

He sat in a Roman chair on his palace balcony, looking vacantly out the window at the new construction around the capital as Antonina prepared their new apartment in the palace. He noticed again how beautiful she was and how fortunate he was to have such an intelligent and lovely wife. He started to fall asleep when suddenly, he heard a "Psst…" at the door to the apartment and saw a shadowy figure standing there.

Antonina looked in his direction, and Belisarius pretended he had fallen asleep under the spell of the wine and deliberately dropped the empty chalice in his hand on his lap. Antonina walked toward him, picked it up, and placed it on a nearby table. Another "Psst…" sound filled the room, and Antonina hurried toward the door and whispered something he could not hear. Belisarius cracked open one eyelid to see who the guest was. A thin figure dressed in a provocatively short white tunic appeared and looked at Belisarius as Antonina pointed to him and laughed softly. It was Theodosius.

The two embraced affectionately, and Antonina put on a pair of shoes and a shawl. She quietly closed the door behind them so as not to wake her sleeping husband and departed the bedchamber with her godson. Belisarius heard them running down the hallway together, then heard another door open and close. And then silence — a loud, long silence that made him put his hands over his ears as he was carried back to the moment when he descended in Gelimer's wine cellar and discovered his wife with Theodosius *in flagrante delicto*.

# Epilogue

I have relied extensively on historical documents (particularly Procopius of Caesarea) to create a canvas on which to paint this picture. Where history is silent or obscure, I have filled the gaps with a literary narrative that aims to conform to the consensus of historians. Drawing on all known historical and literary accounts, I have attempted to reconcile narratives that made the most sense amidst conflicting versions of events. Brevity required me to eliminate or merge some characters who were part of the historical narrative. For readers interested in knowing where there may have been major departures from the known historical narrative, I offer the following:

First, while Procopius mentions in *The Wars* that a Persian knight challenged anyone in Belisarius's army to fight him in solo combat, the challenge was ultimately accepted by a man named Andreas.

Second, the legend of the Holy Grail is an early medieval story that never accounts for its movement from the Holy Land to the West. While Procopius states that Belisarius did recover the "temple treasures" in Carthage that Titus's army had pillaged in Jerusalem in 70 AD, there is no specific record that a chalice was among them.

Finally, Pharas the Herulian and Sunicas the Hun drop off the historical record after the battles of Dara and Tricamaron (respectively). Their continued presence is this novel is purely literary conjecture.

# Major Historical Characters

## (In Order of Mention)

**Flavius Marcus Belisarius**: general, reconqueror of formerly Roman lands

**Pharas**: Herulian cavalry captain of Belisarius at Dara who later negotiated the surrender of the Vandal king

**Sunicas**: Roman-Hunnish cavalry commander whose actions were decisive at Dara

**Perozes**: Persian general defeated at the battle of Dara in the Iberian War (526-532 A.D.)

**Kavad (aka Kabates)**: Persian shah from 488-531 A.D.

**Baresmanas**: Persian captain of Perozes who led an unsuccessful flank attack on the Romans at Dara during the Iberian War

**Justin (I)**: shepherd from Illyricum turned imperial guard. Emperor from 518-527 A.D.

**Flavius Petrus Sabbateus Justinianus (aka Justinian the Great)**: nephew of Justin. Eastern Roman Emperor from 527-565 A.D.

**Theodora**: former courtesan, later Justinian's wife and Roman Empress

**Procopius**: Roman secretary to Belisarius, primary Greek historian whose *Wars* and *Secret History* document the reign of Justinian and the Persian, Vandalic, and Gothic wars

**Antonina**: former courtesan turned adulteress, wife of Belisarius

**Hypatius**: aged nephew of Roman Emperor Anastasius raised as an alternative to Justinian during the Nika Rebellion

**Mundus**: Roman general in charge of troops in Illyricum and suppressor of rioters at Nika

**Archelaus**: admiral of the Roman armada that invaded Africa

**Theodosius**: adopted godson of Belisarius and paramour of Antonina

**Hilderic**: deposed Vandal king whose deposition became a *casus belli*

**Gelimer**: Vandal king who deposed Hilderic and was later defeated by Belisarius at Ad Decimum and Tricameron

**Tzazon**: brother of Gelimer sent to put down a rebellion in Sardinia before the Roman reconquest of Africa

**John of Armenia**: brilliant Roman-Armenian cavalry commander and victim of friendly fire at Tricamaron

**Ammatas**: rash brother of Gelimer who murdered Hilderic and whose impetuous attack cost the Vandals the battle at Ad Decimum and their kingdom

**Gibamundus**: beloved nephew of Gelimer whose defeat by Hunnish archers hastened the collapse of the Vandal front at Ad Decimum

**Uliaris**: drunkard who accidentally shot Armenian John after Tricamaron

**Narses**: Armenian eunuch who served as Justinian's Grand Chamberlain and as general under Belisarius before getting his own command in Italy during the second Gothic War

**Photius**: troubled son of Antonina and informative stepson of Belisarius

**John of Cappadocia**: greedy minister of finance and chief tax collector in Constantinople who helped write the Justinian Code until accused of murder

**Constantinus**: brilliant but insubordinate commander of Roman forces in Italy under Belisarius

**Joannina**: only child of Belisarius and Antonina

**Euphemia:** wife of Emperor Justin

# GREEK AND LATIN TERMS

*Bucellarii*: a late Roman/early Byzantine cataphract (armored knight) who was a hybrid of the Hunnish mounted archers and the heavily armored mounted lancers used by the Goths and Persians

*Caldarium*: a room with a hot bath

*Clibanarii*: Persian knights famous for their cuirass that Latin speakers nick-named "bread-ovens" for the heat they brought to the wearer

*Dromone:* the primary Roman warship

*Excubitor:* a member of the palace guards in Constantinople

*Foederati:* non-Latin allies of the Roman Empire often with a particular specialty who assisted regular army troops; ex. Hunnish mounted archers

*Impluvium:* the sunken part of the atrium in a Roman villa designed to carry away rainwater coming through the open roof

*Limitanei:* Roman soldiers assigned to garrisons on the frontiers

*Magister Militum:* Master of Soldiers or General

*Paludamentum:* semicircular cloak or cape fastened over the right shoulder with a large square brooch called a tablion

*Praetorium:* the residence of the city's governor

*Quaestor:* an official responsible for police and judicial powers in Constantinople

*Tablinum:* an office and library in a Roman home that often doubled as a conference room

*Tribuli:* caltrops or iron tripods thrown on the ground and used to halt the charge of cavalry by crippling their mounts

# ADDITIONAL READING

https://www.academia.edu/42765814/The_Role_of_Climate_Change_in_the_Decline_of_the_Roman_Empire

This paper explains the science behind the theory that a climate catastrophe and the Pandemic of 542 contributed in no small way to the Roman Empire's decline. The bibliography at the end of the paper has a suggested reading list for anyone interested in learning more about the historical and scientific backdrop behind this book. For the characters, this author relied primarily on Procopius's *Wars* and, to a lesser extent, in his *Secret History*, which, while fraught with invective against Justinian, Theodora, and Antonina, offers valuable insights into their characters and motives.

# ACKNOWLEDGMENTS

This book emerged as a follow-up to my Master of Arts in World History thesis work at Norwich University, which addressed the role of climate change and the world's first pandemic in the decline of the Roman Empire. I would like to thank Robin Pierson, the creator of the *History of Byzantium* podcast, whose elucidations on the reign of Justinian inspired me to choose Byzantium as the object of my graduate research. I would like to thank the friends whose feedback on the short-comings of early drafts made this a better story. Special thanks my developmental editor, Lyndsay Stanley, my "blacksmith," whose creative genius helped turn a narrative history into a real novel, as well as my line editor, Joie Davidow, whose gift for an economy of words every reader should be indebted. My gratitude to Florin Safner, whose artistic cartography created the beautiful maps for the book. I wish to thank my wife and family, who patiently tolerated my obsession for this fascinating period of history during the many hours needed to tell this great story. Finally, I owe some thanks to the coronavirus pandemic that afforded me the free time to write.

# ABOUT THE AUTHOR

Robert Bruton is an award-winning American author and a former CIA operations officer who served in many countries once part of the Roman Empire. He has a BA in history from the University of St. Thomas and a MA in world history from Norwich University, where he did his thesis on the role of climate change in the decline of the Roman Empire. He lives near Washington, D.C. with his wife and children. https://www.authorrobertbruton.com

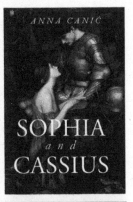
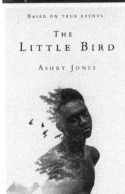